KEEGAN'S WRATH

The Katori Chronicles
Book 5

A. D. Lombardo

BOOKS BY A. D. LOMBARDO

The Katori Chronicles:

The Half-Light

Mariana's Secret

Rayna's Sacrifice

The Traitor

Keegan's Wrath

Keegan's Wrath

The Katori Chronicles Book 5
A. D. Lombardo

This work is a work of fiction. Names, characters, organizations, places, events, and incidents are either products of the author's imagination or are used factiously. Any resemblance to actual persons, living or dead, or actual events is purely coincidental.

Published by Nichols INK

ISBN (Paperback): 978-1-7333376-8-7
ISBN (Ebook): 978-1-7333376-9-4

Cover design by A. D. Lombardo
First Edition 2021

www.ADLombardo.com

5

*I dedicate this final book in The Katori Chronicles
to my dog, Buddy. He often led me into the office encouraging
me to write each night.*

A. D. Lombardo

ACKNOWLEDGMENTS

I cannot believe this is the end. My mixed emotions range from delighted and proud—what an accomplishment—to the overwhelming surprise of Kai's story coming from ME. And yet, I am thrilled to start something new. The freedom to explore new ideas leaves me giddy like a kid in a toy store with birthday money to burn.

I must always thank my son, Connor; I would have never found this passion without him. Fifteen years ago, a bedtime story with a missing mother started it all. I still remember his joy in the grocery store parking lot. His excitement to read and hold an actual book in his hands and then insist that the world also read it brought this story to life.

A big thank you to my devoted husband; he supported me in so many ways without question. There were countless hours spent listening to my ideas, all while keeping the house running as I feverishly typed through the weekend.

And then there is my editor, Keith. Any editor can critique, provide comprehensive editing and developmental reviews, but the best coach. As my guide, Keith led me over, around, and through complicated scenes and writer's block. I am thankful for his support which has helped me improve my craft while writing this series.

I look forward to our next collaboration.

Special thanks to my family and friends for your continued support. I hope you have enjoyed the journey.

And as always, Buddy, thank you for walking into the office every night reminding me to keep writing.

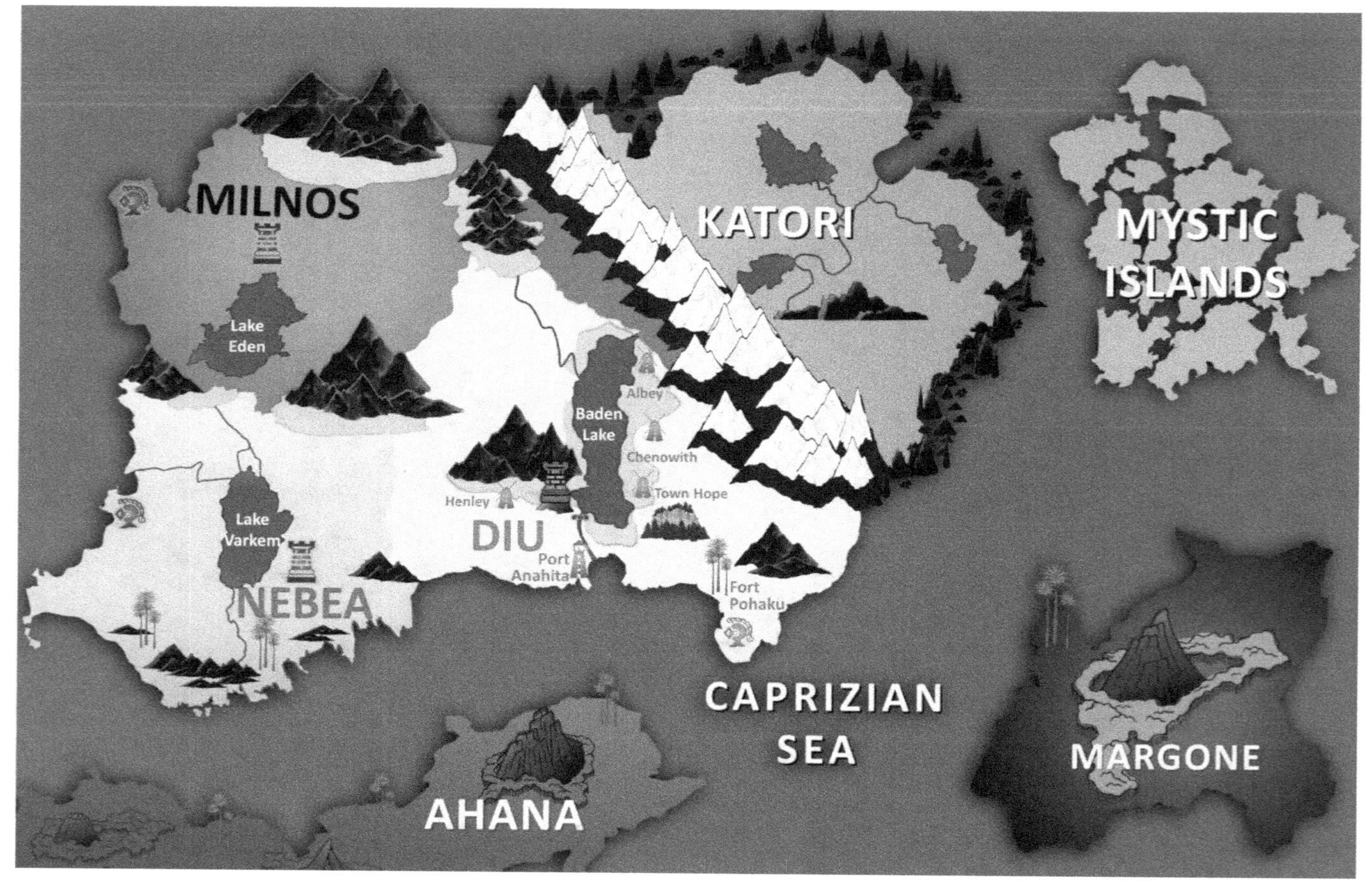

MILNOS
KATORI
MYSTIC ISLANDS
Lake Eden
Albey
Baden Lake
Chenowith
Town Hope
Henley
DIU
Lake Varkem
NEBEA
Port Anahita
Fort Pohaku
CAPRIZIAN SEA
MARGONE
AHANA

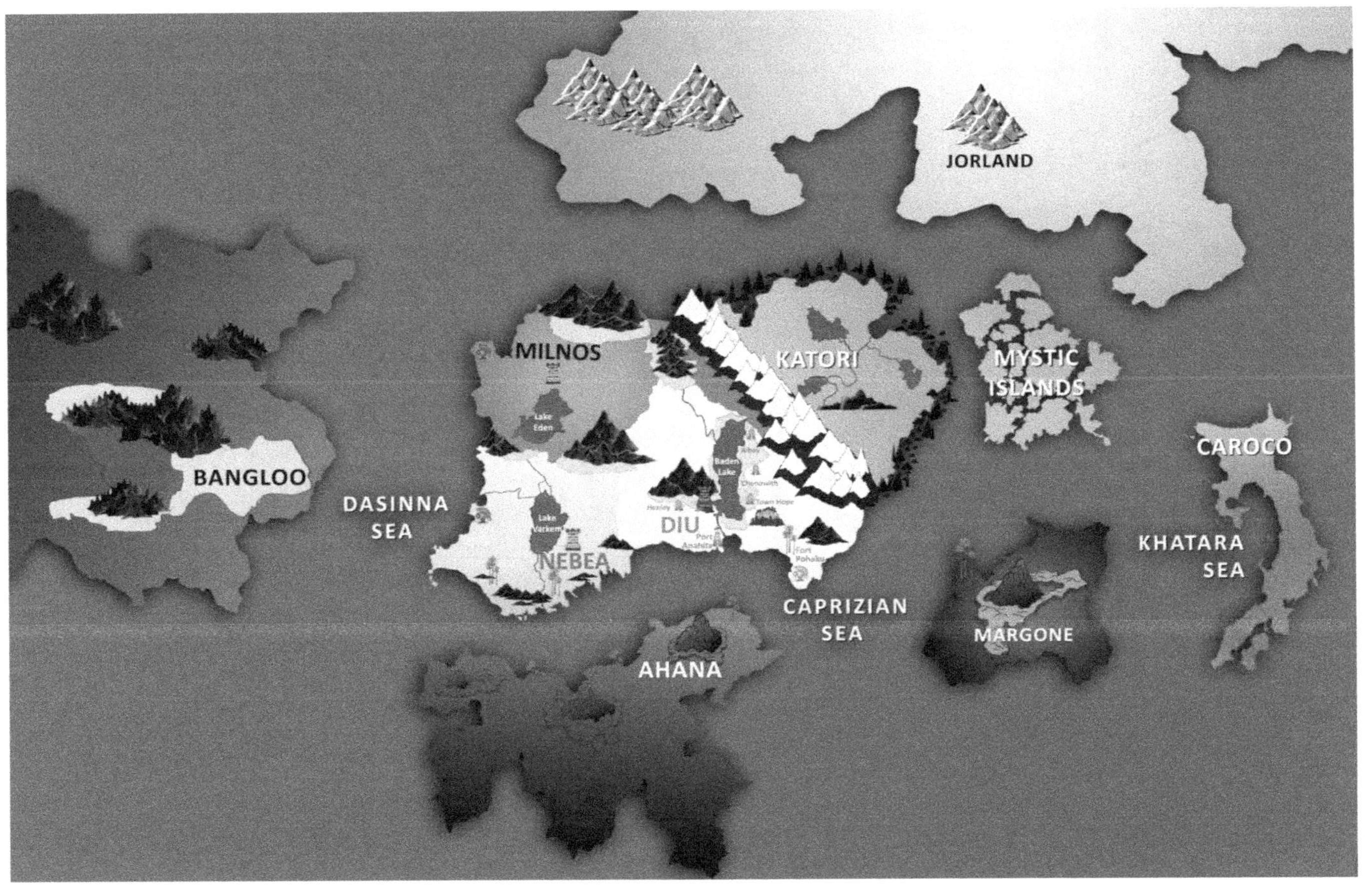

JORLAND
MILNOS
KATORI
MYSTIC ISLANDS
CAROCO
BANGLOO
DASINNA SEA
NEBEA
DIU
KHATARA SEA
CAPRIZIAN SEA
MARGONE
AHANA

A. D. Lombardo

CONTENTS

PROLOGUE

Tears blurred Amelia's silver-blue eyes as she stared down upon her once-beloved homeland, Milnos. A newly discovered hatred bubbled in her chest—one she never thought possible. How could her father be so cruel, locking her away in a tower? Did power mean so much to him? She felt lost and alone, forgotten like a worn-out shoe. The love she once harbored for him was now as lost to her as her freedom.

The small balcony of her chamber beckoned her toward its edge. The cold winter breeze kissed her wet cheeks as she gripped the iron railing, its frozen black iron biting her hands and sending chills up her arms, but she did not let go. The dizzying heights made her tremble. She did not remember ever being afraid of life, but now, everything terrified her. Her heart pounded in her chest, making it hard to breathe. She looked to her abdomen and thought of the little one growing inside her. How could she possibly protect them both?

Her tower was isolated from the black iron castle which sat up the hill, attached to the original keep. The behemoth castle towered over the sprawling city, surrounded in the distance by massive black iron gates. Dramatic spires and ironworks glistened in the midday sun. Amelia had once been intrigued by their elegance, but now their fierce display had become oppressive symbols of rejection and imprisonment.

Would anyone come to her rescue? What of Kai and Diu? Did they no longer care for her? Years ago, Amelia had been betrothed to Prince Kai Galloway, and she had thought he would attend her wedding, but nobody from Diu came. Diu was her second city, where she spent many formative years, but when she needed the people of Diu the most, they all left her forsaken, which made no sense to her. Her heart ached for her husband and news of his fate. Letting go of the railing, she wiped the wetness from her face. Since her mother would not come to comfort her, she would need to soothe herself.

A delicate winter breeze blew around Amelia, and she ran her fingers like a comb through her golden hair, trying to calm her fears. No longer a Maxwell, she was now a Roark, married to the love of her life, Kempery-man Tolan Roark of Diu and Port Anahita. She needed to hold her head high; Tolan would want her to be strong.

Memories of her wedding day brought new tears streaming down her cheeks. Months of planning her perfect day had given her hope for the future. Their wedding day was beautiful; noble lords and ladies had attended the union, offering the couple promises of support in their impending coronation as king and queen of Milnos. The crowning ceremony had been planned for the eve of the new year—a little more than a month ago, now. Sadly, the day of their coronation came and went. Now a prisoner in her own country, Amelia wondered if justice would unlock her door.

Angry and confused, Amelia stepped back inside. That awful evening, a fortnight after her wedding day, guards came into chambers and ripped Tolan from their bed. Her husband's frantic last words to her were, "Don't worry, I'll be fine. I love you. Stay safe." But she saw his expression, and it did not support his statement. He was afraid. All she could do was promise to speak with her father, a fruitless effort in the long run. Even her letters to Admiral Roark, Tolan's father, came back undelivered, tossed in her face. She was alone.

Forbidden to visit her husband, she went to her parents, hoping for answers—or, at the very least, solace in the arms of her mother. Two guards followed her while two more stood outside their chamber doors. The men blocked her path but offered no retort to her demands. Her shouts went unanswered, echoing down the corridor, fading into despair. Her parents refused to speak with her, leaving her wondering why the sudden change.

Whispers about her father's disdain for giving his city to her and Tolan trickled from maid to maid in the coming days. But everyone knew that upon her birth Diu and Milnos had signed a treaty; with no

Milnosian heir, the Regent's daughter would inherit the throne and marry the Prince of Diu, uniting the two cities. Together they would start a new age of peace with a new royal family.

But all that seemed a lifetime ago. While nobody in her family had spoken with her since she was imprisoned, she heard their rumors and hoped they were lies. The people saw her as tainted by Diu and unworthy of their loyalty. Many whispered about a lost heir returning to Milnos—a Penier who would once again sit on the throne. With each passing day, the servants avoided her more and more, and those who did service her room turned their nose up at her as if she were now below them. Lingering around corners, she listened as workers whispered about her husband's imprisonment more times than she could stand. Some even whispered speculations she would be next.

It was not long before Amelia again started demanding an audience with her father. She waited outside his council chambers in hopes of getting his attention. The years of living in Diu had strained their relationship, something Amelia hoped might improve with her return to Milnos. A fantasy, she now realized. He was, after all, the power-hungry regent first and foremost, and she was property.

Each morning and evening, she tried—and each time he saw her, his gaze renounced their relationship a little more. It became apparent that, as a woman, she had little value and no power, something her mother had tried to teach her time and time again. Something her father made sure she understood the following day.

When the Milnos guards came in force, a heavy fist pounded on her chamber door. "Amelia Roark, by order of Regent Maxwell, you are to be remanded to Raven's Tower, where you will live out your days."

Her refusal to come out ended in a broken door. It took three guards to subdue her. The iron shackles chewed at her wrists, and her blood had stained the lace fringe of her dress by the time they reached the tower. *This cannot be happening*, she repeated in her head, but it did not make it any less true. The room was small and confining, but she paced it with such vigor and anxiety that she thought she might wear a rut in the stone floor.

The weeks wore on, but that did not diminish her tears. Her chamber door opened three times a day, and two Milnos guards stomped inside, escorting a maid with a tray. In the beginning, she had begged for her mother, desperate to understand why she was now a prisoner in her own home, but the maids refused to speak. Keeping their eyes cast downward, they placed the tray on her table, cleaned her room, and hurried away. She addressed the guards with a false sense of entitlement, insisting this had to be a mistake—after all, she was to be their queen. Sadly, her words fell on deaf ears, and she remained alone to ponder her fate.

After months in captivity, her frustration began to cloud her judgment, and she punched a guard while trying to escape. The man shoved her into a wall, pinning her with his arm under her chin. Unable to breathe, she stared into his dark, disrespectful eyes. Her hands grabbed at his unyielding strength, his hot breath in her face. "You will be silent. Going forward, you will stand here. Nowhere else but here! You are no queen of mine," he barked.

Those were the last words anyone had spoken to her. She began standing in that very spot whenever they entered. She often tremored in fear, but she never left that spot until the door closed once more. Each guard kept a keen eye on her standing proudly by the door while the servants cleaned her room or brought her food.

Then, one night, she found a note tucked into her freshly made bed. A letter penned in her mother's handwriting supplied painstaking details on Tolan's deplorable treatment and news that Landon Penier, the rightful heir to the throne, had been crowned king during the Winter Festival. Her mother closed the letter informing her that her father, Lucas Maxwell, would be the new Grand Duke, advisor to the king upon his return from Diu.

More importantly, Amelia's child would be taken upon its birth, and she would spend the rest of her days locked away in the Raven's Tower while her treacherous family told the world that she and the baby had tragically died in childbirth. Crushed by the news, Amelia rocked back on her ankles. She had no hope of ever seeing Tolan ever again. While she would live out her days in solitude, and her child would be taken and most likely killed. Her world began to spin inside her head, and everything turned upside down. How could this be happening? There is no way her parents could be this cruel, yet her mother's words were etched in black ink on white parchment, now burned into her memory forever.

Milnos—The Iron City, once her homeland, was now her prison.

A. D. Lombardo

CHAPTER 1

Routine

Whoever thought wielding magic gave you an advantage had never faced a squadron of magical Guardians. For the fifth straight hour, Kai's team drilled—and once again, he found himself pinned in the dirt with his arm bent at an odd angle and his right leg paralyzed. Bits of decayed leaves and pine needles pressed into his face, the smell of defeat trickled down his throat. A Beastmaster, beaten by a Weathervane. Somehow it felt wrong, but he took the loss in stride.

Gail punched the pressure points to restore movement to Kai's leg before offering him a hand up. Her golden-brown hair was pulled tight into a bun, intensifying her stern expression. "You are determined, I will give you that." She dusted her hands. "I applaud you for not using your dragon, but a healthy mix of magic might be the edge you need. Might I remind you, the smallest bits of power pulled from plants and sunshine can go unnoticed."

"If we fight Keegan and his Katoris," Kai said, "I do not want to alert them to the draw on magic, nor do I want my dragon to be my only weapon. They have dragon-killer crossbows."

"Practice siphoning magic in small doses, then push with your dragon's claw for maximum effect. The swift transformation will be difficult to defend if your opponent has little time to feel it coming." Gail nodded, then added, "There is another way. Consider an always-on approach. A constant tap on the vein keeps you charged, allowing you to respond with instant thought. Learn to keep the energy, almost like holding the memory of a kiss. Fight with parts of your dragon: armor plating, claw, or wings."

The pain racing down Kai's arm subsided as she rotated the shoulder and punched a few more points. He had never considered the idea. If he kept even the slightest amount of magic within him, he would not need to acquire as much in a rush to do real magic. "I appreciate the advice," he gave her a nod.

Guardian Mekael, the intimidating brawny Stoneking, smirked. It was the first sign that they respected him. The man's usual stoic profile cracked, and he looked almost kind. "Kai, remember to read the signs of magic when facing a fellow Katori." Mekael sheathed his battle axes. "Even with Gail's method, you can feel the magic. You may not feel anything when she first attacks you, but the moment before she wields the energy, you will notice a spark. Still, it is smart to overcome the dependency of magic. Not every situation will allow for your dragon. We have hidden our gifts for so long it is second nature to me to fight without them. You must be able to face off with any adversary on their terms within your given surroundings before you can bend the situation to fit your desired outcome."

Kai's look of disappointment must have shown because Gail offered a kind pat on his back. "We have decades of experience, and you have a few years of training with a few average fighters from Diu. These past few months with us, you have learned a great deal, but it does not give you our experiences. Give yourself time."

Kai knew they shared their advice to lift his spirits, but instead, he continued to critique each mistake, searching for perfection. On the next round, those with Beastmaster gifts practiced partial transformations, and Kai tried a few midflight shifts. Although he added his magic to his arsenal, he still felt he needed to hone his battle skills before his magic. While they made it farther down the mountain to their goal, they still lost. Chastising himself, he knew he needed to get better at sensing magic before it caught him off guard.

Through the pines, he saw his Uncle Haygan recovering from having the wind knocked out of his chest. Haygan rubbed the black stubble across his chin and leaned against a tree. His newly cropped black hair stuck to the side of his sweaty head. "Well, that was fun."

His uncle's sarcastic tone deflated his self-pity. If his uncle could find humor in defeat, so could he.

Above him, Rayna dangled in an ivy trap in the trees. Her dark brown hair spilled between the vines as her sister, Imani, slowly lowered her to the ground.

"I have to admit, I thought I had you, sister," Rayna said with a laugh. "But this trap caught me by surprise." Rayna jumped free of Imani's cage. "Being hunted, I am sure, is not the same as being on the frontlines of a battle, but this is good practice." Rayna wrapped an arm around her sister and entered the clearing.

Even in defeat, they all kept a positive attitude, yet this was only practice, not war. The real thing would feel much different—and have a deadly outcome. Somewhere in-between, Kai needed to find a balance.

Perched on the rocks, Yulia waited at the finish line. Above her, the brilliant blue sky was dappled with pillowy white clouds that offered little shade from the harsh summer sun. Studying Yulia's features, Kai could not get over how much she resembled her daughter, Riome. Both had green eyes and deep auburn hair, which Yulia kept in a loose braid down her back. A slight breeze danced around her, and a strategically placed cloud cast a faint shadow around the seasoned Katori Weathervane.

Kai leaned into the rocks and spoke to her. "Where is Riome? I heard she was coming to Katori, yet she has not come to see me. Why?"

Yulia slid from her perch and landed at Kai's side. "She is testing a theory before she travels on spy business for Diu."

Kai wanted to ask more, but the Weathervane walked away. Both women were so similar it was scary. Neither took to questions; both loved discovering secrets and floating where the wind took them.

Ryker stood in the shade, avoiding the summer heat, his long black hair pulled away from his clean-shaven face. With him, Smoke and

Shiva, the Nabean black wolves, sat at attention. Unfazed by another defeat, Ryker inspected the edge of his large hunting knife while Rayna healed the various cuts and scrapes along his arm. To Kai's surprise, none of them left a scar against his friend's olive complexion, unlike the jagged scar across the bridge of his nose and right cheek, which made him wonder if Rayna's abilities were growing stronger.

A cool breeze tousled Kai's sandy hair, and he felt something scratch his scalp. Removing the bits of pine needles and dirt, he followed Basil to join the others.

"I warned you to watch out for Basil, Haygan," Ryker teased, "but you never get past him. How is it you get gut checked every time at the same point?" Ryker showed no mercy punching Haygan on the shoulder with his fist. Ryker liked giving Haygan a hard time, but everyone knew they respected one another. The brotherly bond between them continued with a quick return jab from Haygan to Ryker's ribs.

"I have spent the last several months chasing a baby," Haygan retorted, "and a decade or so before that training horses. I am no Guardian." Kai watched his uncle recover his sword, ready for another go.

Kai dusted off his shirt. "We are all tired. Look, we have tried several different tactics—well, everyone but Haygan." Kai laughed, joining in torturing his uncle. "Sorry, uncle, you run against Basil down the same stretch, and in the end, he gets you every time."

"In my defense," Hagan said, running his fingers through his thick black hair, "the last time Basil came through the treetops, he caught me from behind. So that was different. Yet I still say the man is cheating." Everyone laughed, but Haygan's smirk faded. "Every time Basil uses those pressure points, he leaves me helpless. I cannot defend against these new techniques. I need to learn them now more than ever."

Basil, his grandfather, Lucca's best friend and Kai's teacher, turned to face Haygan. Sunlight danced through Basil's black hair, accenting his graying temples. "Cheating." He approached Haygan and jabbed him in the ribs. "But to be fair, I did punch you with my gorilla Beastmaster arm this time, but it was all in good fun." The jest made everyone laugh, even Haygan.

No truer words had ever reached Kai's ears. They all needed to learn them. The method was very new, and only a handful of Katori knew them well. Riome knew only a few and only ever taught him one. The few he knew he learned from Gail, but they required precision for results. Otherwise, they were just sharp jabs that led to confusion on both sides.

His uncle continued. "Most of the Guardians believe Keegan is coming, and I agree. Our magic is too often a crutch, and if I remember anything of the man Keegan was, he relies heavily on his powers. But our gifts were meant for creating beautiful things and the betterment of others, not war. We must outthink the enemy; they must believe they know how we intend to strike. If we use deception and tricks that draw no magic, we may have an advantage."

Kai thought about his various fights against the Caroco. During his first battle against them in Port Anahita, they used no such moves. His second fight was on his journey to save his mother; they used no such defense or attack then either. And even on the ship, during the assault on another vessel, they used nothing remotely similar. If a war was coming, and everyone believed it was, could these pressure points be an advantage for them? While some strikes incapacitated the body, others permanently damaged nerves or stopped the blood flow to the heart.

Ryker tossed up a hand. "Why are we spending time practicing drills if Keegan and his men might attack us at any moment? We should be attacking him. Take the fight to Caroco with dragons and bows. Find him before he finds us."

Kai wanted to agree, but none of them knew anything about the country of Caroco other than it was a very dangerous place on the other side of the world. As far as he knew, not even Admiral Roark had traveled that far.

"Enough speculating about war," Yulia insisted, bumping into Ryker as she passed. "And enough practice. I have things to do over the next few weeks, and it does not include any of you."

Like Kai, everyone felt the finality of her dismissal and departed. It had been a long day, and he, for one, wanted to go home. With an exhale, Kai transformed into his dragon, then he lowered a wing to Rayna and Smoke. While they were only an hour walk from home, flying was faster— and safer. Strangers were commonplace now in Katori. Even though he and his wife were Katori-born, many people made Kai uncomfortable as they stared at him. He knew they beheld him with contempt for turning their world upside down by exposing his Beastmaster powers to the outside world. News of magic now flooded every kingdom on the continent, and many Katori citizens found themselves scorned by their once-fellow neighbors, forcing many to return to their Katori homeland for safety.

◆ ◆ ◆

Midnight dew hung on the pines and dripped on Kai's head, which made him wonder why an unnatural fog filled the city of Matoku. Closing his eyes, he let his energy seep from his bones. Not so far that it floated away in the new breeze that kissed his cheek, but far enough. The air pricked the hair on his neck; there was a Weathervane nearby. He searched the pine barrens along the edge of town.

Yulia's rhythmic, prolonged movements gave him pause. *I thought she left the city.* With each tamp of her foot, wave of her arms, and fold of her hands, she splashed her magic into the air. The collection and expenditure remained so subtle that he might have never noticed had he not been practicing detecting magic with nearly every breath he took. Not wanting to disturb her practice, he backed up the way he came. Before he reached home, something struck him—not physically, but mentally. It drew him like a moth to a flame, summoning him to the Agora, and so he went.

Kai noticed the rolling mist from Yulia billowed into the Agora, filling the ancient building. On edge, he entered and gleaned the space. A silhouette moved through the fog—a Half-Light, his spy teacher and friend, Riome. "What are you doing here, little sister?" he called to her, entering the Katori sacred place.

"Testing a theory." She dangled a white crystal from a chain within her hand. "Orin shaped it for me . . ." she started.

"Why would the master of crystals help you by shaping a crystal meant to perform the rites of Conhanspriga?" Kai interrupted as he crossed the room. "I know Yulia would do anything for you, but why Orin? You are only a Half-Light, and accessing magic is not meant for a Half-Light, no offense." He may have aimed the question at Riome, but he felt it ricocheted back at himself. Kai had not grown up here in Katori. Did he deserve the crystal that dangled around his neck any more than her? Even his grandfather Lucca and the Guardians judged him as unworthy and tried to prevent him from acquiring magic.

"My mother took me through Alenga's restored temple," Riome explained. "It is beautiful, not only in design but the entire essence in that part of the mountain hummed with a harmonic tone filled with a magical serenity. I cannot explain it, but I felt compelled to try this."

It was only a little over a year ago when Orin created the hexagon stone which dangled on a chain around Kai's neck. "Everyone knows a Half-Light cannot enter the sacred water. Which now explains the fog and where your mother went these past few days, but not Orin's participation. Riome, tell me what's going on."

"You will have to ask him yourself," she said sharply. "All I know is when Orin looked deep into my eyes, I felt a connection and a peace I have sought for too long. When Orin took the stone from me, crushed the unwanted dark bits of rock, and shaped the crystal, I cried. As a child, I grew up here and witnessed the blessing of many Katori at the end of their Conhaspriga. I know everything about being Katori—except for this last bit. Orin said the triangle represents strength, balance, and enlightenment. Please, Kai, let me finish." Riome stepped closer to the pool.

Straight above them, the dark starlit sky sparkled with promise, and Kai wanted to let her. At the bottom of the natural spring, Kai noticed the three interlocking loops with no end, the symbol of Alenga. The design was set in stone and illuminated in blue crystal.

Remembering the words that had been told to him and Rayna, Kai directed her to wade into the water. "This is the celestial spirit pool. May Alenga restore your health, replenish your spirit, and bless your future." With a bow, he backed away and sat.

They both looked at the water's shimmering, smooth surface. Light glistened down from the aperture in the roof above. As instructed, Riome waded into the pool. The surface bubbled and beamed with light. Even from where he sat, Kai felt the energy-charged water invigorate his body. Pure magic seeped into his skin. He could feel the power build as the water beckoned Riome deeper.

A pang of jealousy pulled at his chest, filling him with the desire to speak with Alenga. He rose to his feet, and his heart pounded with the knowledge Alenga was coming. Then Riome's eyes caught his as she looked back. Her glassy eyes brimmed, and a solitary tear broke down her cheek. The lift in her mouth said "Thank you" as she eased off the last step.

As her dark hair sank beneath the water, Kai leaned forward to watch her sink. Profound energy filled his aura, and his sense of clarity brightened with the glow in the room. To his surprise, Riome began to rise to the surface quickly. As was done for others, he slipped off his boots and slid into the lukewarm pool. The charged water seeped through his clothing, sending magic up his spine and through his entire body. Taking another step down, he reached for Riome's hand, pulled her into his arms, and carried her out.

Gently placing her on the stone floor, he sat back and waited. Everything he knew assured him a Half-Light could not wield magic, so why would Alenga come to Riome? He could not let it go. When he took note of the stone around her neck, he noticed the delicate triangle was no longer white; it was now aqua blue with purple, red, and green flecks. Desperate to conceal what she had done and what he had allowed to happen, he yanked on his boots and picked up Riome. He could not risk being found in the Agora should someone else feel the power of Alenga's presence.

Outside, the thick fog continued to roll down from the pine barrens, and he darted across the stone bridge and up the embankment toward Yulia.

She asked as he approached, "Kai, did my daughter survive?"

The question struck Kai like lightning. "You mean she could have *died* in there?" He clutched his friend's limp form in his arms. "I never should have let her go into that pool."

"I have no idea," Yulia admitted. "I never expected anything more than my daughter getting wet, but I could not deny her again."

"Yulia, why did Orin help you? He is practically an Elder within Katori."

"Rules do not apply to family. He is my great uncle."

Kai lifted Riome's mouth to his ear. The gurgling sounds from her lungs sent him into action. "Hurry," he insisted, placing her on the ground and rolling her head to one side.

Water trickled out Riome's mouth, and her mother pressed on her chest, followed by the swirling of her finger above her daughter's lips. Water swirled out of Riome's mouth, and then Yulia switched movements, filling Riome's lungs with air. Once, twice, three times before she coughed and gasped for air.

Yulia wiped her daughter's face and helped her sit up.

A million questions danced around Kai's head. "What happened?" Kai said, still holding onto Riome as she regained her breath. "I felt the magic of Alenga's arrival, and I know how it works. You are under for only a brief time to everyone else, but the experience is different on the other side. For you, it could feel like hours."

Riome nodded and took hold of the crystal. "Alenga was there. She spoke to me. She was everything I ever dreamed of and more. She told me many things, some of which are fading now, but what matters is that she reminded me I am only a Half-Light. Any power she granted me would be too powerful for me to wield."

This news did not surprise Kai. "But your stone, it is no longer white. Alenga did something to the crystal. What else did she say?"

"I did not say she did not bless me," Riome said weakly. "Only that the magic would be too powerful for my Half-Light blood to manage. Alenga said there would be a price each time I use the magic. For some, it corrupts their soul. For others, it ages them dramatically and takes their mind. Aging does not frighten me, but I have done some dark things in my life, and forgetting those might be a blessing. So, I would say I will choose the latter when the time comes. Either way, I need to go."

Yulia helped her daughter to her feet. "Tell no one about this, Kai." Her tone left little room for doubt on how important this secret would be between them.

"Riome, wait . . ." he called after them, but she did not turn, nor did Yulia. *Where are you going?* He finished in his head.

CHAPTER 2

Momentary Bliss

Sunshine crawled across the room like a lazy child as Kai's eyes became aware he had slept through another night. The air smelled sweet, like cherry blossoms with a hint of crisp pear. Kai let his hand dance in the sunshine, and the heat of a new summer's day warmed his skin. Months of peaceful sleep left him refreshed and happy, yet he felt anxious. While no nightmares of impending doom plagued him, he could not help but worry when Keegan would strike.

Bliss was not a familiar emotion to him, but surely this was how it felt. His hand slid behind him, searching for Rayna; she was already up. Letting his ears listen, he heard her downstairs, the clink of a spoon against a cup. The teakettle sang out as his feet hit the floor, and he grabbed a shirt. Venturing downstairs, he wiped the dread from his expression, hopeful he could conceal the darkness looming in the recesses of his mind. He owed her that much.

"Good morning, wife," he said as he approached, and she stopped to greet him. The smell of strawberries and cosmos flowers lingered in her hair. Everything about her drew him closer—the warmth of her smile, the curve of her neck, the sparkle in her eyes.

Rayna kissed him with delight and then poured them each a cup of tea. "Good morning, husband," she mocked with a sweetness he loved. "Sleep well?" Her slow delivery sent mixed emotions down his spine. He imagined she too feared any news his gift of visions might bestow, but again he had no dreams to retell. Shaking his head in near disappointment, he reached for his chair.

The smell of vanilla reached Kai's nose as she set the teakettle on the stone hearth. She smoothed her silky green nightdress, and he noticed how the silver band around her finger sparkled in the sunlight. He gazed at the matching ring on his finger. Maybe it was over, and maybe there was nothing to fear. With the safe return of his father, King Iver, and the peace talks between Diu and Katori, war no longer seemed a concern. Although their training to become Guardians consumed much of their time, maybe he could let go and enjoy his new life with her. His mood lifted; he swept her back into his arms. "From the first day I saw you, I knew we were meant to be together. Have I told you I love you?"

"Not today." She giggled, raising on her tiptoes.

Thunderous footfalls echoed up the stairwell, followed by concern-filled shouts and a knock at his door. "Kai, Rayna, come quick. The Elders are about to make an announcement. Your grandfather instructed me to collect you both. We must ride to Hiowind immediately."

Five months of bliss were gone in an instant. A sense of dread bubbled in Kai's stomach with the anticipated news. He let Rayna slip through his fingers as he turned to open the door and let Ryker storm into his living room. His wolf Smoke leaped from his resting place near the large window, ready to join in the action. "What is wrong?" Kai demanded, already reaching for his boots, "I know there is some important news, but please do not make me wait for an official Elder announcement."

"Ten Caroco ships were spotted off the Mystic Islands. We need you both in Hiowind immediately. I have Ember and Snowflake saddled and ready downstairs." Ryker left them to get ready.

A renewed sense of dread swelled in the pit of his stomach. Keegan was coming. Every horrible thought and feeling that he ever had about his birth father rushed through him once more. This man would never stop coming for him and his mother. Lacing his last boot, he looked up to find Rayna's silky green nightdress replaced with a dark green shirt and black pants. She held out a dark blue shirt. "You may want this," she offered, then she reached for her boots.

The bright white shirt Kai wore felt soft against his skin and reminded him of his earlier feelings of bliss. He did not want to change it—or let go. It was impossible to separate the feelings Keegan stirred in him, and he imagined the very mention of the man's name pierced his wife as well. But all the same, he knew Rayna was right. *How quickly our day turned*, he thought, switching out his shirt. While she strapped on her boots, he grabbed a pouch of supplies.

Memories of his younger years stirred at the sight of Ember, his chestnut brown horse with a black mane. The horse was like a second companion who had been left in Diu until recently, and Ember stood proudly near the path. Next to him stood Rayna's horse Snowflake, a dark bay horse with a white dappled pattern—a rare wild Moroka horse from what Kai remembered.

Kai's horse neighed with enthusiasm. "Good to see you too, Ember." He ran his hand over his horse before hopping in the saddle. Their connection remained true as if no time had passed during his adventures traveling around Katori over the last year.

Ryker and Rayna climbed onto their mounts, and Ryker led the way to the road that ran out of Matoku toward Hiowind. Shiva and Smoke followed. With each heart-pounding hoofbeat, anxiety swelled in Kai's chest. If a fleet of Caroco ships were bound for Katori, what did that mean for his mother? Was Keegan coming to take her away? The fear of his mother's safety propelled him to push Ember harder, as if reaching Hiowind faster would ensure her safety and stop Keegan from stealing her away from him.

◆ ◆ ◆

Inside the Agora, all eight Elders stood in a circle around the sunbathed pool of sacred spring water, facing the crowd. Kai watched their robes rustle around their feet as a breeze swept amongst the group.

Knowing they seldom dawned, their Elder robes gave Kai a sense of the serious nature of their situation and the message they planned to deliver. Each Elder wore the color of their discipline: Lucca, Yana, and Kam in shades of yellow for the Lumes; Jin and Rochelle in shades of red for the Stonekings; Wilda wore purple for the Weathervanes; Zook in blue for the Beastmasters; and Noreen in green for the Kodama.

In his many months living in Katori, Kai had come to know each of them. He knew which ones believed change was necessary and which valued Katori tradition above everything else. Even though the Elders decided to show the world their truth—a decision which had saved his life and revealed the return of dragons—some people held firm to the old ways. Kai had no idea how this would go.

Lucca, his grandfather, stepped forward to address the crowd. For the first time, Kai noticed a few gray streaks in his grandfather's pitch-black hair. "Peace between Katori and Diu remains delicate—" he clasped his hands together in a symbol of unity "—but we are hopeful. At this time, we have no news of Milnos moving on our country, but we keep a keen eye on the mountain range to the north near our shared borders. Some Katori citizens living in Milnos fled in fear once news of magic reached the city. They were not pushed out, but they felt a change in the city. In addition, we have word that Caroco ships were spotted sailing around the Mystic Islands toward the coast of Kahoma."

This news did not surprise Kai. He imagined it would only be a matter of time before his father came to Katori, either to take his mother or him or both to join his radical cause. What did surprise him was the lack of warning Alenga had provided. Did she no longer trust him with the future? Why had he not dreamt of Keegan's return?

But then his grandfather Lucca began to speak, and Kai could not believe what he heard. "We are one people, and it is time we started acting like the wise Chiefs and Unie we were appointed to be, instead of scorned parents with spirited children who wanted to explore our world. Same as we welcomed home the outcast Katoris we must also give Keegan a chance. Now that the world knows our truth, things will change. Maybe they needed to change years ago. We must welcome

Keegan and his followers back to Katori and make peace with them if we can. We must avoid war at all costs."

The crowd murmured and stirred. Kai kept his eyes focused on the Elders, searching their poised expressions for any indications that one of them disagreed. Thunder cracked in the cloudless sky, and Wilda's purple silk dress fluttered in a breeze, engulfing only her. She stood proud and waited to address the crowd.

Silence fell over the people, and Wilda stepped forward. Her short black hair was decorated with strands of white and purple crystals that trickled down to her exposed brown shoulders. "In showing the world our truth, we set in motion an inevitable event that will change our world forever. First, Alenga bid us welcome Davi and his people, our lost Katori, back home from Diu. Now, I believe this includes Keegan and his followers. No longer should we hide in fear of the world. That does not mean we wish to rule as Keegan thinks we should, only live in the open. The adjustment will be difficult enough without fighting amongst ourselves. The grumblings must stop; no more whispers about the old ways. We elected to offer peace to Keegan. If we can extend harmony, we may yet avoid a civil war here in Katori."

Murmurs trickled again through the crowd. This time Wilda tamped her hands, sending a delicate gust of air through the gathering. Again, they fell silent and turned their eyes to her. "I know this is unsettling to those who trust in centuries of tradition. It was through considerable deliberations that we made the decision to show the world magic exists and to offer peace to all."

Whispers again weaved through the crowd, and many shifted toward Zook, the youngest chief standing near the end. The Elder for Matoku stroked his trim black goatee but said nothing. The hesitation balanced by the wisdom in the man's dark eyes gave Kai the impression he was an old soul.

A few shouted Zook's name, and he waved a hand to silence them. He used no display of power, not even a growl, keeping his Beastmaster form hidden. In the stillness, Kai observed the Elder and then the crowd.

Zook made the people wait. The respect he commanded spiked Kai's curiosity, keen to hear this man finally speak.

When the Elder raised his dark eyes to the crowd, he let his gaze wander. The midday sun spilling into the Agora gave a bronzy glow to the man's dark complexion. "You all know my heart. And I know what you expect from me is to hold tradition. While I spend a large portion of my day studying the past, let me remind you, the future is not defined by the words in our scrolls but by the actions we take in the present. Still, there is much we can learn by examining history. Our earliest historians wrote about harmony and togetherness, yet after the great war, we hid away. We have lost our sense of truth. We judge any who choose to explore the outside world unless they become Guardians, and we exclude any who choose a different life. We demanded secrecy at all costs, and that choice took much from our society."

A long pause fell over the crowd. Zook glanced at his fellow Elders. "Most Elders are traditionalists who believe in the secrets we keep and the mountains we raised to keep us all safe. Our border creates a sanctuary to be ourselves, but they are walls nonetheless. My dear friend Chief Lucca reminded me that harmony and togetherness are the foundation of our society. I implore you all to welcome our lost children and give the world a chance to accept our truth. The richest part of our history is steeped in tradition, and we must change the deepest part of ourselves if we are to heal the wound between us."

The crowd grumbled again, and Elder Jin spoke over them. "We are united in allowing our people to explore a new openness with the world, which also includes letting them come back," his thick voice bellowed, hushing the crowd. His red robe rustled in the breeze, and the depth of his dark complexion held a richness of earthy tones. His dark eyes smiled before his mouth curved up. "Being more progressive, I have made it my responsibility to listen to these new ideas and understand them. I know many here are true Katori traditionalists, and for you, this change will be harder. It is these very ideas that drove a wedge between us and those who followed Keegan to Caroco. Some who believe as he does live among us, and I hear you, but your words hint at war. Had we been more open to his concepts, would we be facing war on our soil? I think not. Our struggle to trust the world gave power to a movement which festers under the surface of our country."

Again, the crowd complained.

The people shocked Kai. They argued against their Elders. "Is there no way to unite Katori behind a new future?" Kai whispered to Rayna. "I do not trust Keegan, but if we cannot make peace with him and his Katori followers, we will be at war. We must find a way forward that does not involve bloodshed. I cannot say I want to see my father walking around Katori like nothing ever happened, but surely Keegan will listen to reason and accept the offer of peace now that the world knows the truth about Katori magic."

Rayna whispered back, "Change is never easy. The Elders are asking the people to break tradition. And given the flood of Katori who have traveled here to seek shelter, they fear living in the open. I have heard some say their friends now look at them like strangers. The world is not receiving them with open arms but with whispers and rejection. Many Katori living outside of our homeland are called witches or sorcerers. People fear what they do not understand. There are many frightening stories of families cast from their homes just because they are Katori."

He shook his head. "You are right. I wonder how I would feel if I were on the outside of Katori. Still, I fear making peace with Keegan and his followers. Katori or not, they are criminals, and my father wants world domination. He will push for Katori to insist the world bow to us." He knew peace was their only chance, but Keegan was not a peaceful man.

Rayna continued to keep her voice low. "See, even you struggle to make a choice. The traditionalists insist Keegan and the others abandoned Katori for the outside world. Like you, the traditionalists know we must fight for peace. People here remember how Keegan preached for us to stop living in secret, and the Elders cast him out. But they have not seen firsthand how dark he has become."

From the corner of his eye, he saw Elder Yana sit on the floor, her yellow robe pooling around her. Soon, the other Elders followed her example. Stunned by her boldness, the crowd joined them one by one in silence on the Agora floor. Only those near the archways remained standing.

Once the people fell silent, Yana addressed them. "Compassion." Her voice echoed over their heads, and a tiny yellow glow blossomed around her. The golden braids of her long hair shone bright, giving her an angelic presence. "Whenever we meet another, we have the opportunity for kindness. One tradition remains—love others. We must spread peace and love to others. We are a community of givers. Not one of us can lay claim to a perfect life. Within the teachings of Alenga, we can come to no other conclusion—bring her children home." Yana looked to Elder Kam and motioned to the group.

The crowd froze as everyone held their breath, waiting for the next Elder to speak. Kam was the eldest chief, so his words carried the most weight in the Katori nation. His opinion worried Kai the most. In recent talks, the older man argued against the outsiders returning—against Keegan especially. Kai wondered if Kam agreed with today's announcement.

Kam's warrior-like physique and youthful complexion gave him the appearance of a much younger man. His square jaw jutted out to the crowd, and only the wind dared to tussle his long salt-and-pepper hair and the edges of his yellow robe. Eyes focused straight ahead, Kam seemed to look through the crowd to another place and time.

A softness washed over the old chief's expression. "As a scholar of Alenga's teachings, I am reminded life is not about want I want, or what you want. Yana is correct. It is our practice to give. If one of you were in need, I would give you the clothes off my back. All that I have is yours— I can offer no less to any lost Katori. Alenga bids us bring them back within our hearts. She wants them here in her city. I agree with my fellow Chiefs and Unie. We will welcome Keegan home. We will find a peaceful way forward."

In the remaining silence, the Stoneking Elder Rochelle added, "I hope that united we can deliver this same message across Katori. We leave this morning for the coast to greet Keegan and his followers. We expect some may seek out old family members to welcome them and shun them no longer. I bid you each to do the same."

Lucca stood to address the entire crowd. "You all know I lost the most from Keegan's treachery against my daughter; however, for the sake of Katori, we must find peace with him. If the world cannot accept our truth, we do not need the distraction of fighting amongst ourselves."

Silence fell over the crowd as the other Elders stood and bowed and mingled with the group. Lucca walked straight to Kai. Kai knew what his grandfather wanted. The regal yellow robe fluttered around Lucca. "Kai," his grandfather raised a hand to direct him closer.

Kai folded his arms over his chest. "Grandfather, I know you disagree with this. You are as against this as I am. Welcoming Keegan back into Katori is a mistake. I do not trust him around my mother. I will travel with the Elders to Kahoma, and you are welcome to speak with him for the sake of peace. If I see another way, I would offer it. But do not let him near my mother."

"As an Elder, I do what is best for my people, even if I do not always agree." Lucca stepped closer to Kai and glanced around the Agora. "I believe Milnos is not finished with war. Even with the knowledge of dragons, they have immense hatred for Katori and Diu. Milnos has never forgiven our involvement in stopping them from conquering Diu. Roark may have come to Diu and saved the city, but he has gone home now, back to his fort in the south. As allies to Diu, we must protect our neighbors, lest Milnos turn their eyes on us next. We cannot be in a civil war and fight Milnos at the same time. If I can make peace with the man, we all can support Diu."

"I understand," Kai lied. "Rayna and I will be ready to travel with you." He would never understand welcoming Keegan home, peace or not. The more he thought about the return of his murderous father, the more he hated the idea.

A. D. Lombardo

CHAPTER 3

Keegan's Message

Kahoma, the seaside Katori city, clung to the coastal cliffs as far as the eye could see. A beautiful community surrounded by a lush tropical forest on one side and a sheer precipice on the other. Kai peered down the stone stairs secured to the cliff wall, which provided access to the beach a hundred feet below.

He turned to Rayna. "Wow, the cliffs are much higher than I remember."

She held his hand tight and pointed out to sea. "There. Do you see them, the first two ships coming around the cliffs? They seem rather close. Are they not worried about the rocks?"

The white cliffs met the rolling blue waves of the ocean in steep grandeur. The ocean waves crashed against them in angry protest, searching for the sandy beach set back inside the protected cove. A steady stream of people fled the beach, scaling the stone steps on the cliffs as the foreign ships came into view. Kai understood their fears. The Caroco ships were not known to be peaceful. Confused by the Caroco sailor's belligerent disregard for the dangerous shoreline, Kai stepped closer to the edge.

On one side, the beach carved into the cliffs, and on the other, rocks of all shapes and sizes jutted out of the ocean floor, each created to protect the Katori coastline. These looming spires of rock were meant to ward off sailors and anyone wishing to scale the cliffs to reach the Katori mainland. The beach was the only safe access point, and the Caroco ships were not coming into the inlet. *What are they doing?* Kai wondered.

"Why are the ships not coming into the pier where the shore is safe? We should inform the Elders, something is not right. They are making their announcement in the local Agora." Kai turned to see his grandfather approaching and waited.

"How did it go?" Rayna asked Lucca.

The expression on Lucca's face and the Kahoma tribesman following behind the Elders told Kai the news was not good. The tension on their faces concerned him, and he imagined the local citizens did not take it well, especially knowing they were at the forefront of whatever happened today.

Lucca stepped next to Kai and Rayna, but he kept his eyes on the approaching vessels. "It went as well as you can imagine. The Kahoma tribe, like those in Hiowind and Matoku, were torn between the past and the future. Many argued for tradition, while others embraced their new freedoms and the return of Keegan. He has far more followers than anyone imagined. It frightens me to think we would welcome this man back so easily, but then, fear is a strong motivator. War could tear us apart, and none of us want that, so we must try peace. But Kahoma sits in the line of fire. If this goes wrong today, they will pay the price first."

The citizens of Kahoma swarmed the cliff's edge, watching the Caroco ships advance toward their shoreline. To Kai's amazement, their speed seemed to increase as more and more ships came into view. As the ten Caroco ships cut across the open sea, they sailed onward instead of coming ashore along the beach. Then a gray fog engulfed their vessels, and they disappeared. Everyone stood speechless at the cliffs near the corner of Kahoma beach.

He looked to his grandfather. "What now? It will be dusk soon. Do they mean to come ashore after nightfall? Are they passing us by? I hate to jump to conclusions, but their movements make no sense. If they offer peace, why does he not come ashore at the pier? Does he mean to attack us while we sleep? I do not understand." Kai felt afraid, as he imagined many others did, not knowing what his father's intentions.

Lucca did not answer. Instead, his grandfather stepped closer to the cliff's edge and tilted his head. Kai held his ground, angling his head to search for whatever his grandfather heard. The ground began to shake, and Lucca reared back, waving his arms in the air. "Get back!" he shouted, pressing the people backward.

As the crowd ran from the cliffs, Kai stayed. He studied the white cliffs and the rocky shoreline below. The gray fog rolled toward the cliffs through the jagged rocks. The ground continued to rumble as white stones broke free and tumbled into the lifting fog. When a wave of water splashed the grass to the left of him, Kai sniffed the spray.

Salt water, Kai thought. *They must be lifting the ocean!*

Thunder shook the ground, and Kai stepped away from the cliff's edge. The rumble vibrated his body, and he struggled to stay on his feet. Again, attempting to run away from the chaotic earthquake, an unnatural gust of wind struck him, knocking him on his back and propelling him thirty feet away. Each subsequent air gust pulsed with magic.

Rising back to his feet, Kai saw a geyser of water punch through the thick haze and then slosh across the ground. The gloomy mist engulfed Kai as he ran away from the gush of ocean water, which continued to flood the land around him. The next quake brought another rush of water and a massive shadow rushing upward. Turning away from the rolling fog, Kai cleared the haze seconds before a massive vessel sloshed through the water-soaked grass and veered in his direction. Followed by three more ships, each vessel came to rest atop the coastal cliffs.

The four ships leaned awkwardly on their keels in dead silence. No gangplank was lowered, and no faces appeared along the railings. The Kahoma continued to race backward; some even changed into beasts, grabbing citizens as they fled. Kai held his breath. Then hundreds of gunports opened and cannons jutted from their openings—and Kai took hold of his crystal and transformed into his silver dragon.

So much for offering peace, he thought as he flew over the crowd in search of Rayna. He spotted her and scooped her from the rush along with his grandfather, Lucca. Lastly, he found Ryker and his uncle Haygan and offered them a wing, tipped down low. They grabbed hold and climbed up his back.

In rapid succession, the cannons fired. Four flashes of smoke and fire erupted from each ship, then four more. Splinters from destroyed trees and rubble from buildings exploded in a blaze of fire around the blast zone. Keeping a safe distance, Kai circled overhead, holding the treasures of his family within his claws and along his back. He could not believe his eyes.

We need to get on those ships, Kai, he heard his uncle Haygan say to him within his mind. *If we can take the fight to them, we may stop the destruction. But be careful! Each ship has two dragon-killer weapons.*

The black point of each bolt swiveled to follow his flight pattern. Three men maned each weapon; one stood ready to launch a deadly blow while the others rotated the dragon-killer as Kai circled. They were prepared for him—him or any other dragon that may try to get close. Kai veered wide beyond the cliffs and dropped into the thick mist, not wanting to risk being shot down. His amber eyes blinked and gleaned an angled stone ramp, which Kai now understood was how the Caroco ships reached the top of the cliffs.

Hidden from view, Kai landed below the ships on the ramp and released his dragon form. The ramp was wet, but no water flowed from below. "There are five of us and four ships," he said to his passengers.

The second round of cannon fire commenced, and the ground shook. One, two, three, the cannons fired. One, two, three, they fired again. A steady pattern from each ship repeatedly shook the city.

"I gleaned hundreds of men below decks on each ship, more than we can handle alone," Kai shouted. "We need to get them off the ships and stop the cannon fire. Maybe even disable the dragon-killers."

They climbed the steep ramp, and the mist evaporated, giving them a clear line of sight to the ships. The back gunports remained closed.

Lucca pointed to the first vessel. "Rayna and I can handle one ship." Then he pointed to the next. "Ryker and Haygan can take the next two ships. Kai, you go to the last one. Disable the dragon-killers and subdue the men, six men each, and get off."

The thought of Rayna not by his side pulled on Kai's heart. He wanted to protest, but he had to trust her skills and his grandfather. Rayna pulled a few seeds from the leather pouch at her waist. "My vines can get us up top. Ryker and Haygan, you can get up the same way and jump to the other ships. Lucca, if you can distract them with light, my vines can restrain the men."

Everything trembled with the next round of cannon fire. Three or four blasts in succession shook the ground.

"We will need to do more than subdue the men," Ryker shouted over the thunderous cannon fire. "We need to remove the firing pins and cables that fire the bolt, then between the two of you—" he gestured to Lucca and Kai "—you can set the ships ablaze. Fire will drive the men off the ships. There are no Katori among them, so once we eliminate the cannons, we improve our odds, and we can make short work of the army inside."

Before they could react, seven eagles dropped behind them and transformed. Unsure if they were friend or foe, Ryker drew his battle axes, and everyone else drew a sword. Haygan stepped forward, his blade angled at one man's head. "Which side are you on?" he demanded.

A tall rusty haired man held up his empty hands. "We fight for our homeland. How can we help?" The others stood ready to accept orders.

Ryker pointed to the remaining two ships. "Spilt up and take out the men manning the dragon-killer crossbows on the middle two ships. Once the deck is secure, remove the metal pins securing the cable to the bow and the firing mechanism. As a dragon, Kai can set fire to the ships and drive the invaders out into the open, but he cannot risk being shot by one of those weapons."

The Beastmasters nodded and took flight toward the middle ships. Their massive wingspan glided on the updraft from the cliff's edge, and they kept low near the ground. "Haygan, you go with your father and Rayna," Ryker ordered. "Kai and I will take the last ship."

Lucca, Rayna, and Haygan ran to the first ship, and Ryker took off in the opposite direction. Kai followed Ryker around the curve of the cliffs toward the last vessel. Concerns for Rayna drew his eyes behind him. He could no longer see the first ship, but his mind raced to her as if his thoughts could keep her safe.

The final ship came into view. Kai looked up at the massive ship as he collected the last bit of energy needed to transform. The golden braid of his dragon spun in his mind, and his hand touched his white crystal. Controlling his magic, he focused on the wings of his dragon, the only part of his sliver dragon needed to scale the side of the Caroco ship.

Thick scales erupted across his chest and flowed down his back, widening the structure of his body. Although the transformation was painless, he felt every adjustment to his spine, ribs, and shoulders. His biceps bulked with mass and hundreds of smaller scales. As his massive wings sprouted, his leg muscles enlarged to compensate for the strain.

"I will lift you to the top," he instructed Ryker.

With the beat of his wings, they lifted from the ground. Kai flew slow and kept an eye on the ship for surprises. The silhouette of his form cast a massive shadow over the gunports, but they remained closed. As he flew above the ship's railing, the white sails billowed in the wind. At either end of the ship, the dragon-killers sat at the ready. Light as a feather, Ryker jumped from Kai's back, took two steps, and indicated the vessel's stern was his.

While the roar of distant cannon fire concealed his approach, Kai drifted effortlessly above the wooden decking; the tiniest beat of his wings kept him airborne. Even though his stealthy approach made no sound, the ever-watchful boatswain turned at the sight of his dark shadow blocking the sun. Lost on the wind, the man's angry shouts went unanswered, and he wrestled with the dragon-killer, trying to yank it into position on his own.

Drawing on a bit of magic, Kai extended the reach of his arm, and his dragon arm increased in length. He yanked the man from his post. A flick of his wrist sent the man flying toward the cliff's edge. The bombardments stopped and shouts from the stern alerted the other two men to the intruders on their ship. They turned and attacked him without fear.

Their blades flickered in the sunlight, slashing and cutting at Kai. Withdrawing his wings, he landed on the deck with a thud. His enlarged form remained covered in dragon scale, and he towered over his opponents. The sharp blades sparked and pinged with each strike but did not cut through his armored scales. His adversaries looked determined and half-crazed in their attempts to fight him.

Kai knew there was no time to bother with these men. His dragon's claws swiped both men off the deck, and his powerful Beastmaster arms cast them into the mist in the same direction as their predecessor.

Keeping his form, he inspected the dragon-killer weapon. Across the top, he noticed the metal pins securing the cable to the bow. His hands were too large to remove them. Instead, he used his immense dragon strength and ripped the weapon from its base. Splinters spat in protest in every direction as the bowed wooden frame snapped and the firing mechanism broke in half.

No sooner did he finish his task than dozens of Katori warriors land on the deck, all poised to fight. Weapons drawn, they approached the hatch to access the bowels of the ship. Kai released his dragon form and joined them. Ryker reached for the handle to open the entrance. The silence below was deafening and something felt wrong.

Kai stayed his friend's hand. "NO!" Kai gleaned the hatch and then the depths of the ship again. "Why do they wait?" he questioned more to himself than Ryker.

This time Kai focused on the warriors poised to strike, or so he thought. Their swords sagged in their hands, and their shields hung more like decoration than battle-ready. Kai took note of their poorly shaved heads, their half-closed eyes, their barely noticeable breathing. Like the morning mist, the illusion faded away. Wooden posts held the men like statues in position, with their weapons nailed in place. Only two men moved deep within the ship. They poured a black powder from small barrels across the wooden planks before hopping through a hole at the ship's bottom.

"It's a trap!" Kai shouted and yanked Ryker from the ship's deck as his wings burst from his back and he soared into the bright sky. Heeding his warning, the other Katori warriors fled. Desperate to warn the others, Kai flew toward the first ship. In complete dragon form, he cradled Ryker in his claws. Each vessel he passed was the same; half-dead men posed to give the illusion of warriors in waiting. Ryker shouted to the other Katori warriors as they flew overhead.

Behind him, the last ship exploded. Fire and heat engulfed it, sending wood and metal shrapnel into the air. His fellow Katori brethren fled; whether they heard Ryker's warning or gleaned the same as him, he could not be sure.

In the distance, on the first ship, Rayna's eyes lifted to the sky and she pointed in his direction. Kai could not hear her words, but Lucca and Haygan knelt, poised to open the hatch the same as them. The second ship exploded, right below him. He rolled to protect Ryker. His wings wrapped tight around his underbelly as the ball of fire engulfed his backside. Clearing the explosion, he dove for Rayna as the third ship exploded in the distance.

There is no time to land, he thought. Extending his wing, he dipped low and scooped up his family. He felt each of them cling to the edge of his wing. He pumped as best he could with only one free wing, but he gained very little lift. They were falling more than flying. He cleared the railing with a final push. His solitary wing cupped the wind in an attempt to slow their descent, sending them into a downward spiral. As they fell from the sky, he gleaned the flames as they raced through the guts of the remaining ship. Moments before the explosion, he curled into a ball and struck the ground.

Flames and heat engulfed his dragon body with a flash. Inside, he held his family close, hoping it would be enough. As the temperature cooled, he opened his wings. Rayna's face was the first one he saw.

"I'm alright."

Lucca, Ryker, and Haygan stood; they were all safe. Kai released his dragon form. "It was a trap." Kai gestured as he led everyone around the burning ships toward the chaos in the city. "The men inside were victims . . . maybe. They had shaved heads to trick us into thinking they were Caroco men." His group came around the ships and took in their first glimpse of Kahoma. "Keegan deceived us. He knew we would glean the ships, and maybe he even knew we would try to board them. The cannon fire was a distraction to keep us on the run and conceal the real Caroco warriors escaping underground."

Lucca pointed to the ground. "They have tunneled under our very feet." His grandfather knelt to touch the soil. "There is at least one Lumen among them, maybe two. Only a Lumen is capable of this deception—using an illusion of light that even I did not see through, but then again, I was not really looking. Everything about this attack was staged to confuse us."

Ryker stepped forward. "We need Stonekings to track them. Chief Jin and Uni Rochelle need to gather as many Stonekings as possible. We need time to discover their intent and stop them."

Kai looked to the setting sun as it kissed the horizon, and he thought about his father's deception. *He sent us a clear message—there will be no peace.*

◆ ◆ ◆

Like divining rods, Jin and Rochelle meandered through the tall grasses in search of the underground tunnels burrowed by Keegan's men. Their fellow Stonekings roamed behind them in staggered formation, searching for the invaders with their bare feet. Slowly they formed four lines.

Jin motioned to Rochelle. "Here," he pointed. "They came through here, but they are restoring the ground behind them as they go. This technique explains why only Stonekings can follow their trail. We can see the residual magic they leave behind."

Unie Rochelle pointed down the various paths. "I see two more here." Her long flowing black hair trickled down to her waist in tiny ringlets, bouncing as she walked. "We should split up. Some of you follow those two paths. I will follow this path. Jin, you take the next," she ordered, taking off at a brisk walk. Kai followed eagerly, desperate to get answers. Ryker and Rayna came with him while Haygan and Lucca followed Jin.

The various Lumen-powered streetlamps and embedded crystals within the road highlighted the folds in the fabric of Rochelle's red pants. Streaks of orange and gold gave Kai the impression her legs were on fire. Mesmerized by the Elder's furious pace, Kai's heart pounded with anticipation. He gleaned the ground but saw nothing, not even a hint of a tunnel or residual magic. Yet, Rochelle weaved through the city, and everyone followed.

Around buildings, through gardens and pavilions, each step sparked a renewed connection that Kai wished he understood. However, when Rochelle crossed over a bridge, she stopped on the other side as if lost. Up and down the embankment, she traced the river's edge in frustration. Her dark black eyes narrowed, and she jumped in the river. The water sloshed around her knees. "We are close!" she shouted.

Other Katori joined in the hunt, many with weapons and some with wild animals by their side; Beastmasters and their companions. Kai, Rayna, and Ryker kept to the riverbank and followed the group. When Rochelle suddenly leapt up the embankment and veered right, Kai caught sight of Jin and his group. They were on a collision course until they stopped twenty feet short of each other.

Kai felt their concern as the other two groups converged on their location. The silence lingered only a moment and the ground erupted at the intersection. White stones and black soil shot into the air, and three Katori Stonekings rose into the air. Their stone pedestals thrust them skyward then receded, leaving a gaping black hole.

The men landed with ease and gazed at Kai's confused group as a golden light beamed from the blackness. Emerging from the depths, two women dressed in white climbed a set of carved steps. Their flowing clothes reminded Kai of angels from a children's book. Their yellow halo-like glow gave them a majestic presence, and everyone fell back in awe. All but Lucca.

"Parlor trick," his grandfather muttered loud enough for everyone to hear. Rochelle joined him in a few inaudible whispers.

"We have come to show you the way," the women proclaimed in unison. Their delicate lilt sounded almost harmonic and left a sweetness in the air. The lovely curve of their mouths gave the impression they were graceful and kind, but Kai did not trust their fake display.

"Where is Keegan?" Jin challenged as the ground trembled with the thunder in his voice.

The fair-haired Lumens motioned to the pit with a burst of hideous laughter, a horde of Caroco warriors spewed like ants from its depths. Weapons drawn, the Caroco flashed their swords, and the Katori responded with weapons of their own as they charged into the fray. Steel sparked off shields and claws and fangs. Fists flew in every direction. With everyone bunched together, the Caroco drew their hand cannons from their holsters and fired. The spray of metal pierced chests, arms, and legs, dropping many where they stood.

Blasts of light broke the night sky, and tremors shook the ground beneath Kai's feet. His sword clashed and pierced with accuracy and speed. As he slashed and blocked, the ground lifted skyward. He reached out with his mind and started to read the flow of magic. He noticed what looked like tendrils of light emanating from the Katori fighters—some fighting against the Caroco warriors, while others stood with Keegan's men. He punched the man in front of him off the pillar, but before he could jump back on solid ground, the column collapsed.

From every direction, more Caroco came, and Kai knew they were being overrun. Even with his increased speed, he could not battle them all. He felt Rayna shout in his head—*look out!* His head snapped to the left, and Kai felt a massive drain on magic as energy was ripped from the air. Through the trees, he spotted Rayna and Imani as they drove their fists into the soil. Kai drew magic from the starlight, and his crystal glowed. Something was coming, and he needed to be ready.

Giant thorny vines ripped across the soil and thrust into the Caroco warriors. Kai leaped into the air as his wings burst from his back, pulling him skyward. Below his feet, the thick brambles curved and bulged, taking with them everyone in its path. Towers of stone erupted, lifting the Stoneking men to safety, but the vines continued through the battle.

Kai shouted to Ryker and his uncle Haygan. "Get out of the way!" he ordered. Hearing his cries, Rochelle and Jin launched pedestals, lifting themselves and their fellow Katori kinsmen in the path of the vines safely above the erupting chaos.

The wicked Lumens grabbed the vines and poured light into the greenery, causing them to wilt and burn. Lucca dropped his sword and fired back, catching them off guard with his first magical attack. His fierce blast of light showed no mercy and struck them hard. The women stumbled, shielding their eyes as they tried to hold the light back. They gave a reasonable effort attempting to strike back, but Lucca's decisive aim broke their might. Their cries for help alerted their fellow Stonekings. With a thrust of Stoneking magic, a stone slab plucked the women and several other Caroco from the battle and swept them away. Kai flew in pursuit, but they all disappeared into the darkness, leaving only a wake of rubble and the faint sound of thunder in the distance.

"Why show your might so soon, Keegan?" Kai muttered to himself.

Kai circled back to the others, thinking about the strategy. Considering Lumen magic was rare and powerful, why use them this early? Revealing your greatest weapon so soon was typically a mistake, but his father did not make mistakes. *What am I missing?* he pondered, landing amongst his fellow warriors.

With the retreat of Keegan's Lumens and Stonekings, the remaining Caroco fighters fell like leaves in autumn. When it was over, most were dead, but Ryker took one prisoner. He wrapped a rope around the man's leg and hoisted him over a tree branch, allowing Ryker to use him as a punching bag until Kai forced him to stop.

"Enough, Ryker, we need him to be able to speak when the Elders get here."

Ryker pulled hard, lifting the man higher. "Fine, let us hear whatever message Keegan wishes to deliver." Ryker let the rope slip, dropping the man to the ground. "So, speak. How is it that among all those Caroco warriors there were only five Katori? Where is Keegan? When does he plan to attack?"

The anger in his friend's voice shocked Kai. He knew Ryker had a temper, but he never knew this side of his friend.

Kai knelt next to the bleeding man. "I am Kai Galloway. Tell me something, anything. Do you have a message from Keegan?"

"Yes, for you, Keegan's son." The man lifted himself up on one elbow, his sweaty bald head leaned in close. "I have a message for you. Keegan is not coming—he is already here. He has been here for weeks, listening, watching, and learning. Do not hide away in Katori; it is not the sanctuary you seek. Know that we, his acolytes, stir doubt and season this land for civil war. Join him or die; that is your only option. In the end, there will be one ruler, but first, he must cleanse this land of weakness. He will show you all a better way to live and rule this world. Time to go home, Kai—your real father is waiting for you."

CHAPTER 4

Warning Lights

In the aftermath of the battle, Kai and several others searched the dead for survivors. Kai came upon Thomas, one of Jin's students. He was barely alive and gasping for hair. Blood oozed from his ribcage. "Rayna, Imani, Thomas is dying!" He held his hand over the man's wound. "You will be alright. Help is coming." He saw hope in the man's eyes as he clung to life.

Kai moved his hand so Rayna could take his place. The smell of death lingered in the stale air, and the sight of so much lost life on both sides shook him to his core. The Katori losses astonished him, but the hand cannons the Caroco carried were deadly.

Catching up to his uncle, Kai asked. "What about the other six ships? Could there be more ships we did not see?"

Haygan and Ryker lifted the dead into long wagons, clearing the battlefield. "If they can propel their ships up our cliffs, no border is safe. Keegan's remaining ships could be anywhere by now—*he* could be anywhere."

Thoughts of his mother raced through his head. "We need to warn Hiowind and Matoku. The rest of Katori must know about this before Keegan attacks again. And he will attack again."

Ryker turned and pointed back to Kahoma city and the stone monolith near the Agora, which usually shined with a dim blue light but now beamed brilliant white in every direction. Atop the tower, a glass lens on each side magnified the large luminous crystal within. Kai assumed that the Agora's light signaled a warning to the citizens. Then his friend motioned toward the cliffs and a stone platform supporting multiple decorated stone columns, each topped with brilliant crystals. Up until now, Kai had no idea the structure served any purpose beyond beautifying the city.

The crystals flashed a set of signals Kai did not understand. Still, he imagined that they conveyed a great deal in their complexity as the operators swapped between the different stones, hiding or revealing the light in specific patterns. Farther in the distance, he saw a repetition of the same flickering signal. And as he watched, he noticed the tiniest lights blink the repeated message. If he were not anxious and frustrated, he might be impressed by their network and communication system.

He turned to Ryker. "What are they saying?"

"The crystals spread the word of what happened here today." Ryker pointed in the opposite direction, revealing more signal lights along the coast and some deeper inland. "There is a network of beacons built on carefully chosen mountains or atop pylons. I do not understand the code myself, but with light, our message races across all Katori, informing the operators within each city of Keegan's betrayal and the Caroco attack here today. The Agora beacon warns the citizens here to be on alert, and word of mouth will spread through the city to instruct citizens what to do. Don't worry, we will find Keegan. I will not let him hurt your mother ever again."

Kai's impatience was burning. "I am going to Hiowind to check on my mother."

Ryker reached out a steadying hand. "I am as eager as you, but you must not be so hasty." He jutted his chin toward the signaling station. "Once our news spreads around Katori, other reports will come back from our cities. They will either report an all clear, or . . ." Ryker dropped his head.

"Or they are under attack." Kai paced with intensity. "That's why there's no time to waste!"

Ryker's eyes followed his movements. "We are stronger together. You are still a young Beastmaster, so there is little chance you will make it the entire way in one flight. If you stop and get caught by Keegan's men when your magic is depleted, it may be the end for you. No, it is best to wait. We need to know the way is clear and where the Caroco men are going. Keegan still has six ships, maybe more for all we know. Wait until the news comes back."

Kai opened his mouth to protest, but then he saw Rayna helping survivors, and he let it go. He knew Ryker was right—for as much as he wanted to protect his mother, he couldn't help her if he fell into Keegan's grasp. And he couldn't risk making Rayna a widow. As a young Beastmaster, his limitations on distance were frustrating but real. The flight from his grandfather's place in the Katori mountains to Diu took hours, and he still found that distance challenging. They were now nearly twice that distance from Hiowind.

Kai sighed and resumed his agitated pacing. He didn't have to wait long, however. The signal lights to his right began to blink in a new pattern; short bursts mixed with long. He saw it repeat along the shoreline. A third, a fourth, and a fifth set blinked against the night sky.

"What does it mean?" He turned to see Ryker already on his toes.

"Follow her." Ryker gestured to the Weathervane leaving the station, heading to the Agora. "She is the message keeper."

Kai followed her feverishly as she sped to the Agora. She reached the Elders and spoke softly. Their nods and calm expression gave Kai hope, and his feet moved of their own accord to his grandfather Lucca.

Before he could inquire on the news, a second person burst between them. The man's dark eyes glanced from Elder to Elder as he shared his report. It was all Kai could do not to step into the conversation and get the news firsthand. Once the message keeper left, Kai crossed the Agora to Lucca.

"Well, what news of Keegan and the Caroco?"

Lucca looked to Jin. "Give me a moment."

Jin nodded and stepped away.

"There is good news and bad," Lucca began. "So far, all the stations are reporting an all clear. Besides the two battles here today, no other attacks have occurred yet."

"That is obviously the good news," Ryker interrupted. "What about the bad?"

Lucca took a breath. "Three ships were spotted along the northern shore, where the Katori Mountains form our border with Milnos. That leaves three of Keegan's ships unaccounted, lost in the night. I wish I could say that is the only bad news, but we have news a dozen Caroco ships are sailing to attack Port Anahita. Without reinforcements, that city will fall—if it has not already. I am sure they will attack Diu next. We have sent word to Fort Pohaku to warn Roark, but either way, his ships would need over two days to reach Anahita and his men would have another half a days to march inland to Diu. If Roark is also not under attack."

Kai's heart sank. Keegan was attacking all sides, he is dividing our forces. After Port Anahita, Diu would be next on his list. Torn between his mother and father and his new country, his decision caught in his throat. His mind could not put order to the desires in his heart. "We must see to my mother's safety," he finally worked out the words.

Ryker nodded in agreement. "We may have the all-clear, but three missing ships could carry hundreds more enemies into Katori. We know Keegan will come for her, sooner or later. We cannot waste time on the river, and Kai is not strong enough to fly the distance. We will need at least a dozen warriors to secure our entourage. How many can you carry, Kai?"

He had not considered the limits on how many he could carry. "Four, maybe five, certainly not a dozen. Such a large group will only slow us down. We need to move swiftly."

"We will need more Beastmasters capable of carrying others or flying themselves." Ryker twisted his head to Haygan. "My Shuk can carry two, and Haygan another two. That is twelve, I will recruit the others, but we need a good mix of all disciplines. Lucca, will you come as our Lumen?"

The hesitation in Lucca's eyes shot through Kai. He wanted to challenge his grandfather, but he saw the look the other Elders gave. "I am an Elder first, and we are needed here," Lucca responded. His shoulders sagged under the decision, but his voice remained steady. "Lumens are rare. Unfortunately, I know of no others nearby. Yana remains in Hiowind, and Kam is in Matoku. Keegan having two under his command was certainly a surprise to us."

"Understood. We will send news once we reach Hiowind," Haygan said.

Lucca placed one hand on Haygan's shoulder and the other on Kai's and pulled them all together. "Come morning, if the news is still favorable, those who can will travel to Hiowind. I intend to be among those who do. I trust you two to secure Mariana, but know I will not be far behind. Basil is here somewhere. Find him and take him with you. Should you need to take the river, he is an excellent rafter."

Kai respected his grandfather and he knew that only his obligation as a Chief could keep him from his daughter. "We will make it to Hiowind, grandfather, you have my word. I will not let Keegan anywhere near my mother." He said it as much to assure himself as to assure Lucca.

"Thank you, grandson." Lucca stepped back and motioned to a group of Katori. "Take these warriors with you. They are seasoned Guardians. The two Beastmasters, Hannah and Narin, can take the shape of vultures, which fly very fast. Maybe not as fast as a dragon, but you should hold an even pace. They can keep a keen eye out for invaders. These two Stonekings, Braden and Holly, just arrived and are among the very best. They will be a good match should you reencounter Keegan's Stonekings. In addition to Yulia as your Weathervane, allow me to recommend Madrone. The Kodama, Sarah and Joleen, are very powerful plant wielders and healers, which I pray you will not need. Stay together."

It was easy to see the affection Lucca had for them all. His stature remained proud, but his eyes gave him away, and his overprotective nature surprised Kai. Glancing around the compliment of fighters his grandfather offered, he recognized a few. They were a good mix of Katori disciplines. Their goodbye was more of a feeling conveyed with a look, but the depth of their relationship swelled in Kai's chest as they parted.

◆ ◆ ◆

Glistening stars filled the night sky. Kai's wings beat against the wind and he set a fierce pace. The race to Hiowind to protect his mother consumed his thoughts, and more than once, Rayna had to remind him to slow down and stay together. Below him, in the darkness, he sensed Ryker and his uncle Haygan in Shuk form running fast to keep pace while carrying two people each.

For Kai, the weight of five people on his back was hardly noticeable. Their constant shifting, however, made it challenging to maintain a level flight path. Aware his passengers struggled to avoid the sharp spikes along his spine, Kai tried to keep things steady to prevent any unwanted injuries.

The recent events again consumed his fears. If Keegan was already here, why had he not come for his mother already? Why the display on the cliffs? Nothing made sense. Why all the subterfuge? Why did his father not come straight at them? Keegan should be happy. The reveal of magic should open the world to all Katori, even the Elders agreed— Katori should no longer be a cage, keeping their borders closed and their people hiding in secret. But even Kai knew that would not be enough for his father. It felt like they were chasing their tails, trying to catch something that was already in front of them.

Each question offered no answers, only created more doubt. With the whole of Katori set against Keegan, Kai wondered how his father hoped to win. Even with hundreds of Caroco, Kai imagined only a handful of Katori were loyal to Keegan. But even so, he had no idea how many here in Katori believed as Keegan did—that Katoris were gods who should rule the world. He wanted to believe that all Katoris, at their core, hoped for a peaceful existence.

Miles blurred one after the other. Below, a single light caught his attention. Kai watched the bold—or maybe foolish—rafter navigate the rapids and the bidirectional water changes up the Makani River, the same river down which he chased Lucca last summer. Remembering Basil's advice that it was the fastest route between the coast and highlands, he studied Ryker and Haygan's progress along the riverbank. There was very little difference, but the Shuk had the advantage. The hanging lantern attached to the raft bounced in the night and slowly lost ground to their relentless stride.

The vultures, one on either side, were every bit as fast as his grandfather promised. While he could fly faster, these beastmasters kept a quick pace. The rhythm of their wings kept a steady tempo, but he could tell the distance taxed them both. Below him on the ground, Kai reached out with his mind to sense the burden of both Ryker and Haygan. He felt their hearts pound and their lungs heave. They were struggling to keep up.

Torn between wanting to continue and giving a break to his struggling entourage, Kai considered continuing without the others. The shift in his weary passengers reminded him of his responsibility to the group, which meant more than his desire to proceed. Heeding his grandfather's warning to stay together, Kai called to the other Beastmasters as he spotted a small trading post a few miles ahead.

There is a town on the next ridge. We can get food and shelter. Let us stop for a few hours or until dawn.

The rolling hillside teamed with travelers, many seeking shelter within the grove while others packed their belongings to resume their journey, which he was surprised to see at this hour. Above the trading post, three small clusters of tree homes twinkled, and the occasional campfire glowed in the darkness. Circling overhead, he found a suitable place to land away from the hustle and bustle of the crowds.

With cupped wings and an arched back, Kai landed in the tall grass. His extended wing offered his passengers an easy dismount. Before transforming, Kai stretched his wings and dragon spine, surprised to find he, too, was feeling the strain. Letting go of his dragon form and changing back to his natural body was as easy as releasing a breath, but the soreness remained. The gratitude for the chance to rest went unspoken, but even his riders shared silent glances while stretching to relieve their stiff bodies.

"Best I can tell," Ryker said, taking note of their surroundings, "we are a little over halfway. Not sure we can keep up with your pace, Kai. Come morning, we may need to consider rafting."

Although Kai knew the route well, it felt like Hiowind might as well be on the other side of the world. His mother's safety plagued his thoughts. Every moment they delayed allowed Keegan to take her away from him. "Agreed." Kai looked down the hill to the trading post. "Basil, see if you can get a raft and a night's lodging. We have nothing to trade at present, but I am sure you can negotiate something. Since we have no provisions, Rayna and I will see to food and water if the rest of you can find a decent campsite."

Inside the small town, Kai and Rayna relied on the good graces of strangers to acquire supplies. He learned many travelers were seeking shelter in the mountains after hearing about the attack on the coast. For the first time since he came to Katori, every passerby seemed to regard one another with a sense of distrust. Concerned by the lack of pleasant faces, Kai kept his hand on his sword as they meandered through the settlement. When they ventured back into their campsite, they found Ryker stoking a fire for their acquired fish.

Sitting around the fire, Kai's eyes were transfixed on the pulse of the glowing embers as he sorted through the surreal nightmare of the day and the coming challenges. It was Rayna's shoulder leaning into his that snapped him free, only to realize everyone else also appeared lost in contemplation.

Narin, one of the vulture Beastmasters, a towering giant of a man, yawned as he rose to his feet. "Wake me at dawn. I, for one, need a few hours sleep if we mean to hold this intense pace the rest of the way to Hiowind." He marched up the hill behind their campsite toward the large tree built by the trading post as lodging for travelers.

His mate, Hannah, a raven-haired woman with dark eyes, nodded in agreement and followed him to an empty sleeping pod, leaving Basil and Yulia to stand watch. The rest followed the Beastmasters' example and found pods to catch any sleep their chaotic minds were willing to allow. Kai did not imagine he could sleep as he wrapped his arm around Rayna and they lay in the dark. His mind raced to replay the moments of the day and the possibilities of what might happen once they reached his mother.

A. D. Lombardo

CHAPTER 5

Frontlines

The sound of chatter woke Kai. His ears caught his uncle Haygan's voice just outside his pod. "I will wake Kai and Rayna. Make sure everyone is ready to leave by dawn."

Kai squeezed Rayna's shoulder. "Time to go."

Kai stepped out of the pod as the first show of pink pushed against the deep purple sky, then the faintest arrival of yellow woke the heavens. *Dawn never looked so beautiful*, he thought. All felt right with the world. Relaxing into the uneventful morning, he followed Rayna's movements through camp as she joined her sister Imani.

Ryker's voice caught Kai's attention.

"Kai!"

Kai followed the sounds worming his way through the trees. Letting his eyes close and his aura wash over the landscape, he felt the power within his surroundings and the essence of each creature nearby. In the distance, he heard marching and voices echo through the trees.

They were not alone. Moving swift through the trees, he crept up to his friend. Rayna ran to the left and perched on a rocky knoll.

A bead of sweat rolled down Kai's temple. Each vibration ricocheted around the Katori landscape in magical shockwaves. The energy within his aura floated through the forest, connecting him to the beasts of the woods. Pain electrified Kai's spine and rolled down his arms and legs, and his skin grew hotter.

They were less than a day from Hiowind and his mother. He did not have time for another distraction, another Caroco battle. "Do you feel that?"

Rayna sidestepped through the trees closer to him; her hand brushed his arm. "I feel your suffering, but not the source." She adjusted the longbow slung across her back and knelt on one knee. Her hand fingered the tall grasses before she pressed her hand into the soil. Kai imagined she took a reading from nature.

The woods fell silent as if waiting for Rayna's assessment. Fearing what she might find, Kai opened his mind to peer into his connection with the animals of the forest. He had no idea what to expect, but what he saw horrified him.

"Blood." Rayna retracted her hand as if the touch burned. "The grasses taste of blood. Kai, we need to move, someone is killing wild animals." She took off down the hillside without him.

Each fatality Kai felt drove him faster: wolves, birds, and bears cried out as they died. He gleaned the area, trying to figure out what could be causing this, and then he saw it— a large group of men marching through the foothills. Caroco warriors. Nearly a hundred of them, heading north toward Hiowind. His gleaning mind beheld a six-man deep row carving a line of death toward the forest. Keegan's men killed any beast they could find, but why, he did not know. Kai searched the attackers for his father; he was not among them. Then he searched for any Katori warriors, there were none.

Yulia raced a few feet ahead of Rayna, and fog exploded beneath her feet and engulfed their position. On either side, Kai sensed his fellow Katori warriors—a few against a hundred of Caroco warriors, but they had defeated them before, and they could do so again today.

Standing on the front lines, Kai kept an eye on Rayna's position as he moved toward the danger. Sounds of lighting cracked the sky, and a bolt struck the ground. He heard the distant screams through the pines and saw smoke as he continued to charge.

Arrows pierced the mist, and Kai dodged right then left, letting them sail by his face; he did not stop. He charged out of the forest and caught his first sight of the enemy. Two Caroco warriors stepped through the fog, and his sword caught the first man unaware, but the second deflected his blow and jabbed his dagger toward Kai's ribs. He saw the blade but stepped into the strike, surprising his opponent. The metal tip pierced Kai's shirt, followed by a plink—the sound and the halt of his blade startled the Caroco man. A look of fear enlarged his eyes as sweat rolled down his bald head.

Kai raised an eyebrow and the corner of his mouth. The man's blade carved a long line in Kai's navy-blue shirt, revealing a silver dragon scale protecting Kai's abdomen and chest. Kai freed his sword from the man's shield and stole the dagger, which he used to dispatch the man and move to the next. Chaos erupted in a fury of weapons and bodies. Three new warriors replaced the man Kai eliminated. Their numbers were growing right before his eyes.

They will overrun us. How are there so many? How did they catch up with us in the night? Kai wondered. It must be the Stonekings, able to slide through the soil at great speeds, he decided. Then he realized: LUMENS. His mind recalled their abilities to hide the truth of things. This is how they got so close to Hiowind without us sensing them earlier.

He moved faster, eliminating as many as possible with sword and the Guardian pressure points, but they continued to attack, fiercer than the last row. On his left, Basil and Joleen joined the fight. Then Haygan, Braden, and Imani joined on his right.

Wavy dark shadows passed overhead, Hanna and Narin in vulture form carrying Medrone and Holly. He figured that they hoped to flank the Caroco men and create weak points in their assault. Although he had faith in their execution, and the strategy was sound, he knew they were taking risks that none of them could afford.

Yulia continued to bring lightning down on the enemy until a blast of light ripped back through their ranks and struck the cluster of pines around her. "

Yulia!" Kai shouted, watching and waiting for a sign. A sign that never came. Unable to get to her, he pressed on, his swords doing the work before him lost in the repetition of each new enemy before him. His eyes darted between his next attacker and the burnt trees where Yulia once stood.

Behind the enemy fire blossomed through the pines a blast of brilliant white light, followed by hideous laughter—Lumens.

A flash of lightning ripped across the cloudless blue sky and punched the ground, scattering men and dirt like playthings—*Yulia! She is back.* He searched the trees but could not find her. The man in front of him punched Kai's cheek, pulling him back into the fight.

Smoke seeped across the battlefield and flames licked around the periphery. The ground rumbled and heaved; dirt punched through a swath of Caroco, launching Haygan and Ryker skyward as a pillar erupted along the front lines. All Kai could do was keep fighting.

Feeling the seriousness of their situation, Kai drew heavily upon the energy from nature: the wind, the sunshine, and the grass around his knees. Willingly magic flowed into him, and in a flash, he transformed into his silver dragon. His large arching wings expanded, taking out a swath of men to his right. With a twist and a pivot of his spike-covered tail, he caught another section of men. He had hoped pure fear would send the men into retreat. Between claws, fire, and fangs, he thought he had the upper hand being a dragon.

He was wrong.

Instead of retreating, the Caroco army swarmed him like bees to honey. Caught off guard, Kai reared back. *Would they willingly die for Keegan's cause?* He had little time to contemplate their intentions, which became all too real in an instant. Hundreds of cuts slashed through his dragon scales. While he roared in pain and blasted them with fire, they only came harder. More men, one after another, charged at him with black knuckle-blades. The Lumen women joined in the attack, blasting his eyes with light. Unable to see to defend himself, he closed his eyes and tried to glean, but the Lumen magic left him blinded.

Each swipe of the Carocos' knuckle-blades cut into his thick skin, leaving him bleeding and lightheaded. He lashed out, burning a swath in all directions, but he could not think straight. Something was terribly wrong, and they kept coming. The enemy only had eyes for him.

He could barely hold his head and defend himself now. He felt cuts covering his entire body as the Caroco warriors began tearing his wings, and considering how his head felt, he imagined the weapons were poisoned.

He felt some relief when the Lumens stopped their attack, and he tried to open his eyes. His blurry eyesight left him disoriented, and he stumbled and fell. Confusion and screams of terror echoed all around him. His large amber eyes blinked several times, and in-between, he caught the devastation. A thick network of thorny vines ripped through the Caroco army, attacking every man around him. Hundreds of vines coursed along with the ground, punching through men like parchment paper. Kai's amber eyes blinked, capturing the moments in slow motion.

Between the darkness threatening to take him, Kai saw the Caroco men lash out with their swords. Their eyes screamed in fear, but their mouths called charge. They did not want to die, not really, but they refused to retreat. The dark green thorns chased, coiled, and strangled the enemy.

When everything fell silent, he heard shouts. Imani and Rayna rushed to his side.

"Do not transform Kai. You have lost too much blood." Rayna pressed her hands into his scaly face. "Let the Kodama heal you first. Together everyone," she shouted.

Kai felt the warm, powerful hands of the Kodama's touch. Magic coursed through his ravaged body. Although the gashes carved into his body healed, his insides were burning from the poisoned blades of the Caroco. *Poisoned,* Kai used his mind to communicate with Ryker.

Ryker grabbed a vial from his belt. "He has been poisoned by the Caroco blades." Ryker poured the contents of the glass container into Kai's dragon mouth. "Hurry, Kodama. Everyone else, give him your sacred water. We must heal him before it is too late."

Blackness threatened Kai's vision, but the sacred water slid down his throat, and he felt its healing power seep into his body, cooling the fire burning through his nervous system. As if fighting a fever, his body trembled with chills and then swelled with heat. His constant view of Rayna kept him calm and clinging to life. Unsure if he saw the truth of her, he watched his wife. Her skin glowed with a radiance he never noticed. *Did she always shine like that?* He could not help but be fascinated by her beautiful glow.

With the poison and the cure battling within him, he let his eyes close, and he listened to the sounds of his friend's whispers. He knew they said words, but he could not make out a single word until her voice called him back. "Kai, wake up." Rayna's voice danced through his mind. "Wake up. Transform back, and we will take you home."

On instinct, Kai let go of the golden braid of creation that formed his dragon. His dragon body shrank away, and his proper body lay on the bloody, wet grass. As he rolled onto his back, a comforting blue sky welcomed him with open arms. They may have healed his body, but his mind would not respond, shattered into a thousand pieces. His spirit floated away. A thousand miles away, his mind traveled the stars.

A sense of harmony called him to a new place, a place he somehow knew would be happy and safe. There would be no pain or suffering and his soul wanted peace. Yet, Rayna's memory pulled at him, and he wanted to go back. He *needed* to go back. Unsure how to stop moving through time and space, he prayed. *Alenga, please remember me. I understand if it's my time, but I beg you to send me back.*

Be at peace, my son. You have done more than your share.

Her words seemed final, but Kai could not accept this was the end. Please give me strength because I cannot go on without your blessings, and I know this is not over. Keegan must be stopped; I cannot abandon my family, not now.

The silence around him left a hollow fear in his heart. When his spirit stopped, he beheld the dark sky and the brilliant stars and planets. He was nothing, no physical form, only an essence, yet he felt connected to everything.

Go back, Kai, Alenga's voice soothed his soul, and his spirit raced back through space. *I am with you. There is much you can still do.*

Her words slammed him back to his body, and he gasped. Rayna's face was the first he saw. Wet tears stained her face as relief filled her sad eyes. His uncle, Haygan's face, came into view next to her. "Kai, there you are, I am with you. Steady now, let me help you up."

Kai took the offered hand and stood on wobbly legs. Still covered in blood, he felt wet and uncomfortable. His head was spinning, and his limbs were heavy; he wanted nothing more than to sleep. Rayna, Sarah, Joleen, and Imani stood nearby, and their eyes beheld him with sorrow and relief. Imani wrapped her arms around Rayna and whispered. "See, little sister. Kai made it. He is strong, like you."

Afraid of what he might see, he slowly looked at his hands, then he rolled up his shirt sleeve to the elbow. He expected to see hundreds of scars from the knuckle-blades that shredded his dragon wings, but there were none. He touched his face and neck, expecting some proof of the wounds, but he was completely healed.

Rayna took his arm. "You are alright, Kai. I am here."

"The sacred water and the Kodama healed you in time," Haygan reassured him. "There are no scars. The sooner they repair the damage, the better. With the added sacred water, Rayna and the others were able to heal every cut as if they were never there."

Kai let his eyes gaze around the circle of Kodama. "Thank you," he rasped.

Ryker stepped forward. "Come, let us get you home. According to Narin, the way looks clear from here to Matoku, but he did not fly far enough toward the mountains to see all the way to Hiowind. I know we all hoped to reach Mariana today, but without your dragon, we will be lucky to reach Matoku."

Exhausted and broken, Kai collected himself. He refused to slow the group down or risk his mother's safety. Through strength of spirit, he pulled at nature, collecting magic. With each breath, he felt a little stronger; although every part of him felt weak, he continued to gather energy. When he felt strong enough, he shook his head. "No, I am not ready to give up. Let me at least try. I can do this. I will fly us as far as I can."

Dread rattled his transformation, and for the first time, it came slow and painful. Needles prickled down his spine and out his core. He resisted the change, but golden braid forced his shift. Behind his screams, he heard Rayna call. "I am here." Her warm hand came to his restless dragon and touched his face. "You can do this, Kai. Time to go," she assured him.

At first, the countryside rolled by with ease. Kai felt almost bold under the influence of his renewed Beastmaster magic. As the hours passed, his weary bones weighed him down. Flying became exhausting, no matter how much power he collected along the way. The heaviness in his wings showed as he flew lower. Each beat of his wings pounded in his head, yet on the horizon, Hiowind remained a spec he could not reach.

He realized they would have to stop in Matoku as Ryker suggested, which stirred insurmountable anxiety in his ability to reach his mother. Only his determination kept him in the air. If only he could rest a few hours, but there was no time to sleep. This was a race to save his mother, and Keegan would not rest, so neither could he.

When they reached Matoku, he could not fly another inch. Hiowind and his mother were still deeper into the mountains and beyond his reach. After his passengers disembarked, he dropped his dragon form, and slumped to his knees. His head hurt, and his muscles shook. Barely able to catch his breath, he tried to collect more magic, but it would not respond.

Rayna's hand touched his shoulder as Haygan took hold of him and wrapped around Kai's waist.

"Let's get him home," Haygan said. His uncle lifted him to his feet. "A good night's rest will do him good. I will travel to Hiowind tonight and check on my sister. I will see you both tomorrow in Hiowind."

It was late, and the streets of Matoku were quiet. Too quiet for Kai. He wanted to hear music and laughter, to go back to normal, but it was as if everyone was afraid to make a sound. Keegan's warriors could arrive here at any moment. How many were lurking, ready to pounce at his father's command?

"I must get to my mother," Kai mumbled.

Ryker patted Kai on the back. "You need rest. I will go with your uncle to Hiowind. I will protect Mariana. No amount of magic can heal your condition. Only rest can help you now."

"I need to see my mother," Kai insisted. "Either you carry me, or I will crawl, but nothing is keeping me from her." The determination in his voice sounded like thunder in his head.

Haygan stopped and looked at Ryker. "He is right. Neither of us would stop if we were in his condition." His gaze panned around the rest of their entourage. "I will carry Kai and Rayna. Anyone else willing to continue is appreciated, but we will continue traveling to Hiowind."

Silent nods of agreement flowed around the group as everyone decided to see the journey to the end.

"Thank you," Kai responded.

◆ ◆ ◆

Kai opened his eyes at dawn to see his mother sleeping in the bed across the room. Tucked in beside him on the sofa, Rayna stirred in her slumber. He did not remember much about the previous hours, only the memory of his mother's being safe and refusing to leave her side. Although he hoped Alenga might show him how to keep her safe, his unanswered prayers left him conflicted. While the few hours of sleep had done him good, Alenga kept him in the dark, leaving him alone in peaceful slumber.

Rayna opened her eyes. "Did you sleep well?" she asked, attempting to sit up.

Kai nodded, swinging his legs to the floor and helping her. "I suppose, but I cannot remember the last time I had a vision," he responded. "All those years, the dreams were a curse, a burden I hated to carry, but now when I want them, Alenga leaves me in the dark. What is the lesson I should learn from her silence? Why can't I dream?"

His pleas lingered in the air between them as Rayna let a few minutes pass before she responded. "Do you really want a vision?" She paused, and he felt the weight of her question.

"I . . ." He could not answer, not truthfully. He wanted to say yes, but he knew the answer was not really.

"Is it a gift or a curse?" she asked, and her suggestion made him think again. "Maybe you should come to terms with the answer. You cannot have it both ways. You either want the knowledge, or you do not. There is always a price or, in your words, a burden."

Kai nodded. "You are right. If I had known what was coming over the past few days, would it have made it easier?" Even he did not know the answer.

"I think learning to accept the bad with the good might lessen the dream's power over you." Rayna's confidence gave him strength. "Let go of your doubts, and you will destroy the emptiness that eats at you. But if you accept the gift, then you cannot hate the messenger. Alenga blessed you, and you have saved people. Her visions should not cause suffering but enlighten you."

Kai thought about the possibilities he had rejected his gift. There were plenty of times he hated knowing the future, even when he could change the outcome. Rayna's words rang true; he feared knowing or even seeing the tragedy, but it did allow him to alter the outcome. Now he needed to open his heart and mind to the idea that the burden was worth the information.

Sounds of his grandfather's voice echoed into his mother's room. "I must see my daughter," Lucca's voice thundered. "When did you all arrive?" he questioned, entering the room ahead of his son, Haygan.

Haygan stood near Kai and Rayna while his father sat next to Mariana. "As I was mentioning, we ran into a spot of trouble on the road. We arrived here just after midnight. How are you here already?"

"You remember Kakan, Elder Jin's friend, the old dragon Beastmaster?" Lucca said. "He brought us home. We saw no Caroco on our journey, and we came straight here without stopping."

Lucca turned to Kai. "You look rested." His grandfather's weary eyes glanced around their battle-torn clothing. "We should get cleaned up. We need to take your mother to the Agora this morning."

Ever since they brought his mother back from the sea, she remained catatonic. Her broken Beastmaster mind locked her in endless slumber, and only Agora's magical water sustained her life. Kai nodded. "Yes, grandfather."

CHAPTER 6

Strangers

The Agora was a sacred place. All who entered held a certain level of respect and reverence for Alenga. Bringing his mother, Mariana, to the Agora days after a battle made him nervous, but he knew the waters of the sacred pool were the only thing keeping her alive. One of four, Kai helped carry the bed supporting his mother's unconscious body. His uncle Haygan, Lucca, and Basil maned the remaining corners, with Rayna and a few other Kodama following them.

While Ryker kept his distance, he brooded near a column of the Agora, anxious as any to see Mariana wake from her slumber. Although he honored the location and the day with his rarely worn blue Beastmaster robe, his body language told Kai he knew that this was a pointless task, as they all did. Keeping Mariana in this state was no way to live, but the alternative—letting her starve to death in her sleep—was just as cruel.

It was often the responsibility of Unie or a Kodama to ease Mariana into the sacred waters, but today, Kai felt compelled to step forward. He knelt next to his mother and touched her warm hand. His eyes met Elder Yana's, the Unie of Hiowind. Her sincere blue eyes offered him understanding. Carrying his mother, he looked at the water's shimmering smooth surface. Sunlight glistened down from the aperture above him. As he stepped into the celestial pool, he felt a sense of peace within his mind. A tinge of blue light emanated from the depths as he stepped lower into the water and his mother's body touched the surface.

A surge of hope filled Kai's soul when the water began to bubble and glow. The light never blossomed unless Alenga was coming. The Elders stepped close to the outer edge of the pool.

Lucca nodded to Kai encouraging him to continue. "May Alenga bless my daughter today."

His mother's body floated on the surface like a leaf on a lake. Her dark brown hair fanned out around her head like a crown, and her blue dress drifted softly across the bubbling water. She looked like a sleeping princess in a story waiting for her prince to free her with a kiss. Kai took the last step, and they sank beneath the surface.

Alenga's presence pressed on Kai. Her angelic form blossomed with light, and she touched his chest. "Breathe my child. You are made of this water."

Kai took in a breath, and his lungs filled with the sacred water, yet he could still breathe. His body and soul felt invigorated by the magic-filled water, and he could feel the power coursing through him. His restoration, although intense, was instantaneous. A thousand questions flooded his mind, but his mouth spouted only one. "Why will you not wake my mother?"

Alenga touched her fingers to his forehead. Again, she spoke. "See, my child." His mind flood with images of war and destruction. Pockets of peace mixed with the chaos of hate as Katori erupted in civil war. The endless supply of Caroco warriors and unrest ran rampant across their country. Milnosian soldiers took advantage of the Katori rivalry and marched on Diu. Behind it all, a man stood in shadow, his dark soul spread like fingers of darkness from person to person. Each beautiful bright crystal turned black as night, and hatred spread like fire across the land consuming all it touched.

Alenga floated in front of him. "I gave you a gift, a connection, and you closed your mind to me. I know the images are not always pretty, but the variables are endless, and I can only show you one because your mind could not handle the realm of possibilities. You, like everyone, have the freedom to choose your path. None are doomed to live out an inevitable fate. The moments I reveal offer insight to potentially improve the outcome or prepare you for the inevitable end. Those pivotal decisions are still your choice.

"Much like the death of Iver, the only version I foresaw his survival was the one where you held the blade. And even that moment had multiple outcomes."

He heard what she said, and it gave him understanding, but he repeated his question. "Can you help my mother? Please wake her."

"I cannot give you what you seek," Alenga spoke, and with the wave of her hand, Mariana stood at his side, still locked in her slumber. "She must find a way to wake herself. I can only offer you this small moment together. A darkness pushes me away, and your time together will be short."

Alenga touched Mariana's forehead and she whispered in her ear before stepping back. "My son." The sound of his mother's voice swelled his soul. "I am so proud of you and all you have become. But I know that I have let you down as your mother. I am sorry that I choose Katori's secrets over you."

Tears, if they could flow in water, ran down Kai's face. The tightness in his chest made it hard to breathe, and his mouth would not respond. His arms wrapped around his mother in desperation to cling to whatever this moment gave. Her body felt real in his arms even though he knew the moment only existed in his mind, a construct of Alenga's magical plane between worlds. "Please, mother, come back to me," he whispered, fearful this instant would end.

Mariana's hand cradled the back of his head. "I don't know how." She stepped back and looked into Kai's eyes. "My mind is filled with beastly natures. I spent too many years trapped as a dragon. I knew the risks of holding my Beastmaster form, but I thought I had no choice. The golden braid we use to transform will not release my true form. Instead, it bubbles and twists with all the creatures I know, all trying to emerge at once. The person I was feels foreign and lost to me. Even now, I hear them call to me. Alenga's might is all that stands between the beasts and me. My path holds a horrific future. Do not let me become a monster, Kai. I will do terrible things."

"You are no monster, mother." Kai felt like a child once more. "Please, please try to come back to me," he begged.

"I see my future, son, and it terrifies me." Her eyes glazed over by the memory she beheld. "Death, so much death. Please, Kai, set me free. Destroy my crystal and let me die. Do not let the beasts out. The Lioness will consume everything in its path."

Her words were confusing. Kai knew of no such creature called the Lioness. *What is she saying? How can she ask me to end her life?* He clasped his mother's necklace, which dangled next to his own. He did not trust anyone with his mother's crystal, now that he knew the crystals controlled the owner. "I cannot kill you! I will not! I must find a way to save you." Intense emotion poured into his heart, and his mother's magic connected with him through her crystal.

Alenga placed her hand over Mariana's heart. "My dear one, I know I ask a lot of you both, but the darkness is drawing near, and this moment must come to an end. Kai, stay close to your grandfather, Benmar. You will need. . ."

The light around them waned, and the shimmer in Alenga's form started to fade. "The barrier between our two worlds is bending away from each other. Our time is over. Stand firm, both of you, and destroy the darkness."

Alenga's face disappeared, and Kai felt his mind return to his body as he floated to the surface. The water turned cold and unwelcoming as unfamiliar hands pulled him across the celestial pool. His eyes fluttered, and he saw his father's face. The last time he was in the sacred pool on the day of his blessing, his mind lingered blissfully between two worlds—but today, he felt ripped from Alenga's heavenly presence. The intensity of his fellow Katori standing around the pool shined brightly, and he blinked, trying to clear his eyesight. His mouth tried to form words to call for help, but he could not speak, and his body felt disconnected.

Kai slowly crawled out of the water, but immediately, he sensed something was wrong. Haygan was standing in front of him, unmoving, frozen.

Alenga's warning of a spreading darkness set Kai's eyes to search the Agora for Benmar. Kai found his other grandfather, also frozen in mid-sentence with Ryker. Kai felt a tingle at the base of his neck, followed by a gut-wrenching fear.

A wave of darkness pushed unnaturally against the light within the Agora. The room's enhanced energy rolled swift and robust, emanating off each person in their frozen state—that is, until it struck the one man who was still moving through the crowd. Keegan. A dimple in the light surrounded his father like a black hole. Although he was Katori, he lacked the enhanced brightness that Alenga's recent visit generated within everyone else.

Kai's throat seized, and his knees buckled. He wanted to scream out and charge his father, but he could not move.

No, no, not like this!

Keegan knelt next to Mariana, his face lowered next to hers, but he spoke to Kai. "My Lumens have given us but a moment, my son. Seconds outside of time, a moment for you to consider your future. Join me as an equal—or a puppet."

Kai struggled against the invisible bonds that held him. A golden knot swirled in Kai's mind, and he reached out to Mariana with his gleaning, desperate to connect with her. Inside the tortured depths of her mind, he saw three—no, four—Beastmaster braids intertwined with each other, tugging and pulling and screaming to be released. In the distance, the voice of his mother echoed in his head. *Stop the Lioness,* she begged.

In a gush, time resumed, leaving Kai gasping as the Agora chatter filled his ears, and he struggled to regain his breath. Gasps and shouts came at an alarming rate as everyone realized Keegan sat among them.

"Keegan!" Lucca shouted. "Get away from my daughter!"

Keegan's laughter shattered the light around Mariana. Connected to her Beastmaster mind, Kai watched as his father unraveled the golden knot and expelled Kai from his mother's mind—*be gone, boy.*

Kai dropped back on his heels and shook his clouded head, and then he watched in horror as Keegan stood and pulled Marianna to her feet beside him. The glee in his victory broke the world around Kai as his mother's eyes turned black and dark veins crept across her face. Her statuesque form was frozen in a dormant state, and Kai wondered if she was indeed awake or—as Keegan put it—a puppet.

He stood and reached to touch her. "Mother?"

Shielding Mariana, Keegan grabbed for Kai with his other hand, but Benmar stepped between them. "Son, stop this madness! Release Mariana."

A snarl curled Keegan's lip as he eyed his father, but his hand slid down Benmar's arm and let go. The disappointment in their relationship left a sour look on Keegan's face as he stepped away. Then Keegan laughed and he pulled Mariana toward the archway to leave.

Lucca grabbed and pulled on Mariana's other arm. "Mariana, come back to us. Hear me, daughter. Let her go, Keegan! You are hurting her. It's not too late for us to find peace, your followers and ours!"

"Not so fast, old man," Keegan seethed, and Kai saw years of hatred twist his father's face. "Do you know how long I have waited for this day? This moment to face you again. You convinced the Elders to banish me; you even tried to kill me. You bested me in the past, but not today. I control the power within your daughter, and she obeys me now— Mariana." Keegan grabbed her neck, forcing to face her father, then he whispered something in her ear.

Still able to see the crowd's aura, Kai watched every drop of magic in the room flow like visible ribbons of power into Mariana.

"Mother!" he shouted, unsure what was happening.

Benmar pulled Kai to the ground and shielded him as light beamed from Mariana's mouth and eyes. Lucca was cast backward in an explosion of light and crashed into a stone column. He shot beams of his own light from his hands in an attempt to defend himself, but wave upon wave of light from Mariana rolled upon him. His own light turned against him, engulfing both him and the column. Flames licked the column turning it all shades of orange, yellow, and white.

Kai felt the blast of magic flow around Benmar and himself; it was hot but did not burn. He watched Lucca struggle. His silhouette prone against the thick column, his hands outstretched fighting against the blast. With the next pulse of light, Lucca collapsed. The light faded and the column cooled, leaving a black, sooty outline of Lucca's body. Kai watched and waited; his grandfather did not move. Smoke floated around his charred body.

"NO!" Kai shoved Benmar off his back and ran to Lucca's steaming form. "What have you done?" Tears ran down his face. The smell of Lucca's burnt flesh stung Kai's watery eyes. His grandfather was dead.

"Time for the old ways to die, my son." Keegan offered a hand to Kai. "Join your mother and me as we set the world ablaze. We can be a family. Rule the world. Let us return to your city, Diu, and claim it as our own."

There were no words, only anguish. Kai's mother's necklace clinked into his chin as he hovered over his grandfather's lifeless body. He had no idea if he could use her crystal, but he refused to crush it and kill his mother. He could still feel her compassion and kindness radiate from the crystal. The strong connection comforted his broken soul, but it did not squelch the fury forming in his chest. Tears dripped from his eyes onto his grandfather. *Keegan is to blame, not my mother.*

Rage boiled within Kai, and he spun on heels to attack his father. "I will kill you for this! Release my mother!" he demanded, but Benmar caught him by the shoulder and pulled him back. "Grandson, no, you are not ready to face him," he cautioned in a whisper. "Mariana, you must fight my son. Fight Keegan to break free. You are stronger than he is." He stepped back, taking Kai with him and adding more space between them and Keegan.

"Let me go, Grandfather." Kai writhed but could not free himself. "Keegan, I will kill you for this! Let my mother go!"

Keegan spun around, addressing the crowd. "Time to choose. Join me in the fight, my fellow Katoris. Listen to my acolytes. They walk among you, spreading the word. We have spent centuries in hiding, afraid to show the world our truth and the power of our magic—afraid they would reject us, torture us, or weaponize us. Now that the world knows who we are, we should not be afraid. The world may lack the character to recognize the beauty and elegance in our creation, but they will bow all the same. The world rejects you, but we are divine. Let me show you a new way."

Keegan spun again, careful to keep his grip on Mariana's neck. "If they do not love us, then they can fear us. In the first great war, our dragons served as weapons used to secure power to others. Many of our dragons lay on the ocean floor or across countless battlefields. Some hang as trophies. And what did we get when it was over? Freedom?" Keegan gazed around the listening crowd, then shouted, "No! Our people brought home our scars of anguish over the lives we took in the battle for a cause that was not our own. In shame, we vowed to never fight for another again, and then we hid behind a mountain range created by the earthquake that shook the world."

The more Keegan spoke, the more Kai hated the man. Every ounce of his energy boiled with rage, and in his efforts, he pulled Benmar a step closer to the man who was systematically destroying his life while everyone else just watched, too stunned to move.

"Our Beastmasters and our swords saved the world for everyone but us," Keegan continued. "How will the world remember us? As weak slaves—freaks of nature? Let me tell you, the world will remember my name. Alenga will remember my name because I fight for my birthright. I will give you the world. All you must do is stand with me. Spread the word through this great nation. The time is now."

Keegan pulled Mariana's face close to his face and whispered something Kai could not hear. Then they turned back to the crowd. "My fellow Katoris, I will give you a few days of peace to consider my offer. Join me against the world, or be trampled under my wrath."

A scream resonated from Mariana's open mouth, and everyone covered their ears. Kai watched in horror as his mother's body twisted and contorted. Wings sprouted from her back—not the elegant shimmering wings of a dragon, but blood-red wiry wings edged with bony spikes. Her hands and arms stretched into bulky menacing lion's paws, and she fell on all fours.

Her agony stabbed Kai's heart. Without her crystal, he knew the pain she suffered in transforming. Her mass grew with each twist and pivot; her face stretched to compensate for the massive teeth emerging from her jaw. Her sounds changed from screams to shrills to a roar. Thick red and gold fur filled in around her new lioness face, and a golden horn grew from her head. Her eyes glowed red, and fire seeped from her jaws. The rest of her erupted in the same gold and red-streaked fur, followed by a long-forked tail, both ending in a sharp hooked spike. She was part lion, part dragon, and who knew what else.

"To Diu, my love!" Keegan shouted proudly, climbing onto the Lioness's back and taking a spot behind her horned head. "Time to teach Iver a lesson and create our new kingdom."

"No!" Kai shouted, reaching his hand up to her massive head. "Mother! No!"

ROAR! ROAR! ROAR!

The beast snapped at Kai, sending him rearing back in fear. Its massive front foot pounded the stone, leaving a black paw print in the pink Agora stone. Then Kai watched his mother spring off the Agora floor and take flight. Her menacing wings pumped the air and she flew through the open aperture, scraping the edge and breaking bits of stone from the rim of the Agora dome.

His hopes were dashed. The empty skylight held only blue sky and clouds.

A. D. Lombardo

CHAPTER 7

No Time to Mourn

Kai fought back the tears. He was distraught over the loss of his grandfather Lucca, but there was no time to mourn. Diu was in trouble, and he needed to stop his father. Rayna and Benmar were speaking to him, but he could not hear their words. Haygan embraced his dead father lying next to the scorched column, and Yana placed her hands on Lucca's charred forehead. Kai waited, but he knew it was too late. Nobody could bring Lucca back.

The crowd surged with new people from outside while others departed in a rush. Those who entered covered their mouths at the sight of their dead Chief. Whispers and tears overtook the crowd and sent most running from the sacred place. Their Elder had been murdered by one of their own, and Keegan demanded their loyalty in taking over the world.

"Do I stay and bury my grandfather when I must go and stop Keegan to save my mother?" Kai asked in a low, barely audible voice. "Who will come with me?"

Yana stood, covered in black ash from Lucca's burnt form; Kai felt sick at the sight.

A Beastmaster approached, and Kai recognized the man. He was a message keeper, one of the people who operated the light stations. Yana whispered a few words before the man departed. "I am sorry, Kai, there is no time to follow your mother. We must stand together here. Keegan will be back, and we must be ready."

Before Kai could rebuff her, an explosion drew everyone outside. A giant stone obelisk crashed to the ground. Flames and smoke billowed as dozens of armed Caroco men aimed hand cannons at the unarmed crowd. Many fell while others retaliated and fought back. The Katori began to fight one another, and Kai recognized a few from Keegan's ship.

One such man shouted, "Join us, or we will crush you along with the rest of the world!" In the distance, more explosions rang out. Large plumes of smoke erupted along the horizon.

Ryker brushed past Kai and entered the fight with his Katori-infused speed, propelling him into the air. The Katori man reared back and raised his blade to deflect Ryker's assault. Together they battled, and Kai watched their seemingly choreographed maneuvers as each man raged against the other. Benmar was drawn into the battle and disappeared, moving invisibly through the crowd and systematically attacking the Caroco men. He stole a blade from one and dispatched him along with two more. One man got lucky and cut his grandfather's abdomen seconds before Benmar cut the same man down. Kai watched blood land on the white stone path beneath his grandfather's invisible feet.

"No!" Kai shouted, fearing Benmar would be the next casualty in his family.

Anxious to put an end to the fight, Kai took to the air as the silver dragon. No sooner did he reach the sky than two black-winged vultures swooped in and attacked his head. They dove at his head and scratched his thick dragon skin. Their claws held black steel weapons, sharp as razors, and they dug into his neck and head. In a tight roll, he coiled around himself to protect his face. In freefall, he opened his wings, striking one black vulture while he blasted the other with a spray of dragon's fire.

Moments before he struck the ground, Kai propelled himself back into the sky. He could not believe what he was seeing. Small fights broke out across the city—some Caroco-driven, some Katori-supported. It was hard to tell friend from foe. He looked back to search for his grandfather.

Standing with him, Kai saw Rayna touch the bloody wound, healing the gash with her Kodama magic.

Kai landed next to his grandfather and transformed back into his natural form. Warm blood dripped down his neck and around his eye. Again, they were ready for him, attacking with this new black steal capable of piercing his dragon scales. He looked at the freshly healed line on Benmar's stomach fade as Rayna's gentle fingers trickled across the cut around his eye. He felt her magic seep into his skin and heal the wound. She did the same for the cut around his neck. "Thank you, Rayna," he whispered, taking her hand in his. "Yana, what about my mother? And Diu?"

Yana's blue eyes turned serious and narrowed on Kai. "We have troubles of our own here, Kai. Stay and fight with us. We need you. They attack us with two new weapons we do not understand. Keegan planned this well. We are not prepared to fight. This is not the time to divide our resources."

Noreen, the only Kodama Elder, appeared and pulled Rayna away. "I need you to come with me," she ordered more than requested.

Rayna complied but gave Kai a look as Noreen pulled her from him. He knew very little about Noreen—she rarely spoke in the Agora, and when she did, she was an advocate for silent introspection. To see her charge into battle shocked them both. The woman stood nearly a foot taller than Rayna, and her porcelain skin and strong frame made her look like a white stone statue. The Unie offered Rayna several seeds from three different hidden pockets within the sash tied at her waist and then whispered something into Rayna's ear.

Standing in the tall grasses, they both closed their eyes and prepared to turn their powers on the battle around them. Kai watched the earth beneath them ripple in several directions, and he had a feeling about what was coming. Giant vines exploded from the ground beneath several Katoris. The tendrils did not discriminate. Instead, it yanked both friend and foe apart and secured them to the ground. Rotating in silence, the pair continued to subdue men and women lost in the heat of battle.

With silence falling over the surrounding city, Noreen and Rayna opened their eyes. The Unie Elder turned to Yana. "I have no patience for fighting. Secure everyone and determine on which side they fall. I will not let my people spiral into chaos and civil war. We need . . ." Her eyes drifted back to the Agora.

Kai imagined she needed Lucca, but he was gone, the first major casualty of this war. A Chief who offered strength and leadership to all—and her friend. There was no arguing the point; they were at war, and Keegan's threat to return had them all on edge.

"Yana!" Ryker called, running toward them.

Kai was relieved that his friend had survived.

"There are several more fights breaking out around the city," Ryker explained, "and many called for freedom while others demand tradition and the old ways. And there are Caroco marauding all over the countryside! I have no idea how so many managed to get this deep into Katori. I can only guess the Stonekings continue to travel underground."

Basil joined them and offered his report of more Caroco men within the city.

"Thank you, Basil." Yana acknowledged his update. "We will need more men like you in the coming days. Stay with us and fight. We must secure our borders and put down these invaders. We must find the other Elders. Only together can we bring an end to this nonsense."

Kai wanted to listen to their deliberations, but he had his own concerns. Keegan and his mother were on their way to Diu, and it was up to him to stop them. He backed away and took note of who followed: Benmar, Rayna, and Haygan.

Once they were a suitable distance away from the others, Kai stopped. "I cannot ask you to come with me, but I am going to Diu. They have no way of defending themselves against my . . . whatever that monster was Keegan created." He recalled the name his mother used. "The Lioness."

"Grandson," Benmar said, "we must be smart about this. You are not ready to face Keegan. He is too powerful. I was able to protect you, but your mother did not attack us directly. I need to teach you how to bend light, all light, which includes Katori magic, not just nature's energy.

The light was Lucca's gift, yet your mother destroyed him. She killed a Lumen with his own magic. I felt her siphon your grandfather, and I saw her turn it back on him. This is serious, Kai. How do we even begin to fight Keegan with her at his side? We need to stop your mother. Neither of us, even as dragons, are a match for her unless we work together and destroy this Lioness."

Rayna touched Kai's arm, and he shook his head, overwhelmed by all the ideas swarming his already cluttered mind. Her eyes drew him in, and he let her calmness quiet the others. "I am with you," she whispered, placing her hand over his heart, "but we should see to Lucca."

Haygan's eyes avoided the Agora. "The burial of a Chief takes days. We have no time to bury my father. Kai is right. We must stop Keegan and my sister first."

Yana approached their little group. "Haygan, Kai, I am sorry for your loss. Let me see to your grandfather's body. He deserves a Chief's burial, and when this mess is over, we will send him to Alenga with honor. Noreen and I will seal him in the catacombs beneath the Agora. I wish you would stay and help us fight, but I see that your minds are made up. I only hope that you can better serve us all by finding a way to stop Keegan." She paused, her eyes heavy with concern. "Mariana should not spend any more of her life as a weapon in someone else's cause, especially Keegan's."

Although he now had the Elder's approval, her words planted a twinge of guilt in Kai's soul. Divided was no way to win a war, but someone had to stop Keegan. Was he really the man to do it? "If stopping Keegan puts an end to this madness, I will chase him to the ends of this world," he promised.

The golden tips of an eagle circled and swooped. Kai recognized Sabastian's Beastmaster eagle as his friend dropped amongst their group. "Kai, I have come to help, but I had to secure Kendra first. She will not be able to come with us. Her pregnancy requires constant Kodama healing and regular access to the sacred spring."

Kai knew how important a child was to Kendra, and given Sabastian's Lumen heritage, she needed special care to help her and the child survive. Plus, with child, she would be unable to transform without risking the child's development. "I understand. Maybe you should remain here," he suggested.

Sabastian disagreed. "My place is with you. I know Diu well. Even before Kendra came to be your governess, Benmar and I watched over you. Mariana meant more than you could ever know to many of us. I will fight at your side," he insisted, stepping into the collective.

"We need a Stoneking," Ryker suggested, "but there is no time to recruit volunteers."

"This close to the mountains, finding a Stoneking will be easy," Benmar interjected, motioning the ridges in the near distance. Hiowind was a large city nestled along the rocky hillside located at the thinnest part of the Katori mountain range. "Many live in the foothills, but getting one to abandon this fight for another in a place they do not know will not be as easy."

No sooner did the words leave his grandfather's mouth than the sound of thunder rumbled through the ground.

"Keegan's Stonekings are returning," Haygan shouted, drawing his sword. "We may as well meet them head-on."

His uncle charged over the bridge and across the gardens toward the rumbling noise.

The ground shook, and Kai clenched his jaw. A*nother lie*, he thought, chasing his uncle through the gardens toward the sound. *A promised peace, broken,* he seethed in a renewed hatred for his father's choices. The stone mountain ahead of them began to rumble, and tiny pebbles tricked down the crag. Laughter came out from the darkness into the sunshine. Behind the joyfulness, Liam and his band of Stonekings emerged.

"Thank Alenga, it is you and not the other Stonekings." Kai shouted.

Casual and unconcerned, Liam leaned against a nearby tree. "Good to see you too, Kai," his friend mocked, seemingly unaware of the events of the previous days.

"Have you not heard about the attacks on Katori?" Haygan barked in annoyance.

Wren, the older man in their company with a bright red beard, wormed around Liam. Although he was thin, Kai perked at his boldness. He knew the man and his power. *He would be a valuable ally if he will join us.*

"You do not hear much under a mountain." Wren cocked his head to the side. "We were in Albey these past few weeks finishing some support work under Alenga's temple. What attacks?"

It was not easy reliving the events of the past few days. Keeping to the facts, Kai held his emotions in check while informing Liam and his Stonekings about the civil war erupting around Katori, the traitorous Katori supporters, and the Caroco warriors within their borders—and the new weapons they wielded against their kind. When Kai finished, he addressed Liam directly. "Join us on our mission to Diu or stay here. Either way, you are needed in this fight."

"Liam, we need you," Basil said, motioning to the group, "or any Stoneking you can spare. Our ability to glean only goes a few feet into the ground. Your Stoneking magic allows you to scan deeper, travel through stone, and even track Keegan's Stonekings. You are certainly needed here, but we would be grateful if you joined us."

"I cannot speak for another," Liam said, shaking his head, "but I will not have these pirates destroy our home or start another great war."

Kai nodded. "I understand. I suppose if I had only one home, I would do the same. But then, it is more than my love for Diu that sends me after Keegan. You all know that man is my natural father, but what you do not know is he woke my mother today and turned her into a beast— the Lioness. The truth is, stopping him is the only way to stop this war, but saving my mother is my true motivation. If any of you choose to come, I thought you should know. I do not want her harmed—leave her to me."

A boulder of man puffed up his chest and spoke. "My name is Maxen," he announced, "I wish to stay and fight here at home. If these other Stonekings return, they will not know what hit them."

Behind the older man, Wren, a young woman with piercing black eyes waved. She pulled a black leather band from her pocket to secure her long black hair, exposing her bare shoulders. Like Liam and most other Mystic Island natives, her skin tone was dark bronze. "My name is Oléon." Liam's face quirked, and Kai nearly felt Liam's stomach flutter as she introduced herself. "I prefer to stay in Katori if it is all the same to you."

Their shared affections announced their relationship, and Kai now understood why Liam would not come with him.

"I am not one to tell you what to do, Liam—" Oléon motioned to Kai "—but he needs you. We all need you. If you can stop Keegan in Diu, then you should go. Fight with your friend and end this war." She nudged his arm.

Liam's eyes clouded with deliberation. "I . . . agree." Liam nodded first to Oléon and then to Kai and the others. "There are others here in Katori who can stop these infiltrators, but if stopping Keegan ends this war, then I will go with you, and I will help you save Mariana."

The last man in their group stepped forward. Tenoch. Kai knew him well. The son of Elder Jin, a year or two older than Liam, three years older than himself. Like his father, he had a peaceful confidence and a clever mind, which made him an easy choice—if the man was willing.

Kai met the man face to face. "Tenoch, your father is safe, but he remained in Kahoma after the attack. Other ships are missing along the coast, and your father would not leave. I would appreciate your support, but I would understand if you wanted to join Chief Jin."

Tenoch's dark eyes lingered on the sky. "I will travel with you. You need another Stoneking, and I know my father would bless my crossing to Diu."

With his group assembled, Kai took a moment to himself to step through the trees and take a breath. He knew he should not let his guard down, but the death of his grandfather shook his core. *I am sorry, grandfather. I should have protected you. I should have stopped Keegan, stopped . . . the Lioness.* His heart broke and a tear fell down his cheek.

"Grandson," Benmar said, pulling him away from the others. "I know you want to mourn Lucca, and you will, but if you plan to chase Keegan, you must be prepared. I wish we had more time, but there is none left. There is a way to stop my son—or at least protect yourself."

Kai dried his eyes and swallowed his pain. "How? With a single touch, he can control me or drain the life from my bones."

Benmar shook his head. "Today, Keegan went to grab you, but I stepped in between." Benmar paused, and Kai thought about that moment. "When I came near you, did you notice that my son stepped back? He knows he cannot control me. He never has because I understand the magic more than he does—more than most. I think you do too. That is why we can become invisible, or Sabastian can wield light as a Beastmaster. All magic comes from the same place. You cannot change or create the weather, but you have pulled power from a Weathervane's storm. You cannot move stone, but you could stop a Stoneking when he wields his magic if you focused."

Kai thought about the possibilities. "If I understand, you are saying that while they wield the original source of magic, I can turn their energy around on them—or at least drain it."

His grandfather nodded. "Yes. I know it is painful, but that is what your mother did to Lucca today. Her light would have never been enough to destroy a Lumen as powerful as your grandfather, but by turning his power back on himself—well, let us just say the more energy Lucca used, the more she twisted and turned it back on him. You must learn how to bend light, steal magic, and repurpose it. You are the best of us, Kai."

Kai wanted to follow his grandfather's notion that he could be something special, but everything returned to her. "Can I use this to save my mother?"

"This is bigger than your mother. Keep your secrets close, Kai. This knowledge is something Keegan most likely does not know or understand. He may control Mariana, but he does not know how she uses the energy. There are a rare few who understand anything beyond their obvious talents and the label their crystal suggests. Be careful with this precious gift. Study it in your mind because that is where all real power starts—with a thought. Do not give this ability away in a panic or the first chance you get. Wait for the right time to show your greatest strength. Your mother will save herself. She is a fighter, and Keegan cannot control her forever."

CHAPTER 8

Returning Home

Desperate to catch Keegan and his mother, Kai flew over the Katori Mountains with Rayna, Ryker, Liam, and Haygan on his back. Yulia's vigilant efforts created a healthy dose of clouds to camouflage their approach. Next to them, his grandfather Benmar's silver dragon transported Yulia, Basil, Tenoch, and Sabastian. Although capable of flying as an eagle, Sabastian suggested speed was of the essence. In the time it took them to reach Baden Lake, dusk began to darken the landscape, and Kai began to imagine the worst for Diu and his adoptive father, Iver.

The hours of flying left little to occupy the mind but worry. And worry Kai did. About everyone: his mother and her trapped mind, his family and friends and their vulnerabilities, his own mind and the scars this civil war would leave behind. His history books said war was ugly. Battles and death were nothing new to him, but he was learning that war, especially a personal one, was a different beast. Once created, the war took on a life all its own, giving leaders the illusion of control and power and even the desire for more. He saw how hatred fed the beast, allowing the darkness to spread to others. He knew enough soldiers and the scars no one could see; fighters changed forever, leaving them in darkness. He did not want to end up like Keegan or his acolytes. *Do not get lost,* he told himself.

Letting go of his worry, Kai shifted his thoughts to the vast range of advice from others, especially from his grandfather, suggesting he needed to see energy in a way no one else did. *You must learn how to bend light, steal magic, and repurpose it.* He knew how to bend light, at least to become invisible. What else could his bending do? And he knew how to siphon magic, at least from a Weathervane. Could stealing magic be much different?

Below them, the thick clouds rolled, and Kai studied their design. He could see the energy the same as he did that day on the ship, but it looked no different than the power within any living thing—the air, water, or even starlight upon which he could draw magic. Then there was Guardian Gail's advice to keep a constant tap on the vein. A transformation took a great deal of power; to maintain the form, one strengthened the connection to magic and, in a fashion, constantly drew on nature.

Finally, he mused upon Benmar's theory that he should go beyond the label of his Beastmaster crystal. His white stone meant . . . nothing. And yet it meant everything. A blue crystal would label him as a Beastmaster, but his white crystal left him open to being more.

To test his theory, Kai focused on the particles Yulia dispersed with her hands. First, he pulled on the magic she pushed into the sky, clouds meant to camouflage them from the ground redirected back at Yulia. Within seconds, a small developing cloud consumed Benmar's dragon and its passengers. Kai chuckled to himself. *Sorry, grandfather,* he spoke with his Beastmaster mind to Benmar.

Do not apologize—learn. Bending light goes beyond becoming invisible. With practice, it can become a shield. The real test will come when you are in battle. That is how you defeat Keegan.

In the distance, a sickening glow was building on the dark horizon, leaving him little time to consider the principles behind his grandfather's advice. They were approaching Diu—but this was not the usual city lights but thousands of torches and fires. The closer Kai came, the more intense the light became and the more devastated he felt. By the time he and his group arrived, nearly half of Diu was set ablaze.

On one side of the city, the horde of Caroco men attacked—a sea of black warriors swarming the lower end of his city, bombarding the walls with siege weapons and launching volleys of arrows one after the other. Besides barraging the city gates, they attacked the harbor, setting aflame all three piers and five ships moored in Baden Lake. All while the Lioness swooped and scorched through the air, attacking clusters of Diu soldiers and setting fire to various buildings around the city.

What horrified Kai the most was knowing Keegan's out-of-control beast was his mother. Fire spewed from her mouth as her dark wings angled her around the city. Dragon-killers fired in defense, but they could not hit their target; she was too fast. Cannons fired on the Caroco, barely holding them at bay, scattering men with their destruction only to reform their ranks as if they had an endless supply. Arrows volleyed in both directions and commanders shouted to instill courage in their men and direct the next attack.

Kai and his grandfather landed near the smoldering harbor to let their passengers disperse. "We need to put out those fires," Benmar ordered, pointing to the docks.

Yulia nodded and set to work on creating rainclouds.

"There must be ten thousand Caroco warriors, and we are only ten." Kai looked around his group for suggestions as the sounds of hand cannons echoed on the wind. "For those of you who have not fought these warriors before, be warned: they carry a weapon that fires a metal projectile more dangerous than an arrow. They also use black blades and arrows which can cut dragon's scale and are sometimes poisoned, and these men are fearless."

"We cannot risk engaging with them directly," Basil suggested, "or they will overwhelm us, and we are finished. Stealth and speed will allow us to flank them, pick off their numbers around the fray. But as you said, there are too many, and it would be a futile effort to try. And any use of magic will alert the Katori among them—or at the very least Keegan and Mariana, provoking her to attack us."

"Do not use her name," Kai insisted as the rain started. "That beast is not my mother."

Ryker placed a hand on Kai's shoulder. "We need another army." His eyes moved to Sabastian. "You need to find Admiral Roark's men. He should be close by now—a day, maybe two, away—on the road between here and Fort Pohaku. The Caroco army came through Port Anahita. I doubt there are any Diu soldiers left there to help us."

"Would Roark not come by sea?" Kai asked.

"We learned about the attack almost three days ago. If Roark were coming by sea, he would already be here. My guess, if it were me, I would send a fleet across the sea to engage the enemy ships and another army on land. A backup should the fleet be otherwise engaged or outgunned. You can bet Roark is moving two armies, and he is most likely with the group on foot. There is only one other possibility, and that is Keegan also attacked Fort Pohaku. Either way, we need help, anyone they can spare. Sabastian, you need to inform Roark about the situation in Diu. Get him here as quickly as you can."

Sabastian nodded, "The Admiral will remember me." Then he disappeared into the night.

Scanning the battle for Diu city, Kai searched for hidden Katori among the enemy. He hated surprises, and so far, his father was proving to be full of secret weapons. There were none, at least not that he could see. Given that the Lumens were still in Katori, he hoped what he saw was all the truth of things.

Kai looked to the others. "How long do we sit here in the shadows? I cannot very well hide here and do nothing. I must at least try and help fight Keegan's army. I am sure these Caroco soldiers have the same weapons that can cut dragon scales, so I will stay airborne."

Liam leaned toward Tenoch. "We can distract the enemy while you fly over."

"The rains will continue without my constant influence," Yulia offered, "but they will be slow to dowse the flames. We need more Weathervanes or a greater source of water. I will follow the Stonekings to provide cover." She followed Liam and Tenoch into the darkness.

A dark looming fog crept over the land, and the ground rumbled. Kai said, "Rayna, go with the others and search for Keegan's Katori rebels.

They are here, hiding. I'm sure of it. We need to be ready, not surprised."
Kai kissed her cheek before she left. *Be careful,* he thought.

As everyone split up, Kai transformed into his silver dragon and took to the skies behind his grandfather's dragon. Like two silver darts, he and his grandfather flew toward the rear of the Caroco army. Unaware of their approach, the enemy pressed forward, launching arrows and trebuchets and firing hand cannons at the city gates and towers. Still, no Stonekings aided in knocking down the walls. Kai wanted to believe they stood a chance, but he knew Keegan was here—somewhere.

Below the sounds of battle, he heard the ground rumble and shake. He half expected the ground to open and swallow the enemy whole, but nothing happened. A second time, the ground rumbled and then fell silent. Sounds of thunder shook the sky above him and light briefly illuminated the clouds. To his left, he saw a bolt of lightning crack and arch, its wicked finger racing toward the ground—yet seconds before it struck the enemy, it sucked back into the clouds.

We are not alone, he thought.

Between the rain and smoke, he searched for a line of attack. Benmar dove first; his stream of fire scorched three rows of Caroco. Kai went next. The fire started in his belly and built as it rolled down his throat. His blaze carved a path of destruction and scattered the Caroco warriors. Men screamed in terror, but others drew their weapons in a last attempt to attack him. The hand cannons fired, and their projectiles ricocheted off his scales and wings with no effect.

Halfway through the gauntlet, Kai saw a dragon-killer crossbow aimed in his direction. The Caroco man fired the bolt. Kai rolled under the shot, escaping with his life, but his new path took him closer and lower to the front lines. As they raised their hand-held crossbows, he took note of their black-tipped arrows. Unable to pivot in time, he felt the steely teeth bite into his body and right wing. Hundreds of tiny pricks pierced his skin.

He limped into the night sky with one good wing to avoid crashing into the city walls. His amber eyes looked down his belly and across his wing. Covered in tiny arrows, he felt like a pincushion. One arrow pierced his chest near his heart, making it challenging to fly. Kai circled back to the forest where he left Rayna. As he landed, Rayna, Basil, and Haygan rushed to his side.

"Are they poison arrows?" Rayna called up to him.

He shook his dragon head, lowering his chest to the ground. Her eyes scanned him, and he felt her hands press into his scales near his heart. The arrow clawed at his flesh as she tugged, and the wound gushed with blood around his pumping heart. With the critical arrow removed, everyone followed Rayna's instructions to quickly remove the rest.

Each one hurt as they ripped free of his flesh, but Rayna healed the momentary pain. Benmar dropped his dragon form as he landed near Kai and began to help as he informed them what he saw. "We are not alone," he whispered. "Their Stonekings must have been hiding underground; either way, they counter every attack Liam and Tenoch attempt. Even Yulia has opposition. Our only good fortune is there are not more Katori here. I can only guess Keegan is spread too thin to do any real damage here, or he is holding back his real Katori numbers for a larger battle."

Kai imagined it was the latter. His father had a flair for trickery. With the final arrow removed and the wounds healed, he transformed back into his human form. He felt weak from the blood loss, but the wind and rain restored his magic. "I need to go after Keegan directly. If we stop him, the others may retreat. Not to mention if I have any hope of saving my mother, I must risk getting close. I can feel her from here. She is losing herself to the Lioness—her sense of who she was is fading."

The look from the others told him they were confused about this connection to his mother, but they knew he was right.

Basil patted Kai's shoulder and said, "We will help the others retreat. You can do this, Kai. Speak to Mariana, remind her who she used to be, who you are, and call her back to us. She is a fellow Beastmaster, and Keegan is not; only she can hear your mind. Benmar, you had best go with him. Help if you can, and be careful both of you."

Kai searched for the Lioness, but from the ground, he did not see her. He needed to get back in the air. He drew upon nature and collected the magic he needed and wrapped his mind around his Beastmaster's golden thread. His body erupted in silver scales and spikes as his human body transformed into his dragon.

The on-again, off-again deluge of rain helped squelch the fires, but the Lioness continued to create new ones across the city. Swooping wide, Kai angled away from the battle as he flew over Diu. He spotted her perched on the Master General's tower, clawing and ripping the shingles from the roof. Her roar carried on the wind. Taking the opportunity, he flew circles over the Lioness. *Mother, hear me!* he called to her with his mind. She did not respond. Her sharp claws dug at the tower, ripping away the black slate.

Your name is Mariana, Kai heard Benmar call to her. *Come back to us, Mariana.* Still, the Lioness did not budge. Instead, she snapped with her jaws and roared.

Desperate to get her attention, Kai dropped and hovered in front of his mother. The wind he created stirred the fur around the Lioness's face. Kai warbled and roared at her, adding a bit of heat behind it with his message. The Lioness flapped her menacing wings and roared back.

MOTHER! Kai shouted with his mind. *Hear me and remember who you are. Fight Keegan.*

The mention of Keegan's name provoked the Lioness, and it roared and spat fire. The flames licked Kai's dragon scales; he barely noticed the warmth on his face. As a beast of fire, it left him unharmed. But to give her space, he circled and landed on the palace roof. His sharp claws scraped and cracked the tiles, but the palace held his weight. *Come back to me, Mother. The Lioness is not who you are. You still have a choice.*

Benmar continued to swoop, and Kai heard his grandfather's Beastmaster mind call out to Mariana, but all she did was spray fire when he came close. Unwilling to listen, the Lioness attacked the palace and then again blasted Kai in the face with fire.

This time Kai sprayed fire in response to her attack. Worried their fight might cause damage to the palace, Kai took to the sky, and she followed. Together they flew and swooped. Memories of their time as manta rays gave Kai an idea. He darted ahead of her, swooping up over the walls and then down over the city below. Dodging right then left, she kept on his tail, matching him beat for beat.

Find me, mother, he called to her, swooping down toward the lower gardens. *Find me in the maze.* He hoped she remembered their day together in the gardens. Kai turned and darted around her with a quick pivot and a roll, bumping her with his wing. She flew after him, her temper remained intact as she raced after him.

He flew around the outer wall before he shot high in the dark sky. He played with her in a cat-and-mouse game, and she stayed right behind him, matching his twists, climbs, and drops. He dove back down. Within his dragon form, her crystal remained bonded into his structure next to his stone. He felt her anger fade and her happiness grow. *Come find me, mother,* he called once more. *Remember the maze and our game.*

She needs to see me, he thought. Altering the magic and the golden braid of his dragon, he dropped the beastly form around his body. Most of his body shrank, maintaining only his large shoulders and wings. The two glowing necklaces dangled about his neck, strengthening their emotional connection. Hanging in mid-air, he floated and waited for her. His heart pounded in his chest, and the Lioness neared. The closer she came, the stronger her heart's desire rang from the crystal.

He called again. *Mother, come back to me.* She slowed and swooped around him. A low growl caught in her throat and turned to coo and a purr. Feelings of love spiked in her stone. Her massive form hovered in from him, matching his location. Eyes on him, she came closer. He waited. He called again; this time, he spoke out loud. "Remember me, Mother. I am your son, Kai. Come back to me," he pleaded, lowering to the palace grounds. He dropped his wings and with them the rest of his dragon form, leaving him vulnerable in his human body.

Happy to see her follow, he watched her land. The Lioness was huge, and her immense form emanated heat. He looked up at her, and his outstretched hands reached for her. "Mother!" he called, risking a step closer.

He could feel the heat roll off her form. Her paw reached forward and pressed into his chest, touching her glowing crystal that hung around his neck. The Lioness receded, and Mariana's form returned. Their fingers touched. "Kai . . ."

Her sadness overwhelmed him, and he stared, afraid to startle her.

"I cannot control the beast." Mariana's flesh rippled between fur and skin. "I hear the monster even now. Keegan's voice is in my head. You must destroy my crystal," she begged.

"I will not kill you, Mother. There must be another way. Maybe if you wore the necklace, it would give you the control you need. I feel the essence of your true heart, and it could help you heal." He placed his hand over her crystal, lifting the chain from his neck.

"No," Mariana whispered. She held her hand up, refusing the necklace. "Alenga meant for you to have it. She told me I must never take it from you, no matter how much the beast hurts. You need the crystal more than I do. I trust Alenga, and I trust you to do what is right."

Kai did not see them approach, but the burst of wind from two angry black vultures caught his attention as Keegan dropped behind his mother. "Not so fast, boy. She belongs to me." Keegan grabbed Mariana's neck and yanked her backward. In the same motion, he invoked the Lioness.

His mother's screams pierced Kai's ears, and in the same action, Kai transformed himself, returning to the sky and putting distance between him and Keegan. He did not yet know how to repel his father's dark magic, and he could not risk becoming a puppet-like his mother with his father's touch.

The Lioness shot into the air and attacked again, burning a swath over the city's tallest structures. Kai dove ahead and turned his fiery breath against her with little success. Fire against fire; they remained locked in a standoff. Her renewed anger drove the Lioness into a mad frenzy. She pounded him with fire, and he returned fire with a blast of his own. Not enough to hurt her, only push her away, directing her away from the city.

Swooping over Baden Lake, Kai saw their reflection in the water. That is when he decided; if he could not stop her with fire, maybe his leviathan could stop her with water. The cold black waves of the lake called to him, and he dropped his form.

Falling, he collected every ounce of power around him; he consumed magic like a greedy child in a sweet shop. From the Weathervane's energy in the sky, Kai siphoned magic, dissipating the nearby clouds. The moon and starlight bathed him in power seconds before he crashed into the waves and sank into the darkness of the lake. His skin rippled with power as his mind recalled the great leviathan. Energy flowed through his body like ocean waves crashing on the beach.

His crystal shimmered against the blackness as he took hold of the golden braid capable of creating his leviathan. He thought of the dark red eyes, spine-frilled neck, and black diamond-shaped scales. His body stretched and grew at an alarming rate, faster than he thought possible for such a creature. As he slithered from the deep, his head rose out of the water. His elongated body rolled out behind him, and his long wing-like fins fluttered at his sides, balancing his movements. Driven by a broad tail, he maneuvered through the water toward the shore.

With a belly full of water, Kai doused the city walls, parks, and homes in water. Each spray gushed over the flames, smothering them. Angered by the change, the Lioness attacked him. Her fiery breath smacked the side of his head, but the blaze did not burn. He fought back, and a blast of water struck the Lioness and sent her spiraling out of control. Her beastly body crashed into the hill and slid to a stop. Her massive wings flapped and her body shook, spraying water droplets in all directions as she worked to remove the water from her fur.

In between extinguishing the flames consuming his city, he doused his mother again, this time hitting Keegan with part of the spray. His mother pivoted to block the strike with her wing as Keegan's vultures flew to their aid, pecking at Kai's head. Kai snapped his jaw in retaliation, catching a few feathers of one bird before sending them both crashing to the ground beside his disoriented mother.

Filled with what felt like an endless supply of water, Kai sprayed down a row of warehouses set ablaze by the Lioness. As he attempted to douse another fire, the corner of his eye spotted the vultures swooping behind his head. Surprisingly, he felt someone land and take hold of his horn, and a sense of hate washed down his massive spine. The depth of anger crushed his already sad heart, and in an instant, he knew his passenger's identity—Keegan.

"There you are, my boy." Keegan almost sounded proud. "I would know you anywhere. Such an exquisite creature. Does your magic have no limits? Well, you must get that from me because I have none."

Desperate to dislodge his passenger, Kai shook his head. His heart pounded with waves of hate, and he found it difficult to breathe, causing him to twist and coil uncontrollably. His long body thrashed, carving deep ruts into the soil as he slithered toward the water's edge. Confused by Keegan's magic, Kai let his Leviathan body collapse. His head crashed into the lake, but Keegan maintained his grip, and his evil thoughts rippled into Kai.

Swimming into the depths of the lake, Kai attempted to drown Keegan. If the man would not let go, then he would willingly kill the man whose wrath caused so much pain in his life. But then a persistent voice whispered in his mind—rise—*Rise*—*RISE*. Kai darted for the surface. He did not need the air, but he realized Keegan did, and the man's power willed him to rise. Kai burst above the water's surface, his entire body exposed and his head above the clouds. He swayed like a drunken soldier.

Keegan's grip intensified along with the deluge of unwanted emotions.

"I have learned a great deal over the past few months, mixed with years of practice," Keegan hissed. "I understand better how to control you. Remember, I gave you a choice to join me as an equal. Now you will be my slave."

Fear of his father's power sent Kai into a panic, but Keegan's hold on him was irresistible.

Keegan laughed. "The eyes of the world are upon you, my boy. Time to show them what we all know to be true. We are GODS. Now I will have two monsters to do my bidding."

I am not strong enough to stop him! Kai cried inside his trapped mind. Then Keegan pressed his black crystal into Kai's skull, and the darkness within clouded Kai's mind. The voices of tangled souls whispered to him: *Obey.*

Keegan spoke again, "Show them who you really are. Show them they will bow or die. Attack!" he ordered. "You cannot resist me. I have been controlling others my entire life. Who do you think first taught Nola's mother and gave her the dark crystal? Nola's hatred for Iver made her easy to corrupt."

Kai's head spun and his mind went black. Visions of the past flashed before his eyes. He saw a youthful, spirited Nola clutching a small dark crystal in her hand as a younger Keegan whispered in her ear. Kai watched her wield magic and hypnotize others to do her bidding.

Again, Kai heard Keegan speak. "Yes, that's right. I was the one who taught Nola magic, and I set her on the path to destroy Iver. I hated him for stealing your mother's heart." Kai's vision returned to the present, and he saw Diu burning in the night. "Mind you, my crystal is not the first dark crystal. There were dozens over the centuries. These crystals are proof we can be more than we thought. We are all-powerful and we Katori must rule. Now, like your mother, you will yield and obey, joining her at my side."

The truth of Queen Nola's hatred and dark soul now made sense. Any hate she felt for Iver, Keegan's darkness amplified through a power not meant for the average human. Kai felt the strain on his mind and the overwhelming desire to smash the city with his beastly form. Slithering across the lake, he sloshed toward the harbor and his beloved city.

Unable to block Keegan or siphon his magic, he let go of the golden braid in his mind. The snap was painful but swift. His water serpent vanished, and Kai plummeted with Keegan grabbing the back of his head. His father's grip pulled them closer, and Kai watched in horror as Keegan's face became his face. "FINE. I will steal your face and convince those closest to you to follow me, and then I will rip out their hearts." Kai felt fog cloud his mind. "There you are, my boy. I need just enough to take your face."

Keegan let go as the Lioness returned, swooping under him and carrying him away as Kai continued to fall.

"I am not done with you yet, boy!" Keegan shouted as the Lioness flew back toward Diu.

Spiraling to his death, Kai could not find focus; up was down, down was up, and his mind did not care. When a razor-sharp dragon's claw wrapped around him and a blast of fire burned through the dark sky, consuming Keegan and the departing Lioness, Kai righted himself. Holding onto the dragon's claw, he watched the angered Lioness turn and deliver a blast of light from its open mouth.

Two giant dragon's wings wrapped around him, and Kai closed his eyes and prayed. Again, he felt the heat but was unscathed. A second blast of dragon fire engulfed the angry Lioness. The smell of burning flesh followed by screams sent the Lioness retreating into the night. As the heat blew back from his face and his head rolled around, he saw the silver underbelly of a dragon. *Benmar.*

◆ ◆ ◆

Kai woke to the sounds of battle and Rayna's whispers. Her right hand lay on his forehead while her left pressed into his chest.

"What happened?" he asked as sat up and looked to Benmar. "I remember Keegan trying to control me, demanding I smash the city, and then he stole my face. He planned to trick all of you and murder you."

Benmar pulled Kai to his feet. "My son is gone, again. I broke my son's hold on your face the moment I burned him. He can only hold another's face for a short time. Burning him left him no choice but to heal himself and let go of his dark magic. But the good news, your mother fights against Keegan; she could have done more in that last attack against you, but your water blast shook her mind, and she wandered on the hillside shaking her head while Keegan came after you."

Kai remembered the smell of burnt flesh and screams. "What about Diu?" Before anyone could answer, he fired off more questions. "What about Iver, and Ryker and Haygan? Where are the others?"

"I don't know about Iver. He is still on the inner walls around palace grounds, last I saw. When I saw you in trouble, I flew in your direction, and then I brought you to Rayna." Benmar motioned to the Caroco horde still attacking the city walls and the remaining dragon-killer weapons aimed at the sky. "Diu will fall without reinforcements, and we are in no condition to stop them."

As his friends all returned, he looked around at his humble, tired group. "We must go to the palace," Kai directed before changing into his silver dragon and letting Rayna climb up his wing.

He learned two important things today. First, there was still hope for his mother, and second, he was still afraid of Keegan. A problem he would need to overcome if he hoped to stop the man with the dark heart.

CHAPTER 9

Distractions

The dragon-killer crossbows along the outer walls of Diu aimed at Kai's underbelly. His heart pounded in his dragon chest as he and his grandfather flew over the city. The crossbows followed his flight pattern but did not fire. He could only hope they would remember that the silver dragons were friends to Diu. Only when they landed on the inner walls around the palace did he truly feel safe.

Iver was the first to welcome him, running headlong at the two silver dragons perched on the walls of Diu. "Kai!" his father shouted. "You came. Thank Alenga, you came. We have been under attack since early this morning."

Returned to his true form, Kai greeted his father. "I am here, but not for this." Kai motioned to the enemy encircling the outer walls. "I am chasing Keegan and the Lioness."

"The monster, the beast which set Diu ablaze?" Iver glared in remembrance. "I saw the creature. Fierce beast, why did it retreat?" he asked, grabbing Rayna's outstretched hand and offering her a warm welcome.

Kai gulped at the word monster. "The Lioness, it . . . she is my mother," he admitted with a heavy heart. "Keegan is controlling her mind. He was able to wake her, but she is confused. We followed them here. Keegan means to rule the world, and he planned to start here in

Diu. With my mother as his puppet, he is unstoppable. I need more time to turn her back. My Leviathan's water blasts are the only way to slow her down. She is stronger than Keegan. If I could keep them apart long enough, I could free her."

"The serpent! That was you?" Iver marveled and then chuckled. "There are tales of a water serpent in Baden Lake. Sailors now fear crossing the lake, and I have to pay nearly double to get them to venture away from shore for fishing expeditions or supply runs to Chenowith, Albey, and Town Hope."

Kai remembered all too well the terror his creature instilled when he rescued Rayna from Nola's grasp. "My apologies for my first appearance. I was not in complete control the night I saved Rayna, but tell the people the Leviathan is on their side. As for the Lioness, I believe Keegan retreated to regain control. We should follow them. If she is fighting him, and grandfather believes she is, now is our best chance at turning her back."

The ground began to shake, and Liam and Tenoch shouted at once. "Stonekings!"

Liam wedged between Iver and Kai. "Kai, you must get us to that tremor. NOW!" He pointed to a plume of dust rising within the city and the sound of the ground grumbling.

Benmar's back erupted with the wings of his dragon, and scales rippled across his evolving form. Kai followed suit and started to transform. "Not so fast, Kai Galloway," he heard a familiar voice shout, and he spotted Dresnor running across the wall behind him. "You are taking me with you."

"Run faster, old man," Kai shouted with a mouth half full of oversized teeth.

His grandfather's wings swelled to full size, and then he extended them to Liam, Tenoch, and Ryker as Kai completed his transformation. Ready to leave, Haygan climbed up Kai's back along with Basil and Rayna. Kai turned his head and caught sight of Dresnor joining without hesitation.

Together they flew into the fray. Gliding over Central City Gardens toward Rimtown, Kai spotted a gaping hole created by the Stonekings deep within Rimtown's warehouse district. The newly opened tunnel spewed Caroco warriors like ants, each man attacking anyone they could. Their hand cannons fired on the nearby citizens, cutting them down where they stood.

Tenoch jumped from Benmar's back, his hand outstretched to the raised soil around the opening. Kai watched in amazement as the dirt swooped skyward into a smooth slide, ready to catch the falling Stoneking. Liam jumped next and attacked the enemy Katori Stoneking warrior working to enlarge the entrance. From then on, it was a battle of rocks, dirt, and debris slung from one to the other.

Tenoch's foot punched deep into the loose soil, and his hands rolled and pushed in various directions, both working to close the gap and stop the horde of Caroco pouring into the city. The ground rumbled and shook as the dirt started to seal shut.

"Let me off here!" Rayna shouted. Kai extended a wing, and she hopped to a large warehouse, notching an arrow in the process.

Benmar landed and sprayed fire at the approaching horde. Some retreated, while others ducked and charged.

Grandfather! Kai called out. *They have weapons that can carve through your dragon scales, be careful.*

No sooner did he speak to his grandfather did a dozen Caroco warriors charge Benmar. Their fists bared the black knuckle-blades designed for slicing through dragons. Instead of flying away, his grandfather lowered his head level to the cobblestones. His amber eyes narrowed at the oncoming attack.

What are you doing, grandfather? Kai asked with his mind.

I am waiting for them to get closer.

The Caroco warriors approached with shouts of attack, which only turned to screams as his grandfather engulfed them in a ball of fire. Their angry, fiery forms swirled and swayed like drunk men unable to maintain their path until they fell dead in the street.

Meanwhile, Kai landed on the other side of the rapidly closing tunnel entrance only to notice the dirty bald heads of more Caroco warriors emerging from the darkness. Their battle cries echoed into the streets before a second enemy Stoneking shot rocks at Tenoch, distracting him from his mission.

Moments after their arrival, the street swarmed with Diu soldiers engaging in battle against the Caroco warriors. Blades and shields clanged in protest on every corner. Haygan and Ryker joined in the conflict, each wielding a double-headed battle-ax and a sword. As more enemies rushed out from the black void, Kai charged toward the tunnel, spewing fire into the opening. Dresnor launched arrows at any enemies approaching Kai's back, hoping to take a chunk out of Kai's dragon scales.

Kai tried to maneuver in the crowded street, but his wings restricted his movements. Like his grandfather, he sloughed off his dragon form and collected the weapons from a fallen Diu soldier. Like old times, Kai and Dresnor stormed the streets, searching for Caroco—those men in black with their scared, star-tattooed necks.

Between his speed and Dresnor's unequaled skill, they were a formidable pair. From the corner of his eye, he spotted the occasional arrow as Rayna leaped from rooftop to rooftop, defeating as many enemies as her quiver would allow. They spent time combing the streets until they turned the wrong corner.

Through the smoke and fire, Kai spotted the enemy lying in wait, their hand cannons aimed and ready. Taking hold of Dresnor, he held his friend back before he could run into the open. "There are too many," he insisted, "and they are armed."

From across the road, ten Diu soldiers poured into the street, ready to attack. Kai shouted, but they did not stop. From his viewpoint, he spotted a second set of Caroco warriors emerge behind the first group. Kai tilted his head and noticed each man carried a hand cannon. He shouted again to the Diu men and ran into the street behind his fellow soldiers. The Diu men raised their shields in defense.

Seconds before the enemy fired, Kai spotted Ryker coming from his left. The first shot tore through the dark-blue fabric of his shirt. His arm oozed with blood, but he kept moving.

Kai's crystal sparked with power as he ran into action after his friend. Smoke, fire, and debris filled the streets as the Caroco men fired their second round of hand cannons. The projectiles pinged off Kai's chest, arms, and leg. Two consecutive arrows flew over his shoulder, eliminating two men at once from the enemy's ranks. More arrows rapidly followed, one, two, three, four. Ryker sliced through the second row. Kai took on any left standing after the volley of arrows.

As the last enemy fell, Kai looked back to find Dresnor dropping to his knees when the shots stopped firing. He had taken a shot to the chest.

"Rayna!" Kai shouted. His wings sprouted from his back and he rose to the rooftop where Rayna perched.

She jumped the gap and landed in his open arms, and he lowered them both to the ground. Dresnor coughed blood, and Ryker pressed his hand against the spurting wound.

"Hold on, old man, I am here." Kai took hold of his friend's hand and lowered his head to the cobblestones.

Rayna's hands glowed with power. "The ball missed his heart," she reported as she ripped open Dresnor's damaged shirt to clean the wound. "Hold him still. This is going to hurt."

Kai held Dresnor's shoulders while she worked. Her hands pulsed over the hole. Dresnor groaned but held back any actual display of agony. Up and down, she moved her hands until he saw the surface of his friend's chest bulge and the silver ball popped from the cavity. "The hard part's over," she whispered to Dresnor, who then passed out in a massive pool of his own blood.

The golden Kodama light sealed the hole in his friend's chest, leaving a slight scar for the memory.

"Will he make it?" Benmar asked, joining the group.

"He will," Rayna announced, letting the light fade as she sat back on her heels. "He lost a lot of blood and will need rest. We need to get him to the palace. When he wakes, I can give him some herbs to help continue the healing process, and even a little magic to restore his strength."

Thunder shook the ground, and Kai rose to his feet.

"I will take him," Benmar announced. "That sound is Liam and Tenoch sealing the breach. I just came from the walls. The other Stonekings escaped. The rest of you should search the city streets, make sure there are no Caroco left, then come to the palace. We need to regroup."

Wings sprouted from Benmar's back and he scooped Dresnor into his arms. Kai offered a nod and joined the others as they circled back to the place where the Caroco broke through, where they found Liam and Tenoch replacing the final stone in the outer city walls. Joining them, Kai saw Rayna turn the corner.

"Anyone else need healing?" she asked.

"Everyone is fine. How is it you never run out of arrows?" Kai asked, noticing her full quiver.

"Kodama grow them from seeds," she opened her hand, and Kai watched the tiny seed elongate into the perfect wooden arrow with green leaves for fletching instead of feathers.

"Clever," he pulled her in close, and she noticed the gash in the shoulder. Her warm glowing hand pressed into his skin, and Kai felt the wound close. "Thank you, my dear."

When they returned to the palace, Kai was not surprised to find Dresnor propped up on the King's council chamber, but he was pleased to see his friend much improved. "Father, the best we can tell, there are no Caroco left inside the city. I hate to leave you at this late hour, but I must find Keegan and save my mother," Kai insisted, unwilling to take a seat.

Basil leaned into a chair but remained standing. "None of us are in any condition to travel, Kai."

It was apparent that his group was tired, but Kai refused to quit. "Stay here and help fight, if you wish, but I am going with or without you."

Dresnor chuckled. "And you call me stubborn. I am in no condition to travel, even with your wife's healing touch. I feel lightheaded, but if you go, I go. I am with you to the end, my friend. But consider this: the cries of war have stopped, and even the enemy sleeps. They have attacked for nearly two days straight, first Port Anahita and now Diu, but now they rest. We should take advantage. You are not exactly sure where we go from here, am I right?"

The truth was he did not know where to go next. "I wish I knew for sure, but I am unsure how to track them. We only came here because Keegan announced his plans. But I don't understand why the Caroco army holds back if they have two Stonekings and a Weathervane?" Kai scanned the group for answers.

"They are a distraction," Cazier announced, entering the King's council room with Captain Drew Henley. "Information is coming in from various spies within my network. Keegan is fighting on several fronts: Katori, Port Anahita, Fort Pohaku, Diu, and he has finally attacked Nebea. There must be a limit to the number of men he can throw at this war. With the majority of his Caroco men here in Diu, I wonder where his Katori brethren hide."

Iver's head bobbed in agreement. "But these men here, they do not attack to conquer. As you said, they are a distraction. What are they waiting for? Why amass your army here, then abandon it?"

Kai thought about everything Keegan said to him about his cause. "The enemy of my enemy is my friend," he suggested. "Everyone knows Milnos already hates Katori for their part in the great war. The Katori dragons came Diu's aid, crushing the Milnosian forces. I can only speculate that Keegan wants to seize control of Diu to punish Iver, so it would be smart to consider Milnos as a possible ally. Why waste your own men? If you can get another to do your dirty work, you save your men for the occupation after the war. Keegan's men are merely toying with us."

Benmar was not one for words in large gatherings, so it surprised Kai when his grandfather spoke. "I can see it now. The civil war within Katori keeps the Katoris busy and potentially converts followers to his cause; meanwhile, he is courting Milnos to crush Diu. How else could he bring down both Katori and Diu at once?"

"What is his cause, exactly?" Dresnor interrupted.

"Originally," Benmar started and then sighed heavily, "my son wanted to live freely anywhere in the world. He wanted to show the world our magic. The Chiefs and the Unie refused, and Keegan led a rebellion that ended in him and his followers being banished. Then Kai changed everything when he revealed our magic to the world. I know Keegan; it must sting him greatly to know his son is accomplishing more than he ever could."

"But the world knows about magic now, so why start a war?" Dresnor countered.

"Hate and power," Kai offered, removing any personal feelings from his statement. "Years of darkness has changed any good intention Keegan once held. He does not only want Katori. He wants Diu. Because my mother chose this place over Katori. Because I defend it time and time again. Think about it. Every attack has been personal to me. He wants me here. The final battle in his mind happens here—my home. The only thing he did not count on was my Leviathan beating the Lioness. This attack inside the city happened because it kept me here and gave him time to get away to regain control over my mother."

"If all of these assumptions are true, then we need to prepare," Iver said, making his way around the room. "And you need to rest. If you mean to go after Keegan, and I know you do, each of you will need all the strength you can muster. If they are traveling to Milnos to gain an ally in this war, it will take them days to get there. They may have a few hours lead, but if you go ill-prepared, you will save no one. Son, I know very little of how your magic works, but I imagine it requires a focused mind and a rested body." Iver took hold of Kai and ushered him toward the door.

Thoughts of protest caught in Kai's throat. He knew Iver was correct, but he wanted to save his mother. She needed him now, more than ever. "I really should go," he insisted, taking Rayna's hand.

"You have dreams, correct?" his father whispered. "Maybe a good night's rest will shine a light on the whereabouts of your mother and confirm what we already believe. Better to go after them prepared than get blind-sighted. Take the advice of a father, or should I order you as your King?" He grinned, ushering Kai and Rayna down the hallway toward Kai's old room.

◆ ◆ ◆

Once alone, Kai took hold of Rayna's hand. "I need to ask you a favor. Do you remember when you pressed your hand over Senina's mouth and moss bloomed under your hand?" He kept his voice low, hoping not to upset her with the memory of the time she lost control, and, in her anger, used her powers against another Kodama.

Rayna's eyes narrowed, and her expression of guilt and confusion made him reconsider. "I remember," she whispered, her eyes cast down. "Why do you ask?"

"I need you to do the same to me, only say here on my arm." He touched the exposed skin above his wrist. "Over and over until I can stop you from doing it. If I am to beat Keegan, I need to be able to block his magic. You are the only person I know who can force your magic on another, and change them. You are also the only person I trust to help me."

Her delicate touch barely grazed the hair on his arm and the bright green and yellow moss sprouted beneath her touch. It did not hurt, but it felt permanent. Using his own magic, he tried to remove the growth, but it would not recede. He sensed the energy within the plant, but the magic used to make it grow was spent. There was nothing to siphon.

With a second touch from Rayna, the moss vanished—but this time, Kai gleaned her efforts. He saw the energy around her fingers. It came from the air like tiny dust particles, and the moss itself became magic. Some went into Rayna; the rest floated away and disappeared.

"Again." He slid his shirt sleeve further up his arm. "This time, can you be bolder. I want to see you draw in the magic, hold it, and wield it against me. I need to study the flow around me, feel the change so I can understand how it moves. And if I can steal it."

She nodded. Her palm hovered over his arm, and he saw her pull energy from the plants in the room and even the air to ignite her crystal—but, more precisely, the moonlight coming through the balcony windows. He tried to take the magic from her as she held it within her. The light in her crystal waned, but she was still able to create the moss running down his arm.

"You did something?" She cocked her head sideways. "Only because I was attuned to you trying, but you took part of what I collected."

He smiled. "Good to know you felt it. Try again." He felt giddy in their experimenting.

Each time he could siphon a little more and prevent her from fully growing the moss down his arm. "Again," he insisted. The magic flowed, and he pulled upon it, but he could not stop the fuzzy plant from spreading. It trickled across his skin like peach fuzz. "Well, that is new . . ." He tried to sound hopeful, but it was still not the result he wanted.

"You are holding back," Rayna lowered her hand. "With Keegan, you cannot hold back. Do not be afraid to push back on me—the most I end up with is a green hand, which I can reverse. I am not Lucca, and you are not your mother. Do not wield in anger as Keegan would. Your power does not come from hate. I am no sage, but the greater the purpose, the better the outcome."

Her honesty struck him hard, but she was right; he had held back. The possibility of hurting her kept him from pushing the limits of what he might do. "I think we have done enough for tonight." He raised his arm, and she removed the moss. "I am just not willing to take risks, not with you."

CHAPTER 10

Mariana's Message

Thankful that even the enemy needed sleep, Kai climbed into bed. Sleeping with the fear of war looming felt surprisingly easy given the burden that weighed on him. With an open mind and humble heart, his head settled on the pillow. Rayna snuggled close, her breathing peaceful and easy. Although he had spent years hating his gift of visions, he now understood they were but a glimpse into the future, not meant to torture him but illuminate the possibilities of change.

Closing his eyes, Kai relaxed and did his best not to search for answers. His breathing slowed as he remembered that an open mind worked the best. His consciousness settled at that moment just before sleep takes you, yet your mind still clings to this world. A rush of anticipation mixed with a sense of magical awareness raised the hair on his arms, a cue that often preceded an impending vision.

Years of practice preparing his mind for receiving and remembering flooded back to him. His consciousness opened in the hopes of catching the finer details of a vision. When he finally slipped away, something called to him. A knowing feeling bloomed at the front of his mind.

The dream exploded in a vision of white. A blinding light as bright as the sun, yet he felt no heat. His eyes watered, but he refused to look away. He searched for the source. At the center of the brightness, he noticed a figure on its knees, and he tried to focus, staring into the light, but the light collapsed, and he found himself in utter darkness.

Within the depths of a prison, men shouted and went mad, lost in the darkness—Kai's bloodied knuckles wrapped around black iron bars. The cold metal fit snugly against his palm as he yanked on the door. It did not budge. In the next flash, he found himself running through the dungeon; torchlight splashed across the low ceilings and dirty walls. Men rattled chains and called for freedom. A boney hand reached for Kai, and he stopped as a gaunt face appeared in the darkness. The eyes seemed familiar, but he could not connect the name. The man mouthed words, but Kai could not hear the request over the clanging and the screams of men.

The next flash dropped him in the middle of a battle with the Hiowind Agora in the background. His sword clashed against dozens. The first warrior's silver-and-black raven armor glinted in the sun and the next, a bald man, was dressed in black with an ugly scar, a star branded on the side of his neck—Caroco. Sliced down in a fit of fire and black knuckle-blades, Benmar's dragon chomped and clawed, but they were too much for him. The men moved like angry wasps after meat. Behind him, Haygan and Ryker fought for their lives, and the horde engulfed them in a sea of swords.

Chaos ruled the field as the thousands of enemies became uncountable. Surrounded, each Elder fell, then Basil, Dresnor, and Yulia. Above him in the sky, dark shadows loomed, their shape blocked by the clouds. Kai turned his head as he raised his shield to block the curved blade of a Caroco sword. In the next flash, he saw himself running headlong into Keegan's open hand.

◆ ◆ ◆

"Good morning," Rayna's voice called him back to the waking world. Her head leaned on his shoulder, and she wrapped her arm around his stomach.

The faintest hint of sunlight peeked through the curtains of their bedroom as Kai searched for distant sounds and was pleased to hear the war had yet to resume. Sleep clung to his mind; he was not ready to wake, so he let his eyes close once more. Thoughts of his mother danced around the shadows of his thoughts. Eager to connect with her, he touched the crystal of her necklace, which hung around his neck.

The crystal warmed to his touch, and he felt magic from the stone race up his arm. His mind bloomed with light, and his mother's silhouette stood within the golden hue, the details of her face almost visible. His mother's voice echoed in his head. *I am here, my son. Only now, while Keegan sleeps, did I discover I have the strength of mind to reach you. I am sorry I did not give you a better life. Know that I love you, and I am proud of you. You are not alone.*

The sound of her voice made his heart weep. He knew her form was only in his mind, yet he wanted to race to her side and hug her close. *Mother,* he called back to her. *There is much in my life I celebrate. Do not let this one moment steal a lifetime of joy. You are not to blame for Keegan's choices. Where are you? How can I save you and stop Keegan? Can you get away from him?*

He fired off a rapid succession of questions then felt sorry that he wasted his moment of connection with his mother asking about Keegan and this pointless war. *Forgive me, Mother,* he pleaded, hoping she understood.

It is I who seeks redemption for the past, she replied. *I need your forgiveness. You must be willing to crush my crystal to stop the Lioness. Her wild nature is stronger than I am. I do not see the future as I once did. Only darkness surrounds my mind.*

The brightness around his mother made it difficult to look directly at her silhouette. *I forgive you, Mother, but I will not kill you. There must be another way. Tell me where you are, and I will come.*

We are going to Milnos. We arrive tomorrow, and Keegan means to join Milnos in attacking Diu. Then his new army will join the Caroco in attacking Katori. Do not let him merge his troops. Everything else is a diversion to buy time—even I am a distraction. I see blood filling the Agora's sacred water.

Dragons die by the hundreds. You and Benmar must stop him before his hate fills the world. Hate is all I feel now.

A million thoughts raced through his mind; how could he help her feel the love he knew she carried? *Remember who you are and the truth of your heart,* he begged. *Do not let Keegan control you. How can I save you?*

He wakes . . . His mother's voice and the golden light faded. She did not return.

The crystal turned cool within his palm. His mother was gone, and the connection lost. Her words echoed in his mind along with a low hum of peace.

He opened his eyes. "Rayna, I know where Keegan went. We must travel to Milnos to save my mother. I can turn her back to our side and stop him before he can return with Milnosian reinforcements."

◆ ◆ ◆

When Kai opened the door to his chambers, he found Dresnor and Drew about to knock.

"Good," Kai motioned for them to follow. "I have news about Keegan's plans. I need to speak with my father before we leave."

After everyone gathered in the King's council room, Kai shared the details of his vision, validating their assumptions from the previous night. Providing only the bits he felt mattered, he concealed the fact his mother was the source of his information, fearing her information would only raise suspicions or fears that his mother's message was a trap. Given his father's constant upper hand, he had considered the possibility that Keegan was feeding him misinformation through Mariana, but it did not matter. He would find a way to stop him and save her in the process.

Kai watched the Grand Duke Dante Carmelo and his cousin, Master General Adrian Cazier, accept him as if no time had passed and Nola's deception had left no taint on their relationship. Sigry, the palace physician and king's council member, however, stood near the balcony archway, unwilling to act as nothing had happened to his King. His narrowed gaze left Kai with the feeling that he still blamed him and the Katori for everything.

Kai addressed the group. "If Keegan expects us to stay here, then we need to leave Diu without being noticed. Meaning, some of us will need to remain behind."

The news sent glares and aggressive posturing through the group. "Ryker, Uncle Haygan, I know you want to come, but I need as many Katori to remain in Diu. We need them to believe we are all still here." He could only hope if they remained behind; it would change the outcome of his dream and save their lives.

"If you think I am staying behind, you have another thing coming," Ryker argued and glanced at Haygan. "I do not imagine you agree with this either, right? Keegan murdered your father two days ago using your sister as a weapon."

Haygan clenched his fists. "Don't you think I know that?" he spat. "I want to avenge my father's death, and I want to save my sister—but if Kai needs me here, I must see the bigger picture. Dresnor and Drew can take our places with Kai. Sure, they lack our speed, and they are not Beastmasters, but their skills as fighters will more than make up for that. Besides, Keegan will sense you or me coming, but Kai's friends stand a chance at helping without detection, should they get close to Mariana."

"Basil, Yulia, Liam, and Tenoch," Benmar addressed the group, "Kai is right. The other Katori will be gleaning our movements, and they might follow us or even try to prevent us from leaving. Keegan has a plan for us here, I am sure of it. We need everyone to cluster together to make it difficult to tell who's who and then provide a distraction while the rest of us escape. I have an idea that requires . . . "

"No," Ryker interrupted. "I will not stay behind. Forgive my rudeness, but I am not asking. I am telling you. Even if I must walk myself, I am going with Kai. And you will not convince me otherwise. I am not chasing revenge or even a lost love. Kai needs me more than Diu. I know what I feel, and I am going to help him bring back Mariana."

Kai raised his hand to calm Ryker. "Fair enough, I will not argue. I trust your instincts." They exchanged nods, and Kai turned back to his grandfather. "If you have a plan for our escape and a way to beat the other Katori warriors, all the better."

"I have an idea on how we escape without detection, but it requires giving up these." Benmar plucked a glass vial from his leather pouch secured to his waist. "These vials contain enough magic to give a false sense of light within the average man and in addition bestow a little strength and speed. The last part of my plan involves a little misdirection and hiding our true Katori light."

Basil shook his head. "Giving up the one thing that can cure internal injuries or heal on the battlefield? I'm afraid I must disagree. I do not see the wisdom in giving up several vials of sacred water moments before we head into war."

Rayna cleared her throat. "If Keegan's Katori warriors are gleaning our location, and I am sure they are, we need to deceive them. Use the gift of gleaning against them. From this distance and the vast city with its stone walls, we appear more like sparks of light than people. If we give a non-Katori these vials to drink, from a distance, they will look like one of us. This will fool Keegan's followers into thinking that all nine of us still remain here in the castle, giving the others a chance to escape. But for the escape to work, those who leave must hide their Katori light."

Iver pointed to the vial and then looked to his son. "I understand what the water can do. But what does Benmar mean, exactly? Hiding your Katori light?"

Kai let out a short sigh. "Benmar means we need to become invisible, in every sense of the word. We must hide the essence of our energy and become not only invisible to gleaning, but also to the naked eye."

"Invisible?" Iver's brow furrowed. "You can do this, turn invisible?"

Kai understood his father's disbelief. "I have only done it once, technically. Hid another person besides myself."

Kai watched Iver nod his head, listening with intent. Then he noticed his Kempery-man Ian Farwick maintained a wary eye, standing a respectful distance from his king with a hand on the hilt of his sword. When Benmar motioned to the King, Ian stepped closer.

"Iver," Benmar continued, "you drank the water and bathed in the Agora five months ago. I am surprised at the extra light you retained. I believe if you drink another vial, you will again appear as bright as one of us. Now we only need to replace three others, decoys who will stand in our place allowing us to escape undetected. Two vials each should be enough—Cazier, Dante, and perhaps your Kempery-man. I imagine he will feel better knowing he has the speed to protect his king." Benmar motioned to the overprotective Ian hovering behind Iver.

The suggestion of the king consuming more of this sacred water brought Sigry into the conversation. His serious eyes narrowed on the blue vial suspended by Benmar's fingers. "Your Highness, I must protest you drinking this unknown substance. We do not know the long-term effects or the addictive properties it may possess."

Iver stayed Sigry's objection. "I trust my son and Benmar. The water, if anything, removes the years from your bones. I feel twenty-five again, and I have no burning desire to consume more. I merely wish to provide the illusion necessary for my son's escape. If Kai cannot stop Keegan, we most likely will not live to care about possible side effects."

Sigry backed away, and his continued scowl made it obvious he disagreed, but he would not publicly challenge his king a second time.

Master General Cazier leaned across the table. "Sire, I will send for the rest of your Kempery-men and several captains—anyone not already engaged in battle along the southern wall. We could also use these hand cannons the Caroco carry. Many were recovered from the battle within the city and we have several crates of them, if memory serves. And then there is Nola's Arkin oil, a sticky syrup that burns white-hot and explodes when introduced to fire. As far as I know, most of her supply remains intact. We only need a way to deliver it to the enemy."

Kai stepped close to Iver. "Father, we must go. Keegan is a day ahead of us on his journey to Milnos. Liam and Tenoch can keep the others out of the city, but you need to consider taking the battle to them. If Sabastian cannot find Roark's troops, you are on your own. The rest of

Katori is not coming to our aid. It will not be enough to keep the balance of power—you must outsmart the enemy and take it back, you must win more than the Caroco. In every battle, the Caroco had something special just for me. They will hold back, waiting for me to show. Keegan is overconfident in his plan, and that will be his undoing."

"Have faith, son." Iver placed his hand on Kai's shoulder. "You may be leaving in the middle of a battle, but stopping Keegan and saving your mother saves us all. Besides, my collection in the armory contains a few surprise weapons. We will give them a good show if nothing else. Bring back your mother and we will win this war together."

CHAPTER 11

A King's Time

An overwhelming sadness pressed on Iver's chest. The anxiety building in his heart forced him to grab Master General Cazier's arm. His cousin did not ask how he was doing, and for that, he was grateful. None of them were all right—this was madness, but then war was not a sane man's business. Guilt and grief toyed with his emotions, and Iver wanted to crack, but this was not the time.

Years of believing Mariana was dead and then seeing her, even asleep, woke a joy he did not know he still possessed. Walking away from her, leaving her in Katori, took every ounce of strength he could muster. Now he struggled with the thought that she once again belonged to Keegan, and it angered him. She deserved better. He had promised to keep her safe, and so far, he had done anything but.

Following his son, Kai, and his friends to the courtyard, Iver recalled various items stored in the armory. "There should be seven crates of hand cannons," he instructed one of his guards. "Look for the crates from three years back, and the marking should be a falcon with the Bangloo word SUCUN stamped on the boxes. Also, send someone to collect the Arkin oil in the old granary near the training field. There should be several barrels and crates filled with ceramic jars. Collect everything, bring it to the courtyard, and await instructions."

"My King?" Cazier asked, waiting for the approving nod from Iver. "Five years ago, we brought back a pump of sorts—a brass or copper contraption, I cannot completely remember. It is nearly four feet tall. Your men will know it by the strange hoses attached. One tube will siphon from a barrel, and the other sprays liquid. It was meant to pump and spray water, but I believe we can use it to distribute the Arkin oil."

"I recall it; it was meant to put out fires." Iver chuckled. "How ironic today we will start a few with this forgotten machine."

"Sire, if I may." Sigry trotted to catch up with the group. "I believe I could also provide a few surprises to our enemy. If you allow me a few men, we can collect the items from my supplies. Nothing poisonous, I assure you, but I have a few herbs capable of inducing tears or coughing fits. They could aid in the disruption of their attack and aid in your turning the tide."

Cazier swiveled his head to turn to Yulia. "After you create the cloud cover for their escape, we may need you to ensure the wind blows in our favor. We would not want Sigry's concoctions coming back on our troops."

Iver watched Yulia sprint toward the apple orchard to create a magical storm. He watched her, intrigued by her magic. Her stance was bold, and she moved in slow, methodical movements that Iver found to be graceful yet forceful. He could only imagine what her choreographed magic did to the air around them as her hands rolled over and scooped air. The wind began to stir, and with the next fold and upward push, the small clouds in the sky slowly merged into a larger mass.

Following the creation of her cloudy weather, the sounds of war pounded in the distance as the Caroco army resumed their bombardments. Iver imagined they feared whatever Yulia might be planning, and he anticipated retaliation in magical form from the enemy's Weathervane, yet none came. After several quick tamps of her feet, fog bloomed through the courtyard, giving the air a damp quality.

"King Iver," Liam said, forcing his way into the conversation. "I have a few ideas on how we can relocate the Caroco army. If Tenoch can keep their Stonekings busy, and Yulia can distract their Weathervane.

Meanwhile, I think I can wash a few of them away. Provided you allow me to redirect the water behind the Baden Lake dam."

"Do you mean to bring down the dam below the lake?"

"Well, not bring it down, per se. Merely expand the overflow servicing the river. With a few minor adjustments to the landscape, I can . . ."

"No," Iver snapped. "Will we have nothing left after this war?" The thought of destroying his countryside on top of the suffering within his city was more than he could stand.

"Father," Kai held up his hands between the two men. "Liam and a few Kodama can put right the land. Maybe not replace the water, but I doubt he means to drain the lake. It may be a sacrifice worth considering."

"We need to go," Ryker interrupted. "It is time."

Benmar distributed the vials to Iver, Ian, Cazier, and Dante. "We need to time this just right. While you four drink the sacred water, we must conceal our own light as well as Ryker and Rayna's light. Kai and I must do everything in our power to hide those of us traveling to Milnos."

Although Iver understood the concept behind their plan, it baffled him how their magic could possibly include becoming invisible. "Kai, Benmar, are you sure this is the only way?" He did not want to doubt his son, not after everything, but this seemed too impossible.

Kai looked resolute. "I am sure."

Benmar said nothing, but a bit of trepidation welled in Iver's belly. Behind the confident tone, he could see that the fear in his son's eyes matched his grandfather's concerns.

"Good luck, son. I believe in you," Iver added, hoping the reassurance helped one of them.

Basil pointed to the small blue vial in Iver's hand. Resting in his palm, it seemed insignificant, yet he knew even a tiny quantity held incredible power for someone like him, a man without magic. Hoping to boost the confidence of the others, Iver went first, downing the cool liquid. Within seconds, he felt magic surge through his core and down his arms and legs. The energy electrified his thoughts and instilled an exuberant desire to use the power to save his city. Even before he drank this dose, he felt more alive, more aware of his surroundings. He felt capable of extraordinary speeds, like he could move a mountain.

Looking to the others, he realized Benmar no longer stood among them. A slight gust of wind tussled everyone's hair and clothing, and Iver felt the hot breath of a dragon among them. Then he heard the rustle of Benmar's wings and his claws scraping the cobblestones.

Kai motioned to the space behind his friend. "You are next, Drew. My grandfather will do all the work, just relax and trust me. Once you touch my grandfather, you will once again be able to see him, but you will fade from our view."

Drew felt for Benmar's wing. "This is so wrong," everyone heard Drew utter as he climbed up Benmar's wing and faded from view.

Kai motioned to the vials in the Grand Duke's hand. "Dante, if you will go next, to replace Ryker."

Dante hesitated only a moment but drank the vial, and Ryker disappeared, same as Drew.

"Our turn," Cazier said as Kai let go of Rayna and stepped back. "Do me a favor, will you? Find Riome. I sent her to Milnos. She was supposed to bring back news of Tolan and our missing spies, but I have not heard from her. She is my last spy, the only one I trusted to bring back the truth. Promise me you will find my daughter," he only half-whispered.

"I will find her," Kai nodded, taking hold of his crystal.

Iver watched Cazier remove the cork from his two blue bottles and raise them both to his lips. Then the Master General downed the contents, and Kai disappeared. Again, the sounds of dragon's wings and the scratching sounds of claws on cobblestone gave the fog an eerie, haunted feeling. The thought they stood among invisible dragons was almost too much for Iver to fathom, but then this was no time to question reality.

Dresnor reached outward. "This better not be permanent." He wrapped his hands around Kai's wing and vanished, but Iver could still hear him speak, "Oh, I can see you now, how reassuring. Thank Alenga because I did not fancy riding an invisible dragon floating in the air all the way to Milnos."

Rayna and Ian were the last two to switch places, and then it was done.

Iver reached both hands into the air like a blind man searching the heavens. "You can do this, Kai." His hands found the side of his son's silver dragon, and he saw a faint silver glow of the dragon above him. "I know this is new, even for you, my son, but you are so like your mother. Your magic comes from her, but I believe in you, and you can draw strength from my faith." He offered one last vote of confidence to his son and stepped back.

Kai offered a draconic warble in response, and Iver could only assume it was some form of thank you.

Multiple gusts of wind stirred the fog around the courtyard as Kai and Benmar took flight. Their hidden forms left no indication of where they were or the passengers they carried. Keeping his eyes trained on the thick clouds for signs of their departure, Iver breathed a sigh of relief when two swirls disturbed the gray rolling mist.

Knowing there was not a moment to lose, Iver turned to address the people gathered in the courtyard. As he continued to feel the extraordinary effects of the magical Katori water, he knew by the behavior of the others that they too were feeling the same.

"For the next several days," he said, "you will feel and move like a superhuman. We must take every advantage if we hope to defeat the Caroco. They attack from the south with the intent to wear us down. While they bide time for a second army to attack from the north. They mean to wipe us from this world and take our city. I will not allow that to happen, not while I draw breath."

132

CHAPTER 12

Too Many Minds

Invisible, Kai flew into the clouds over Diu as he balanced both worlds—his Beastmaster dragon form, and his true mind. His magic flowed easier than ever before. Even the ability to maintain their cover and go undetected was surprisingly effortless when he did not force the result. In fact, trying, he now realized, was the only thing ever stopping him. His questioning mind kept his doubts at the surface, blocking his ability. The awareness made him smile—as if a dragon could smile. *I understand now, grandfather,* he said with his Beastmaster mind to Benmar. *I could do this all along. It was only my mind that got in the way.*

Well done, Kai, his grandfather replied. If you can remember it even when your emotions race and the situation seems dire, there will be no limits to what you can do.

Gaining speed, they flew around Thade Mountain toward Milnos, and Kai spotted the town of Henley in the west. The city sat peacefully with patches of sunlight piercing through the thinning gray clouds. Behind them, the sounds of war faded like last night's nightmare. Even though he could no longer hear the expositions or battle cries, they still haunted him. Doubts about staying pulled at his gut.

"Look, everyone!" Rayna called out. "Diu soldiers. They must be coming from the northern outpost along the border. This is good news."

Kai scanned the ground. Between the trees, he spotted the Diu banner, a silver wolf on a field of blue. He estimated that maybe two or three thousand soldiers snaked along the road toward Diu. His father must have sent word that they needed help. And the fort must have sent nearly every man stationed along the Milnosian border at the Black Bear outpost. They were many, but nothing compared to the Caroco horde swarming the southern walls of his city. He knew he should be thankful reinforcements were on the way, but they were no match for the Caroco warriors and their ruthless Katori conspirators.

Again his guilt for choosing to leave reared its ugly head. Had he made the right choice? Or was he again following the plan Keegan laid out for him? He had been so sure staying in Diu was his father's plan, but now he questioned if they were merely flying into another trap. Taking a breath, he chastised himself. *This is no time to question every decision. Trust yourself, trust Alenga. We are where we are meant to be.*

But even so, he imagined the worst was unfolding in Diu. In its prime, his city once boasted thousands of soldiers. However, during Nola's reign, she dispersed many soldiers who were loyal to Iver, and only some had returned in the past few months. Those soldiers who remained in the city were the first to be attacked. Two of the five barracks lay in rubble and consumed by fire. Once again, he recognized Keegan's strategy: He wanted Diu to suffer before he took possession. It was not enough to wipe them out in a quick and painless strike. No, Keegan wanted the battle to last for days and days.

And that gave Kai hope. He prayed that the enemy's hesitation in ending the fight would provide them with enough time to find a way to stop this war.

Searching the landscape, Kai noticed the sandy desert that was Nebea's territory as the burnt orange earth cut a line against the green of Diu. They were close to the border, but he was unsure exactly where they were in relation to Milnos. *Where are we?* Kai asked his grandfather. *I have never traveled to Milnos. I have studied plenty of maps of the region, but I see no landmarks. Everything is green on one side and sandy on the other.*

Benmar replied, Keep watching, grandson. The peaks of the Kuro Mountains should be within range very soon. We near the center of this land, the point at which everything intersects. Where Diu and Nebea meet Milnos.

Years of studying geography helped Kai orient himself toward the Kuro Mountains. Like his grandfather mentioned, he recalled that the black mountain sat at the edge of Diu, Milnos, and Nebea. Topped with puffy white clouds, Kuro's graceful peaks cut into the sky. It was a gray haze at this distance but surprisingly beautiful. If only it did not mark the edge of his father's country and the beginning of his enemy. Was he too far to turn back? He knew he could be of help to his father, but could he really save his mother? Reaching Kuro meant the southern end of Lake Eden was on the other side, and they were a little over halfway to the Iron City of Milnos.

We should stop soon, Ryker spoke to Kai's mind. *Once we pass over Kuro, hang to the right and stay away from Lake Eden. There are too many people living around the lake. Fly high and avoid lingering over the main road. We should find a farmhouse, someplace established yet a little worn-down. We want a farmer of means but not of importance—someone who will not turn us in for money or status. Tomorrow, we can walk into Rieko city for supplies and fly the last part to Milnos.*

Kai thought about what the Milnosian citizens might think of Katori travelers or Diu soldiers. He knew of the unspoken hatred for Diu, a prize that had been stolen from Milnos thanks to the Katori dragons during the great war. And yet, he wondered if the years of peace between the two cities were a lie. A deception fabricated by Regent Maxwell to lull them into a false sense of security. With the return of many citizens back to Katori in recent months, Kai was unsure if they fled home in fear or were driven from their homes.

Have you traveled to Milnos? Kai asked Ryker in return.

I went to many places searching for Mariana all those years ago, Ryker stated flatly. *Even Milnos, although I did not linger much in the city.*

Reaching the summit of Kuro, the valley below unfolded. Lake Eden sat along the horizon bedecked with a rim of various structures and a hive activity. Benmar banked right just as Ryker instructed, and Kai followed. They kept to the clouds and continued into the heart of Milnos territory. Through the occasional opening in the clouds, Kai caught glimpses of the beautiful countryside spreading in every direction. Farms and trading post towns dotted the landscape south of the well-traveled main road.

Circling south of Rieko, they searched the landscape for a farmstead that might not question a foreigner's purpose this far from a major city. At least, that was how Kai hoped it would go, but he knew they could not be too careful. Most likely, they would need to split up to avoid drawing too much attention.

The hour was getting late, and the summer sun had already started to set. Kai was tired and hungry, and he imagined that everyone needed a moment to stretch their legs, eat, and rest. It was Benmar who spotted the ideal farmhouse and directed their descent. It was south of the main road and just far enough from Rieko; even Kai's dragon eyes could barely see the twinkling lights from the city.

They went unseen, landing in a small clearing a few miles away. The sky was a lovely golden orange, and within a mile, the first show of red then purple painted the sky. "We should split up. Rayna, Benmar, and I will approach the farmer and inquire about lodging in the barn while the rest of you circle through the woods. I will signal if it is safe to approach."

Ryker agreed and convinced Dresnor and Drew to allow Kai to go on without them.

By the time they reached the farmhouse, the stars twinkled above in a sea of midnight blue. A dark gray-headed man slid the large barn door closed and turned to walk up the hill toward the farmhouse. The first thing Kai noticed was the older man's ocean-blue eyes. They were wise beyond measure. Even though deep lines on his face carved the length of his story—he was clearly a man well into his seventies—the farmer moved like a much younger man.

Kai addressed the farmer from a respectable distance. "Good evening."

The farmer took a step toward them and angled himself between Kai's group and his home. Kai recognized it as a defensive posture, one a person might take if they were sizing up a stranger trespassing on their land after sunset.

The farmer glared at Kai and his group. "You are mighty far from the main road. Why are you on my land?" He stepped forward, puffing up his chest.

Holding up empty hands, Kai took two steps back, giving the man the high ground. "Forgive the late hour, but we need a place to sleep for the night. We are weary travelers on the road to Rieko. I know the city is only a few hours walk, but we are at our limits, sir."

The older man scanned the group and their lack of supplies. His gaze left them each stripped bare for the trouble, but none said a word while the man gauged their purpose. It was Rayna's voice he heard next.

"These are troubling times, sir, and I am sure the arrival of strangers at your door at this late hour may give you pause, but we only need a place to sleep. We will go now if our presence grieves you or your family." She motioned up the hill to the older woman and a young girl standing in the doorway of the farmhouse.

"You are Katori, aren't you?" The farmer glared at Kai and Benmar. "But the young lady, you were born and raised in Port Anahita with a few recent years in Diu." He jutted his chin to Rayna. "I want no trouble. Milnos is no place for any outsiders, especially those from Diu."

Surprised by the man's astute observation, Kai felt driven by the truth. "We are from Katori, Port Anahita, and Diu," he acknowledged. "We seek only shelter for the night. We mean you no harm." Again, Kai displayed his empty hands.

The farmer's decerning eyes traveled from his family to Kai's group, then he extended his thick meaty hand. "My name is Waldon, and my wife believes in hospitality to strangers." He motioned to the woman, now standing outside the door, giving her husband a nod. "I have a keen sense around others, and you and your group are running from, or maybe toward, something. I want no trouble; you stay one night only. I have no time for freeloaders. You had best be gone before my workers arrive."

"Thank you." Kai accepted the outstretched hand. "I am Kai, and this is my wife Rayna and my grandfather Benmar. We appreciate the offer and, if possible, we prefer to go unnoticed. I hope you can understand—strangers in a strange land. Maybe a place in your barn?" He pointed to the large barn a short way down from the house.

"What is your purpose, if you do not mind me asking? Foreigners in Milnos these days are a rare thing—and unwise, if you do not mind me stating the obvious."

"We are traveling to Milnos," Kai answered honestly, knowing Waldon would sense his truth. "My mother is unwell, and I hope to see her before it is too late."

Waldon again measured Kai's words. "There is talk from the other farmers—stories of a Katori beast that came through here in the wee hours. It hit several places along the road. An angry creature with wings and teeth that spits fire and kills everything in its path. Are you with them?"

The guilt of his mother's destruction weighed heavier than he knew it should, given the blame belonged at Keegan's feet. "We saw the creature yesterday as well, but we managed to avoid any casualties. Thank you for the warning. Any idea where it is going?" Kai asked, knowing the truth but wondering what the man knew.

"It is gone. That is all I know." There was little fear in Waldon's tone, which he held more around the eyes. "Rumor says it was headed toward Lake Eden or the mighty Iron City, but again I am a simple farmer. I have no interest in such things. I know your mother draws you to Milnos, but maybe you should reconsider."

"I appreciate the advice, but my mother needs me. Not sure I have a choice if these are her final days. I hope you can understand my urgency."

"Your choice." The man's eyes relaxed, and Kai hoped the truthful bits gave sincerity to his story. "You are welcome to stay the night, and I agree it is safer for all if you go unnoticed. It would be unwise to invite you up to the house, but my wife can prepare a basket of food. Milnosian soldiers travel the main road, and they rarely venture this far—but if they do, they will come to the house and need access to my barn. I am a loyal citizen, so if they seek you out, I will deliver. If you understand my intentions."

"We are in no trouble, Waldon," Benmar offered. "Truly, we are merely passing through on our way to Milnos, and we wish to keep to ourselves. Thank you for your hospitality."

"Fair enough," Waldon accepted the explanation. "I have another option. The old barn down the hill near the trees. It looks precarious, but she will hold." The farmer pointed, and Kai followed the man's gesture.

The moonlight outlined a sagging form half consumed by vines, dilapidated and beyond repair. Surrounded by tall grasses and framed by two ancient oak trees, the old barn sat nestled into the landscape. It looked sad and almost forgotten, a perfect place to avoid detection.

"Thank you. We will keep to the old barn and leave at sunrise." Kai nodded as Benmar shook Waldon's hand. "Would you mind if we made any modifications?"

"Make any changes you need to feel safe. I intend to tear it down at the end of summer, so it makes no difference to me. A few old boards may shore up the broken section in the roof if you feel the need. Wait here, and I will bring you some food and water."

Waldon darted up the hill again, giving Kai the impression that the man was in a hurry to be done with their exchange.

"We should leave before they wake," Kai suggested to Benmar. "No use testing the man's loyalty between his country and his hospitality."

"Agreed." Benmar nodded and jutted his chin toward the returning farmer.

"We have plenty of corn and potatoes," Waldon said, handing them a basket and a jug. "I am sorry I could not spare more meat and cheese, but they are costly resources. I cannot offer you wine, it is too precious, but this water should satisfy your thirst."

"I appreciate the kindness." Kai nodded and started to walk away.

"Magic is new to the world," Waldon called after Kai and his departing group. "These many months, I have seen amazing things. What is your gift, if you do not mind me asking? I know not all Katori have powers, but you strike me as extraordinary, given the way you carry yourself."

The question sliced through a lifetime of secrecy he was not willing to break. "We have no real magic, only an affinity for plants," he lied. "I served in the military until the world turned upside down and my heritage became a liability. We seek only shelter for the night and no trouble."

"Fair enough." The farmer turned back to his home without further question.

Joining Rayna and Benmar, they all moved across the grassy field, getting a close look at the old barn. Thick angry vines clung to the siding and climbed toward the second story in an attempt to reclaim the land. The old door hung at an angle and groaned in protest at Benmar's forceful entry. Every step inside the empty barn reminded Kai of a simpler time. It was mostly dark except for the shaft of moonlight punching through the hole in the roof. The place smelled of hay and age. Cobwebs clung to the corners and appeared to be pulling the barn down from the inside.

Dresnor climbed the ladder to the loft. "The place has seen better days, but the beams are sound. We should all sleep up here, off the ground, and pull up the ladder."

Kai and Benmar joined the Kempery-man to inspect their accommodations. "Rayna, can you do anything to secure the structure?" He leaned over the ladder to speak to his wife as she pressed her hand into the ground.

Rayna dropped a seed near a thick post. The vine sprouted and shot up the support, taking her up into the loft. "I can secure the exterior with stronger plants. Nobody will get within ten yards of this place without me knowing." She let her vines ooze through the hole above the loft, blocking the moonbeam.

They enjoyed a quiet meal with everything secured before finding a place to rest for a few hours. Kai imagined he would fall asleep swiftly; however, the previous day's chaos kept his mind racing. He could not possibly justify leaving more people behind without good reasons, and currently, he was out of excuses.

CHAPTER 13

Rayna's Secret

The small heap of moss-covered hay beneath Rayna felt better than sleeping on the hard ground, but she still felt restless. Grateful for the few hours of sleep, she sat up to sense their surroundings by connecting to the outside landscape. Her fingers danced over the leaves of the delicate ivy. The vine connected to another thorny briar plant, which crept out into the tall grasses surrounding the barn; each told her that no one was approaching the barn.

At her side, Kai slept, a peaceful yet eventful slumber, which she imagined—or rather hoped—offered new insights into their uncertain future. Letting him rest, she took a moment to herself and slipped out of the hayloft using a few vines to lower her to the barn floor. With a few taps and a nudge, the woody vines parted, she stepped out into the moonlight.

Quietly she strolled through the pasture, and the wet grass kissed her ankles and bare feet. She missed Katori and the land she called home. This soil was rich and inviting but foreign and rocky. It was strange to her how she could feel so much history in the ground. Years of potatoes, corn, and spinach that the farmer had rotated through the fields. Even the animals left their mark, telling her this pasture once held many cows and a few horses.

Happy to have a moment to herself, she closed her eyes. The air was sweet and clean. This was the first moment of true peace she could remember in weeks. Maybe even as far back as her wedding day. The ensuing chaos made her wonder if she and Kai would ever be free from Keegan and his hateful heart. But then she needed to keep the faith. Alenga would show Kai a way, and she would help him end this war.

It was the old oak tree that spoke first, then the grasses. They warned her of an approaching man. The care they took watching over her made her smile. "Benmar," Rayna spoke to him without turning around. "You should be resting. We have another big day of travel, and you will be doing the dragon's share of the work."

"I doubt we will do much flying," he replied. "We are too close to civilization. Once we leave Reiko, there are a few paths that may be free of people, but there are many communities between here and Milnos. Lake Eden is a rich resource for food, and it harbors many. I can think of only one section safe to fly over."

Considering the hour, Rayna turned so that she could wake the others. "Dawn is coming, and we should go before the farmer changes his mind."

"You should tell him." Benmar stepped in her direction, stopping her departure. "He has a right to know before we reach Milnos."

"Tell him what?" she responded, letting her eyes fall to the ground, avoiding Benmar's gaze.

"Tell him you are pregnant." Benmar touched her chin and lifted her gaze to meet his. "I care for you both, and I mind my own business, but this is no time for secrets."

The fear of letting Kai know caught in her throat. "How did you know? I am only ten weeks along or so. I have not told anyone. Between Keegan and the Guardian training, I have not had the chance. I did not want to make things more complicated than they already are. I wanted it to be a happy moment when I told him. When news of Keegan's ships arrived, everything turned upside down and then . . ." She could not complete the thought.

"When you are alone, or you think you are alone, you hold your stomach—the way an expectant mother would. I suspected something before we left Katori. I saw you in the Agora the day Keegan came to steal Mariana. You touched your stomach when my son addressed the crowd. In battle, you hold back and find ways to fight from a distance, something you never did before. The baby is small but noticeable, three or four inches. You are a liability to the group if you cannot push forward when we need you."

Rayna took Benmar's hand in hers. "Please, you must not tell Kai." She begged, hoping he would understand. "He is under enormous pressure. Leaving Iver to save his mother, for him it is like choosing who lives and who dies. And he still has no idea how to stop Keegan. His dreams, now that he has them, only show war and death."

"You are starting to glow," Benmar spoke, turning the conversation back to her, "which is natural for a mother. You have a new life growing inside of you. By the way, I hope you know you can no longer transform into a tree. Much like a Beastmaster, you cannot risk harming the baby."

It had not crossed her mind, but it made sense. She remembered Simone's inability to become a dragon when she was pregnant. "Thank you for the reminder."

"But what gave you away is the heightened sense of smell I have as a dragon. Today I sensed the baby when I gleaned you. I am surprised Kai has not detected your changes, but perhaps my grandson is too distracted to notice, but he will. Most likely at the one moment he needs his focus the most."

The thought that she could put Kai in harm's way quickened her pulse. "I will not turn back," she insisted. "You need me. Kai needs me. If anything, I am the only one who can heal. We gave most of our sacred water vials to hide our departure. Dresnor and Drew are more of a liability with their lack of Katori gifts."

"Please, Rayna, at least let Kai make a choice. Do not blindside him."

"I cannot. Besides, where am I to go? Where is safe these days? Katori is in civil war, Port Anahita is besieged, Diu is under attack and will most likely be destroyed in the coming days. I am only a liability if he knows.

Now is not the time to tell him. He cannot waste time worrying about me. Help me hide this!"

"There are places I could take you," Benmar said slowly. "Places nobody goes. Believe me. You would be safe. Alone. But safe. Please, I hate to force your hand, but we have no time for debate. Either you tell Kai, or I will."

Her heart pounded in her chest. She could not bear the thought of Kai going to Milnos alone.

"You would give me an ultimatum? Really? No, you would never come between us. I do not wish to be alone. I couldn't live with myself if I was the only one who survived. No, that is not an option. We must all stay together to help Kai, to help us all. Now is not the time for his mind to be divided." She waited for him to respond, hoping her argument was sound.

The seconds dragged on, and Benmar started to pace. "Seems I have no choice." He approached and put his arm around her. "You are right. He does not need another burden. I will try to help you, but I will not lie to my grandson. May I?" he gestured to her abdomen.

She nodded in acceptance, and Benmar placed his hand a few inches from her stomach and moved it in a figure-eight motion. The tiniest glow emanated from his hands. There was no heat, only a feeling of peace that swept up and down her entire body. "I am no Lumen. Lucca would be better suited for this task. His magic lasts longer."

Rayna heard the sadness in Benmar's voice as he uttered Lucca's name. They all missed him and wished he were here now. "Thank you." She watched him continue to perform the same steps a second time and final time.

"I have blended your two auras. Your stomach should not stand out as the baby develops. We will need to do this every so often. You will appear naturally bright, but not just around the belly. This way, if Kai does look at you, he will see one source, and hopefully, he will dismiss the exaggerated glow and not delve deeper to see the baby."

"Thank you, Grandfather." Rayna kissed his cheek and turned back toward the barn.

◆ ◆ ◆

Dawn's earlies rays broke through the darkness, driving away the night with each inch it gained over the landscape. "We should go before Waldon wakes or his workers arrive," Kai said as looked to the others. "It will be better if we are just gone and if we avoid the main road."

Ryker nodded and was the first one down, followed by Dresnor and Drew. Kai waited for Rayna and Benmar to return, his legs dangling off the loft edge. Rayna smiled up at him, and he hoped she would not see the contemplation behind his eyes. The doubt in what he was about to do.

He hopped down and landed in front of her. His strong arms wrapped around her and pulled her close. "Thank you for being my strength." He kissed her forehead. "Even with the risks, I know we are stronger together. I must speak to my grandfather alone. Can you walk ahead with the others?"

She nodded and stepped in line with Drew as they all walked outside.

Kai and Benmar trailed behind the others as they left Waldon's farm through the forest, avoiding the main road.

"Grandfather," he said, taking a deep breath. "I wish there were another way, but you cannot come with us. We need you to go for help."

Benmar pulled Kai to a stop. "Grandson, I will not leave you."

"You are not leaving me. If I fail to turn my mother, we must return to help save Iver. Diu will not survive without aid. The Elders in Katori must know that Keegan plans to hit them next. They must come to Diu. Each scuffle in Katori is only a distraction to keep them busy and thin out our numbers, all while Keegan gains a second army. You know as well as I do that if Diu surrenders, its soldiers will eventually join him. Better to fight for the winner than die. Natural survival instincts. Keegan's army will grow. Preventing Diu from falling is our best strategy. If we put all our resources there, we at least stand a chance."

There were so many things he wanted to say to his grandfather, and they all came out in a jumble. The look in Benmar's eyes stabbed at his heart. Sending away the one man who was always there for him felt wrong, but he had no choice. "Kai, I do not understand how my leaving changes anything. Why can you not send Rayna or Ryker?"

"Ryker is no dragon; he cannot fly over the mountains. We Katoris either fight in Diu, or we will face Keegan's combined forces in Katori. That is what my dreams show me. If we lose in Diu, Keegan will attack Hiowind and Matoku. The Caroco and Milnos armies destroy the sacred Katori cities and any who oppose him. We must not let him merge all his men together. Even now in Diu, I fear my father, Iver, is already dead. Unless Roark reaches Diu, it will fall. Alenga does not show me their fate, but I can guess."

Benmar started to pace. "I am not sure I can convince Katori to come." His grandfather shook his head. "I am a man of few words. I am practically an outcast living up on the mountain. How can I convince Katoris to abandon their homeland and fight on foreign soil? We are in a civil war, and some of the people supporting the uprising are good, loyal Katoris. People hate that the Elders broke tradition—that they did so for you, not to mention you are the son of the man behind all of this. My son is the enemy. Why would they listen to me? Why would they fight for you?"

The truth was hard to hear, but his grandfather was not wrong. Many disapproved of revealing their magic to the world—and that it had been done by a child not raised in Katori, taught their ways, and dedicated to their secrets. It was a valid question. Even he could not see why they would fight for him or Diu. "Ask Davi and his people," Kai suggested. "Davi and the other outcasts call Diu home." He hated calling them outcasts, but it was the truth. They had no more settled in Katori than he had.

"The outcasts are not fighters. Keegan's men will slaughter Davi and his people, and anyone who gets in the way. The Caroco are in this war for blood, and they will win by stepping on the bodies of others. You cannot bring Davi into this."

The sunrise poured through the valley, and Kai continued to follow the others. "You are right. This is not his fight. But I cannot ask the

Katori because they are not my people—not completely. I cannot ask the real dragons because they do not care about the world of men. There is no one coming to save us. The battle must take place in Diu. We cannot let him merge his armies. I cannot promise we will win there, but we will not in Katori." Kai waved his hand toward some ominous distant event.

Kai could see the argument swelling in Benmar's throat. "This is wrong–leaving you is wrong."

"Grandfather, if you continue with us, we will die in Milnos or fleeing back to Diu. My visions change each night slightly as we travel, but one thing remains the same: Diu is the turning point in the war. What happens there decides our future. Left unchecked, the growing unrest in Katori will feed Keegan's cause, and we will all die in Katori. Most do not want to fight, so they will fold and follow just to end this nonsense. Any who remain opposed will die."

Doubt hung on his grandfather like a wet blanket. "And you believe they will make a difference? That enough will listen and change the odds?"

"I cannot say you bringing help will make any difference in our fates, but Diu stands a far greater chance with help." Kai wanted to say yes, but it would be a lie, one he could not fully sell. "Light up Katori with the truth—this war is not about me or secrets, nor is it for Katori's betterment as Keegan would have them believe. This is his desire to rule and spread hatred. Some part of Katori must be willing to stand against him."

Benmar's contemplation took longer than Kai hoped. The moments passed with agony before his grandfather responded. "You left your uncle because he died in your dream, same for Basil, and you tried to leave Ryker. Tell me I am wrong. Was last night's dream so awful you would now send me away? If you think removing one link in the chain will break the future, let me take Rayna with me. Let me save her. Why risk her life going into Milnos?"

Kai thought about the suggestion, but she was the one person who did not die in any of his dreams. "Last night, I dreamed Keegan killed you. There, yes, I admit it. You and Keegan are drawn together like a moth to a flame. He will sense your presence, and then you sacrifice yourself to save me. No, I cannot let him take another person from me. But Rayna, I need her here—I see her here in Milnos. I am not sure why, but I know I need her. Leaving the others changes things. I can only hope that Ryker survives whatever happens in Milnos, all I see is him surrounded by fire. Bringing Dresnor and Drew, leaving you behind. These changes matter. Please trust me. Katori is no longer shrouded by secrets, but they still have their traditions. Convince them to fight, or Keegan will take their freedoms."

They walked on in silence nearly a mile before Benmar spoke. "I will make better time flying alone." He stopped, and Kai did too. "There is a mountain city in Katori near the border. I will send word through the beacons. If I can bring back Katori help, I will, but I will not linger. I will return to Diu. Either way, with or without help, I will meet you there."

There were no words to say. Instead, Kai hugged his grandfather and let him go. Watching him fade from sight, Kai prayed for his swiftness. The gust of wind that fluttered through Kai's hair was enough to know Benmar was gone and with him all of Kai's hopes. He had not the heart to tell his grandfather no one would come, but at least he managed to save one more person from an awful fate.

Rejoining his group Kai pulled them all together to hatch out a plan to ensure their safety and success before setting out on the last leg of their journey to Milnos.

CHAPTER 14

Amelia's Choice

A welcomed breeze drifted in through Amelia's open balcony door, providing a reprieve from the sweltering heat. The Raven's Tower felt unbearable between the warmth of summer and her seven-month belly. Wearing only a chemise, Amelia crossed the hardwood floor to her stone balcony. Above her, the stars smiled and mocked her lonely existence. They were free to dance in the night sky and sparkle while she withered in her forgotten tower.

The jingle of keys clinked against Amelia's door, and she hurried to her dedicated spot. As the door swung wide, the guard glared at Amelia, reminding her it was best not to look at them. The maid was new, someone she had not seen before, a woman so bold she looked into Amelia's eyes. The kindness she saw almost made her smile, but she looked down, holding her frail body and crouching as if she could get small enough to recede into the cracks between the stones of the wall.

A grunt from the guard startled Amelia and shook her with fear. The maid raised a hand as if to calm her nerves, but the guard shouted, "Do not touch the prisoner!"

The maid did not quake in fear. Instead, she lowered her head to connect with Amelia. "Miss." The woman's voice was sweet music to Amelia's ears after months of male grunts and shouts. "Can I get you anything?"

Amelia turned as the guard yanked the maid from her room. The woman's eyes were intense, and she was not afraid. The door slammed shut. *Foolish woman, you should not defy the guard*, Amelia thought, looking at the simple tray of food that was her dinner.

With barely enough food to survive, she waited to give birth. Her frail hand rubbed her swollen belly. She wanted to love this little one, boy or girl, but there was no hope for it. Once the guards noticed her evolving figure, they informed her mother and the news that came back broke her heart. Her survival, although unloved, was the only kindness her mother could guarantee. The child, however, had no such promise. While her mother did not specify what would become of her baby, the midwife said she would take away the child on the day of its birth.

Thoughts of jumping to her death fluttered in her chest and pulled her back to the balcony. The sparkling lights of the city left an amber glow that drew her to the railing. The hard stone felt warm on her feet. A sweet breeze caught her nose, and the darkness below opened its arms to her. Tears ran down her cheeks as she thought of her husband. "I am sorry, Tolan. I am not as strong as you. I cannot live without you, without our child. I cannot let them take it away from me."

A flutter moved in her stomach and her unborn child punched at her ribs. Once. Twice. Three times. Amelia let her hand rest on her stomach. The pressure of a tiny hand pressed into hers. The realization she was not alone broke through her sadness. She stepped back from the railing and cradled her stomach. Sorrow and joy overwhelmed her with a new set of tears. Her baby wanted to live, and she wanted to live. Together they would find a way.

◆ ◆ ◆

Come morning, Amelia set her mind to regaining her strength. Before the guards arrived to bring her morning tray of stale bread and dried meat, she dropped her glass on the stone threshold of her balcony. It shattered and the guard outside her chambers went to unlock her door with his jingling keys. As quickly as she could, she lay on the floor next to the broken glass and closed her eyes.

She heard the door open, and the guard entered. "This better not be a trick, girl!" the man shouted, but she remained motionless.

His thick, meaty fingers grasped her shoulder as he rolled her on her back. Amelia commanded herself: *Stay calm.* Inside, her heart pounded with fear, and her frayed nerves implored her to run through the open door, but she kept still.

The guard shook her roughly.

Amelia let her eyes flutter. "So hungry. Please may I have some food?" she begged.

To her surprise, the man lifted her from the balcony and placed her in the bed. "I will get food. You rest." His hand brushed her stomach, but she continued to fane frailty. "It is not right they starve you and your unborn child, even if this little one is a Diu . . ." The guard did not finish, but she knew he wanted to say something hateful, but even he saw the innocence in the unborn baby.

He left her alone only a moment, as the maid soon arrived with her breakfast just as he closed the door.

"The girl fainted," the guard explained to the maid. "Send for the midwife, and when you return, bring me some food as well. I have two hours left on my shift, and I need something to eat." The man's dark eyes narrow on Amelia. "Do not make me regret this kindness. Now sit up and drink some water."

Amelia sat up and took the cup, sipping the water slow and easy. "Thank you." She let her eyes meet his before shying away, afraid of being punished for being too bold.

"Same as yesterday." He poked at the plate. "Stale bread and smoked turkey. You need fruit. Vegetables. And way more meat than they offer." He took her cup and handed her a chunk of bread.

"Forgive me for my honesty"—Amelia caught his eyes again—"but my parents do not care if the child lives, only that I do. Why, I am no longer sure, but you should go before the midwife arrives. She will tell my mother if you do anything more than guard my door."

He nodded and reached for the door. "My name is . . ."

"No names," Amelia interrupted him. "I appreciate your kindness, but names create familiarly, and neither of us can afford to slip. Someday, if I ever leave this place, you can tell me your name." She took another bite of food, and he left.

It was well over an hour before her door opened again and the midwife filled the frame. Amelia rose to her feet as Dextra entered. Trying to look presentable, she stood and smoothed the front of the blue dress she now wore and ran her fingers through her dirty hair. Dextra's pert lips, narrow nose, and sharp black eyes scanned Amelia, and then the midwife stepped to the side.

Amelia all but fell over when her mother entered. Like Amelia, Lady Grace had golden hair and large silver-blue eyes, which frowned when they fell on the tattered white lacing left undone to allow room for Amelia's expanding stomach.

"Mother!" Amelia cried, reaching to touch her mother's arm. "You came."

Her mother recoiled at the sign of affection. "I am Your Royal Highness, Duchess of Milnos, if you please." Her mother rolled her eyes and then turned to Dextra. "I do not appreciate this distraction in my morning. She is too frail. Even I can see you are not feeding her enough. I never said starve the girl. The babe is draining the girl's strength, and while she is a prisoner of Milnos, she is still a lady. This will be my only visit. If you cannot manage, I will find another caretaker who can. And I do not have to tell you what will become of you should you fail."

They continued to talk as if Amelia were not there, bantering about what Amelia should eat, the state of her ratty dull hair, and dirty nails. The words civility, lady, bath, soap, books, and a new dress trickled into her ears through a renewed sadness. Her mother cared more about her appearance and her behavior than she did about her imprisonment. Amelia wanted to collapse when her mother left, but she stood tall and defiant as Dextra instructed the maid to bring more food, as well as a few additional servants and two guards, to her tower prison.

When the maid returned, she brought a tray of meat, cheese, and fruit. The young girl's arms bulged with books, which she placed on the small table and fresh linens for her bed. The two guards carried in an oval copper tub while the two male servants heaved large pales of water to fill the squat tub.

"Measure the girl for a new dress, one that will accommodate the growing bump over the final months," Dextra ordered the seamstress and then left.

Amelia watched the seamstress eye her like a filthy dog. She knew the woman well. Over the years, Rubina had measured her for hundreds of dresses, and now suddenly Amelia was beneath her. Once they were alone, Rubina yanked off her filthy dress.

"Bathe," she ordered. "I have a clean chemise in my bag you can wear while I take measurements and an oversized dress that I believe will fit until I can bring you a suitable new dress."

The tub was small and the water was lukewarm at best. But this was Amelia's first real bath in months, and she wanted to savor the moment. Sitting on one end, she tucked her knees against her belly and slid her long blonde hair into the water. The clean water felt refreshing against her scalp, and she closed her eyes. For the first time since her imprisonment, she felt almost human.

Tap, tap, tap. Amelia felt a finger poke her, and she opened her eyes. Above her, Rubina glared, so she sat up, covering herself. "I do not have all day." The seamstress took a seat and tapped her foot as if that might hasten the situation.

Amelia picked up the soap, which smelled of jasmine and orange peel. Her wet hair clung to her shoulders, and she began to scrub. By the time she finished, her white skin was rubbed raw, but she felt whole again as she put on fresh clothes. The measurements were quick and quiet, and when Rubina left, Amelia again found herself alone.

She fingered the books on the table. "Finally," she spoke, rubbing her belly. "Something to help pass the time. Let me read you a story, little one." She took the top book, sat on her bed, and began to read. All this time, she never realized the child was her salvation.

156

CHAPTER 15

The Insider

Rieko city was much larger than Kai first realized, and the Milnosian military presence was more substantial than Port Anahita ever boasted. Although it was an outlying town, and there was little chance that he would be recognized, it was not worth the risk to walk around without some sort of disguise. At the first chance, he liberated a hat he found on a covered wagon in the long line waiting to pass inspection. Keeping his head down and pretending like he owned the place, he and his entourage passed through the gatehouse. Luckily, the guards asked no questions, but they cut several looks at Rayna, which left Kai feeling uneasy.

If anyone knew where they came from—Diu vermin treading on Milnos soil—they would most likely be strung up in the square or chased out of town. Even being from Katori would not be much better. "Best keep talking to a minimum," Kai suggested, using a Milnosian twang he knew well. "Any foreign accent will raise unwanted attention we cannot afford."

Kai and his group crossed the street and stepped onto the raised sidewalk that lined the wide streets. Both the sidewalk and the roadway were made from large square stones, unlike the rounder cobblestones used in Diu. The people reminded him of High Town in Diu—clean, well-dressed, with their noses in the air. That is when he realized he and his group were totally out of place. They looked like foreigners. Even the Milnosian security dressed better.

Stopped short by a boisterous group of high-society gentlemen entering a cigar shop, Kai caught the disapproving looks on each man. The last overdressed man scanned him and his fellow travelers, and his upturned face made his judgment clear. Unfazed by the rude rejection, Dresnor followed the men inside, leaving Kai dumbfounded.

Through the picturesque window of the shop, Dresnor approached the group and the owner. Their conversation was a mystery, but their body language and facial expressions left Kai pleasantly surprised. The two men conversed at length, and when Dresnor rejoined them, he carried four cigars. "Kuwani cigars are a rare treasure beyond the shores of Ahana." Dresnor spoke with a deep voice, drawing out his vowels in a way that surprised Kai.

Kai looked at his friend with new eyes. "Since when do you come from Ahana and know anything about cigars?"

"I was born on Ahana, where my parents raised me until a terrible accident took my mother. When I was twelve, my father moved us to Diu, and the rest is history. The accent comes in handy when needed. My father worked as a sommelier, and he taught me much more than ancient fighting techniques in those early years before I joined the service of Diu."

A group of refined ladies strolled around their group, leaving gasps and disapproving looks in their wake.

Rayna jutted her chin at their rudeness. "My pants are unsettling for the women in this city," she said. "Every woman here is wearing a dress. If we mean to travel to Milnos, I should buy a dress."

Kai looked at the rest of the group. "If we hope to follow Keegan and my mother to Milnos, we all could use a wardrobe adjustment. The Milnosians will hang us all if they learn we are from Diu. Especially you three." He nodded to Dresnor, Drew, and Ryker. "Even without the Diu armor, you carry yourselves like soldiers, and without the Milnosian or Bangloo branding, that leaves Nebea or Diu. We need something in a lighter color with embroidery around the cuffs and collar. Since I am the most recognizable, I will stay out of the shops to avoid any unwanted attention while the rest of you acquire what we need."

Ryker scoffed. "I prefer black." His fake accent left it a little unclear as to his origin, which pleased Kai. "And I do not wear embroidery. I am not interested in fitting in with these people, but I do not wish to end up in prison or jeopardize the mission. I will see what I can find."

Dresnor passed their supply pack from Waldon to Kai. "I agree. If we are to walk into Milnos, we need to start looking like them. I am no spy, but I know if we want to go where we want, we need to look the part. I will get you two a better shirt and a vest. And I will see if we can find a room. We could all use a clean shave." He sized Kai and Drew, looking them up and down before walking away.

Ryker glared at a group of men looking down on him. "I will see what I can do, but there is no way I am wearing anything with lace on the cuff." He stomped off following Dresnor, leaving Kai and Drew to wait for Rayna outside a dress shop.

It was a gaggle of women who drew Kai's attention to a local shop. The open doors, the smell of perfume, and the laughter of ladies trickled into the street. Kai stepped closer to eavesdrop. Inside, ladies played with masks, batting their eyes at one another, and fanning themselves with ornate feathery fans. "Do you like the blue one or this gold mask?" A woman with golden locks held up one and then the other. "Blue is my favorite color, but the gold seems very elegant."

Her raven-haired friend pawed at some lace on the nearby table. "Are you even going? I mean, you have no escort. Did you really think Lord Heller's son would ask you to the King's masquerade ball? He has known for a month, and the event is in Milnos tonight. He left two days ago by carriage. Willa, he was never going to ask you. You cannot go to even the local festivities without an escort, so why bother?"

Willa dropped both masks and stormed out of the boutique, bumping into Kai in the doorway. "Humph," she glared at him as if it were his fault, but the tears forming in her eyes knew better.

Kai turned back to find Drew scanning the streets. "There is a masquerade ball in Milnos tonight," Kai informed him. "If we hope to get into the fortress to discover Keegan's plans and save my mother, this may be the perfect cover. Now to find—or perhaps steal—an invitation."

Dresnor turned the corner and joined them, carrying a brown paper package. "We have what we need to enter Milnos," he motioned for them to follow. "Everyone in town is talking about the King's birthday celebration: a masquerade in Milnos tonight. It could help us gain access to the city and avoid anyone recognizing the Diu Prince. Not sure yet how we will get access to the event at the fortress. If Regent Maxwell means to offer men to Keegan's cause, we could find out. Getting close to your mother might be possible if Keegan is attending the event."

"We heard," Kai nodded, "and I agree."

Dresnor nodded and handed Kai a brown package. "This should be suitable attire. According to the shop owner, the selection of masks he offered was minimal, but given the party is tonight, I am surprised he had anything left at all. It seems even those not in attendance plan to celebrate here. Once we collect Rayna, we can leave town. I used the last of my Milnosian coin. They do not accept anything but their own currency, so I hope the others fared better if any of us intend to eat more than the meager supplies from Waldon's farm."

Kai took the packages meant for him from Dresnor as Ryker joined them, crossing the street behind a white open-top carriage. Then they heard a commotion coming from the lady's dress shop. Well-dressed ladies laughed and fanned their faces as the shopkeeper berated Rayna. "Get out!" She waved a hand, motioning to the open door. "We do not serve filthy women like you. Milnosian coin or not, you are Port Anahita harbor trash." The woman shoved Rayna in the chest, pushing her outside, and closed the doors behind her.

Off-balance, Rayna stubbled backward, catching two ladies in the process. The women took one look at Rayna's appearance and shouted, "How dare you touch me, you filthy woman? Are you trying to rob me? Guard! Guard!" The high-society woman feigned distress, waving her hand in the air, calling for help.

Kai stepped toward the confrontation, ready to defend his wife, but Ryker pulled him back. "Best not make things worse. We should go, and quickly before the authorities . . ."

No sooner did his friend state the obvious, several armored guards converged across the street and marched in their direction. Their shouts sent Rayna rushing down the nearby alley, with Dresnor and Kai quick to follow. Calls from the guards echoed after them, and the sound of heavy boots set Kai's heart pounding.

"Stop that woman!" they called, but Rayna slipped out of sight.

Turning the corner on the next street, Kai caught sight of his wife darting between two horse-drawn carts toward another backstreet. He and Dresnor dodged traffic and bystanders, doing their best to follow. Yet when they reached the backstreet, there was no sign of her.

"Where did she go?" Kai questioned, quickening his pace.

Fear and desperation propelled him blindly down the street and onto the main road, yet the crowd showed no sign of her. Dresnor pulled Kai out of the flow as the guard's shouts grew louder.

"Spare a light," his friend tugged on a nearby stranger as he waved the cigar in the air.

The stranger and his friends eyed Dresnor, then he noticed the red and gold band around the cigar and smiled. "Kuwani, a fine cigar." The man offered Dresnor a box of wooden matches with a hint of respect.

Drew and Ryker joined them, mingling with the locals as the guards entered the intersection, shouting after Rayna.

"Ah yes," Dresnor puffed on his newly lit cigar, "there is nothing finer than Kuwani." His Ahana accent brought smiles to everyone's faces, and the other men nodded, tipping their heads in agreement. "Thank you." Dresnor handed back his matches and ventured down the sidewalk.

Kai and the others followed. "What about Rayna?" he asked, still searching the streets in both directions. "We cannot just leave her."

Behind them, the guards dispersed into the street in different directions. Kai did not know if they would continue to look for his trouble-making wife or if they had better things to do. Either way, they were gone, and he took a much-needed breath.

Dresnor chuckled, "Your nimble wife is three stories up." He jutted his chin but kept walking. "I would say the newly grown ivy in the last alleyway was her doing. It certainly made for a swift escape."

Kai had missed the vines, but it sounded like her. He cut his eyes upward, scanning the rooftop, then he spotted her on the corner just ahead of them. "We need to put more distance between those guards and get out of town."

Kai's group zigzagged through town and reunited with Rayna. Kai took Rayna's hand, relieved they all escaped capture. "We must leave now. Once we reach Milnos, we will get you suitable attire and find a way into the King's event. I will fill you in along the way." He crossed the street, keeping a watchful eye for any suspicious guards searching for his wife.

"Once outside of town we can find a secluded place to depart. It takes two days by carriage to reach Milnos, and we do not have that long. We must continue with our alternate means of travel if we hope to arrive in time. Benmar told me the route to avoid prying eyes from the ground."

Making their way through town, Kai passed a small chapel and heard a Nebean accent echo across the square. "Spare a few coins for a sister of the cloth?" The lilt in the woman's voice perked his ears but he kept moving. "Support a good cause, young man, and Alenga may yet bless you and yours."

Kai stopped dead in his tracks. He knew that phrase—Riome. "I have a coin to spare for a good cause, little sister," he called out. He weaved through the crowd with his hand tight around Rayna's, hoping the others would follow.

The ocean blue robe and white head scarf concealed the woman's hair. She wore little makeup, yet she did not look like herself. The pale skin, fair eyebrows, and eyelashes combined with a splash of red freckles over her nose and cheeks left her completely changed. The age around her eyes caught in his throat; this feature was not make-up or a trick in her disguise; she was truly older. His best guess, Riome had used the Katori magic stored in her crystal. Alenga had warned her: magic was not meant to be wielded by a Half-Light. The power was aging her.

Kai dropped a coin into the woman's basket and offered her a nod. "Could you offer a good word for me with Alenga in your prayers, Sister?" He stared into Riome's eyes.

"You will need more than a prayer, my brother." Riome pointed to the nearby chapel. "Perhaps a moment in communion this very hour would ease your soul. I have time if you need counsel."

She did not wait for him to respond. She simply crossed the street, opened the large wooden door, and entered the chapel through the stone archway. Kai turned to the others and handed Drew his packages. "Keep watch. Rayna and I will find out what Riome knows. Cazier sent her to Milnos in search of Tolan and some missing spies. She must know something we can use."

Kai opened the door for Rayna, and they entered the chapel. He was pleased to find it empty, with Riome sitting near the middle. The stone structure was simple except for the ornate glass window in front of him, depicting the tree of life set in front of a blazing sun. The building smelled of wood and burning candles, making him wish for quieter times.

"What are you doing here, Riome?" Kai whispered, slipping into a pew beside her. "Your father worries about you. He said you went to Milnos, but he has not heard anything since."

Riome maintained her posture, but she let the Nebean accent fall away. "We could not very well sit and wait for news. Master General Cazier, my father, sent seven spies into Milnos over the previous months, and not one has returned. We needed to know why. The honest ones are dead, and the dishonest—well, they are dead too, only before they died, they shared secrets about the other Diu spies within Milnos— coming and goings, names, identities."

Kai thought about the implications of so many lost spies within the network. Good men and women who served their country kept the peace and maintained the balance of power. "I am sorry for the loss of"—he wanted to call them her friends, but he knew better—"your associates, but I am headed to Milnos. What else can you tell me?"

Riome cut her eyes at him. "Yes, well, as I was saying, I came to Minos for answers. I knew the Regent would not simply walk away from Diu like nothing happened. Dragons or not, he wants war, and I was not going to sit around waiting for Roark to muster an army to march on the great Iron City looking for his son. Nor could I wait for you to return to Diu."

Rayna leaned around Kai and whispered respectfully, "Did you find anything out about what became of Tolan and Amelia?"

Her silence was deafening. Kai began to imagine the worse until Riome spoke and confirmed the horrible truth. "Alenga, keep Amelia in your arms." Riome gave a moment of silence, which surprised Kai. She was not a religious person, yet her experience had clearly changed her in ways he did not expect. "She is not faring well. As for Tolan, I could find no proof he is still alive."

Kai saw her wring her hands in her lap. "Is she . . ." He could not bring his mouth to form the word.

"Alive, yes. At least she was ten days ago. Again, I could not confirm Tolan's death, but men boast, and he was a Diu noble in a Milnosian prison. The worst of the worst happened to him. Not sure anyone could survive what I heard. Amelia, however, still suffers in isolation. Her spirits . . ." Riome hesitated. "Well, after say six to seven months locked away in the Raven's Tower with no hope of rescue, I cannot imagine a delicate flower such as her faring any better. They do not feed the girl enough. From what I can tell, she will likely starve to death before she ever leaves."

Kai squeezed Rayna's hand and took a deep breath. He could not imagine what it would be like to be forgotten and locked away, never seeing each other again. "Did you tell her you would come back for her?"

"I most certainly did not." Riome's tone implied foolishness he did not fully understand. "You cannot give hope to someone without showing them a light at the end of a tunnel. I had no idea if I would make it out alive or be able to return with help. Giving her hope and then never returning would be much worse."

The idea Amelia had no hope broke his heart. Not wanting to wash over the news about his friends, he let a moment of silence linger. Considering they needed to focus on stopping Keegan and saving his mother, he needed to know if Riome knew anything of use. "Any other news I should know about in Milnos?"

"I suppose you want to know about the mysterious man who came to court requesting a private audience with the King. Rumors spread quickly. Regent Maxwell—no, wait, *Grand Duke* Maxwell—denied him access to the King and sent him away. But like magic, Keegan sat on the balcony of King Landon's bedchamber without anyone knowing how he got there. While I do not know the terms of their agreement, I heard that Keegan wishes to ally with Milnos. If Landon helps him attack Diu and then Katori, he will share a few secrets of his magic."

"Surely Maxwell told Landon about the return of the dragons." Kai saw her expression and felt foolish for thinking it, but he said it anyway. "Maxwell fears dragons. He would never attack Katori, not directly."

"That may be true, but Keegan claims to have weapons besides the dragon-killer crossbows that can slice through dragon scales. Once infused with some black powder Keegan brought, the iron gets forged into metal-tipped arrows and handheld weapons used for close combat. Part of the terms include this secret new metal he wants King Landon to make. Also, Keegan claims to have a new monster capable of fighting fire with fire against the dragons. For the support of the Milnosian army against the world, Keegan offers a level playing field, and Maxwell encourages the King to accept these terms."

Kai cringed at the thought of those menacing black knuckle-blades. Although the damage was invisible on the surface, the pain of being ripped apart shuttered down his spine. Letting the memory go, he thought of his mother—Keegan's new weapon, manipulated and bent to his will. "Did you see the Lioness?" He hated the idea of referring to her as a monster.

"I did not see the Lioness"—Riome used his term but gave him a curious glance—"but then, I was long gone before Keegan arrived. As I hear, there will be a demonstration tonight at the event. I was on my way to Nebea to find a spy worthy of helping me. I sent word through the network to Diu asking for help days ago. I had hoped my father might have someone who can help me rescue Amelia, but I have no time to wait for his response. Maybe you can help me save Amelia and search for Tolan."

"You will get no help from Diu," Kai stated. "They are overrun with Caroco warriors." Guilt ate at his insides for abandoning his father and his city. His mother had asked him to stop her, and now his grandfather Lucca was dead, Diu was under attack, and he had no clue how to stop this war. But crushing his mother's stone was not an option, not yet.

Riome did not say it, but he could tell what she was thinking. *What are you doing here if Diu is under attack?*

"I must stop Keegan," he said firmly, "although I am not sure how given all this new information. I know firsthand how the black knuckle-blades work. They slice through dragon scales like a hot knife on butter. With the black-tipped arrows and the dragon-killer crossbows, we dragons cannot take to the sky. On the ground, he cuts us down like weeds. And the Lioness is my mother. He controls her like a puppet on a string, and we must find a way to break his control."

Rayna leaned into his shoulder to address Riome. "Keegan's Katori warriors shift the balance of the war. We cannot let him gather more men and weapons from Milnos. We are here to bring Mariana back to our side if we can."

Kai tapped his fingers, weighing their options and considering the risks. "I know the right thing is to save Amelia, but she offers no advantage for the detour, and without proof, Tolan still lives, I am not sure how we can help you." He felt terrible saying it out loud, but it was the truth. "You must have a plan, but I cannot spare anyone to help you if it takes us away from stopping Keegan." He hoped she had an idea.

"I mean to rescue Amelia, but it will not be easy. I am surprised to hear you give up on her so quickly. Iver considers her family and insisted we investigate her situation. She was your friend and betrothed since childhood. Does she mean nothing to you now?" Riome got up and walked away, and her glare left him heavy and sad.

She was not wrong but hearing it out loud stung. Caring did not change the facts. He had left so many behind in his wake to stop Keegan and rescue his mother. Were they really all victims because he prioritized his mother over everyone? Did his twisted, tangled mess of a relationship with his estranged father control his every thought? *NO!* Kai could not accept this.

He slid down the bench to the aisle behind Rayna. "You know I would if I could," he called after her. "I thought you were the master spy here. Surely you could rescue one girl." He half teased, trying to soften the mood, but her eyes cut him deep.

"Until I confirm Tolan is dead, there are two souls left in Milnos needing our help." She brushed past Ryker and Dresnor, pausing briefly when she saw Drew.

The group slipped down a few back alleys, exited a side gate to the west, and followed a narrow road away from Rieko.

"Even I cannot be in two places at once," Riome said as they walked. "Otherwise, I would have tried to save Amelia and Tolan myself. They might as well be on opposite sides of the world, one in the tallest tower and the other in the deepest dungeon. It will take a coordinated effort. We must liberate both at the same time. If I save Tolan, Amelia's guard detail will quadruple, but if I save Amelia, they will most likely just kill Tolan. It would be easier for me to save Amelia. I have visited her once already, and I know the routine. Please, you must help me." She stopped to allow Kai to gain ground but continued before he reached her side.

Feeling responsible for everyone was becoming a burden Kai could no longer carry. "I left my grandfather's dead body on the floor of the Agora, still warm, to chase after Keegan, to stop this war and maybe save my mother. I left my father in Diu with less than a thousand men against ten thousand or more. I could have been a great help to him, but I left him to continue this chase. Forgive me if I am finally coming around to your way of thinking. They are all casualties in a war I did not start, but apparently, I am the only one capable of stopping it, or so everyone keeps telling me. So, yes, I am letting Amelia rot because I am only one person, and I must make choices about who lives and who dies."

Kai quickened his pace to put distance between him and the others. He could not face them. Any of them. His ever-evolving visions showed him deaths, too many to count, and yet there was no clue how to heal the spreading hate.

It was Rayna's hand that slid around the crux of his elbow. She said nothing, only kept pace.

"There will be a limited window in which to free Amelia after the evening guard change," Riome continued. "They do not search her room after lights out, so we have until dawn. Acquiring access to the gardens below the Raven's Tower will be easy. Scaling the tower is another matter. Even if I could get my hands on stone spike climbers, I doubt Amelia could climb down in her condition." Riome raised an eyebrow at Rayna. "What do you say, Kodama? Can you get me up a tower and help rescue Amelia?"

Rayna's shocked expression brought a chuckle from Riome. "Yes, I know what your kind can do. You wear your green like a declaration as my mother does with purple. I lived in Katori until I was twelve. I know everything. The rich garden soil near the tower should provide adequate to our purpose, but you should see the space beforehand."

Rayna held her hand over her crystal and nodded. "It will take time, but I can grow a vine long enough and strong enough. But what do you mean by—her condition?"

"Amelia is pregnant."

A baby changed everything, and Kai's heart twisted in a knot. The guilt of leaving his friend broke his heart, but the idea of an innocent child stirred something deep. The bond between mother and child brought thoughts of the early years with and without his mother.

Rayna brought them to a stop. "Kai, we must help," she insisted. "We will help Riome—I will help."

His wife's insisting eyes implored him, and he relented. His hand pressed his mother's stone beneath his shirt; he could feel the hope pour into him. "I must focus on this war, Keegan, and my mother, but Rayna can help you. I am not sure how to help Tolan. You do not know if he is even alive, so I am not sure we can afford the diversion to search." The torment of abandoning his friend left a tightness in his chest.

"I know you do not need the detour, but you must find a way into the prison and get inside information. He is not dead, I am sure of it," Riome huffed.

Riome's continued insistence that he search for Tolan weighed heavy on Kai.

"Getting yourself arrested would be easier than posing as a guard," Riome continued. "They would spot you a mile away. You are too lean, and you do not have the time to study their protocols, secret signals, and guard rotations. The catch is this: you will have to do something serious enough to get yourself close to Tolan. Only the worst of the worst go to that prison, and the interrogator I questioned said last he knew Tolan was kept on the fourth level down."

Kai indulged her plan a little longer and let his mind imagine what she meant by something serious. Thankful she paused to let the idea settle; he was not sure he could go that far. "How far?" he asked, hoping he did not have to cross a line if it came to that.

"Knifing a Lord should do." The glint in Riome's eye gave him the impression she had just the man in mind. "Someone in the gemstone district, a man of means and power, will get their attention. He will demand swift justice and severe punishment. The King's masquerade birthday celebration is this very evening in the fortress, which means we are going right into the lion's den, but we have no choice. Once you are in place, the following evening Rayna and I can set about saving Amelia. Once we have them both, we will meet you outside of the city as soon as possible."

"And while you three are saving Tolan and Amelia, what are we supposed to do?" Ryker prodded once he had finally caught up with them. "What of Mariana? I thought we came here to save her and stop Keegan, remember? I know it is cruel to say, but we do not have time for this distraction."

"At the ball, find out where Keegan's men are hiding—the Katoris," Riome called over her shoulder. "This mastermind Keegan is not here alone, and it would be helpful to know how many we are up against. And find out about the knuckle-blades, too."

"I will find them," Ryker acknowledged. "But how do you suggest I go about it? As Kai said, the man thinks ahead."

"Take Dresnor with you, sabotage the black powder that makes the metal stronger. And find out if they have any more surprises for Kai, but keep your distance; we've no time to rescue you. Drew can escort Rayna and me. Ladies do not travel in Milnos without a male escort—unless they are *that* kind, and we do not want to be mistaken for that kind of woman. Kai, you should keep your distance from Rayna. No need to draw attention to you two as a couple in case one of Keegan's spies sees you. Avoid direct contact with Maxwell and Landon. If they get their hands on you, you are finished."

Kai stopped at the edge of a small clearing. "This seems far enough away from town. If we hope to reach Milnos in time for this event, we need to move and move fast. And just to be safe, I think traveling invisibly will be our best bet." He stepped clear of the others and transformed into his silver dragon, and for good measure, he pulled at the light around himself to turn invisible while the others climbed up his wing.

CHAPTER 16

The Iron City

The summer sun climbed across the sky as Kai flew at a swift pace. Keegan and his mother were a day ahead, and he was certain that his father used that extra day to secure troops and weapons to lay siege on Diu and anyone else who stood in the way of his world conquest. Although Kai's passengers were now seasoned dragon riders, he did his best not to forget their presence lest he soar too high or too fast in his haste to reach his mother.

Hours rolled from one to the next, and although the clouds concealed his movements most of the time, it fell on him to hide them from prying eyes on the ground when the blue sky opened wide to bathe the landscape in sunshine. It was those in-between moments he was most thankful for; those critical moments kept his mind preoccupied on balancing between his dragon and absorbing and bending the light to conceal their existence.

It was in the clouds he remained lost in thoughts of Keegan, his mother, and the lives he felt were his burden to protect. At this point, he saw no way to save the others and stop Keegan. The only positive he had was the repeating vision, Rayna years from now chasing two little girls through a field of wildflowers. Why Alenga had blessed him with the memory, he did not know, but it was something to cling to in his moments of doubt.

It was Rayna's touch on his neck that brought him out of his funk. He felt the silver scales tickle and itch under her influenced Kodama magic. She was testing him, offering him a chance to spend their trip practicing his ability to block or redirect any magic forced upon him. A skill his grandfather, Benmar, claimed was possible—yet it still eluded Kai.

Twice in his past, he had mentally flown over the mighty Iron City using Katori magic, once in search of his mother and once again when Riome went missing, but this was the first time seeing it in person. The great city did not blur underneath his sailing spirit; instead, it morphed on the horizon into a towering, dark monster. The city was both beautiful and terrifying, steeped in history and grandeur while also menacing and angry. The sprawling metropolis of Milnos dwarfed Diu in every way, with dozens of towers and battlements dotting the skyline. While the foundation of the city appeared rooted in old history, there appeared to be many modern mechanical additions.

The black, ironclad city loomed in the distance, a city that gave Kai nightmares as a child when he thought he would someday live in a city that hated Diu. How his father, Iver, ever thought these people might accept him as their king if he married Amelia, he would never know. Every story since the great war told of brutal Milnosian warriors and power-hungry lords bent on world dominance. It was home to the evil King Panier, the man who killed Iver's father and brother.

While Diu history painted Panier as a mad man filled with hate, the Milnosian people considered his family line to be heroes sent by Bangloo to conquer this land. A lump caught in Kai's throat. For him, the city was a place filled with people who hated everything about Diu and would see the Diu prince strung up if they got the chance. He could only pray the stories were exaggerated and their hatred did not run so deep.

The closer he flew, his dragon eyes zoomed in on the various networks of walls and turrets, a city designed for war. At its heart, the black fortress clawed at the sky with menacing spires. From a distance, it was formattable, which meant up close, it would be a behemoth. Any nerves Kai had were now magnified. What was he thinking bringing them all here? *This is a mistake.* The thought bubbled up without his blessing.

Searching the ground, Kai turned his eyes toward Lake Eden and the grand estate nestled between the lake and Milnos. The estate was more prominent than anything around Diu or Port Anahita. Riome suggested someone there might be the solution to attending the masquerade ball hours from now. Landing a few miles away, he hoped they went unnoticed.

As Riome led his group through a pine forest, she removed some garments, such as her head covering, which became a shawl, and she flipped others like her skirt inside out. With the pale makeup on her eyebrows and face wiped clean, the color in her cheeks returned, yet the aged skin remained. By the time they reached the estate, she looked completely different with a dark skirt, a pink blouse, and a white shawl.

Nestled amongst the rolling hills, General Niren's estate offered a view of Lake Eden on one side—a beautiful blue ribbon on the horizon surrounded by lush green terrain as far as the eye could see—and the dark city of Milnos on the other.

Kai noticed the estate's lush, sprawling lawn, which offered an unhindered view of the three-story mansion at the end and hundreds of grapevines stitched across the landscape around the back. When they reached the main gatehouse, Kai studied the cream-colored hut with a single door and three windows. The guard inside spoke with a gentleman and his wife. He imagined the man consulting his list was responsible for deciding who entered and who he sent away.

"Your man lives well, for a General," Dresnor noted. "Better than any Diu Lord or General I know."

"The wealthiest nobles in Milnos come from old money." Riome sidestepped the line and nodded to a second guard who motioned her through without question. "Niren is a fifth-generation oil man. He's also the only one in his family to serve in the military and maintain a profitable business. We should be able to get a carriage from here to take us into the heart of the city without any delay at the gates. Provided the General is in a receptive mood."

Kai noticed the dirt on his arms as he carried the packages with their Milnosian attire for the masquerade. He smelled of dirt and sweat from the miles of traveling, and the smoke from Diu still lingered on his skin.

"How exactly do you intend on getting us into the King's birthday celebration?" Rayna clutched their remaining supplies and followed Riome past three horse-drawn carriages. "I overheard a gentleman waiting at the gate mention that he tried getting invited. He is here to inquire with the General for admittance since they are old friends."

"General Niren," she stated flatly, "is very fond of me. Or at least the me I pretend to be when I visit. As head of security, he can grant us access to the ball. As far as he is concerned, I can come and go as I wish, for a price. As for your gentleman at the back of the line, he is never attending the event. The man at the front, his business partner, is selling secrets to their inventions. Niren will pay money or do favors for the right price. It pays to be first."

"Harsh rules," Drew said, cutting his eyes at Riome, "when a man sells out his friend for an invitation to the King's ball?"

"I do not make the rules." She glared back, and Kai caught the hidden tension between them. "Power and influence stand shoulder to shoulder with wealth. There will be both at the King's event. As I said, there is a price to play in the arena of Milnos. One best learn the rules and ruthlessly engage."

Kai did not want to know the price of their admission. His imagination and her expression suggested it was not for polite conversation, and he was better not knowing. Near the estate, a young man approached. His pristine blue uniform with gold cord showed no rank but gave the illusion of service. "Lady Sheerin, General Niren is in the gardens if you will please join him. I can care for your guests, and they will meet you at the stables when you are ready to leave."

"Follow the footman to the guest quarters to get freshened up, and I will meet you at the stables." Riome's Bangloo accent flowed freely as if she were a native, reminding all of them to hide their Diu and Katori origins. "I will join you when I can." She left them, and Kai watched her follow the man around the house through a large black iron gate. He wanted to follow her, but he knew she could complete her mission better without another soul to worry over.

◆ ◆ ◆

When Riome returned, she was refreshed and clean like the rest of them. The stableman brought four horses connected to a large black carriage that he had pulled near the front of the estate, ready for her departure. She carried four white envelopes, one of which she handed to the driver. The man with her carried two large white parcels, and two small boxes, which the footman promptly stowed in one of the many trunks secured at the back with the remainder of their packages.

Behind her on the estate's top step stood a man in uniform. His tanned, weathered skin showed years in the sun in service of Milnos. Smoke from his cigar encircled his hand as it dangled at his side. Then the general took a long drag, and it burned bright red. The man's dark eyes never left Riome's back until she entered the carriage. Unsure how he felt about this strange man offering them passage, Kai gave the General one last look before climbing in behind Rayna.

There was an uneasy feeling between Drew and Riome. Kai imagined Drew wanted to know what she offered to gain them a no-questions passage, but then her locked jaw and cold gaze gave him the impression she would not speak of this day to anyone. When she did speak, her tone was cold and direct. "Good," she kept her chin high, and eyes focused a spot over Kai's head. "You each look much better for our entry into Milnos. This carriage belongs to the General, which means it will not stop for inspection when we reach the gates, but either way, keep your eyes down. Do not give them a reason to break that rule and question us."

Their bumpy ride through the country gave Kai time to think and ponder how they would save his friends and his mother—and stop Keegan.

"Lady Sheerin," Kai mocked, "I see you managed three invitations, and we need six, so how do the rest of us get in?"

Riome lowered her eyes to Kai. "We become who we must. Yes, the General could only give me three. I will need to seek another. Lord Luedke can part with the remaining invites. He is a wealthy gem dealer in Milnos with four children. Three are old enough to have an invitation. You simply attend in their place when his children come down with an unexplained illness moments before they plan to depart. I will acquire those once inside the city." She peered out the window of the horse-drawn carriage, paying everyone little attention while they rode toward the city.

Drew cocked his head. "You do not like this Lord Luedke? Offering him up as Kai's victim and poisoning his children for access to the event."

Her nose twisted at the question, and Kai could see her disdain for Lord Luedke as she turned toward Drew. "Let us say I had an opportunity to witness the kind of man he is, and you're right, I do not much care for Lord Luedke. He has trouble keeping his hands to himself and taking no for an answer. As for his children, a mild stomachache is a small sacrifice for the greater good. He owns half a city block. I will use the servant's entrance and deliver the potion myself and be back out before the horses even have time to circle the block."

It had been five months since the wedding when Drew last saw Riome, and Kai could not help but notice his friend could not take his eyes off her. Kai knew his friend found her alluring, but he was unsure if they ever managed to tell each other how they felt. So far most of this trip they seemed at odds, and he could only imagine thoughts of any man touching her drove Drew mad. Kai did not have the heart to explain that the life of a spy meant sacrifices beyond imagination were a given.

When they reached the city gates, Kai tilted his head to look outside, careful not to draw the guards' eyes as they approached. The black gate towered overhead, and the clickity-clack of the carriage wheels on the drawbridge made his heart pound. They were entering enemy territory with a little more than a hope and prayer for how they would come out of this alive.

While most wanting to enter the city waited in a long line, their carriage took another lane, only stopping at the gates, where Kai witnessed an exchange between the driver and the guard. The driver offered the white envelope from the General, and they were free to proceed.

The sounds of Milnos city were loud, the streets thick with people and carriages. Poverty-riddled streets near the wall flowed into the wealthy hustle and bustle as they neared the heart of the city, which looked modern and yet steeped with old iron and stone architecture, giving the city a mysterious nature far greater than anything Kai knew.

When they reached the appropriate block, Riome exited the carriage alone, spoke to the driver, and mingled into the crowd. Kai tracked her movements as the driver resumed their progress down the block. Anxious to ensure her safety, he gleaned her activities. Her steps were swift down the alley to the back entrance. A butler answered the door. A tiny glow emanated from the crystal around her neck, and the man let her enter.

Kai gasped. *She is using the crystal.*

Thoughts danced through his head on how she could use magic. Nola's crystal gave her the power to manipulate the mind. He could only imagine Riome used hers likewise. As the carriage started to circle the block, her obscured essence became a little more than a sparkling silhouette. Up the stairs, she darted, down one hallway and then another.

Her form came into view as she turned the next corner. It was then she appeared to enter a room and dose her first victim. A man much taller than her pulled on a dress shirt one arm at a time. A pinprick from her ring on his neck and she was already heading into the next room. The next young man sat in a chair, lacing his shoes; he never saw or heard her enter. She was quick, and it was painless. The man reached to his neck and then grabbed his abdomen as Riome slipped back into the hallway.

Her last victim was a young girl. She was not alone. The woman with her, a lady's maid, opened the door. Again, the crystal glowed, and Riome gained unquestionable access. Her movements were slow and graceful as she appeared behind the girl, pulling aside her hair to expose her neck. The maid offered Riome a necklace to secure around the young girl's neck, and she did as requested, but not before she pricked the girl's skin with the necessary potion and left.

In Riome's haste to escape, she darted down hallways right then left; Kai could see her struggling as he gleaned. Then he noticed a momentary pause in her step as she reached the entrance to the last room. Her eyes closed and her hand covered the crystal, and he could almost see her mentally count to ten—*breathe*, she mouthed.

In the next instant, she dashed into the library, scooped up three envelopes from the desk, and ran to the open balcony doors. Then their carriage turned another corner, and Kai noticed her path would converge on their impending arrival on the street up ahead. In the next movement, she leaped to the rose-covered trellis and shimmied to the ground. Then, she sprang through the gate just as the carriage pulled into position. Kai flung open the door and scooted over to give her room.

When Riome entered the carriage, she was calm and collected, but he saw the new wrinkles around her face, the age in her green eyes, and the new gray hair amongst the auburn. The use of the crystal was taking its toll on the Half-Light. He wanted to caution her, but she knew the risks—and he imagined if the roles were reversed, he would choose the same as her. Although he wondered what magic Alenga gave her, it made sense. What other gift could a spy want but to be able to convince others that you were who you needed to be in any given moment—or persuade them and bend them to your will?

Three blocks later, Riome broke the silence. "General Niren has two rooms at the Sedalia Inn. A glamours place, two streets over." she knocked on the roof of the carriage and it came to a stop. "Show the owner this token. It will allow you to come and go." She handed Dresnor a copper coin with a diamond-shaped ruby set in the center. "Once you are ready, proceed to the fortress with a local carriage on the street showing the same token to avoid payment. Niren's carriage will take Drew, Rayna, and me. Here are three invitations for you. Dresnor, and Ryker—enter separately. Remember, it would be best if we avoid each other at the festivities. People in Milnos watch people, if you understand my meaning. And just in case I am unclear, consider everyone to be a spy or a gossiper. Be careful who you speak with at the party. We are strangers here, and gossips love a mystery. No need to draw attention to the rest of us."

Ryker swung open the door to the carriage. "I guess we need to make sure none of us get caught," he stated smugly and hopped out. "I will walk from here."

Dresnor joined him. "Kai?"

Kai shook his head; he still needed more time with Riome. "I will catch up with you." He pulled the door closed and his friends proceeded without him.

The carriage lurched into motion again, turning the block. Each building they passed, each corner they turned brought them closer to separating, and Kai felt his heart pounding. What if this was all part of Keegan's plan? Or even worse, what if someone spotted him and Rayna suffered because he brought her into enemy territory?

Riome touched Kai's hand. "You are worried."

"Of course I am worried." He took a deep breath and let it out slowly. "I have no idea your plan. Every person in this city would turn us into the authorities—or worse, beat us on sight. Milnos is the last place we belong. Look how they treated Tolan; a man meant to be their king. They were not very kind to Rayna, and all she wanted was to buy a dress, but . . ."

"Milnos is a dangerous place," Riome interrupted, "and there are bad people here, but not everyone is out to kill you. Just breath and trust your instincts."

Rayna's hand squeezed his arm. "After tonight, either you will have Mariana by your side, or you will rescue Tolan. Whatever you choose, I will be waiting for you outside the city tomorrow night after we rescue Amelia."

Drew kept his eyes focused out the window, but Kai wondered what he thought about his choice. They were like brothers, and he valued his opinion. "What do you think I should do," he asked Drew.

"Strategically, we should focus on capturing Mariana if Kai can control her or bring her to our side; that changes things in our favor. Sabotaging their black powder supply, finding the other Katoris, discovering if any other surprises are coming—those things make sense to me. Amelia is alive and most likely will be after this war, which I cannot say the same of us. Having said that, I have known Amelia for years, and she has been in my parents' home several times. It would be difficult for me to walk away from helping her. The same goes for Tolan. If there is a chance he is still alive, I could not leave him in this horrible city. I am sorry, Kai, but this is your decision, not mine. We will follow your lead, and I will respect either choice."

The carriage came to another stop.

"We will be fine," Riome assured him, "and besides, we have Drew to protect us. You know I always have a plan. To set your mind at ease, Rayna and I need to get close to a particular botanist tonight at the ball. Tomorrow he will invite us to the garden near Raven's Tower where these rare, exotic flowers grow. Rayna needs to see how challenging the growing space will be, and if possible, set a seed in place, or we may have to find different seeds than what she brought. Do what you must, Kai. Confront Keegan or try to whisk your mother away from him if you can, or take your chances with Lord Luedke and gain access to the prison to find Tolan. Everyone is right, I have no idea if he is still alive, so I will understand either way."

The use of Keegan's name set Kai's hands to fidget. Riome opened the door to the carriage. "Give us a moment, if you please." She motioned to the others, and Drew and Rayna hopped out.

"You are afraid," she said to Kai once they were alone.

"I am not," Kai answered too quickly. He had a lot to fear, really. The Milnosians wanted them all dead, and Keegan had nearly succeeded several times. His mother was under the influence of dark magic. He still did not know what he should do to save her, and he had no idea how to defeat his powerful father.

"Your current state is a good thing," Riome explained. "Your apprehension means you are not going in overconfident. I need you thinking. There is a fine line between caution and fear. Do not let it control you, or you have already lost. The question is what, or should I say who, are you afraid of?"

His first thought was—everything. But he held back to allow other possibilities to ruminate. A strange city in a foreign land filled with people who hated anyone from Diu. Landon, his childhood nemesis, now King of Milnos. Keegan's abilities. Amelia and Tolan. His mother. He had so much he was afraid for, and everyone was counting on him.

So, his first thought was correct. "Failure. I am afraid of failure. Keegan is stronger, better, more in control. I do not stand a chance against him. I have a theory on how to control my mother, but I have not tried it yet. Everyone is counting on me, and I am guessing from one point to the next."

"That is not fear as long as you move forward. A healthy dose of caution is a good thing. Considering all your options keeps you alive. But find that deep desire to win and do anything to succeed, risk it all. Stay sharp, Kai, and hold nothing back. The smallest detail in your strategy matters but you should change instantly if a better option presents itself. The best spy is not perfect, only adaptable. I have faith in you because you are stronger than you think."

Kai thought about Riome's advice, yet he could not help wanting to know if he was doing the right thing. "Keegan is always ten steps ahead of me. Like he knows what I will do, and he puts me in the dirt every time. His power is greater than mine. He could kill me with a touch, and I can do nothing to stop him. Add in the Lioness, my mother and . . ."

"Stop it!" Riome corrected his downward spiral. "With thoughts like that, you have already lost. FIGHT!" She pounded her fist into the carriage cushion and leaned in close to gaze into his eyes.

The sudden burst of anger hit Kai in a wave, followed by a surge of confidence. He saw the necklace glow through Riome's blouse as she squeezed his knee. New thoughts entered his mind—courage, anger, confidence, and with it, power traveled outward from his heart.

"STOP." Kai pushed her hand away. "Do not waste your limited gift on me." The surge dropped away suddenly, and he felt a cold chill run down his spine.

She sat back and braced herself with one hand on the carriage door. "You are right. Not that I wasted my gift on you, but you need to feel those things for yourself. It is time, Kai. Stop relying on visions to show you the ever-changing outcomes. Trust your gut and if you are wrong— improvise. Choose and own it. None of us blame you for Keegan or his war."

Her words cut to the quick of him. She was right; he needed to believe in himself and own his choices, good or bad. "How do I get my mother away from him? That is the key to stopping him—I know it. If I could get close enough to her, maybe I could bring her to our side using her necklace." He pulled her chain out of his shirt.

"Sounds like you have a plan." She opened the door and started to get out.

"What if I am wrong?" he spouted, halting her departure. "Or what if Keegan has more control over her?"

"Drop these thoughts. I could push them from you, but my magic fades, and you will drown in overwhelming anxiety. Like I said before, face this fear and move forward or you have already lost. You cannot control everything. Which means neither can Keegan. Sure, he assumes you are coming, but use that against him. Use him. Ask yourself, how can Keegan help you without even realizing it? Figure that one out, and you will take the lead in this war." She patted him on the back as Drew offered her a hand to exit the carriage.

CHAPTER 17

Lord Luedke

Along the short ride to the Milnosian fortress, Kai watched the city spark with life. Exiting his carriage, he caught his first look at the fortress gardens and vast courtyard. Music boomed into the night, and people laughed and danced. The decadence of the masquerade ball left Kai speechless. Never in his wildest dreams could he imagine such a spectacle. The use of gold, silver, and rare gems to decorate columns, fountains, and chandeliers was magical yet wasteful.

Alone in line, he felt nervous and out of place. Even as a prince, he had never experienced such majesty. He offered the elegantly scrolled invitation to the footman standing near the stone archway when it was his turn. The man accepted his card, and another man ushered him into the outside garden. They welcomed him without question.

Following the red carpet, he meandered through the festivities toward the fortress. Heads turned, and eyes stared as they critiqued the worthiness of his attire, head to toe. Finding him acceptable but otherwise unremarkable, each returned to their previous distraction.

Entering the fortress, he followed the trail of attendees eating, laughing, and sipping wine. The banquet hall was three times the size of Diu's great hall and decorated in white, gold, and silver beads, ribbons, and sparkling crystals that cast various rainbows around the room. He pondered the expense and, more importantly, the ego that required such extravagance. From the top of the stairwell, he tried not to gawk. Performers dangled and twirled from long ribbons affixed to the ceiling while men and women juggled fire.

Mingling into the main crowd, he noticed the other men, like him, dressed in decorative attire with gold-and-silver trimmed coats and various colored ruffled shirts. The only item he did not enjoy was the filigreed gold mask that Dresnor had acquired in Rieko. It felt tight against his skin and made him desperate to remove it, but then it was the only thing concealing his identity from any who might recognize him—which would be a great many considering he was the prince of Diu.

Searching the crowd, he noticed that everyone wore a mask, including the performers and even the servants. But masks or not, he could glean the essence of the guests. Nearly half in attendance were Katori, a much higher number than he ever would have expected at a ball for the King and Milnosian nobles. Keegan's missing people. A benefit, he decided, as he would not stand out in the crowd should Keegan or anyone search for him. Thankfully, his would-be father was not in attendance.

Making his way to the back of the room, he spotted Ryker and Dresnor entering one behind the other before parting in separate directions. Both wore more modest attire, with less gold and silver embroidery and more black accents.

At the center of the banquet, the dance floor swarmed with men twirling women this way and that. Dresses flared and fluttered. The rhythm was quick and upbeat, their smiles joyful and their movements carefree. The longest table known to man with a buffet big enough to feed an army sat near the far wall. It was the dais Kai spotted next. King Landon, his childhood nemesis, sat on the golden throne. The jeweled crown on his head was much too elaborate for Kai's liking, and his scepter held a red ruby gem the size of a man's fist adorned with white diamonds and gold vines.

Kai felt Rayna's presence before he spotted her descending the red-carpet staircase into the crowded banquet hall. The only bits he recognized were the color of her hair and eyes and the curve of her face and body. Her usually long brown hair sat intricately pinned atop her head, accented with tiny ringlets and jewels. From what he could see around her mask, makeup glittered her eyes and stained her cheeks. Her red-stained lips matched her shimmering red dress, which was bold, too bold, cut in places and formed in others. The Milnosian style was flattering, but her garment gave away so much, highlighting her in a way he found provocative.

His heart pounded at the sight of her, and he stepped in her direction. Drawn to her like a moth to a flame—their eyes met, and he found himself consumed with desire.

"Excuse me," a man said as he slipped in front of Kai and ventured up the steps to take Rayna's hand. "I must know your name, my lady."

The man was tall, dark-haired, with a chiseled jaw and perfect white teeth. Kai hated him already. "My name is Lord Jameson Luedke. It is a pleasure, my dear." He kissed her gloved hand, and Kai reached to smack the man from fawning over his wife.

"The lady is with me," Drew said, pulling Rayna's hand from Luedke's grasp. "Mind your manners, sir, or I will turn this festive celebration into your memorial." Drew did not wait for a reply. Instead, he brushed around Luedke, nodded to Kai, and made his way to the opposite side of the festivities.

"Well, I never," Luedke huffed and stepped back into the crowd.

Kai caught sight of Riome on Drew's other arm. Like Rayna, her outfit showed off more of her than he felt acceptable, giving Luedke another reason to stare as they passed. Even with the added years, she was still beautiful, and Kai noticed behind her makeup and mask that she had again used magic. Although she chose to age over letting the power ravage her soul, he wondered how many times she could use it before it took her life.

Kai's eyes followed his wife as he leaned against a tall serving table before they bounced around to the others watching her. "Tell me, Lord Stein, do you know who she is?" Kai heard a man ask before turning to discover that Lord Luedke again stood next to him. "I spend a great deal of time at court, and I have never seen her before."

Thoughts of punching the man came to mind, and then he remembered his mission to save his mother. Although Riome's plan suggested he grievously wound the man to gain access to the prison to search for Tolan, he did not believe in the mission. This task was still a distraction compared to the urgency of stopping the war and turning his mother back to their side. Plus, striking a man for no real reason was more complicated given those in attendance. Not that some part of him did not agree the man probably deserved a good punch in the face, but he could not help but wonder why Riome really took such a disliking.

Biding his time for the right opportunity, he followed Luedke as he meandered through the crowd speaking with another gentleman. If Kai did decide to follow Riome's plan, he did not want his mask removed in the great hall in front of the King.

"She is a guest of General Niren is the rumor I heard," the silver-haired Lord Stein answered, strolling with Luedke. "The man she is speaking to is a botanist, here to study the rare plants around the city, a student of the old professor. He arrived last month. Either the scholar knows the young lady, or he respects her. He rarely spends more than a few minutes tolerating women. Says they bore him with their frivolous minds."

Luedke folded his arms and studied the group. "The man with her, I have never seen before. Maybe he is one of the King's new captains. He certainly reeks of military attitude. King Landon makes so many changes it is impossible to know who's who these days. Too many changes, if you ask me. And now he allows this new man, Keegan, to decide the direction of our war. I am not sure we, the real power behind this city, trust this Katori. I, for one, do not, and I know you cannot afford to lose your contract—or the King's financial support."

Stein puffed up his chest. "You are quite right. I have invested heavily in bringing the king's new war machines to fruition. My creations will revolutionize this war and change the balance of power forever. It is time Milnos proved we are superior to the rest of the world. I only wish our King did not entangle our destiny with the Katori. I do not trust him or his magical misfits."

Luedke leaned in close. "Stein, tell me, do these things really fly? I find it hard to believe you designed something nobody else understands or that they are capable of flight. Sounds like fantasy or witchcraft to me. Will they really take us all to Katori?"

Stein's lip curled with delight. "By the thousands. The dragons will be finished once we own the skies. Mountains and walls will mean nothing. This fool Keegan gave us the one element we needed to seal their fate. This black powder will go into every weapon we have: our cannons, arrows, swords, hand cannons. We will destroy the dragons once and for all. The rest of their magic pales in comparison now that we can cut them down from a distance."

This news sent chills down Kai's spine. Milnos was planning a direct assault on the dragons—and on Katori. Was this his fault? Would Milnos be attacking them if the dragons stayed hidden? He needed to warn everyone.

"I hear Maxwell does not like the Katori man," Luedke suggested, "but the King wants Diu, and Keegan promises to deliver. We should be wary of him and his beast. What does the Katori get out of this war? We cannot possibly be considering giving him Diu."

Kai leaned in, interested to hear the response.

Stein laughed. "Makes no difference to me. Maxwell plans to kill him and his monster once the real battle starts. They will be a casualty of war, caught in the crossfire. As will his men. Weakened by days of battle, the Caroco army will be no match for us. While they are distracted fighting Diu, we will surround them and crush them from the rear. We no longer need Keegan or his so-called magic. Entering the heart of Katori with our airborne forces will be just as easy.

"Our flying contraptions should reduce the travel time to Diu, carrying nearly one thousand men each. My engineer says the steam engines will deliver us in three days to their gates—or rather, over them. Maybe faster with the Katoris who claim they can control the wind. Our second wave of soldiers left a day behind the first; they will join in at my command and we will finish them all."

This new information left Kai's mind racing. These airships seemed impossible, but Lord Stein sounded confident. A silver serving tray perched on a server's hand passed in front of Kai. Puff pastries and a cheese block teased his nose, but the small, serrated knife caught his attention, which he palmed and slipped into his belt without anyone noticing. Searching the room, he realized he needed to tell someone what he learned.

An ominous feeling swept over Kai altering the peaceful feelings emanating from his mother's necklace. His mother was nearby. The shift started with dread and moved to fear and finally to rage. Drawn outside, Kai darted up the stairs of the banquet hall and exited into the garden area. The music stopped, and the dancing crowd scattered, pointing to the sky. He followed their gaze and nearly stumbled down the last two steps as the Lioness came into view. Her golden fur glowed in the moonlight as her dark wings flapped slow and easy, dropping her in the center of the courtyard.

"Spectacular creature, almost beautiful," a masked man to his right stated. "We are fortunate this Keegan is on our side."

Kai laughed inside his head. *Keegan is not on your side.* Not that Milnos needed the Katoris at all, according to Lord Stein. His eyes scanned the crowd for Riome as fire from the Lioness streaked across the sky. He needed to warn her of their plans. She was too focused on saving Amelia; she did not even consider the real threat. They needed to focus on turning or capturing his mother.

"Bloody beast, worse than a dragon," a masked man to his left commented. "I look forward to putting her down when we reach Diu. She is killable in her natural state—a mere woman, as I understand, but then we have a new weapon I would not mind testing out on her now. Flames and fur aside, she does not look as fierce as a dragon."

The voice sent a shiver up Kai's spine. He knew the man. Beside him stood none other than Grand Duke Maxwell. Kai took a step back, suddenly thankful for the mask hiding his identity. When the demonstration of the Lioness ended and the beast changed into his mother, he pushed through the crowd, desperate to get closer.

Gone was her Katori dress, replaced with a shimmering blue gown befitting a queen. Her long dark hair flowed down her back, pinned at the sides with tiny white crystals. Keegan stood at her side, his hand around the back of her neck. Around her neck clung a silver laced wrap decorated with a black stone that covered part of her bruised skin. He imagined that Keegan maintained constant control perhaps through this dark crystal and direct contact, which caused the marks. But why not heal her?

She is just a tool. The thought angered Kai.

Making his way through the onlookers, he felt the emptiness in his mother. Her blank, thousand-yard stare pulled him to her. The crowd marveled at her beauty and approached her like a wild beast now tamed. Keegan marched her toward the stairs and the awaiting King Landon, coming to get a closer look at his new weapon.

Moving through the crowd, Kai reached his hand to touch his mother as she passed by, but another hand spun him around and pushed him back several feet.

"Now is not the time," Ryker hissed, pulling him away. "I want to save her too, but think of Rayna and the others. We risk exposure without a plan of escape if you cannot control her. There are too many soldiers." Ryker's eyes scanned the periphery, and Kai followed his gaze.

Reluctant to let her go, Kai's heart tightened. "Now is the time," he whispered, remembering Stein's words. His mother would be a casualty of this war. "I can do this. I can turn her to our side. I have her necklace, and it connects us. I can use it to control her. There is more to Milnos than we thought. We must warn Katori." His mother's face turned to find him in the crowd, and he watched a single tear roll down her cheek. *End this, my son,* she begged, her voice ringing in his head. *Set me free.*

No part of him could destroy her crystal and end her life. He refused to believe that was his only choice, not when he could feel the hope she sometimes felt. His sole existence was predicated on saving her. *I love you, mother. Let me find another way.* He reached out to her mind and felt a sense of love fill her stone around his neck. *Hold on, mother. Let your hope grow. Remember who you are. It will be our salvation.*

To Kai's surprise, she stepped back down the stairs and walked in his direction. Her eyes started to clear, and her face softened a little as if she were ready to smile. His heart leaped at the chance that it was working. She seemed awake, willing, free. With each step she took, her expression improved, and Kai slipped through the crowd to reach her.

Keegan let go of King Landon's hand and called, "Mariana," but her eyes stayed on Kai, and her ears ignored the call until Keegan's hands once again took hold of her neck. The darkness returned to her eyes. In a few quick steps, Keegan maneuvered Mariana away. The glazed-over expression on his mother's face returned as his father's grip pressed into her skin. "Now, my dear, where do you think you are going?"

Keegan glanced into the crowd, spotting Kai. Even with the mask, his father knew it was him.

There was no place to run. Kai thought for sure he could save his mother, and part of him did wake her. Something about the proximity of her crystal not only drew her closer but gave her back some control. It made Kai wonder if there was a way to use it against Keegan and turn his mother against him without knowing what happened. *Now is the time,* he thought again.

"You know, boy, I thought you were smarter than this." Keegan stepped into the parting crowd, pushing Mariana ahead of him. "How foolish to come alone, but then you are not alone, are you? Your little tree spirit is here somewhere. I heard the little Kodama sister survived, so I imagine she is never far from your side."

"Do not speak of her." Kai seethed and risked man-handling his father, shoving him away from his mother. "I knew you were here. I came for my mother. I would never expose my wife . . ." Guilt over giving Keegan too much information swelled his throat.

An elite Milnosian guard pulled Kai away from Keegan. "Wife?" Keegan chuckled as his eyes rolled around in his head while he gleaned the banquet attendees. "Hmmm, you speak the truth. I do not sense the little Kodama sister. A brave choice to come alone. Foolish, but brave."

Considering the possibilities that he was strong enough—and that his mother's own will might be strong enough as well—Kai pulled on the energy around him and focused on his mother, ordering her to attack Keegan. She turned to stand near Kai and made a low, throaty growl toward Keegan.

The king approached and called to Keegan, "Can you not control your beast Katori?"

Keegan spun around to address King Landon, and Kai took hold of his mother's crystal, willing her to come to him. He felt the hope emanating from his mother and her desire to break free, and he stepped back two paces before a meaty hand came out of nowhere and yanked Mariana's necklace from Kai.

"What is this trinket?" The chain snapped, and he turned to see Maxwell seething yet delighted. "Diu brat!" Maxwell ripped Kai's mask from his face and then grabbed Kai with both hands.

Kai struggled to free himself as Maxwell pushed him toward King Landon. "Your Majesty, I have a birthday gift fit for a king." He rammed Kai a second time as the crowd parted, fascinated by the scandalous events unfolding.

A hush fell over the onlookers, and Kai did his best to avoid eye contact with the remaining members of his hidden entourage. Yet nothing could keep Rayna's connection from reaching him. She was frightened, hiding along the periphery behind a stone column as Riome and Drew urged her toward the exit.

Panic sank heavily into Kai's heart. His mother's necklace was now in the hands of his enemy, and he had no idea how to get it back. The king's elite guard swarmed him, searched him, and found the blade, then put him on his knees.

The guard displayed the small, serrated cheese knife. "Have you come here to kill me?" Landon mocked, turning to address Kai with a hint of hesitation. "Pathetic blade compared to what I brought all those years ago. Are you here for revenge for what happened in the Diu palace with your siblings?"

"Sire," Keegan said, rushing toward Kai, clutching Mariana in one hand and grabbing Kai with the other. "Allow me."

Kai flinched as he felt a wave of hate rush down his back. *Focus*, he told himself as he thought of the happiest moments in his life to maintain control of his emotions.

"Allow me to deal with him in a way only I, a Katori, knows best," Keegan seethed. "He is a thorn in my side, and I would relish the opportunity to punish him properly."

Maxwell approached. "No, he is my prisoner—MINE. You are a guest in Milnos, Keegan. Do not overstep, or you may lose our support. We have little need of you and your pet to fight our battles." He waved dismissively at Mariana and whispered to the King.

Mariana's mouth opened, her eyes turned black, and dark veins crept across her face as the ear-piercing scream echoed into the night, forcing everyone to cover their ears. Everyone watched in horror as his mother's body twisted and contorted. Her wiry, blood-red wings sprouted from her back, and her hands and arms stretched into bulky menacing lion's paws, and she fell on all fours. The glamour of her entrance fell away, replaced with terror that forced the crowd to step back even though their curiosity kept them locked on the power struggle before them.

Her agonizing screams reminded Kai her crystal now sat in Maxwell's pocket.

"Do not threaten me with your beast!" Maxwell shouted to Keegan over the din. "You came to us, remember. If you had the means to win, you would not be here. Lest you forget, we now possess the formula to make the dark arrows and knuckle-blades capable of slicing through dragon scale. Your Lioness, from what I can tell, wears no such dragon armor. She should be easy for my elite guards to slaughter." Maxwell motioned around the periphery and dozens of men stepped forward their armor decorated with a silver raven. Some sported knuckle-blades while others notched a black arrow and took aim. Kai could not help but notice the elite guards were also armed with black swords.

King Landon stepped forward. "Do not test our delicate alliance, Katori. Milnos is a force to be reckoned with, and you had best remember your place."

A snarl pulled at the corner of Keegan's lip.

Kai smiled at Keegan and whispered, "You are losing your touch, letting me slip through your fingers. Now you will never know how I took control of her away from you." Guards swarmed Kai and pulled him from Keegan's clutches.

"Be careful of this one," Maxwell commanded them as they pulled Kai away. "He is like her—a beasty, capable of dragon form."

The guards did not flinch, but Kai could see the fear in their eyes. "He is my son, and I can control him," Keegan professed, "as I do her. I can keep him from changing. If you will allow me." He motioned to Kai and stepped closer.

King Landon's cocked his head. "So, you are not a prince, after all? Just a Katori bastard?" He laughed as if he had finally beaten Kai.

Keegan pulled something from his pocket, a black shard, like the one Nola owned. Now that he thought about it, his mother wore something similar that had been sown into her lace collar. It must have enhanced his father's ability to control her. Maxwell nodded, allowing him access to Kai. The guards held his arms wide as Keegan approached. Kai squirmed, trying to break free.

His father undid the top two buttons of Kai's shirt color and searched his neck. "How interesting, you are not wearing your crystal—or your mother's," his father whispered. "Smart. I wanted you to join me of your own free will, but now you leave me no choice. I know you do not need yours, and yours does not work for me, but mine will work on you. I have studied the crystals for years—how they work or do not. The magic is still a mystery, but a piece of mine seems to work on your mother well enough. I believe our shared blood connection gives me more power over you, or have you forgotten that day in Diu? This is your last chance. Come with me, and I can take you away from all of this. We do not need the Milnosians to win."

After the moment on Keegan's ship, when his father compelled him to obey and kept him from escaping, Kai thought he understood how the crystals worked. He had always assumed that his father had used Kai's crystal to control him, but now he wondered if he were wrong about everything. Again he squirmed, trying to free himself as Keegan affixed the dark crystal around his neck. The chain was tight and pressed into his skin, securing the stone against his neck. The hate poured in like a tidal wave, and Kai felt his eyes turn. He imagined they were black like his mother's. Yet, he still had partial control over his mind and his ability to speak. "You might as well kill me because I will never live the way you want."

"Then you will become a slave." Keegan pressed the palm of his hand into Kai's forehead. He felt his body go slack and his willingness to fight faded away. "I must visit him once a day before my influence wears off," Keegan said to Maxwell and the guards, "but he should be compliant. You should secure his arms so he cannot remove the chain."

A roar from the Lioness shook the crowd as Keegan stepped back. Screams sent people scurrying.

"Remember where I found you, Landon," Keegan said with a scowl. "I can put you back in that gutter. You underestimate your value in this war, King, but for now, I will play along. Remember, there is a limited amount of the powder, and some of those weapons you are making go to my men if we hope to win. I expect delivery as promised in the next few days. I will return tomorrow to reestablish control over the boy."

Keegan turned his gaze to Kai. "It is only a matter of time. Think about my offer, boy."

Thoughts of protest danced on the periphery of Kai's mind as the elite guards yanked him through the crowd. He knew the next several hours were bound to be brutal, but there was little choice in the matter since he was helpless under his father's control.

CHAPTER 18

Morning Blues

Darkness lingered around Rayna's room at the opulent and ornate Sedalia Inn, which Rayna had discovered was one of the finest establishments in the city. Only the tiniest bits of dawn spilled through the heavy drapery. The hour was early, and Rayna missed Kai. Memories of the elite guards dragging him away cut through her heart. Letting him go without a fight had left a scar she could not heal, but knowing that Keegan's dark crystal trapped him in a helpless state left her fearing the worst. He was in prison, not because he hoped to save Tolan, but because Landon had discovered his identity—and Keegan had helped.

Tears ran down her face as she peeked through the window to the foreign streets below. In the wee hours, only a few early risers wormed the streets, anxious to get home lest polite society become aware of their dubious exploits. The occasional guard and street sweeper ensured the city would return to normal after the city-wide festivities for the King's birthday celebration.

If she were at home, she would have opened the window, let in the outside world, and embraced the new day, but not here. Not in Milnos. She feared who might see her, somehow knowing that she did not belong. Would they toss her in prison—and what of her baby? She ran her hand over her stomach and gleaned her abdomen. It was such a little helpless thing, a ball of light still taking shape. Would he or she ever know their father? Would she ever see Kai again?

Sadness drove her back under the pink covers of her four-poster bed. Her tears soaked her pillow before Riome pulled open the curtains to let in some light.

"We need to get ready," Riome commanded. "The Raven's Tower is several blocks from here. We do not want to be late." She turned to Rayna, and their eyes met.

Rayna dried her face and swung her legs off the edge of her bed. Her feet dangled a few moments before she hopped down and grabbed her bush to give her hands something to do besides fidget. Riome never seemed like the type to pry, so her questions surprised Rayna.

"Are you alright? Do you want to talk?"

There was a kindness in Riome that made her want to say yes, but if she started, she was unsure she could stop. "I want to go home," she said anyway. "I want Kai back, and I want my life back. I do not want to be brave—I am so tired of fighting."

"For a baker's daughter, I am impressed you managed this long. Kai speaks highly of your skills. I know this is a lot, but right now, I need your help to save Amelia. We need only meet Professor Krane, the botanist in the gardens today, to get a lay of the land, plant a seed, then we will return tonight and retrieve Amelia."

Rayan heard part of what Riome said, but her mind raced through options that might save Kai. The pounding in her heart bounced between emotions. "We could use her as a bargaining chip," she suggested, "Landon always liked Amelia. Everyone knew it—well, at least I did. But she was betrothed to Kai and in love with Tolan, so Landon never stood a chance, and his spiteful nature only ensured she would never see him as a suitor. He would do anything for her if he thought there was a chance to be with her. It must be why she is still alive; I am sure of it."

"Rayna, get a hold of yourself." Riome wrapped an arm around her. "Do you even know what you are saying? We cannot use our friend as a pawn."

"How else are we to get Kai out of prison?" She felt the warm tears roll down her cheeks once more, and Riome pulled her closer. "Keegan's crystal keeps Kai from protecting himself. And now Landon is torturing him and will most likely kill him. He hates Kai, always has, and Amelia is the key to his safety."

"You do not mean that, not really."

"I do mean it." Rayna pushed her away. "This is all your fault. We came to turn Mariana back to our side, and your plan ruined everything. You seeded doubt in Kai's mind. He looks up to you, and now he is trapped with no way out."

"You are scared," Riome said calmly. "Have faith in Kai, have faith in me. I trained him well, and escaping prison is easier than you think. Believe me—I have escaped more than my share. Keegan will visit him, even if it is only to boast, and Kai is smart. He will find a way out. We need to follow the plan and wait for him outside of the city. We already know Mariana is drawn to her son. We saw that last night. He will find a way to free her from Keegan's grasp."

Having faith in Kai was the easy part. Standing by while they punished him was not. She dried her eyes. Riome was right—her emotions were getting the best of her. "I am sorry, I know that is true. But do you honestly think Keegan will let Kai walk right out without attempting to use him too? Then he will have two monsters under his control. We have no hope of stopping Keegan without Kai. None of this was supposed to happen. We were supposed to get Mariana away from Keegan, to stop him and this war."

Riome cocked her head to one side and ran her eyes over Rayna, head to toe. "I could not help but notice yesterday you were rather insistent we help Amelia. Why? And why the change of heart today?"

"I only wished to help my friend," Rayna lied. Her guilt showed more than her truth.

"It is, what, nearly four or five months since the wedding. How far along are you?" she asked flatly.

There was no point playing dumb. "Ten weeks, maybe a little more." Rayna did not feel like lying any longer; she did not have the energy.

Riome was no idiot, and it was better if someone else knew—at least that is what she told herself.

"Does Kai know?" Riome rolled her eyes. "No, he would never have brought you if he knew. Interesting."

"Everything happened so fast over the past few weeks," Rayna tried to convince Riome and herself, "I have not told him. I do not know why I waited. No, that is wrong. I was waiting for him to relax, to realize there was no impending doom coming to destroy us—that Keegan was gone. I guess I was wrong. Keegan was always going to come, and Kai knew it."

She slumped, feeling deflated. Her emotions were out of control. Thoughts of the baby within her, however, lifted her spirits. He or she was a small part of Kai, part of her; for the baby's sake, she must see this through and save Kai if it came to that. One way or another, they would be reunited.

"Well, I hate to dismiss this new development," Riome said, patting Rayna's hand, "but can we get on to saving Amelia? We are her only chance at freedom—or, should I say, *you* are her only chance. Raven's Tower is twelve levels tall, and our little bird has the penthouse view. When I was last there, I noticed the exotic flower beds and the little glass greenhouse. The garden may be twenty feet long, but it is only five feet wide and over fifteen away and surrounded by a knee-high stone wall. The garden is the only source of exposed soil in the entire area. You need to see the ground, and start a seed growing. The closest point to the tower does not provide a straight shot up the spire."

A knock on the door ended their conversation. The arrival of two maids hired to help them prepare for afternoon tea with the professor left them both weary and unwilling to risk any discussion. Riome told Rayna more than once: *trust no one and do not reveal our purpose in the city.* Instead, they kept things light, discussing the King's party, flowers, and their afternoon with Professor Krane.

The older maid opened the door to the oak wardrobe in the corner of their room. "There are four dresses, navy, pink, yellow, and green. Do either of you have a preference?" She pulled at the hems to show off the style on each.

"Rosette," Riome addressed Rayna, "you were admiring the navy dress with the ruffled lace sleeves. I think it will be splendid with your blonde wig. I shall wear the green one," she announced with authority.

The pretend name Riome gave her felt exceptionally fake today, more so than at the party the night before. But using her real name would draw unwanted attention that they could not afford. "I do so adore those sleeves." She lifted her nose, trying to play the part of a wealthy young woman. "Sheerin, you are right. I must wear the navy dress."

She plopped into the chair in front of the mirror, waiting for the younger maid to do her hair. "It will be too hot for a wig today, Lady Rosette," the older maid suggested. "I know they are all the rage, but maybe you should reconsider."

The older woman offered a bemused smile while glancing at Rayna for rebuttal. "I am having afternoon tea with a gentleman who prefers blondes," Rayna said, knowing full well it was to help hide her identity during the day.

Once the girl secured her wig and refined the curls, the maid applied a bit of makeup and retrieved the dress. Eyeing the sown-in corset, Rayna stepped inside the dress, dreading what came next. The lady's maid trussed and pulled at the lacing, and with each tug, Rayna held tight to the bedpost. The tighter it became, the more uncomfortable she felt until she could not stand being jostled anymore. "Stop," she begged. "It is tight enough." She swatted the young woman away and sat on the edge of the bed to catch her breath.

"My apologies, Lady Rosette. Can I get you some water?" The fair-haired girl patted Rayna on the shoulder while the other older woman poured a glass and offered it to her.

More and more, Rayna missed her life back in Katori, living in the trees with Kai and her delicate flowing dresses. She knew they were doing what they must, but this was not how she envisioned starting a life and raising a family. Across the room, she saw the older maid return to pinning the hat on Riome's head while the younger maid kept a keen eye on her condition.

"I am fine, really, thank you. I am a little tired. Where is my hat?" Rayna asked, changing the subject.

The maid brought her the matching hat and secured it before buttoning the lace cuffs at her wrist when Drew dashed into their room. "Time to go," he panted, out of breath. "Forgive me." Then he bowed his head as if he might see something he should not.

"We are both dressed, Drew," Riome responded. "Thank you, ladies. You may go. We can take it from here." She rushed the maids out the door and then turned to Drew with a look of foreboding, giving Rayna the impression the spy could read the clues on the man's face.

"Who's coming?" Riome paused before continuing. "Do they know where we are, or more importantly, *who* we are?"

Drew's expression beheld his astonishment at her accuracy. "There are Katoris searching the city for Rayna. Keegan ordered a city-wide search. They are to identify each Katori and report back personally. If he finds her, we are all doomed."

Butterflies caught in Rayna's stomach. "Personally identify," she muttered to herself, then her strange nervous excitement turned to anguish and fear. They were not coming for just any Katori; they were hunting *her*.

"Your parents," Riome guessed, and Rayna felt the spy search her eyes for validation. "There are only a few of Keegan's men who laid eyes on her that day she confronted Keegan and his followers on the beach of Dragon Spine Island, but according to Kai, she favors her mother. Keegan's followers must hope to capture Rayna. As you said, Drew, if they discover her, any leverage Kai might have will be lost."

The memory of that day shook Rayna. The day Keegan and his followers—her parents among them—came for her and Kai on Dragon Spine Island, attacked them mercilessly, and then tried to burn her out of her tree. The lace on her arms suddenly began to itch, and the bodice felt restricting, causing her to gasp for air.

Drew came to her side. "Easy Rayna, slow breaths." He helped her sit on the sofa.

"We have no time for this. Get yourself together, girl," Riome ordered, grabbing Rayna's hand and pulling her back to her feet. "If Keegan aims to find you, let him try, but he will have to get through me. How much time do we have?" She looked to Drew as he crossed the room to the window.

He pulled back the curtains. "They are at the corner. Now they are crossing the street. There only a few Katoris living in this city, and I heard the man say that there are two staying here. How can there be two full-blooded Katoris here? What do I not know?" He looked between Riome and Rayna.

Riome ignored his question and opened the door to their room. "You must go now. Take Rayna ahead to the tower without me. It is more important for her to continue, she is Amelia's best chance for escape. I will stay behind, draw them out and send Keegan's Katoris away—so long as Keegan is not among them. I can convince them they have successfully eliminated the two girls in this place."

"We cannot separate," Drew refused, averting his eyes. "The moment Rayna steps outside of this room, they will follow her. I listen too, and this gleaning power they have allows them to see you and Rayna, and the truth of everyone in this room. I do not know what you have done to yourself to gain access to magic, or have them believe you are full-blooded like them, but I am not blind. I see the aging effects."

Riome shook her head. "Once they see Rayna, no amount of magic will convince them otherwise. She is the person they seek. I can convince people to give me what I want, do what I want. I can even have them believe I am someone else, but I cannot wipe their memory."

Drew shook his head. "No. *You* are her best chance at survival. And you're coming with us." His eyes insisted before he ushered both women out the door and down the hall.

Riome held her ground, refusing to take another step. Rayna saw the spy contemplate their next move. "There is a servant's entrance at the back," she said, motioning toward a narrow stairwell.

Rayna lifted her dress to avoid tripping as Drew led them downstairs. The heavy door clanged as Riome forced it open and darted outside into the alley behind the Sedalia. The towering inn and neighboring building allowed very little light down the damp street, giving her a chill as her friends pulled her along.

As the alleyway led to another, a putrid odor made her gag; then, she spotted the overflowing trash bins. A loud clang, *the metal hotel door*, she thought. "They are coming," she stepped ahead as if she had some idea of where to go.

The sound of footfalls chased after them, and Rayna's heart pounded into her throat. *What will they do if they catch me?* She could not stop her overwhelming panic. Her shoe caught an uneven stone, and she stumbled, but Drew's firm grip kept her from falling. He stopped and stared at her. "Rayna, I know you are afraid, but think of Kai. He needs you if he is going to defeat Keegan."

The words of encouragement straightened Rayna's shoulders. Drew was right; she needed to be strong; this was no time to panic. She shook her head, and they caught up to Riome at the corner.

Riome smoothed her dress. "Calm yourselves." she took a deep breath. "We need to cross this boulevard and reach the next set of back streets if we hope to lose these Katori hunters." She passed Drew something Rayna could not see. "You may need this."

They stood tall and stepped out into the strolling crowd. The people moved as if they had all day to go nowhere. The busy boulevard made running impossible, yet fearing her pursuers would catch them, Rayna quickened pace. Her rushed movements caught the attention of the crowd, and they cocked their head at her. Their judging eyes tied knots in her stomach, but she did not stop. Her dress swished around her legs, and the lace felt tight on her arms. The hot sun made her head itch under the blonde wig, but she continued to worm her way to the next intersection.

Riome grabbed Rayna's free hand, her tight grip a desperate reminder of the danger of being caught. "Are they coming?" Riome did not wait for a response as she pulled Rayna and Drew across the intersection.

Up until now, Rayna had been afraid to glean her pursers. She did not want to know how many were coming for her, how big and frightening they might be. When the echoes of footfalls behind them announced that their hunters were getting close, Rayna reached out with her mind.

Two Katori. The first was a tall, older man, and the heavy thud of his boots and the desperation in the man's expression sent chills down her spine. With him, an older gray-haired woman, her stride quick and unrelenting. They were determined; Rayna could see it carved into their faces. They needed to catch her.

Rayna's heart pounded in her chest. "They are coming," she whispered, rushing into the next onslaught of bystanders out for a mid-day stroll. "Excuse me," she muttered, "excuse me. Sorry. Again, sorry," she apologized, bumping several more people as she maneuvered down the thoroughfare.

Without so much as a warning, Drew pulled them into the chaotic street. Rayna grabbed her dress as she stepped over a small puddle. They dodged two horse-drawn carriages and a supply wagon making their way to the opposite side before slipping down another alley away from prying eyes.

Running in a dress and lady's dress shoes did not slow Rayna's pace as she darted down three different passageways before she realized she was alone. She gulped. *What have I done?* She took a few steps back the way she came. "Riome," she whispered into the poorly lit alley before the footsteps chasing her turned the corner, and Riome found her. "Where is Drew?" she asked, realizing he had no Katori speed.

Riome looked to Rayna. "You know this can only end one way? They will continue to chase us. Their ability to glean the city makes escape impossible, and no amount of my magic will convince them you are not the girl they seek. I must end this. By the time Keegan notices his missing people, we will be long gone, and it will not matter—*they* will not matter."

Rayna thought about her friend's words—these lives did not matter. "I disagree," she said, refusing to go along with killing someone, even if it was to save her life. "There is always another way. You are the master of potions, use something less toxic. You're a spy, surely you have something," she said, waving vaguely at Riome's many hidden pockets and satchels.

"A spy uses what she has available"—Rayna saw Riome slip a silver ring on her finger—"and right now, there is no room for compromise. I cannot risk a Katori being unaffected by a weaker potion. These people are dangerous, and they will stop at nothing to take you away. Take you to Keegan."

Riome was right, the danger was real, and it was time Rayna accepted the fact that everyone's lives depended on her evading capture. She knew all too well that catching her would tip the balance in Keegan's favor. Taking the lead, she searched for the perfect dark alley to spring their trap. The Milnosian streets glimmered with her magic-empowered vision. The twists and turns narrowed between older buildings. As they fled around another corner, they found themselves trapped in a dead-end street.

"Perfect." Riome looked to the dark windows above. "This should be quick. Stay behind me. They won't know what hit them." Rayna watched Riome tie her dress and puffy petticoat around her hips, exposing her ruffled drawers to improve her mobility.

Before she could ask what was next, the two silver-headed Katoris turned the corner and quickly closed the gap before stopping. Their faces hidden in shadow sparked a fight-or-flight response that sent Rayna's blood rushing to her core. She pictured scaling the drainpipe to her left and the three daring jumps to gain access to the rooftop. But then she replayed her friend's words—they will not stop. Riome was right, and she knew all too well the stakes were high, and both of their lives were on the line.

Rayna's hands felt cold. She was ready to fight.

"Keegan is coming for you, Rayna," the strange man spoke, stepping closer. "There is no escape."

Rayna pulled a dagger from her dress, a weapon she thought foolish at first but that now gave her some comfort. "I will never go with you. I will never help Keegan. You will not take me alive, and my friend here has no intention of letting you leave this alleyway." She hoped her confidence carried with her words.

The woman joined the older man. "Hush, we have no time for this foolishness. You must come with us." Her forcefulness left little room to guess her intentions—they were both desperate.

The older man pulled a blade and waved it at the gloom behind himself and his partner. "Come out, young man," he instructed. "I see you sneaking through the darkness. You cannot trick a Katori hunter so easily. I saw you hiding in the alcove when we passed two streets back. I know you hoped to catch us from behind."

Drew stepped from the shadows, blade in hand, but Rayna also spotted a silver ring around his finger—the shape very similar to the one Riome wore. "I may not be Katori, but I promise, you are not taking Rayna with you."

The man tilted his head and spoke to Rayna. "Clever girl."

The pride Rayna heard in his voice shocked her, urging her to take a closer look. She took two steps around Riome and would have taken a third had her friend not stopped her. The man's face was familiar to her, but the woman, gray and aged as she was, had features that matched her own. "Mother?" she asked hopefully yet not entirely sure.

The woman's sad eyes said it all. "Daughter."

Rayna furrowed her brow, trying to understand. "But how?" Their age made no sense to her, but then it all made sense. "Keegan did this to you. He took the years from you because you helped Kai."

"We were not the best parents," her mother offered, "but we do love you and your sister." Her honey-colored eyes implored Rayna's heart to soften.

"I want to trust you, but why should I? You attacked me on Dragon Spine Island. Keegan tried to kill me, and you did not even try to stop him." Her emotions bubbled to the surface, but she held back her tears. There was more to say, but she let it go.

"I cannot change the past, and I regret so much, but now we are trying to help you," her mother pleaded. "You must leave the city. Keegan is sure Kai brought you, and he means to use you against his son.

I will not risk your life; he will surely kill you once he has no more need of you. We must report back and tell him you are not in Milnos."

Rayna put away her dagger, but Drew and Riome remained on guard. "I cannot leave the city. I must save my friend first. She is trapped . . ."

Riome's fierce stare stopped Rayna from saying more.

"I must see you safely out of the city," her father put away his blade and motioned back the way they came. "We have no time to waste with idle conversation. Your mother and I made so many mistakes. If I can save you now . . ."

"I do not care about the past right now," Rayna raised her hand to stop her father. "I will not leave my friends or Kai behind. Help us save them or help us stop Keegan."

Riome's deep sigh stopped the conversation. "The way I see it," she started, pointing her blade at Rayna's father, "you have only one choice. Let us go. I do not much care what you do after. If Kai is correct, and he usually is, we will all find ourselves back in Diu in the coming days. Decide to help us or fight with Keegan. Either way, step aside."

Rayna's mother took her father's hand. "Let her go. She must follow her own path. We are very proud of the woman you have become, daughter. Your adopted parents raised a fine young woman. Demir, we must report back, or our absence will draw attention to Rayna's presence."

Her parents darted back down the alleyway and turned the corner. They were gone. Riome did her best to smooth her rumpled dress. "Drew, you had best get us a carriage if we ever hope to meet Professor Krane at the tower."

Drew left them alone.

"If you need to talk," Riome offered.

Rayna took Riome by the hand and ventured back to the main street, where Drew hailed a carriage. "Not today," she nodded, and then she took Drew's hand and stepped into the carriage.

CHAPTER19

Darkness

Under the influence of Keegan's dark crystal, Kai saw the world in shades of gray backed with a feeling of anger. His limbs were slack, and his soul felt locked away, out of reach. The torture room smelled dank, with death lingering in the corner. The various oil lamps and torches flickered menacing light up the stone walls. Kai saw the various iron devices through the haze, making him wonder which they might use on him. He was surprised when they chained him up, but then again, the Milnosian guards spent hours beating him—which made sense, he thought. They all wanted their shot at the Diu prince.

While each blow hurt, whatever magic his father had placed on his mind dulled his senses and left him locked away in a dark place, far apart from his body. He felt detached, like a forgotten puppet with no master to animate him. Each guard took their turn, laughing and punching as he dangled from chains affixed to his wrists pulled over his head.

One guard, his fist bloodied from his previous turn, stepped up and studied Kai. "You know, this is not entertaining if they do not scream or cry for mercy. Bleeding is great, but I want to hear him beg, like the others. I might as well be punching something dead. Can we take this collar off?"

"Are you mad?" the next guard asked. "The Grand Duke said that collar is the only thing keeping him under control. Without it, he has magic—dragon magic, if I heard Maxwell correctly. I am not risking being eaten or burned alive by a dragon."

The others murmured in agreement. "Might as well take him to his cell."

The lead guard released the chain securing Kai's hands. His body dropped to the floor in a heap. He had no interest in moving, yet a small part of him screamed. Disconnected from his body was no way to live, and he wished they would kill him to end his misery. Free him from Keegan's control.

Then he remembered his mother, and he imagined that this was how she felt: alone, disconnected, hopeless. For her, he would need to be strong. He would need to find a way to escape—and free them both.

His guard laughed. "I wish all our prisoners were this obedient." The guard shoved Kai into a cell and secured his wrists with chains attached to the wall before adjusting the length, forcing him to stand with his arms wide. "We need more of these collars, but I could do without those creepy black eyes and the lack of screaming. I like the screams." He poked Kai in the ribs and departed with the other guards.

Kai had felt the dulled jab against his ribs, but he lacked the ability to respond. Kai closed his eyes, exhausted by the ordeal, and his mind fell in and out of conciseness. Filled with visions of doom and moments of hope, he struggled to focus. In a small moment of clarity, he thought back to a moment before they came to Milnos, the moment his group hatched an idea to conceal their crystals. An idea that would keep their magic close but concealed.

His mind thought back to that day in the forest outside Rieko, and a plan he hoped might protect them all from discovery or losing their crystals. Kai paced in the clearing, knowing they would soon find themselves in Milnos, and while he knew his mother's crystal connected him to her, he also believed their crystals could be used to control them. His mind raced to ensure if they were captured, the crystals would not fall into the hands of Keegan. "You all know my mother's crystal connects her to me, and I still believe I can use it to bring her back to us. It should come as no surprise that we risk getting captured while in

Milnos, but we cannot risk Keegan gaining control of our crystals." Kai eyed his fellow Katoris. "When I was on his ship, Keegan came close to learning how to use mine against me. Then in Diu, he used his crystal against me. He is very powerful. We cannot let him use our magic against us or his magic to create more monsters."

"What do you propose?" Ryker asked. "I am not leaving my crystal here in the woods. Without it, I cannot transform. I know you can, and after you told me how you did it, I tried several times, but it does not work for me. Maybe you are wrong about how this all works, or maybe you and your mother are special. There is something missing I cannot put my finger on it, but I am keeping my crystal close."

The thought he could be wrong—or that he and his mother were different—had not crossed this mind.

"We could hide them under the skin," Rayna proposed. "Say, on the back of the leg, below the calf muscle. It is not an obvious place, no risk of internal damage if you are in a fight, and I could heal the wound. No one would know. Keegan would have no way to take the crystals and control us."

With everyone in agreement, Kai and his fellow Katoris hid their crystals under their skin. Ryker used his blade to cut an opening just below the calf muscle, inserted the crystal, and Rayna healed the wound. All they wore in remembrance were the simple chains around their necks.

The memory of that moment in the forest—and the fact his crystal remained safely nestled in the back of his leg—gave Kai a slight sense of comfort, even if the dark crystal blocked his connection.

As the hours rolled on Kai, felt the dark fog lift, which he thought was a good thing at first, but then the pain started to grow. He felt his broken ribs, the dried blood around his eye, his busted nose, and the swelling in his face. However, his vision remained dark, and Keegan's hatred clung to his heart like sticky syrup. *Keegan must be asleep,* Kai thought. *This must be the moment my mother feels the most hope, when the mental part of Keegan's mind control fades, a thin ray of hope creeps inside.*

With each passing moment, the pain increased. He struggled against his chains, but it was no use. Pressed against the wall, he had no leverage, and his arm muscles were too weak to use his Katori strength. Unable to free himself, he called to the magic within his stone to give him strength, but the dark crystal pulsed around his neck. The pain shot down his spine. Again, he tried, but his father's hatred blocked access to his crystal. His heart pounded in his ears, his lungs heaved, and he coughed several times. Blood spattered the floor.

Controlling his breathing, he regained his composure. The pain and agony remained, but he could moderate his inhalations and exhalations to avoid breathing too deep. His legs ached to rest, but the chains holding his arms wide did not allow the luxury. Heavy footfalls echoed through the prison, drawing his eyes to the iron gate. For a fearful moment, he wondered if Keegan was coming.

Then the silhouette of a guard holding a bucked filled the doorway. The man dropped a bowl inside and rattled the cell door shut before moving to the next cell. Clang, plop, clang, step, step, step. The sound faded and was gone.

Standing in his filthy cell, he watched the rats scurry about the rotten, slop-filled bowl on the floor. *I guess that is my breakfast*, he laughed inside his head. He tried to find the humor in his predicament to maintain his sanity, realizing he was regaining some of his mind. Moans from nearby cells gave him the feeling everyone suffered in this part of the prison.

Another dark shadow blocked the torchlight from Kai's cell, disrupting his contemplation. He did not need to ask or glean the man's face. He just knew. "Keegan," Kai addressed his father. "Took you long enough. Is it morning already?"

"How did you do it?" Keegan asked, entering Kai's cell. "How did you break my spell?"

Kai gasped for air. His broken ribs made breathing difficult, and he no longer had the will to stand. His knees buckled, but the chains kept him from collapsing to the stone floor. The chains dug into his wrists.

Keegan rushed to his side, and his concerned look took Kai by surprise, but neither man said anything. His father yanked on the chains, once, twice, and with the third pull, the stone securing the chain length broke, releasing Kai. The loud rumble brought the guard.

"Bring me some water and the key for these chains," Keegan commanded the guard while helping Kai lean against the stone wall. "It did not have to be this way, son. I never wanted this to happen to you." Kai felt his father's fingers graze the damage done to his face.

The fatherly concern felt uncomfortable. At a loss for words, Kai stared at Keegan with his good eye. With every fiber of his being, he hated this man—at least he thought he did. The dark crystal pressing into his neck clouded everything in hate, leaving Kai unsure of his feelings. He knew the dark shard affected his mind, but its power seemed to have limits, needing to be recharged. The crystal dangling from his father's chain was long but thinner than it should be. Kai wondered how many pieces he had broken off to use on others.

Kai's wrists remained bound by the heavy chains resting in his lap. The guard returned, with the key to Kai's freedom dangling in his hand. "I am not supposed to unlock the prisoner," the guard insisted, reluctant to offer the key. "Maybe I should call the captain."

The speed with which Keegan turned on the man was nearly instantaneous. His strong hand clutched the man's throat. Kai thought his father would kill the guard, leaving him a vacant husk. Instead, he whispered to the guard, and then Kai saw the hint of gray around the man's temples, the aging in and around the eyes. He did not siphon much, but the man lost at least a decade before Keegan released him, casting him backward.

Disoriented by the ordeal, the guard dropped the key and stumbled back through the open door. In the same flash as before, Keegan knelt next to Kai and unlocked the chains binding Kai's wrists. Keegan pressed his hand to Kai's chest. Warmth rolled through Kai's bones—he felt his cracked ribs heal, his swollen eye return to normal, his broken nose mend. All the bruises and soreness left his body. He was physically whole once more.

Kai wanted to be grateful, but he could not bring himself to say a kind word. "Healing me does not make up for what you have done—or what you plan to do."

Keegan stood up, giving Kai space. "My son, why do you trouble yourself with the lives of these mere men? You, like me, are a god among them. Together we could rule the world. Yet you wallow in their mediocre lives. I gave you a choice, and you chose them. Have you had enough? Are you ready to follow me?"

"You didn't give me a choice. Maxwell unmasked me to Landon, my oldest enemy. What did you expect me to do? Join you? I could be wrong, but you did not seem to be in a position of power yourself. There are whispers that you plan to lead them to the heart of Katori. Give them our homeland."

"Landon is my puppet!" Keegan barked. "He wants justice for the death of his father and mother, regardless of the fact that his father was a tyrant. King Bannon Panier started this chain of events by killing Iver's father and brother. I know Milnosian history, son. Who do you think whispered in the king's ear—made him crazy? I gave him one of my dark crystals so that I could sow chaos. Who knew he would kill so many? He was a touch out of his mind before I came along. But then a boy became King of Diu—Iver—and he killed Bannon. I meant to take my revenge and make Iver my puppet, but your mother had gone missing from my ship. So, I gave the shard to Nola, Bannon Panier's illegitimate daughter, and I left her to corrupt herself and the world around her. It took me years to learn that Iver stole Mariana from me. By then, news of her death left me with little reason to return to this part of the world."

His father's details of the past filled in the blanks as to why so many influential people had been set on a path of hate and destruction over the years. His father was behind all of it.

Keegan paced the small cell. "At the time, I was in the middle of taking control of Caroco. Hearts and minds need constant attention if you wish to make them worship you of their own free will. People are playthings."

"No wonder my mother ran from you. You are insane. You would risk exposing the Katori secrets to the world because you want to be worshiped? They are using you—and your black powder. Maxwell means to kill you the moment he gets the chance."

"He will not get the chance." Keegan stepped to the open cell door. "Come with me, son. I can bring all my armies together and destroy them all, and then we can remake your precious Diu. People will worship us. They will build shrines and monoliths in our names. I could restore your mother. We could be a family."

Kai shook his head in refusal. "Why would I care about you or your future? I took the beating of my life rather than go with you last night. You are not my family."

"You are a brave one, there is no doubt. From the first moment I saw you, I knew. Your face, those eyes. I know my own eyes, my own blood. That night in Iver's palace, you stood in the back and watched me. I heard the Katoris called you a Half-Light back then, but I knew better. I felt your true Katori power. I watched you scurry through the secret passage to save your little sister."

Anger boiled in Kai's heart, but he took a breath, unsure if the feelings were his own or stemming from Keegan's crystal still secured to his neck. "You do not know me."

Keegan ignored his son's words. "My next plan was to take Helena, Iver's beloved sister, in Port Anahita. I wanted him to suffer, and I wanted your attention. I needed the chance to show you Katori power, because you didn't have your magic in those days. You spoiled that, too, by saving Helena and defeating my Caroco men. Bad timing on my part, I could have sent more men, but as I said, you did not have your magic, and I could not risk Katori preventing your access and acquiring your crystal." Keegan's tone had a sense of pride.

Tired of the banter, Kai interrupted. "Why are you here, Keegan? Break me out or leave me be."

"How did you control Mariana?" Keegan stared deep into Kai's eyes as if he could root it out on his own. "The shard she wears, much like yours, comes from my crystal, which gives me control if I concentrate on her. There is no way you should have been able to steal her away. Tell me, how did you do it?"

Kai thought about telling him but hesitated as a new idea formed in his head. "Free me. Free me from this cell, this prison, this city. Help me stop Milnos, and I will tell you."

"This was not part of my plan." Keegan stood and paced. "I knew you would follow your mother and me to Diu. I was counting on it. I left a gift for you, but I do not imagine you stayed long enough."

"What gift?"

"Your Aunt Helena." Keegan tossed his arm out. "My men were to capture her on their way through Port Anahita and offer her in exchange for you. Iver must be beside himself with worry, if he still lives. He has nothing else I want now. A pity you will see his city destroyed behind the haze of my crystal. You will join your mother and me in the coming days as we attack Diu."

Fear swelled in Kai's heart. Was his aunt still alive? Would she die because he left Diu? "Why are the lives of others so irrelevant to you? Milnos is going to slaughter everyone, especially the dragons. There will be no Katori left when they are finished."

Keegan ignored his warning. "I am a little surprised you followed us to Milnos, leaving behind your helpless father and everyone you love. But I had a secondary plan here, too. Here, in the city of your greatest enemy, I hoped you would join me. There is no one coming to help you. I made sure of it. Katori spirals into civil war, and everyone is eager to blame you for my attacks—it surprised me how easily my fellow Katoris believed the idea. A lifetime of secrets and one boy turns that upside down."

His father's arrogance enraged him. How could this man be so focused on himself that he could not see the destruction he caused? Or care?

"Diu will be mine, son. Join me. The Milnos army will fight for me, I can assure you. Milnos will fly in and squash their old enemy, and my awaiting Caroco army will crush Milnos in return. I will rule this entire continent."

Kai shook his head. "So, it is true? They have ships that can fly? And you do not care if it means they can cross the uncrossable Katori Mountains straight into our homeland, unchallenged? They will slaughter the dragons and then our people. Stop this madness, please. Be a better man." The words came out in a begging tone, faster than his mind could process the foolish request.

Keegan seethed at his refusal. "Have it your way, son. I will not offer again. When we leave, you will be my slave, same as your mother. My will is stronger than yours."

His father's grip closed around his throat. The dark crystal pressed deep into Kai's skin, and the detached feeling and heavy depression started to return.

"You will be back." Kai tried to laugh, squirming under his father's influence as his mind returned to the darkness. "If you want to know how I did it, you will be back to free me when my mother begins to rebel."

The iron gate creaked open, and Keegan called for the guard. "I am done with him."

Abandoned by Keegan, Kai stared at the torchlight spilling through the iron gate. As the hateful darkness consumed him, he clawed at the collar secured to his neck, but his fingers could not remove the dark crystal. His mind grabbed for reality, but it slipped out of reach, leaving him again lost in a paralyzing haze.

Beefy hands grabbed Kai by the arms. "Back on the wall, prisoner." The guard jostled him into position and chained him, one arm pulled tight to the wall while the other dangled at his side.

In his solitary darkness, a voice called to him. Real or imagined, he did not know, and the hate swirling inside of him made him wonder if he even cared. While there was no physical pain, the thoughts and hatred of his father left him begging for death. "Mother, I am sorry," he cried out.

"Kai," the voice called again. "Kai, is that really you? Kai, speak to me!"

The voice prodded. Relentless, it called, begging him to respond. The darkness ate at him, and his own voice sounded distant. Tears ran down his cheeks. *All is lost, Rayna. I am sorry I failed you. Alenga, take this heartache from me.*

"Kai, can you hear me?" the voice shouted again.

"You are not real," Kai shouted back, willing the voice to cry for him no more.

"Kai, Prince Kai, of Diu. Is that you?"

Kai's dark eyes kept him from seeing details in the flickering torch light, but when a shadow wisped in front of him, he jerked back, striking his head on the stone wall. "Leave me be," he shouted as the pain of the strike made his eyes water, but again he saw the figure—a face closing the gap and blocking the light. "Who are you?" Kai whispered to the shadow.

"He is a demon, Red. Eyes black as coal. We should leave him to die," the shadow called to the distant voice.

"Ghost, is that you?" the voice called out. "Free me, let me see him for myself."

"No, he is a DEMON!" Ghost shouted.

"If that man is who I think he is, he is my best chance at escape. Please, free me," Red demanded.

CHAPTER 20

Forgotten Man

Ghost's shadow faded from view. Ka blinked and searched the edges of his vision. There was no one there. Red's voice was also gone. In the silence, Kai waited, listened, and heard nothing. Had he imagined the voices, the shadowy figure? Was he losing his mind? Did his father's spell create hallucinations? Kai's mind struggled to find focus under the influence of Keegan's dark crystal.

"Hurry, man, unlock my cell," Kai heard Red's voice once more.

The clink and jingles echoed into his chamber moments before two shadowy figures rushed into his cell. The man named Ghost blocked his view of Red. "See, I told you, he is a demon with black eyes. There is a poison in him that seeps into the skin around his face. We must kill him or leave him to die."

Red pushed Ghost away. "It *is* him," Red whispered, but Kai's clouded mind could not piece together the shapes behind the bearded man in front of him. "Kai, can you hear me? It is me, Tolan." His friend tugged at Kai's restraints.

"They chain him for a reason," Ghost said. "They fear him, as should we. His demon eyes are evil, and we should not free the darkness. They chained him here for a reason, Red." Ghost repeated, as he waved a torch close to Kai's face.

"Tolan?" Kai tried to see, but the dark haze left him unable to see the details of his friend. "Is it really you? The crystal, remove the crystal," he begged.

Tolan's hand touched his neck.

"No," Ghost insisted, pressing something sharp into Kai's neck. "We cannot trust the demon. This crystal could be the only thing keeping him at bay. We should kill him."

"I trust my friend, demon eyes or not." Tolan turned Kai's head to the side. "Do not make me regret this," he whispered, releasing the chain securing the crystal.

The removal of Keegan's crystal shard provided instant relief. The darkness and the hate sloughed off Kai like dead skin. His eyes cleared, and he saw his friend and the man he called Ghost. Tolan was a sight, hair down around his shoulders, a long beard, and missing an eye. Ghost looked slightly better in the sense that his muscles looked strong and healthy, but the older, gray-haired man was every bit as filthy, and his beard reached down to his navel. Both were malnourished and bared the signs of reoccurring torture.

With his father's dark crystal removed, his own crystal roared with power at the base of his calf. Pulling at the dampness and moss of the prison, Kai found bits of life, bits of magic willing to recharge him. "You might want to step back," he instructed, taking hold of the chain that bound his wrist, ready to pull with all his Katori strength.

"Ghost can unlock those." Tolan pointed to the strange man dangling a bone piece with a hook. "He has a gift for locks. He will not leave this place, but he can unlock anything."

Free from his chains, Kai rubbed his arms and wrists. "Thank you," he nodded to Ghost. "If he has a key, why does he not escape?"

"He says it is impossible," Tolan responded. "And I believe him. I tried, got pretty far too, but as punishment, they took my eye." He pointed to the empty cavity.

Guilt hardened like a rock in the pit of Kai's stomach. Tolan had endured so much suffering. How could he have considered not even trying to save his friend? His selfishness kept him from doing the right thing. Maybe if he followed Riome's plan and stabbed Lord Luedke, he would not be in this position in the first place. Keegan, Landon, and Maxwell would never have even known he was in Milnos. It was then Kai considered the circumstances of his capture—and his luck in finding Tolan. He chastised himself for doubting this might be Alenga's doing. *She brought me to Tolan.*

"You are stronger than anyone I have ever met." Kai pulled his friend into a hug. "Seven months in prison would have broken most men. Believe me, I know, I spent a few days in a Diu prison, which I thought was deplorable before today. Milnos has torture down to an art. How did you survive all this time?"

Tolan stood and crossed closer to the light. "Amelia. She gives me strength."

"Still," Kai shook his head and stretched his arms and legs, sore from hours for forced posture. "I do not understand why Maxwell would keep you alive."

Tolan stroked his long, red beard. "Landon visited me once before I attempted to escape. He told me I deserved prison for thinking I was better than him, but he would let me live for old time's sake. He also told me he would marry Amelia once she was no longer pregnant with my child. The next day I tried to escape, but the guards caught me. I am ready to make another attempt—I promise, I have no intentions of dying here. They may break my body but not my mind." To Kai's surprise, he chuckled. "I read that in a book once."

"Good to see you've not lost your sense of humor." Kai caught another glimpse of his face and his missing left eye. "Now, we need to escape," Kai whispered, doing his best not to stare or avoid looking at his friend's deformity.

"Not to discourage you, but you do realize we are four levels down in the worst dungeon imaginable, don't you? Since my incarceration, three men have tried to escape, and all died before they even left this level. I at least made it to the second level. This place is like a maze. The deeper you go, the less they care about you. The only thing that saved me was

Ghost. He brought me food, real food—not much mind you, but it is better than the slop they toss in your bowl. How did you end up here?"

"Lucky and mouthy." Kai chuckled, trying to convince himself he was himself again. "Actually, King Landon imprisoned me. As you can imagine, my showing up at his birthday event uninvited did not go well. Maxwell is working with him, and then there is Keegan, my birth father. The man who attacked Port Anahita. His army is attacking Diu, Katori, and Nebea. Basically everywhere. He wants to rule the world. Landon has new weapons and flying ships. I am not sure of anything anymore. I came to save my mother. Instead, I ended up down here."

Tolan nodded. "Landon never liked you. He never liked anyone, not even me. In the end, he especially hated me. I had no idea he loved Amelia. How is she, do you know?"

The truth of a thing was always better than the lie, even if it is a sad truth. "I am sorry, my friend. She is still pregnant but suffering in isolated captivity, but if all goes well tonight, Rayna and Riome plan to rescue her from the Raven's Tower. Your father came to me and asked for my help to discover your fate. I am afraid another great war kept us from coming." Kai then turned to the old man standing nearby and studied his familiar eyes. "Mister, I cannot very well keep calling you Ghost. What is your real name?"

Tolan twitched with anticipation, distracting Kai. "If your friends are saving Amelia, I want to be there! So, how do we get out of here? You must have a plan because I know, together, we stand a chance."

Before Kai could respond, he heard the sound of stone on stone—a whack and a crack seconds before a gush of magic flooded the room.

"Ghost, no!" Kai turned to the old man standing over Keegan's destroyed crystal with a rock in his hand. "Why would you do that?" he yelled.

Ghosted pointed to the white dust on the ground. "Demon stone."

The man's eyes looked confused at Kai's frustration, sending Ghost scurrying out of his cell and into the shadows of the prison. Curious about the change in the crystal, Kai pressed his fingers into the smashed powder. The hate was gone, as were any hints of magic. "Now that the stone is shattered, Keegan must know I am free, and he will return. We have no time to waste standing here. It is time to go."

"I will not leave Ghost behind," Tolan insisted. "We must find him. He knows the other levels, and he is our best chance at freedom." Tolan stepped into the flickering torchlight outside Kai's cell and darted down the dark corridor.

There was no time to spend literally chasing a ghost. "I am sorry, but we do not have time for this." Kai darted after them. "We need to leave before my father comes back. Where could he have gone?" He caught up with Tolan and followed his friend's lead, searching the surrounding cells.

"I have no idea." Toland pushed open another dark cell. "Most of the cells down here are empty. With his bone key, he can come and go anywhere. Some cells have secondary cells that connect to other hallways. I have only studied this section, but he knows them all. Ghost, come back! We need to leave!"

They searched the adjacent cells, four unlocked and empty; the subsequent five cells contained men spouting nonsense or seething in a fit of uncontrolled rage.

"We must find him," Kai said as they continued to look. "I think I know him, or the man he used to be. The more I think about his eyes, the more I recognize him. How far could he go?" he asked, turning down his third passageway and pressing his face into a locked cell.

"Before we get lost," Tolan said, laying his hand on Kai's shoulder, "maybe we need to go back. I want to help him because he helped me. I am not sure why you are trying to help him or who you think he is, but the man is a lifer. This awful place is his home. Whatever he left behind, the real him died years ago. He may not be worth the risk."

Reluctantly, Kai turned back. Tolan directed them this way and that. Each turn looked the same as the last, but his friend appeared confident. When they reached Kai's original cell, he sighed in relief. He took one last look inside, and Ghost was not there.

"He had his chance," Kai said, pulling the iron gate closed to add the illusion that it held a prisoner.

Following Tolan, they followed new hallways that twisted and turned until they neared a locked gate securing their section. Kai shook the iron door. Kneeling, he inspected the lock. "I wish I had a tool. I could pick this lock." He looked back at Tolan and saw a hand reach out to him from a dark cell.

"Please. Take me with you," Ghost whispered.

Kai moved to the iron cell door. The depth in Ghost's eyes weighed on him. "Who are you?" he asked. He leaned toward the iron gate, trying to study the shadows distorting the man's face.

The man's dirty hand grabbed the bar. His face came into the torchlight. Beneath the age, the dirty beard—the shape of the man's face was familiar. "Please don't leave me here. I've been here so long. If we die in the escape, that is no different than my life now. I am a ghost, the forgotten man."

Kai could not put his finger on how he knew this stranger. Again, he asked. "Who are you? Tell me your name."

"I . . . I am not sure I remember. I've not spoken it in so long." The aged man shrank back into the darkness. "I . . . I am . . . No one. That is what they told me. Repeatedly, they said I belonged nowhere to no one. And I believed them. Then they forgot me. Left me here to die." The man pressed his face into the iron bars. "I tried to escape once, made it to the surface before they caught me. I stopped trying years ago. Others try, but they all die. Red, I mean, Tolan, he tried, but they did not kill him. He is special. I heard the guards say. His wife is a princess or a queen, I think. Please, do not leave me here alone. Not again. I can help you."

Tolan grabbed Kai's hand. "We have to go," he insisted. "We have no time for games, and you said your father would return. I will not waste my chance at freedom."

"Do you know who this man is?" Kai gestured to the shadow consumed figure.

"No. He comes and goes like an unseen ghost, and the guards do not even care anymore." Tolan pulled on the cell door, and it opened.

"We must help him. Whoever he is." Kai could not escape the idea he knew the man, and yet he had never seen him before in his life. The man was a stranger. "Ghost, come back into the light. Would you please tell me your name? You are somebody. I think you are somebody to me." He moved to allow the light to splash into the darkness.

The stranger pushed the gate into Kai, and again he pressed his face to the bars. His hair and beard spilled through the bars. Threadbare clothing clung to his form. Brown eyes pleaded in desperation. "I died here. Leave me. I am already a ghost. I am no help to anyone."

Kai could not help but feel for the stranger. "I will not leave you. Tell me your old name—the one your family used. Someone loved you once."

"They once called me . . . Andrew. King Andrew Cazier."

In shock, Kai grasped the man's hand. Adrian's brother. His cousin. "You went missing over twenty years ago, a few years before I was born. Presumed dead, lost at sea." Kai pulled Andrew into the corridor. "We are family, you and I. Cousins. King Iver Galloway is my father. Your brother Adrian is the Master General in Diu, and you look just like him."

Andrew's eyes darted around the edges of his memory, and then he motioned them to follow. "I know the best routes through the prison. Some stairways lead to the guard's quarters. That is where I find food. Others cross to empty sections, back stairwells, and other ways around the dungeon."

"Thank Alenga, I found you." Kai wrapped an arm around Andrew, pulling him close. He felt the weight of his cousin's wiry frame—skin and bone.

Andrew led their small group around the warren of the Milnos dungeons. Uneven cobble switched to dirt and back again. The haphazard design gave the impression little thought went into the expanded sections beyond the need for more space. The first set of stairs they climbed looked decent at first glance. Andrew's light frame scaled them with little effort, but the rickety structure began to creak and groan with their combined weight.

Kai grabbed the railing and stopped, and Tolan braced himself as the entire staircase swayed mid-step, but Andrew did not stop. Reaching the top, Andrew called back in a low, demanding tone. "No time to waste, these corridors do not stay empty long. We must hurry." Tolan took the stairs two at a time with Kai keeping close behind.

In the following passage, Andrew glanced back over his shoulder. The look was brief, but Kai's stomach turned. He trusted his cousin because he was a Cazier, but the ease with which they dodged guards hiding in alcoves or vacant cells suddenly worried him. Keeping a close eye on Andrew, Kai wormed in front of Tolan. "You sure this is the best way?" he questioned, looking up to the next level.

The second set of stairs were a combination of steel and wood leading to the next level. Andrew never responded; he only darted down a narrow corridor, which Kai realized too late was full of the most dangerous of prisoners, grabbing through the bars. Andrew dodged left then right, ducked, and weaved through the gauntlet. Angry hands reached for Kai, but his speed kept him from capture.

"Take us with you!" A set of hands snagged Tolan's arm and pulled him against the iron bars. Four hands held him in place as men shouted for freedom.

Andrew dropped back. "I can free you. I know your kind. You are thieves. What did you steal? Food? I steal food." He stared at the man and then picked the lock with ease.

The hands released Tolan, and Andrew motioned to continue while he picked another lock and opened a second gate. No sooner were they free than the other prisoners darted around Kai and Tolan, running headlong into the darkness without them. Andrew smiled and unlocked more cells, freeing dozens of criminals. "They will not get far, but they will provide a distraction for our escape."

As they wormed through the dungeon, his cousin's pace increased. He went down corridors, turning left then right, up a spiral staircase and across a wooden bridge, and up another set of stairs. Some of the freed prisoners followed while others took different routes. As they ran, more men in cells cried out. Hands grabbed at them, begging for freedom. Andrew complied without question, freeing more and more men.

Down the next passage, Andrew picked a lock, and they entered a large stone room with high arched ceilings, a processing room of some sort surrounded by holding cells. *We must be near the end*, Kai thought as he waited for his cousin to pick the next lock and lead them out. The room fell silent while Andrew knelt on one knee. An eerie feeling crept into Kai's head. *Where are the other prisoners, the ones following us?* He stepped back toward the last gate, setting half-closed.

The appearance of a guard at the gate behind them cut through his heart. He turned back to Andrew, rising from his knees, and his cousin looked back. The betrayal was there, but it was too late.

"Thank you, Rat." The soldier laughed, pulling Andrew through the gate before slamming it shut in Kai's face.

More guards arrived, weapons in hand. Andrew stood among them, unchallenged for trying to escape. His eyes looked away as Kai searched him for the truth of their situation. But there was no need to ask; his cousin had sold them out to the guards.

"I will get out of here Andrew. Whatever they promised you, I can do better. Remember your name. It means something to me, and it did to you too. I can take you home, cousin." Kai tried to connect with Andrew, the man he used to be a lifetime ago.

"There is no use, Kai," Tolan said. "Call him Andrew, if you wish, but Ghost is a lifer, and the prison is his home. They are his family. And we—we are in trouble." Tolan pulled Kai around as he motioned to their new circumstances.

Several cell doors opened around the large stone room and filled with prisoners. He knew the guards expected him to feel terrified, but Kai was no ordinary man. However, their unlocked doors proved this was a trap, and Andrew had led him straight to them. He imagined these cellmates were the worst possible prisoner: violent abusers, psychopaths, and murders. "Meet your new plaything, boys. He is the Prince of Diu. Good luck, your Highness." The guard chuckled as he and others approached the door to watch.

Out of the farthest cell, a burly figure approached, a man who was a head taller than Kai. The second prisoner came at him from the opposite side, cracking his knuckles in anticipation. Kai gleaned the dimly lit area and discovered they were surrounded by twenty prisoners, each of various sizes and weights, but all in the mood for a fight.

Kai sidestepped around the cell, trying to size up his competition. "I do not want any trouble, but I will defend myself, and some of you may get severely hurt." There was no way to say that and not sound cocky, but he brought his fists up all the same, protecting his body and face.

"Hurt?" The burly man laughed. "All I see is a scared boy about to get beaten to death for being a Diu brat. I could take you without help, but then we share our toys here."

"Diu brats are our favorite," a voice from the shadows mocked.

"I hate to disappoint, but I am not from Diu. I am Katori. The full-blooded variety, not a Half-Light. I will only ask once. Leave me and my friend alone, and we will leave." He knew they would have no idea what he meant, but he did not care.

"Boy," said another man as he stepped into the torchlight. There was a scar cut across his face, and he was missing an ear. "Makes no difference to us. We don't like Katoris either."

He counted seven men with bones fashioned into makeshift blades. Thankful he now heeded the teachings of the Guardians; his crystal fully charged gave him the magic he needed to protect himself. With a thought, his back and chest rippled with dragon scales, as did his arms and legs.

Kai moved back toward the bars and the laughing guards. "I will not ask again. Leave me alone, and nobody needs to get hurt. This is all a mistake, and I will be gone in a moment."

"Oh, yes, boy, you will be gone," the burly man teased. "You see, we have a deal with the guards, so it looks like you are never leaving this cell alive. Either of you."

"Do you believe in dragons?" Kai asked Tolan, but he did not wait for the reply. "I am no demon, but I am a dragon. You have missed a lot these many months in prison. Stand back," he ordered, moving into the center of the room as the mob circled.

The first and second bone shard clinked against his dragon armor, sending the men jumping back in pain as their weapons pushed back on them. Then the rest of the mob charged with blades and fists. The transformation was slow and elegant in Kai's mind, but his metamorphosis happened in seconds. His dragon body expanded, his tail shot across the floor, and his wings expanded, scraping the stone ceiling. Heat poured through his teeth and smoke rolled out his nostrils.

The slightest blast of fire sent the prisoners rearing back in fear, each scrambling for the safety of their cells. Kai's amber dragon eyes scanned the room for any stragglers. Only Tolan remained. Kai used his dragon's claw and ripped the iron gate from its hinges. The guards ran away in fear, but Andrew stood frozen in place.

Kai transformed back. "What say you, Andrew? Are you a Cazier, or a rat? Time to choose."

"You would help me even after I betrayed you?" Andrew's puzzled look changed into realization. "I have never seen a dragon. Not a real one. They do not fly over the desserts of Nebea. In all my visits to Diu, I have never seen so much as a shadow in the sky. I thought they were all dead, and I certainly had no idea they were *people*."

Kai stepped closer to his cousin. "Do you know the rest of the way out?"

"I have been out several times when I do something for the guards. Beyond this point, the men locked in here are drunks and pickpockets. They could be of use to you." Andrew eyed them both with a hint of shame.

"I thought we could, but we cannot trust him." Tolan grabbed an abandoned sword from the stone floor and pointed the tip near Andrew's throat. "Back away, Ghost. I will not let you stab us in the back again. I thank you for helping me recover, but we part ways here. Stay or go makes no difference to me but get out of our way. I will not let you jeopardize my chance to save Amelia."

Kai stayed his friend's hand, lowering the blade. "Remember, Andrew, you are family." He pressed his hand into his cousin's chest. Offering magic in the form of hope, Kai pushed waves of energy into the forgotten man. He was no Kodama capable of healing, nor was he like

Keegan, but his relationship with Rayna and his connection to this mother showed him that emotions have power.

Their eyes met, and Kai saw a shift in Andrew.

"Thank you," Andrew said as a tear rolled down his cheek. "I will not forget this kindness."

"Release some of the prisoners," Kai said as he grabbed a sword and motioned for Andrew to lead the way. "They will provide a distraction for the guards when we reach the exit. Time to go."

CHAPTER 21

Black Hickory

Outside, the soft breeze swept the tiny ringlets of Rayna's wig and played with the lace on her dress. The ash-colored tower stood in angry contrast to the beautiful blue sky. Rayna beheld the unique shape of her friend's prison. It was not like normal towers, round with a turret at the top. Raven's Tower was square with four round turrets, which came to a point made of black iron. From her point of view, she noticed a small balcony on one side.

The balcony would be her entry point—but only if she could grow a plant that high on her own in a short amount of time. Gleaning the tower's top level, she saw Amelia and her pregnant form. Her friend sat reading a book in a simple chair near the open balcony door. Attempting to scan the lower levels and count the guards, Rayna noted the density of the massive structure.

"There is too much stone and steel in this city." Rayna clutched the small handbag Riome gave her and lowered the brim of her hat to conceal as much of her face as a group of men approached.

Drew puffed up his chest as the men came closer, and the mere sight of the lady's protector quickened their pace and sent them on their way. "I do not like the people in this vile city."

Rayna turned to Riome. "How long do you suppose we must wait?" She tapped her toe as if she could somehow speed things along. "Maybe he thought we were not coming."

"We are late." Riome's tone held no malice, but her displeasure with their current situation was obvious. "But we are fortunate your pursuers were your parents and not some other Katori hunters. As for being late, we are still fashionable. Our only cause for worry is the messenger sent to retrieve the General's carriage still waiting outside the Sedalia. I prefer an easy escape, should anything else go wrong. We had best hope our driver returns before we need to leave."

"Why exactly are we here again?" Drew asked, clenching his jaw dusting soot from his sleeve acquired during their morning adventure.

"I thought it would be important for Rayna to see the site, and plant a seed now." Riome pointed to the large stone pavers of the sidewalk. "I am concerned, as you will both see, about the distance between the garden soil and the tower. I am not sure it is possible to grow anything capable of carrying the weight of two, let alone three people. As a guest, I can study the guards, their access points to the tower, and patrol routines. I need to understand the angles of everything to prevent our capture."

"Why three of you?" Drew pressed.

"I cannot very well send Rayna up there alone. I will accompany her and take out the guards. It should be easy enough, but I need you to be our lookout. You are our eyes on the ground should something go wrong."

"Fair enough." He turned his nose away and paced up and down the street.

Waiting at the gate, Rayna took in her surroundings. The stone walls surrounding the tower stood ten feet tall, and the large access gate only offered a small window, which she could barely see through on her tiptoes. Given Amelia's delicate condition, she would need to construct something substantial enough to support them all. She thought about disrupting the stones to provide more soil for her to work with—oak tree roots were strong enough to move stone, but any noise would alert the guard.

"I see what you mean." She dropped back down on her heels. "How are we going to get inside this evening? The professor is not going to invite us in in the middle of the night. I doubt any guard would let us in without him." She again shuttered when she noticed a group of women stare at her as they walked around their group.

"Acquiring access at night will be easy. No lock can keep me out," Riome boasted. "The simple-minded guards should be easy to handle with my crystal, but scaling the tower is another matter."

"You do not mean to hurt them!" Rayna suddenly realized Riome's convictions might be more extreme than she preferred given their earlier encounter with her parents.

Drew offered a concerned look.

Riome laughed, although Rayna wondered if it were mockery or not. "Why do you both think I always resort to killing? My crystal will get me close without causing a commotion, but a sleeping potion should do the trick. I assure you no one needs to die if they stay out of my way. We can hide them out of sight behind the greenhouse, and Drew can take their place."

"The botanist is here," Rayna whispered as everyone turned to see Professor Krane, the gray-haired plant scientist, exiting his carriage. His dark suit reminded her of something Kai's Professor Graydon might wear, but the white pine walking cane reminded her of father and his woodworking hobby, how she longed to be home or anywhere but here.

"Professor Krane," Riome called out to him. "Pleasure seeing you again, and my apologies for being late. After the dramatic events of last night's ball, I wondered if you would still be open to our visit."

Riome approached the professor. "You remember my sister Rosette and our overprotective brother Drew," she jested, offering Drew a sweet nudge as she took his arm.

Rayna felt a rush of magic pour from Riome as her friend stared into the professor's eyes.

Professor Krane eyed Rayna's hair. "I would not imagine a woman of your knowledge gets lost in high-fashion and wigs. Your natural color is much nicer." He pulled a key from his pocket and unlocked the gate.

As any gentleman would, Krane held the gate and then locked it behind them. "Welcome to my humble garden. Might I offer you refreshments from the heat? Again, I apologize for my tardiness."

Entering the garden behind the professor, Rayna caught her first full view of the Raven's Tower and the surrounding stone tiles covering the ground in every direction. The width was overwhelming, and the dizzying height left her astonished. "Thank you, yes, please. I could use a moment free of the sun." She smiled at his kindness.

His mannerisms were nothing like she expected from someone in the Iron City, but then again, he was not from here. Still, it made her wonder why he would welcome them into a sacred place without having them properly investigated. She could only guess Riome's strange magic last night at the ball influenced his decisions and gained them entry. Still, a man of mystery, she decided—one she could not trust, which kept her on her toes and her lips sealed.

Krane ushered them to the tower. "I use the bottom floor of the tower as a study to catalog the various species." He motioned to the tower entrance guarded by two men.

The Milnosian soldiers stared straight, their heads held high and their demeanor fierce.

"I do love a man in uniform," Riome said as she patted the raven embossed breastplate. A moment later she stopped their group with her glance around the tower chamber before nodding the all-clear to Rayna and Drew.

Rayna fidgeted, trying not to panic over her restricting corset. The fabric on the arms looked beautiful, but she suddenly wanted to rip the lace off. Even her wig suddenly became more noticeable and began to itch. To her surprise, the thick stone battlement walls kept the lower chamber room several degrees cooler than the outside air.

The scent inside was old wood, leather, and paper. Three of the four walls had windows, while the other had a large staircase leading to the upper levels. Rayna strolled around the chamber, taking her time to stretch her neck when she reached the stairwell before moving to a window.

Inside, the professor offered them sweetened lemon water, which he poured from a glass pitcher into four small glasses.

"Does anyone else use the tower?" Rayna asked as she walked to the next wall of windows, taking in the view outside and the location of the gate. "It would be a terrible waste of space." She made her way around the room, fingering the spines of a few books on a wooden shelf and inspecting the plants sitting on a table near the window.

The professor took a sip from his cup and looked closely at Rayna. "To be honest, I hardly notice who else works in the tower. I see food come and go, soldiers change in a regular rotation, but then again, I have only been here a short time. I keep to myself—I am not one for people or politics. In fact, you three are my first guests."

Drew sat on the edge of a tall stool near a long table of dried flowers and a few bugs pinned to a scrap of wood. "Excuse me, professor." He held up a small board with three different bugs pinned in a row. "What do bugs have to do with plants?"

A delighted smile lit up the professor's face. "You see, young man, there is more to plants than most people think." The older man adjusted his spectacles and leaned over the table to point at his charts. "Sunlight, rainwater, soil, and even the bugs around them can help or hurt. I study everything. While these beetles damage the leaves, I have found misting with vinegar works to keep them away. These insects help the plants by eating certain smaller bugs. Part art, part science—botany."

Eager to study the area around the tower, Rayna slipped out on her own. The dark stone was hot under her touch. Studying the large stone slabs beneath her feet, she looked for cracks or large joints that might allow seeds to reach the soil. The more she looked, the more disappointed she felt. The tower was not new by any means, but not one crack or gap seemed wide enough for any of the seeds she carried. No weeds grew around the tower or the surrounding courtyard.

"What have you learned?" Riome whispered, strolling up behind her.

"I cannot do this," Rayna admitted. "I am one Kodama. Growing a plant capable of reaching the top, strong enough to hold three people, in minutes—impossible." She hated being negative, but someone here needed to be realistic.

"Now is not the time to give up." Riome looked over her shoulder, and Rayna followed her gaze to the professor and Drew, closing in on their location. "I am not asking you to turn into a tree in your condition because I know you cannot, but I have seen Kodama grow massive plants in minutes."

"Yes, destructive, angry vines, but they are not strong enough to break the stone. They can help us get down, one at a time, but not up. I need something like a mighty oak to lift us and hold us while my vines lower each of us to the ground. I imagine we will need to hurry, scale down quickly without detection. Noting I have in my little pouch can do what you are asking."

Professor Krane caught her eyes, and the corner of his mouth twitched as his concerned look studied her moody demeanor.

"I noticed you have variegated philodendron known as White Princess." Rayna motioned to the garden and a specimen she recognized by the splotches of white, which made her smile at the thought it looked like a painter had spilled paint on them to give them a unique look.

He perked up at her words and motioned around the next row. "Great find. I did not see that plant in my initial review." He smiled and gestured down the row. "I have a Silver Glove and a Pink Lady from the same family. I also have three varieties of Tarin Stalk." He opened a small journal and took notes while everyone studied the plants.

"This is a Blue Harmony rose and a Lemon Vine," she said, pointing at the following species. "I know they are not rare plants, but they are beautiful, and both have medicinal qualities. There should be a companion plant for these, like Rose Weed or Mint Clover. They help with the taste and smell. I did not see either plant, but you should acquire both."

Krane nodded in agreement. "The plants dumped into this garden make no sense unless they are leftovers from other gardens around the city. Maybe I can find the missing plants and bring them together. I hope to visit the other locations in the following days."

Moving along the wall, they continued around the various gardens as Rayna and the professor pointed out more plants. "Variegated Pink Pinnacle and Copper Blaze," Rayna said, letting her hand graze the edges of both. "These are not wise plants to have here. Both are invasive species that rob nutrients from the soil, not to mention their size will overshadow your smaller Pricynthia growing underneath."

Krane stepped around Drew and motioned to a few plants, drawing Rayna's attention. "Right now, I am waiting for these precious flowers to bloom." He looked at her with hope-filled eyes.

"Dear me!" Rayna paused over a grouping of four plants. "I saw this plant in a book once. The size of the leaves and the depth of green, tell me, are they a Tall Bearded Iris? What color?" Part of her wanted to touch the plants; they would speak to her bloom under her magic, but she also liked the waiting, the surprise of their bloom.

"I wish I knew, but the garden society kept poor journals that do not mention every plant. Most of the details are either missing or too faded to read. They may be a pristine white adorned with purple-blue stitches on its delicate ruffled edges or a smoky yellow with a violet center and a dusting of brown. Both plants were listed, but there are no plant locations or dates. You are welcome to visit with me each day until they bloom."

"You do know your plants, sister," Riome marveled, taking Rayna's hand and leading her away down the gravel path, closer to the edge of the garden near the tower. "You must try," Riome whispered. "Plants are capable of growing on rocks with little soil, and can break stone."

She calmed her breathing. "Trying is not my issue. Under ideal conditions, fulfilling the request would be easy, even doing it on my own. But this is not ideal. Speed and stealth matter—not to mention the lack of water, the massive stone tiles, the guards, and everyone in the city. When my tree scales the tower, everyone will see it." Her tone rose a little with her pounding heart.

Riome gave her a look but said nothing. She did not have to tell her that everyone, especially Amelia, counted on her, so she pulled herself together. Fingering the various seeds in her pocket, each responded to her touch; she knew their potential. Most were thorny vines, quicksilver thatch, corkscrew vines, and medicinal plants. One seed sang under her touch, belonging to a black hickory tree, the only seed she had from the rare plant, but there was no other choice.

Deciding on a strategy, she pulled two seeds: a corkscrew vine and the black hickory from her pocket and dropped them into the rich soil along the garden's edge. The vine seed sprouted with the slightest bit of her magic. The green vine wrapped around the black hickory and forced it underground. Acting as a conduit, Rayna pulled energy from the world around her. The magic within her crystal urged the corkscrew to burrow through the rocky soil under the stone pavers.

The distance between her and the tower looked impossible. She needed a greater connection to nature. Wanting to extend her reach, she slipped out of her shoes and pressed her toes into the soil. It felt moist and welcoming. With her eyes fixed on the professor and Drew strolling two rows away, she let her magic flow deep underground. Her mind gleaned the viny tendrils as they searched for any crack or crevice they could exploit and reach the sun.

Meanwhile, Rayna urged the vine carrying her precious black hickory seed to worm through the soil, delivering it to the midway point beneath the stone. In her mind, they were fifteen feet out and a foot below the stone slabs surrounding the tower. The black hickory seed was not particularly big, but the tree itself was massive, and the roots were strong. The sun above glared down on Rayna's head, causing her to sweat. The more she worked, the hotter she felt.

As the professor came closer, Rayna listened to Krane and Drew discuss the importance of plants, but her mind only half heard his story as the corkscrew vine snaked underground, searching for a weak point in the stone—and to her surprise, there were several close together. Adjusting her corset, she took a breath. The lining of her dress felt hot and restraining, but she continued focusing on growing the root system of the great tree. The unseen parts make them strong but can be every bit as substantial.

Taking magic from the sun felt like drinking from a hot teakettle. The energy came swift and faster than she expected. Her head spun, and tiny stars danced at the edges of her vision. Riome leaned into Rayna and smiled at her. She wanted to stop, but they did not have the luxury of days; tonight, they needed to have a tree tall enough and strong enough to save Amelia. The more magic and power she created to strengthen her plants, the more exhausted she felt. Her free hand drifted to her abdomen and her eyes closed. *Take care, little one. Mommy can do this.* She hoped the excessive magic would not hurt the baby.

As the roots of her seed expanded, she commanded them to grow deep underground and then far and wide; she only allowed a few tendrils to force themselves into the various cracks and weak corners. They heaved and pressed into the stone, trying to do the work of decades in minutes, until the sounds of cracking caught her ears, and she stopped. The professor never stopped talking, but Riome heard the noise. "Shhh, be careful, go slower," Riome warned, squeezing Rayna's hand.

"I need a distraction." Rayna jutted her chin to the end of the row. "Those stones, I need you to knock them over."

Riome edged closer to a haphazardly stacked pile of garden stones. Rayna urged the roots of her plant to continue growing far and wide while slowly forcing themselves skyward. The roots moved deep beneath the ground, and she felt them latch onto the rocky soil. Her mighty black hickory tree pushed against the heavy stone slab.

The faint cracking noise turned into a low rumble and ended in a crashing sound when Riome collapsed into the pile of stones. The crash and Riome's shouts brought the guards, the professor, and Drew to Riome's puddled form on the ground.

"Dear me," she said as she fanned her flushed cheeks. "I only leaned back a little. I never meant to knock them over. I had no idea someone so carelessly stacked them." Riome glanced around Drew as he pulled her onto her feet.

Rayna looked from Riome to the bulge in the stone. The smallest leaf started to unfurl, but she pulled it back down as she slipped into her shoe and ran to her friend's side. "Sister," she said as she dusted the back of Riome's dress. "Your gown is a mess."

Drew put a steadying arm around Riome. "Are you hurt?" He swapped looks with both ladies and looked at the guards eyeing them before returning to their posts.

"I am fine, really, do not fuss." She cut her eyes momentarily at the damage done to the stone slab, and then she quickly turned to Krane, trying to distract the man from Rayna's work. "May I ask why you came to Milnos, of all places, to study rare plants?"

Rayna watched Krane's face droop, and his lips pressed together. "I studied plants at the academy where I met a professor born and raised in high society here in Milnos. He retired years ago, and he encouraged my visit, but I never managed to come before he passed away. I arrived last month to start cataloging everything, finish what he started. So far, I have only managed half of the plants in this section. The neglected garden sat for years without a gardener. I found root rot from standing water, a bug infestation . . ." he started to explain, waving his hands like an enthusiastic child.

With the professor distracted, Rayna strolled over to the broken bits of stone. Even though her plant had receded, the damage was rather noticeable.

"Staring at it will not fix the cracks," Drew whispered over her shoulder.

"I know." She continued to stare, wishing a Stoneking could come along and hide what she had done. "I did not mean to make it so large, but my magic is a little out of control today. The best we can do is press the gravel bits back into the hole. Come tomorrow, we will be gone, and there will be a giant tree standing next to the tower. Stand here with me while I offer the remainder of my power to the roots. They can continue to grow fat for tonight."

A breeze kissed her cheeks, and Rayna pulled for the energy it offered. Forcing as much magic as she dared into the black hickory roots, she watched them grow thick. She could feel the tree's desire to punch skyward, but she asked the plant to store the magic. *Keep it safe until it is time to grow.* She pulled energy from the sun and pushed into the soil with her mind through the cracks beneath her feet. Again, the heat flushed her skin, and stars crept into her vision.

She did not remember falling, only Drew's arms around her as she swooned from the effort. His quick reflexes kept her from the ground. "Rosette!" he shouted with enough presence of mind to use their aliases. "Sheerin, come quick."

"Dear sister!" Riome dashed away from the professor's side. "Your cheeks, you are burning up. Professor, please excuse us. We should get our sister home. The heat is too much for her. Besides, we have dinner with the General," she suggested. "Again, thank you for your kindness. We are here under the General's allowance, and I dare say we will not remain long in the city."

Rayna tried to smile as she patted the professor's hand. "I am sorry our visit must end so abruptly," she lied, knowing she never wanted to come back to this terrifying city.

Disappointment washed over the professor. "I see." He nodded and extended a hand to Drew. "It was a pleasure meeting each of you. I will be here for the following year to see all the seasons of these plants should you change your mind."

Rayna offered a smile as Drew escorted them to the gate, but she felt sorry that they had deceived such a kind old man into believing they were interested in his plants; she offered one last wave as he started to close the gate behind them.

◆ ◆ ◆

Midnight came too soon. Rayna felt rested, but the pressure of everything hinging on her felt unbearable. Could she really grow a massive tree alone in an instant? Her doubts nipped at the edges of her faith, forcing her shoulders to curl around her. Drew squeezed her shoulder; his eyes spoke volumes. He believed in her. She let the corner of her mouth curve upward to accept his unspoken confidence.

Above them on the roof, she gleaned Riome perched on the corner of the building, watching the changing of the guard. The spy glowed with an unusual brightness for a Half-Light, but then Rayna knew her unique blessing from Alenga changed her in ways none of them thought possible. Although Kai told her about that night, she wondered why the magic aged her instead of corrupting her as it had Nola. When her friend scaled the downspout and slipped between her and Drew, Rayna held her breath.

"It is time," Riome announced, then she darted into the night.

Dressed in black, they slipped down the street toward the Raven's Tower, avoiding the occasional shower of light from the lampposts on the street corners. The tower's dark, ominous form loomed in the distance creating a void of nothingness, ready to devour them all as they neared. Their quick Katori pace left Drew at times struggling to keep up, but they never slowed until they reached the cross street below the tower.

Drew clasped his hands together, and Riome stepped into his grasp. She leaped as he rose, and he tossed her over the ten-foot wall into the arms of the enemy. There was no sound, not even a thud to indicate that Riome had landed on the other side—only silence. Rayna gleaned the courtyard, and she saw Riome prick the first two guards with her poisoned needles. The spy's sparkling essence darted through the gardens around the far side of the tower. Her form was graceful and precise as she moved through the night and took out the remaining four guards.

The gate creaked open, and Riome motioned them inside. The click of her locking the gate gave Rayna chills. Every noise sounded loud and ominous. She did not feel ready, but this was not the time to back out or let doubt cloud her abilities. At the top of the tower, she saw Amelia's sleeping form and the baby within her belly curled in unknowing splendor. The sight of them both gave her strength as she marched to the cracked stone over her awaiting tree.

Millions of stars twinkled in contrast to the pitch-black sky above. Their magic rained down on Rayna with a warmth she had never noticed before. All energy now carried a heat that she did not recall . . . *before the baby*, she realized. The warm breeze wrapped around her as her mind offered more energy to the tree, ready to explode above the surface. "Can I start?" she knelt, placing her hands over the zigzag cracks in the stone.

Riome paused, and they all listened to the silence. "Yes, but go slow," she cautioned. "We do not want to draw attention to our location. We must wait for Dresnor and Ryker's attack on the weapons facility. They must sabotage the factory and destroy the black powder," she reminded.

"I am not sure slow is going to be an option," Rayna suggested. "There is so much magic pressed into this small space. I am afraid once it starts, it will take on a life of its own. I will not be able to stop it—and I am not sure I *should* stop it if we hope to reach the top of the tower. The roots grew all day with the power I left behind, and now they are massive, twice the size of a full-grown tree. I started feeding it again the moment we arrived. It is the only way I could do this alone."

To her relief, an explosion rang in the distance. It must have been Ryker's attack on the weapons factory, so she pushed her magic into the ground. "Get back!" she shouted only seconds before the tree erupted through the stone, shoving her backward. She skidded on her heels as her hands pressed into the tree trunk. The force cracked the stone slabs and shattered them like brittle crackers. The black hickory expanded in a cloud of dirt and debris with a thunderous vibration that shook the air.

The rapid growth surprised everyone, especially Drew. He rushed to Rayna's side. "My word! If I had not seen this with my own eyes, I would not have believed this possible. Are you alright?"

Sweat glistened around her hairline, and the breeze gave her a chill. "I am fine," she answered, but her unsure tone left Drew's gaze watching her every move. "We need the corkscrew vine," she called to the plant now wrapped around the top of the black hickory tree. Heeding her call, it slithered snake-like down the tree to Rayna's outstretched hand.

No sooner did the vine wrap around her wrist than she heard Professor Krane. "Lady Rosette, what is the meaning . . ." He stopped when he caught sight of the massive tree that was not there earlier. "Did you grow . . . how did you?" he stuttered, and she saw his confused eyes unable to process the full-grown tree the height of the Raven's Tower.

Rayna's heart sank in fear for her would-be friend. "Oh, please, Professor, you should not be here. We are here to save our friend." Rayna tried to explain, pointing up.

"We do not have time, Professor." Riome dashed to his side and took the older gentleman's hand in hers. "You must leave this place. I will not hurt you, but if I must . . ." She did not finish her statement; she simply motioned to the downed guards.

"There are at least a dozen guards in the tower," the professor stated.

"Leave, professor!" Drew ordered, already pushing the man toward the gate and then forcing him outside.

"We all need to get to the top," Riome ordered. "There is no time to lose. We must reach Amelia before the guards take her deeper into the tower. We do not have the time for a standoff."

A second explosion sounded in the distance. Again, Rayna could only imagine that Dresnor and Ryker were behind the blasts, and she could only hope they escaped without injury. As Rayna's vines pulled the three of them up the tree beside the Raven's Tower. Rayna was the first to jump to the balcony, followed by Riome and Drew. Before they burst into Amelia's chamber, her balcony door swung open, and Amelia screamed at the sight of them and then burst into tears. "Rayna, Drew!" Is it really you?" She ran and wrapped her arms around them.

Riome reined in their reunion. "We have no time for pleasantries, Amelia. Fires blaze in the distance, distracting the city to our rescue, but we did not go unnoticed. The guards are aware of the tree. Before I jumped to the balcony, I thought I saw movement on the ground. It will not take them long to discover us up here. They are coming."

The sound of keys jingled at the door as a guard stormed in, sword drawn. "Stop!" he shouted, reaching for Amelia. "My Lady," he motioned to her to join him.

Amelia raised her hands, urging the guard back. "They are friends, people I trust, come to save me. Please, you helped me once. Now let me go," she pleaded.

The guard's sword weaved between Riome and Drew. Rayna imagined he determined them to be the more significant threats. "Please, sir," Rayna said calmly, "you obviously care what happens to her. Let us save her and the baby. Let her go, and I promise we will take care of them both."

The man's dark eyes softened, and he lowered his blade. "Take care of your baby, Lady Amelia." He stepped back to the door. "Come back to Milnos and be our queen if you have a mind to save our city. The people will listen if you give them a chance. Not everyone hates Diu—or you—for marrying Tolan. Maxwell and the high lords do not speak for all Milnosians, nor does the fake king. We did not pick Landon. The lords of the land forced him on us. Money and politics run this city, and a few with power now question our leadership and this coming war."

"Thank you," Amelia said genuinely. "I may consider it if we live to return. Now that I am no longer your prisoner, may I know your name?"

"My name is Christopher, my lady. And I was only ever following orders. I never—"

"We are trapped," Riome interrupted. "They set the tree ablaze. There is no way we are going back down the way we came. Which leaves fighting our way down inside the tower."

Rayna rushed to her precious tree—the last of its kind. Halfway up the tree, she spotted the flaming arrows piercing the trunk and spreading fire. The lower branches burned, and flames licked up the bark at a furious pace. Touching a nearby branch, she spoke to the tree. Her magic seeped into the limb, and she felt its pain. *I am sorry, but I need one last thing.* She begged it to offer her the last of its power.

Smoke swirled around the treetop, causing Rayna to cough; still, she did not let go of the tree. Tears ran down her cheeks and she prayed to Alenga. Several pods puffed amongst the green leaves. As the nuts reached maturity, she started plucking as many as she could and stuffed them into her pouch.

"Time to go." Drew pulled her from the balcony's edge. "We have no time for this. I can hear them coming up the stairwell. We have minutes left. Even with the guard's help, we are four against many."

"You do not understand," Rayna shouted. She pushed Drew back and grabbed hold of the tree, draining the burning tree of that last of its energy before she darted through Amelia's chamber into the stone foyer. "Stand back," she ordered, plucking a seedpod from her pouch.

The sounds of men rushing their position echoed up the stairwell. Holding the pod in her hands, she eased a tiny bit of magic into the seed. Roots and branches spouted, and she urged it to form a small ball that grew to the size of her head before she tossed down the steps and grabbed another pod.

"No offense," Christopher said to Rayna, "but I am not sure those little things will do much to hold back those guards."

Shouts of men in pain echoed back up the stairs, and Rayna glanced back at the guard. "You were saying?" She tossed a second root ball. "The magic is delayed. I can see when the pods reach the guards. Only then do I release the power to expand the tree. They will hack through eventually, but it gives us time to find another way out of here." She tossed a third before turning to Riome.

Riome pointed to a ladder on the wall. "Where does that lead?" she asked. "Are there other guards up top?"

Christopher shook his head and led the way. The view from atop the battlement offered a panoramic view of the city. In the distance, smoke and fire roared into the night sky. "Any ideas?" she asked Riome, who was also circling the tower searching for a way down.

Drew pointed to her pouch. "What about the rest of your seeds?"

"I only have a few black hickory pods left, and they need soil to grow large enough to help us reach the ground. Same with my vines, they need soil. I can get them to grow, but they will not be strong enough to hold our weight—or travel the distance to the ground. Not sure I could even get one of us safely to the bottom."

"Christopher," Amelia said, "you love Milnos. I cannot make you choose to fight for me over your home. You must climb back down. When the others get through, and they will, you must help them."

"I will not let them hurt you," he refused. "I am no monster. I do not kill women and children."

Riome stayed the guard's hand. "Let me help you make your decision." She motioned him away from the others. "If you want to help Amelia, remain her ally here. If she can return, you may be of use to her future. I can offer you a convincing alibi if you do not mind a fierce headache and a bruised face." She directed him back down the ladder.

When she returned alone, Rayna imagined the spy drugged him as she had the other guards and left him passed out on the stone floor with a few punches to the face for good measure.

"May I?" Rayna motioned to the closed trap door.

The others stepped back, and she placed one of the hickory pods in the center. She closed her eyes, exhausted from the magic that she had already expended—she feared for her little one. Giving the last of the energy from the hickory tree, she instructed the pod to grow. She felt the roots punch into the wooden door and into the surrounding stone. It grew in every direction, roots, limbs, branches, but no leaves. There was simply not enough life to make the tree live and prosper. She felt terrible for wasting another seed, but it seemed like her only choice at this point. *I wish Kai were here*, she thought, wishing that she could fly like him for the first time.

CHAPTER 22

A City on Fire

Kai kept a quick pace, each anxious step bringing him closer to the outside world and his freedom. Exiting the dungeon from that point on was relatively easy. Pickpockets and drunks scurried behind Andrew and Kai and Tolan. The fearful guards ran without looking back. "Dragon—dragon—dragon!" they shouted as Kai and his group followed at a safe distance.

Outside, the air smelled sweet and clean. The wild breeze caught Kai in the face with a whiff of smoke. Men ran in every direction across the courtyard. "Hurry, the armory is on fire!" one man shouted while another cried, "Fire in the Raven's Tower!"

The news set Kai to panic. "Rayna and Riome went to rescue Amelia from the Raven's Tower. We must help them." He reached for nature. Magic poured into him, refreshing his energy. Up in the dark sky, he spotted her—his mother—the Lioness.

The Lioness was easy to see flying above—her fiery body shown like a beacon against the dark sky. Her fierce wings twisted, angling her into a dive straight for them. No longer in possession of his mother's crystal, he used his own in an attempt to connect with her. His magic flowed out from his Beastmaster mind, reaching for his mother. *Remember who you are. Come back to me. Fight Keegan.*

Mariana's mind roared in anger back at him. Swooping through the air, she landed with a thud and Keegan slipped from her back and approached. The Lioness stomped a fiery paw, and the ground sizzled. "You must tell me. How you did it?" Keegan demanded, grabbing for Kai. "You broke my control, and I need to know how."

Tolan raised his sword and attempted to run Keegan through, but Keegan blocked the strike and took hold of the young man's neck. He studied his face. "Tell me, or I will kill your one-eyed friend. He has no idea the power I wield, or he would never be so foolish. He looks familiar, a filthy, younger version of Admiral Roark. Could this be his son? I have always had a keen eye and sense of connections, and I can see he means something to you."

"Heal him," Kai said, pointing to Tolan's missing eye. "I know you can restore him."

"You ask too much, boy." Keegan refused as Tolan squirmed, trapped under his grasp. "Bringing back his eye will take too much from me, and he is not worth anything to me."

"Are you sure?" Kai goaded him. "Not worth the secret I hold? When my mother turns on you and kills you, will it be worth it then? Heal my friend, and the secret is yours." Kai knew the risk was significant, but he also knew his mother would understand—she *must* understand.

Still holding Tolan's neck, Keegan pressed his other hand over the missing eye. The glow was subtle at first, then it brightened, and Tolan screamed in pain. The cavity burst with light as the new eye formed. Tolan's hands clasped around Keegan's, holding on for dear life. Kai saw the magic pour into Tolan in a wild gush as his body convulsed and he screamed again. His father's upper body shook out of control. The palpable flow of magic danced around Kai as he witnessed the chaotic overflow of magic bloom around Keegan.

The desperate sounds sent Andrew into a frenzy. "Let him go!" he shouted, "Let my friend go." Andrew latched onto Keegan's arm. The three wrestled, and Kai watched in amazement as Andrew's muscles plumped and his eyes and face regained their youthfulness.

"Let go of me, you fool!" Keegan shouted, shoving Tolan and Andrew to the side. "This idiot could have drained me." He reached for Andrew but stumbled, landing on one knee, holding his chest.

The grassy area surrounding his father wilted and turned black. The leaves on a nearby sapling withered and fell away as the tree shriveled crumbled to dried bits. Partially rejuvenated, Keegan shook and glared back at Andrew. "Give it back! The energy you took, give it back," he demanded, attempting to stand.

"No!" Kai shouted, taking hold of Keegan and pulling him the rest of the way to his feet. "Borrow from nature like the rest of us. Leave him be, or I will order my mother to attack you." Kai shoved Keegan away and moved toward the Lioness. Raising his hand to her, he listened to her Beastmaster mind mumble, and he studied her body language before leaning in close. He hoped in Keegan's weakened state she might be more receptive.

She approached. Heat poured off her in waves, and Kai reached out with his mind. *Search for the hope within, Mother. Your strength and your kindness are all we have left. Everything depends on you remembering who you are.* His mother shook her head and pounced with both feet, huffing at Kai. The glow in her eyes waned, and he felt her emotions swell. The wave struck him in the chest and an idea formulated in his mind. *Please forgive me, Mother, but I must ask a great sacrifice. This is almost over,* he promised.

In a show of faith, the Lioness approached. Magic surrounded her essence, raising the hair on Kai's arms and neck. As she came closer, he felt heat roll off her like a furnace. Hoping to connect with her yet still afraid, he hovered his hand near her head. She nuzzled him with her nose and slid her head under his hand, and her audible purr lifted Kai's spirits. Her fur cooled under his touch and he smiled at her. *You are in control, Mother. Good.* Behind the Lioness, Mariana lingered in the periphery, waiting and willing. Keegan was losing his control over her.

"What do you hope to gain, boy?" Keegan stepped away from another tree he drained, leaving a dried barren husk. "If you hoped to stop Milnos, you are a little late. They want this war more than I do. Their army set out for Diu three days ago. In two days, they will be at the northern gates of Diu. Let me guess. Your friends are behind the explosions around the city. Destroying my black powder now is irrelevant. The blacksmiths had nearly two weeks to make arrows, blades, and such. I had no idea one city needed so many forges. My ships brought the powder here while you stood on the shores of Kahoma. You cannot win."

Kai's heart sank. His father was so far ahead; he did not stand a chance. Milnos was already on the move even before his father had even arrived. Although the news shocked him, he did not let it show as he stroked the Lioness, soothing her violent nature. "Maybe you are right, but I will not stop trying." Kai turned toward his father, noticing Keegan's next long drag on nature. He followed suit, bolstering his own resources. "Let my friends and I go, and I will give you the secret to controlling my mother." He hoped his father's weakened state would buy them time to get away and make a new plan.

"I will never give up, we have that in common—I will hunt you," Keegan promised. "I will come for you and Diu. Any chance of being my equal ends here, tonight. This is the last time I offer. Tell me how you control the Lioness, and I will let your friends go." Keegan reached for the Lioness, and she let a low growl slip through her jaws.

The risks were beyond horrific if Kai was wrong, but he had few choices left. "My answer is still no." He gulped down the guilt stuck in his throat and offered his mother's life in exchange for time and the possibility she was stronger than his father. "Her necklace is here in Milnos. I used it in Diu, and again last night at the event. She will never be yours if I wear it." Giving away the knowledge that Mariana could be controlled with her crystal was risky, but Kai believed the magic could flow in reverse, allowing his mother to influence Keegan. "Even now, our connection remains. You must find Maxwell. He took her necklace before you grabbed me. Retrieve her crystal, wear it, and I will lose my connection. My mother will be all yours without hesitation."

Keegan stepped in close and glared at Kai, searching him for validation. Kai remained stoic, continuing as his father stepped closer.

"Getting through to her was so much easier in Diu. I am guessing you placed the dark crystal on her to strengthen your control. But her necklace is stronger than yours—I am stronger. That is how I beat you. That is how I will always beat you." Kai let his hand slip from the Lioness. *Trust me, mother. Go with him.*

"This better not be a trick, boy." Keegan whipped his head around to study Kai's expression. "Bold words considering you have lost everything, but I believe you. Although I am surprised you are willing to sacrifice your mother for a few more hours of freedom. Once I find Maxwell, I will come for you next." He hopped onto the Lioness and flew away into the darkness.

"The creature, the Lioness," Tolan said, jutting his chin to her fading form. "She is important to you, and she is like you, a person behind the beast—your mother?" His statement felt like a question, but it was easy to see Tolan understood and did not judge him.

"She is my mother," Kai acknowledged, "and I just handed Keegan the one thing capable of controlling her, her necklace. I can only hope she is stronger than he is, or we are all lost. We must get back to Diu before it is too late. I can fly the distance in two days, but we must find the others first. I am the only one who can stop my mother. The only thing we can do now is pray reinforcements reach Diu in time. Give me a moment, I must search for Rayna."

Letting his body relax as much as it could, Kai closed his eyes, took a deep, cleansing breath, and focused on his feelings for Rayna. His mind searched for her around the city like a detached spirit searching for a home. His magic collected like stardust in the sky and shot across Milnos with a single thought—*I am coming, Rayna!* He waited for a response. He saw her hands pressed against a vine woven cage with fire lighting up the night sky behind her.

Please hurry! she pleaded in return.

"Rayna is still at the Raven's Tower." Kai glanced at Tolan and then Andrew. "To reach her and Amelia, we must fly over the city. Do not be afraid. Once I transform, I will not be able to talk to you, but I promise I will not hurt you."

Tolan touched his face around his restored eye. "How can I ever thank you?" His friend's overwhelmed emotions brought tears to the brink. "I am ready when you are. I trust you—always have."

Contradictory to Tolan's excitement, Andrew stepped back, terrified. "I should stay here. I do not deserve to be free." His cousin inspected his renewed strength and marveled at the magical changes. "I betrayed you. I am no longer the man I was. The nightmares in my head confuse me. I do not trust myself, and I want no part of any war."

Kai placed a hand on Andrew's shoulder. "We do not leave family behind. You do not have to fight, but your brother, Adrian, would hate me if I did not bring you home. I do not have time to convince you. Trust me. Now step back and hold on!"

Knowing there was no more time to waste, Kai connected to his crystal and accessed his magic as he gave one last look around the courtyard outside the prison. Most of the guards were gone, and those that remained scrambled to collect escaping prisoners. His swift transformation garnered screams and shouts, but they did not attack. Tolan and Andrew scurried up his extended wing and he took flight.

Along the horizon, he saw two fires at opposite ends of the city. The larger he assumed was the armory, but he focused instead on the Raven's Tower. The behemoth silhouette of the tower cut into the night sky with a blazing tree near its equal. Thoughts of Rayna burning in her tree brought back terrifying images. His wings beat faster as he soared toward the tower. Flaming torches flicked against the night sky across their fortified walls. Tiny lights sprang to life around the dark city battlements. He knew he didn't have much time left if he hoped to save Rayna. He flew so quickly and so single-mindedly that he almost missed the dragon-killer weapon notching into position to aim at him from the fortress walls.

Folding his wings inward, he dropped like a rock. The bolt flew high, missing his head. With a few pumps of his wings, he was back above the fortress and circling into the sky. His amber eyes scanned the surrounding battlements for others ready to attack. There were three more. Torches illuminated various points along the walls, and he caught sight of two groups of men—archers. They shouted something he could not hear. He could not be sure, but he could only imagine the guards aimed black steel arrows at his silvery form.

Kai wanted to remind Tolan and Andrew to hold tight, but he had no way to speak to them. As he reached the Raven's Tower, he spotted a giant ball of bark with dozens of men hacking away at the cluster of vines. As they broke through one section, new vegetation grew in its place. Kai gleaned inside. Four figures huddled within, but one beamed brighter than he thought possible—Rayna. He pivoted to avoid another bolt aimed at his belly and felt Tolan and Andrew shift, but they held fast. Circling back to the tower, he dove low into the streets to prevent the guards from seeing his approach. His wings scraped the buildings on either side. Citizens ran in fear.

As he reached the block with the tower in front of him, the scope of Rayna's tree next to the massive battlement came into full view. Flames consumed the beautiful black tree, and his heart went out to her knowing it pained her to create something so beautiful only to have it destroyed. Raising into view, he spotted the archers, and they were ready. They loosed their arsenal, and this time Kai pivoted but did not divert his approach.

A dozen arrows pierced his dragon scales and lodged into his wing and belly. Still, he focused on his target, leveling before swooping down and latching onto the giant vine pod with his claws. Eager to put distance between himself and the enemy, he flew straight up into the clouds. Each beat of his left wing stung, and his belly ached from the arrows lodged into his scales. His eyes cut to the second blaze glowing against the night sky, wondering if Ryker and Dresnor needed his help too.

The forest outside Milnos swallowed his silver dragon in darkness. After he lowered the vine ball containing his wife and friends, he landed in the small clearing. The root ball broke open, and Rayna emerged. Her hands reached for his massive head, and he glanced at his outstretched wing. She tamped the air with her hands. And he knew she understood.

"Poisoned?" she asked.

Thankfully everything felt alright, and he shook his head no; everyone began to remove the arrows. The jagged points ripped with each yank, and more blood gushed to the ground. While Rayna healed the wounds, he felt the warmth of her magic. His amber eyes cut to her; his dragon nose perked at her sweet scent—honey. Even without trying, he felt her presence, and she pulsed with power. There was something new about her he could not put his finger on until he gleaned her form. Her glow swirled in an unnatural swooshing motion, making him focus until he noticed a tiny radiance in her belly. His heart swelled in a whirlwind of emotions.

Anxious to feel her in his arms, he transformed back into his natural body. His eyes drank her in, and he pulled her close. There were no words between them; they were not necessary. Kai felt as though he were the happiest man in the world. If only he could stay in this moment forever. Rayna spoke first. "I wanted to tell you," she admitted, "but everything happened. . ."

He felt her tears soak into his shirt. He stroked her hair, holding her tight against his chest. "I should have known, but Keegan and the Guardians took me away from you, and I lost focus on what mattered. I love you for being strong enough to follow me. You are more than I deserve." He let her step back, and he touched her belly, noticing the little bump that fit in the palm of his hand.

Rejoining the others, Kai saw Tolan and Amelia standing lost in each other. Tears, hugs, and Amelia's large belly consumed their moment, and Kai felt happy they were reunited. Wanting another moment alone, he gestured to the others that they would be right back. A few steps later, they stopped. A dark shadow darted through the trees. There was no noise, but the silver eyes of a black Shuk glared at Kai, and he knew. "Ryker, you made it. Where is Dresnor?"

A large bundle dropped in the grass and then another before Dresnor hopped down from the Shuk. "We stole all we could manage." Dresnor knelt and unwrapped the tarp. "Two dozen blades. Not much, but better than nothing."

Drew darted through the trees around Kai to inspect the weapons. "How did you manage to get here so quickly? We heard the explosions, but I assumed we would not see you here until morning," Drew motioned to the prearranged spot they selected before going to Milnos. "Kai brought us here, but there is no way you covered that distance with . . ." He started to motion to Ryker, still in beast form, but lost his words.

Ryker transformed and stared at Kai; then he glared around the camp without saying a word.

Dresnor continued his story. "We managed to learn where they stored the black powder Keegan brought and where they made the weapons. We did not find the Katoris hiding place or where the weapons went after, but there is no more powder. Oh, the stories a man will tell under the influence of ale. I thought I had a strong constitution, but Ryker might not even be capable of getting drunk. Anyway, he learned they have Arkin oil in the city. And I actually convinced two workers to deliver two barrels each to the weapons facility instructing them to mix it with the black powder and hot steel. They had no idea what either substance was; I simply convinced him it would increase their durability in a fight."

"Where is she?" Ryker blurted out. "Where is Mariana? She should be here. You had one mission: to save your mother. Why is she not here? You promised using her necklace you could turn her, bring her back to us. Clearly, you failed."

Kai's guilt hung on him like a wet blanket. "I lost her crystal when Maxwell captured me," he admitted. "There is no way I could get it back, so I told Keegan where to look. He is the only person who can get close enough to Maxwell to take it. We must return to Diu and hope we can save the city—if there is anything left. The Milnosian army left days ago, and unless we leave now, we will not get there first."

The anger in Ryker's eyes bordered on rage. He stepped in close to Kai, leaving little room to breathe. "I have nothing to go back to without Mariana. We only came here for her—that was your idea, and you failed. You are as cunning as anyone I know; you could have tried to get the necklace back." He puffed his chest and narrowed the gap between them.

"I had no choice," Kai countered. "Luedke claims King Landon has warships capable of transporting thousands through the air and over the mountains. After they attack Diu, they are going over the Katori mountains to our home. They will not stop until they slaughter every dragon—and Milnos or Keegan rule whatever is left. I cannot waste time searching the city, hoping to find it while this new wave of soldiers crushes Diu."

Ryker's eyes burned holes through Kai's soul. "No," he thundered. "There is always a choice; those are your own words, if I recall correctly. How could you give her away like an unwanted plaything? She is your mother. We must save Mariana. She is here in Milnos, so there is still a chance. I stopped you at the banquet because it was not the right moment, but I assumed you had a plan, a way to call her to you. Instead, you gave away her crystal to the one person your mother fears the most. Tell me it is a mistake, that you can get it back. Get her back!"

There were no words Kai could offer—the crystal was gone. His eyes dropped to the forest floor. All the guilt in the world did not change the fact that he gave away his mother's necklace. Her crystal was his to protect, the only thing possible of stopping Keegan, and he gave it to the enemy. There was no way to undo the deed, but he was unsure he wanted to change his decision.

Putting space between them, Kai took a step back, fighting his own desires to lash out. "Bargaining away the necklace was only a half-truth," he began, wondering how he could explain he felt driven to give it to Keegan. "My mother is stronger than him. She came to me even after I lost her crystal. I know it is a risk, but I think I am right. I need him to think he has the upper hand now that he wears her stone. When did you stop trusting me?"

Kai felt Ryker's spiteful stare turn his blood cold. "You *think* you're right?" Ryker pushed Kai hard in the chest. "We came all this way, and for what? Nothing. Now we turn tail and run because you *think* something different. How do we know your next idea will work? Since when do you give up on your mother? Is this because you are afraid of Keegan?" He pushed Kai again.

"Stop it, both of you," Riome said, stepping between them. "Kai did what he thought was best. Fighting amongst ourselves will not save anyone. Right now, we go to Diu. If we can get ahead of the Milnos army, we will. If we can save Mariana, we will. If we cannot stop this war, we will give our lives, but I will not stand here wasting time. And while I am yelling, who is he?" she pointed to Andrew.

In the chaos, Kai had totally forgotten about his cousin. "Riome, meet King Andrew Cazier. Adrian's older brother was lost at sea and taken prisoner by Milnos. I believe he is the man we have been searching for all these years." He kept her identity secret, not revealing she was Adrian's secret daughter.

Keeping her expression neutral, she looked Andrew over. Kai tried to gauge her concerns and feelings, but she was never an easy read. "We will see you delivered to your brother in Diu. Right now, we are at war. I am sorry, but you must wait to return to your homeland. It will be Master General Cazier's responsibility to take you to Nebea." She nodded and turned back to Kai—waiting.

Everyone looked to Kai, everyone but Ryker; he was nowhere to be found. "Given the number of people and Amelia's condition, the only way for her to travel is in a basket suspended beneath my dragon form. It will be moderately more comfortable than riding a dragon but, more importantly, safer. At some point, we will need to stop, and any who can sleep during the day will keep watch while I rest. Rayna, I know you are tired, but if you could . . ." He could see the weariness in her eyes, and he longed to comfort her.

She leaned into his shoulder. "I can make a basket, something to carry five of us. The other three will need to ride up top." She patted his chest and looked inside her seed pouch.

"I will be back after I find Ryker." Kai walked into the darkness.

Thankful Ryker had not walked far, Kai slipped up beside his friend and stared at the night sky. "I know you are angry with me, but you must trust me. Alenga said I would need my mother's necklace more than her. And she was right—it gave me hope in these past few days more than you can possibly understand, but now I need my mother's hope to feed

Keegan. That is what I believe her crystal can do—transform decades of hate into hope. It is a risk, but my mother is stronger than him. She broke free of him at the banquet on her own. She overcame the dark crystal on her own."

The silence left Kai wondering what else he could say to convince his friend that this was a good idea. But no words came to him. Changing the subject, he announced, "I am going to be a father."

Still, Ryker did not speak. Kai did not need to reach out with his magic to sense his friend was still angry and deserved to be. "We are going back to Diu. Are you coming with us?" Kai waited for a response.

Ryker turned around and faced the way they came, and his eyes hung low. "Congratulations on the baby." Then he walked back to the others with Kai following close behind.

CHAPTER 23

Return to Diu

Night flying was exhilarating when he knew where he was and where he was going, but tonight Kai flew across unfamiliar enemy territory. His instincts, the moon, and stars were his only guides. Knowing his silvery form glistened in the moonlight, he maintained a high altitude and focused on an imaginary target in his mind. His burden went beyond his passengers and his unborn child; he carried the weight of everyone depending on him.

His decision to travel to Milnos had cost him dearly in losing his mother's necklace, and it made the others doubt that he could use the crystal to bring his mother home. Returning to Diu without her and her crystal made him wonder what other mistakes he might make and what it might cost him. Could he be wrong about letting Rayna follow him into war? What if his vision changed again—and now she was at risk?

After hours of flying, dawn peeked above the horizon. With every inch it crawled into the sky, the more Kai worried. It was a constant reminder of time passing faster than him. Time was a precious resource, and he had little left. Milnos marched on Diu somewhere in the distance. Keegan and the Lioness flew somewhere behind him with a new weapon that could counterattack dragons in flight.

Limited by his passengers and the lack of sleep, he flew as fast as reasonably possible, but it did not feel like enough. From his current altitude, he searched for the Milnosian army through patchy pockets between the clouds. Even though the Milnosian army had left several days ahead, they were on foot, and he could fly faster. *I will catch them, eventually*, he thought.

As he flew over the landscape, he looked down at his passengers from time to time. The high altitude left the air thin and cold, which did not bother his dragon skin, but it left the others shivering—the group huddled together for warmth in a bed of green moss in the woven basket. Tolan rested on his back with his wife's head resting on his shoulder. Drew had spent most of the trip speaking with Riome, but Kai noticed they too had given in to sleep. Rayna slept between Amelia and Riome. Her eyes were closed, and her arms were wrapped around Amelia.

The sight of his wife again stirred doubt in all his choices—joining the Guardians, chasing Keegan, following his mother to Milnos, and now returning to Diu to fight a war. Even though he promised Rayna they would always be together, risking her life—and now the life of their unborn child—was a mistake. Losing her and the baby, he realized, was a risk he could not take. Nothing mattered more.

Thoughts of Shane, his childhood friend, came to mind. War and death changed him at an early age. Although his friend did what he did to save Kai, Shane always regretted the outcome. It left a feeling of sorrow in his friend and put an unsurmountable distance between them over the years. And now he understood why Shane made the choice to step away from Diu—and him. Shane wanted a peaceful, simple life with Julia. He had no more appetite for war or adventure.

With very little sleep, Kai did his best to keep a consistent speed, holding the precious basket in his claws and retracing his path back to Diu. To his relief, he spotted Kuro Mountain in the distance, the black mountain sitting at the edge of Diu, Milnos, and Nebea. Reaching Kuro meant the Diu countryside was near, and they were over halfway home. One more day, and he would reach Iver.

Dark storm clouds lingered around the peak, forcing Kai to swing wide to avoid the weather. The detour made him worry he would be too late, and his new path would force him closer to the main road, the one place he did not want to be. They could not afford extra time on the road. Even at his speed, the distance between the city of Milnos and Diu took time. Time they did not have. *Will there be anything left of my home?* He could not help but worry. He had failed to protect his mother, and now he would fail to save the man he considered to be his real father.

We should stop and rest for a few hours. Kai heard Ryker interrupt the thoughts in his head. Although Kai wanted to continue, he knew Ryker was right. Hoping to smooth things between them, Kai did as Ryker suggested and circled the dark clouds toward Kuro Mountain. On the far side, high on the mountain, he spotted a large clearing suitable for their needs. A frosty blanket covered the ground, but the position offered seclusion and security away from Milnosian scouts.

Once they were safely on the ground, he transformed back into his human form. "Anyone sleeping should stay in the basket. It will provide warmth and protection," he said, then stifled a yawn as Rayna took hold of his hand.

Dresnor glanced between Ryker and Kai, noticing their tension. "Kai needs to rest. He is the only one doing any real work. Tolan and Drew, you've had the day to rest. You can take watch. Three hours, I know it is not much, but we all know racing to Diu is our priority."

Ryker's eyes protested, but he said nothing.

Nestled in the corner of the basket, Kai held Rayna; his one hand rested on her abdomen. "I am not sure you should come to Diu," he whispered.

She placed her hand atop his. "We are not having this conversation. You are tired, and I can see the worry and guilt eating at you. Protest after you sleep." She closed her eyes, and he followed suit.

◆ ◆ ◆

Whether it was instinct or training, Kai jolted awake, and his blade flicked at his intruder's neck. Riome's pride beamed as he opened his eyes, her hand outstretched toward Rayna's arm. "There was a time I could sneak up on you. Good to see you are on guard. Time to go." Riome withdrew, and Kai woke Rayna.

The others were awake, preparing for the final leg of their journey. Drew and Dresnor kept watch with one eye on Andrew. Tolan stood whispering with Amelia, and Ryker stood alone; his posture left no doubt the state of his mood. They both looked away, avoiding each other.

Kai kissed Rayna on the forehead. "I only needed a minute. I will be right back."

Kai took a moment to stretch before he turned to go. He watched Rayna collect berries from the vines she planted, offering Amelia something to eat. *I will be right back*—these would be the last words he told her. *Not I love you, not I am sorry—I will be right back.* The lie felt strangely familiar but necessary; he was saving more than just her this time. They would all understand someday; although he might not live to explain, he hoped they knew he left them behind out of love.

Once he was clear of the camp, he took off at a quick pace. Several yards down the mountain, he gleaned another glade, one with an angled outcropping, the perfect place to transform and fly away. His feet crunched through the light dusting of frozen snow. Through the forest, he darted as he drew small amounts of energy, nothing much; he dared not alert the others. He leaped over the small rocks, collecting more power as the clearing came into view.

Connecting to his magic, he searched for the golden braid to create his dragon. The magic within his crystal surged up his spine. The Beastmaster chain spun in his mind and merged with his own. The change felt exhilarating as the scales rippled across his back. His body grew and his wings expanded. As he dove with his wings wide, he completed the transformation into his dragon form. He launched out over the treetops below, and with one beat of his wings, he lifted back in the air.

On his second beat, he felt the thud of four paws land on his backside. At first, the weight was significant, tempting him to roll in flight and dislodge the beast. Then the weight changed, and the four paws became two feet.

Ryker, what are you doing? he spoke through his Beastmaster mind.

Ryker raced up Kai's dragon spine and dove onto his head. The man's legs wrapped around his neck, and his arm hooked around a horn on Kai's head. Ryker's angry face came into view of Kai's amber eye, and then he felt the cold steel press into his cheek. The cut was small, but he felt the blood trickle down his dragon face.

I do not need black steel to hurt or kill a dragon, Ryker spoke to Kai through their Beastmaster magic. *You see, through the eye socket with a long dagger like mine, I can pierce the brain. Land or I will demonstrate.* The cut below Kai's eye left little room for wondering if Ryker was serious, so he complied, circling back toward Kuro Mountain. He kept low and landed at the same spot he left only moments before.

He landed with a thud, and he shook Ryker from his back seconds before transforming. "Are you mad?" Kai thundered in Ryker's direction. "Were you really going to kill me?" He touched the cut on his face and felt the wet blood on his fingers.

Ryker did not shy away; instead, he rushed Kai, closing the gap between them. His friend's hands latched onto his shirt and thrust him sideways into a tree. "First, you bargain with Mariana's life, and now you toss your family away. I thought you were past running off alone, playing the foolish hero. You have no right to leave any of us behind, not even Rayna. Especially not her. We all followed you because we believe in you, and you abandoned us when things got hard. Mistakes are part of leadership, so learn and move on, but do not make a decision for me or anyone else."

"I am trying to protect all of you, especially Rayna and the baby," Kai growled back. "I can fly much faster without the basket, without passengers."

"Right," he scoffed. "You know full well it would take us three days on foot to reach Diu if we could get anywhere near the city behind the Milnosian army. Leave us here, and we will resort to our own foolishness to save you. It is selfish to leave us. You are trying to protect yourself. Mistakes are a part of life, and there will be more. Yes, I am mad you lost Mariana, but we both know you are no quitter. Even if you fail again, which you might. I will fight beside you, and we will live or die with honor."

The wisdom in Ryker's words cooled his temper. "My father was only twenty-two when he became king of Diu," Kai admitted. "I do not know how he carried the responsibility. He challenged Milnos, restored peace, and maintained it for twenty-three years. I cannot say two more years would see me ready, especially if it means leading people into war. I am not ready to ask people to die."

"You are not asking us to die," Ryker replied. "You are asking us to stand up for what we believe. We each fight for our own reasons: country, honor, loyalty, freedom."

He wanted to believe it was that simple. "I cannot take Rayna into this war. Alenga gave me one happy vision, one in which I see Rayna alive years in the future. Dreams of her happy future or not, maybe she only lives because I leave her here. She was meant to save me in Diu and again in Milnos, but I cannot risk her now that I know about the baby. If we keep going, we are flying to our deaths, either in Diu or Katori. I would rather you live and be angry with me than you die because I made a mistake and cannot stop this war. Because I cannot change my mother back."

"You do not have the right to choose for the others. If I die, and I might, that is my choice, to live standing against Keegan and Milnos. Hiding is not living, running away is not living—fighting for what you believe in, that is living."

It was difficult to argue with the Ryker. Kai would not want his choice taken away. "Would you have killed me if I did not return?" Kai circled back on his original question, glancing down at the dagger on Ryker's hip.

Ryker's raised eyebrow and prolonged contemplation turned Kai's stomach. "I was mad—I am still mad, but I have faith in you and your mother. You are both fighters. Time to go." He motioned back up the hill towards the others.

As they reentered the campsite, Rayna caught sight of Kai. "My word, what in the world happened to your face?" She approached, reaching to heal the gash. "Where did you two go?" She looked to Ryker and back to Kai, searching them both for truth.

The heat of her magic and the kindness in her touch panged his heart. He knew it was not his choice, but he would do anything to keep her safe. "Seems I was not paying attention to where I was going." He cut his eyes at Ryker as his friend joined Dresnor near the basket. "But I do have something to say or rather ask before we leave. If anyone wishes to stay behind, I will understand. I cannot make the choice for you, and I would do anything to save the lives of my dearest friends. Cousin Andrew, you said you wanted no part of war, so if you wish to stay here, I will not make you continue."

Behind the filth and torture, Andrew's green eyes fought to control his demons. "My mind is not the same. The voices in my head say, this is not my war. They also tell me not to trust anyone, but they are wrong. Eden Galloway was my grandmother, and you are my family. Nebea and Diu are cousin countries; we fight for each other. I doubt that changed while I was in prison. I may not be the King I was, but I am wild enough to be the warrior you need. It will be good to see my brother Adrian again. And if I may, I cannot ride any longer in the basket, too much like a prison."

Kai nodded, accepting his cousin's answer. "Tolan, you and Amelia have a baby on the way. I will not blame you for choosing to protect your family."

Amelia nodded to Tolan, and he pulled her close. "If I do not fight, there may be nothing left. Amelia and I spoke while you were flying. We will continue to Diu."

Dresnor held out his hand in protest. "Do not even bother asking either of us." He cocked his head toward Drew. "You know where our loyalty stands. We are going."

Riome rolled her eyes, and he knew better than to consider she would stay behind. Finally, he turned to Rayna, and his heart began to swell. He did not want to leave her behind, but she was his world, and now she carried their future. He opened his mouth, but she spoke first. "I am better with a bow than most. I can fight and keep my distance, but do not even suggest I should stay behind."

With everyone in agreement, they set out to reach Diu. Again he kept a fierce pace, flying as fast as possible while carrying his family and friends. The wind tugged on the basket, shifting his balance if he picked up too much speed. The afternoon clouds plumped beneath them as Kai kept one eye on the road below and the other on the horizon. He knew they would catch up with the Milnosian army marching along the main road at some point.

Around dusk, he caught sight of torches sparking to life. Their lights snaked through the darkening landscape below. Every part of him wanted to storm their position, set them ablaze with his dragon's breath and scatter their ranks. Easing down through the clouds, he spotted Milnosian units. Mounted riders rode five wide and countless deep, and archers with both longbows and crossbows were preceded by an endless supply of warriors armed to the teeth with various weaponry. Among the siege weapons were dozens of wagons filled with crates, and he could only imagine their cargo: knuckle-blades, arrows, and swords, all made of the dark metal. Through a parting cloud, the moonlight glimmered off a dragon-killer crossbow, and the men perched alongside aimed at the skies. They may not be watching for him, but they were ready to shoot anything that came close.

Rage bubbled in his throat; they were going to kill everyone he loved. Not even the dark blades he saw from that great height stopped his desire to burn them where they marched, but he did not attack. It was the basket gripped within his claws, which carried the most precious thing in all his world, that kept him from doing anything foolish. He flew back above the clouds, blocked by the haze of gray; he pushed the limits of his wings.

The intensified drag on the basket altered his angle, pulling hard on his grasp. He heard a commotion below, but he did not stop—*anything to reach Diu before the enemy*, he thought, struggling to keep his balance. Along his back, he felt his riders settle against his spine and duck behind his spikes as his head lowered, straining to stay aloft. With each beat of his wings, he dropped until the basket sank into the clouds. While they made progress, he was losing altitude.

Slow down, Kai. You are flying too fast, and the basket is pulling you down, Ryker spoke to his mind.

Kai knew Ryker was right, but his mind raced through the possibilities. If he did not get to Diu in time, his world would crumble under this new military force. *The Milnosians are beneath us*, he responded. *We must beat them to Diu and save Iver. I can do this.* He pumped his wings and pulled them ever so slightly higher while the basket within his claws jerked backward, and he heard vines snapping along the handle.

The weight shifted, and screams rose to his ears. Kai cupped his wings, hoping to slow their progress and resolve the situation, but the basket swung forward like a pendulum, twisting him sideways. The motion rocked his riders, and he felt Ryker, Dresnor, and Andrew slide toward his wing. It was all Kai could do to turn and twist his back before they slipped off the edge. With his riders scampering back into place, he pumped his wings, trying to regain control. The basket's swing slowed, but they were still falling, and the cracking sounds continued.

Sinking through the clouds, Kai thought about the Milnosian army below. They could not afford the enemy seeing them plummet. His head sank beneath the gray, and they were completely exposed. Below them, the torchlight burned a path along the main road. Angling his wings, he directed them south, away from the marching warriors. His talons gripped the woody vines trying not to break the handle when he felt new vines twist through his grasp.

Below him, the basket began to morph. He felt Rayna's magic and saw her crystal glow. Under her influence, she changed the shape of the basket into that of an angled bird. The sides grew sloped wings, the front edge of the basket transformed into a pointed beak, and unwanted bits fell off. Kai flapped his wings, twisting the new creation to match his climb. The new design slipped through the air beneath him back up into the clouds. The bird-shaped basket Rayna created from the vines now moved with him. Although the vines wrapped around his claws, his legs were free to move and shift.

Pumping his massive wings, they rose into the dark sky; the moon and stars were a welcome sight as they leveled off. The new basket felt lighter and easier to maneuver. Aiming both himself and the bird forward, he picked up speed. The bird's sleek design slipped through the air like his own dragon wings. The drag of the old bulky basket no longer pulled him backward; the lighter construction floated with little effort. Going faster, he pitched his claws and the little bird shifted with his movements.

Back on course, he flew toward Diu with an ease he found effortless. The landscape rolled and pitched under his chosen path, and within no time, he overtook the enemy below. When Diu came into view, he expected or rather hoped to see the city's twinkling lights; instead, a golden hue lit up the night sky.

Diu is on fire! Kai panicked. His city burned in the night, and there was no sign of rain. His next worry consumed thought clawed at his heart. *Had Yulia fallen in battle? Why was she not making any storms to quench the flames?*

Although seeing Diu still standing gave Kai hope, he flew faster, anxious to close the gap and discover what happened. Nearing the city, he could barely see the far side of the outer walls which now appeared to be consumed by thick, angry flames. As he flew closer, he saw a new line of walls made of different rock and debris coursed through the center of Rim Town. *Have Liam and Tenoch built new walls around the damaged section?* He had no idea, but he hoped this was a good sign.

Angled toward the city, Kai caught sight of the shadow that his dragon form and tandem bird glider created. It was dark and menacing, so when the dragon-killer crossbows aimed, he climbed high and dodged two bolts. Hoping to illuminate his silver dragon body and remind them he was a friend; he shot fireballs into the sky and circled the city again. Two more bolts flew in his direction, each from opposing sides. He angled, and the first shot missed his neck, but the second fired through the vine bird glider and entirely through his wing.

He had no choice but to land—and land fast—or crash, which was not an option. The tear in his wing burned with pain, and he felt the blood trickle down his wing. Turning toward the palace, he adjusted their trajectory. He pumped his wings, but only one side lifted, dropping his right side. The hole through the membrane of his wing fluttered but no longer created lift. They were flying too fast to land safely. He tried again to lift and slow their speed, but the bird's weight and his useless wing left him little control.

Again he tried to correct their course, but this time he felt heat rush into his clawed foot and travel up his leg. The familiar soothing Kodama magic from Rayna poured through his body and out his wing. As his wife's power began to heal his wound, he caught sight of a black shadow shoot into the air. The creature was swift, a dart across the night sky. He pumped his mending wing and leveled out as a black dragon swooped in over his head.

Risky move flying over a city at war in the dead of night, Kai, Simone spoke to his Beastmaster mind. *They will not fire on me,* she suggested flying ahead of Kai.

Simone darted ahead, dive-bombing the dragon-killer crossbows along Kai's path toward the palace located in the center of Diu city. Her dragon fire blossomed into the night sky, not harming the warriors on the walls, and the Diu men ran from their positions. Slowing their speed, Kai pulled back, cupping his wings, and shifting the vine bird to match his change as they dropped into the courtyard. Diu soldiers converged on their location as the bird skidded to a stop, and the vines released his dragon claws.

Ryker, Dresnor, and Andrew jumped to the ground, allowing Kai to transform. Each of them glanced around the swarm of Diu soldiers. Swords and crossbows stood ready to slaughter them all as Simone landed at his side and belched fire in Kai's defense until the soldiers backed away. As the bird cracked open like an egg, his wife emerged, stumbling into his arms. She looked tired, and he knew why. Healing him that fast without touching the wound directly took immense power, and she had expended a lot.

"Are you alright?" he asked, cupping her face.

"I am, or rather I will be." She glanced back as Ryker helped the others exit the broken bird.

"My son, you returned." King Iver's voice boomed into the courtyard as he rushed to grab hold of Kai, his eyes wild, his face covered in blood. "Were you successful? Where is Mariana?" Iver released his son and searched the faces of the others.

Guilt formed a lump in Kai's throat. "I failed, Father. She is not with us, but she is also not far behind. The Milnosian army will be knocking at our gates within a day." Although he did not know where the Lioness was now that he no longer wore her necklace, he knew Keegan would not be far behind.

His father did not chastise or question what happened, and for that, Kai was thankful. "Seems we are still on our own." He patted Kai's shoulder and turned to address the group. "We lost the lower section of the city this morning as the Caroco advanced. We pushed back the enemy by starting a controlled Arkin oil fire along the lower wall. Tenoch held them back while Simon and Haygan dowsed the area with the oil, and Liam took on the last of their Stonekings. Your friend, Tenoch, is alive but severely burned. He is with the healers now. I can only assume if the Milnosians are close, the end, set long before this day, is near."

Kai could not agree more—the end was near. Listening to his father go on about the previous few days left him in awe of how well they managed without him. Simone's arrival certainly helped turn the tide, even if it was a momentary win. Holding his wife's hand, he pulled Iver aside. "I know this is not the time, but I wanted you to know I am going to be a father."

King Iver wrapped his arms around them both. His joy showed on his face when he finally let them go. "Never apologize for a blessing, my son. Besides, we need all the hope we can get. Forgive me for whispering, but is that Amelia and Tolan with you? They have changed so much these past few years. I can hardly recognize them."

"Father, while we were in Milnos, Riome and Rayna rescued Amelia. Her father imprisoned her in a tower after she married Tolan. Tolan spent many months in prison, where he befriended another man—our cousin, King Andrew Cazier, believed to have drowned at sea over twenty years ago."

Iver and Andrew's eyes met. There was a kindred connection Kai saw between them as they approached and hugged. Two long-lost souls reconnected.

CHAPTER 24

Golden Messenger

Unable to sleep another minute, Kai slipped through the secret tunnels to the library. He let his fingertips dance over a few spines when he realized he heard faint music coming from the next room. Interested in who might be playing at this early hour, he slipped into the hidden passageway between the two rooms. The melancholy melody hung like a heavy cloak around Kai's soul.

The latch released and the hidden panel opened without a sound. Illuminated by candlelight, the music room danced to Riome's solemn tune on the piano. He let the melody linger a moment, caught in its sorrow, before he entered.

"I never knew you played the piano," he murmured, intruding upon her solitude. He took in the stack of books on the table, the half-eaten dinner, and the two empty bottles of wine.

"Seems we have come full circle." Riome let her hands slip off the keys and the music fade. "You, using secret passageways, entering rooms you should not in the middle of the night. I remember the evening I found you in the library. Your little adventure helped me find the secret corridors. I never thanked you, although at the time I did not know if I could trust you. I know all too well the secrets children can keep." Taking the final gulp of wine, she tipped her head to him.

He could not imagine how she felt spending her childhood pretending to fit in among the Katori, knowing all their secrets, and then escaping before they knew she was a Half-Light. Unable to live in her mother's country and the only way to fit into her father's world meant she would need to lie there too. They were more alike than he realized. "Feels like a lifetime ago." He stepped closer and leaned into the piano.

"I have lived more in these past few weeks than I ever did before." She stood and grabbed a brown leather journal from the table before collapsing onto the sofa. "Funny thing, life. I never thought I wanted anything more than to be invisible, go where I should not, be anyone I chose—anyone but myself. I steal secrets, trick people, and do the unthinkable for a living. And up until now, I did so guilt-free. Now it seems I want more. The past haunts me, and I am running out of time— literally."

The newest gray streaks in her hair and the lines on her face spoke volumes, but Kai understood how she felt. He spent so much of his life chasing the past and now he worried about the future. He wasted so much time not living in the present. "We both grew up too fast, but those lessons brought us here. I cannot wish away one mistake without wishing away a blessing. While I would love to follow you down that next bottle of wine you are eyeing, I think we need to discuss the selection of books you have decorating this table. Herbs, poisons, and cures—heavy stuff the night before possibly the fight of our lives."

Riome opened her journal and plopped it in Kai's lap. "How would you feel if you had to poison your best friend's mother, possibly kill her? You are the closest person in my life besides my parents. Kai, you are more like a brother than I ever hoped to have, but I do not see another way to stop this."

Kai looked at the compounds listed on one page and the calculations on the other. Riome was planning on poisoning the Lioness. He clapped the journal closed and tossed it back at her. His pulse thundered in his ears, but he looked at her before he spoke. The sadness in her eyes paired with the excessive wine made sense. There was no use being mad; her own guilt was eating her alive.

"If I cannot persuade my mother," Kai said, "then I want to take her and Keegan down peacefully. Can you redo the composition of the potion? Maybe make it less lethal? We need to hit Keegan and my mother at the same time, but I really do not want to kill either of them."

Her eyes raced from book to book, until she plucked one from the pile. "It is risky to guess. I hate guessing, but I will try to dilute the potion, alter a few ingredients. I cannot make promises they will be as effective or guarantee the results with no time to test. Sleeping potions can be more difficult when you do not know the actual weight of the victim. Not enough, and it does nothing. I will consult Sigry and we will do our best." She grabbed another book and started reading.

"I will leave you to your work," he said, then he slipped back out the way he came.

◆ ◆ ◆

Dawn's awakening cracked the horizon as Kai and Rayna stood on top of the Master General's tower. "Have you ever wanted something so much you've forgotten how to move forward? I have made mistakes over the years, and while I hope I have learned a thing or two, any mistake I make today could cost me the life of a friend or family." Kai wrapped his arms around her and held her close.

Rayna patted his hand. "Every time I notch an arrow, I ask myself, what if I miss, what if I am not fast enough. But neither question keeps me from firing. You are not alone today, and none of us expect you to be perfect. When you lead the charge, keep the group together. Fight as a unit just like we practiced."

Kai thought about the plan and their chances. He knew Rayna was right; he was not alone, so he needed to have a little faith. "Riome wanted to poison my mother, but I convinced her to use a sleeping potion instead. Between Sigry and Riome, the potion they are concocting must be enough to drug them and slow them down without killing them."

"I know she is your mother, but it may come down to you making a difficult choice."

Although Rayna did not finish her thought, he knew what she meant. "Do you want to visit your parents before things start?" he asked, changing the subject.

"If I see them, my mother will know I am pregnant and not let me fight." She leaned into him. "I am surprised you are willing if we are being honest. Why are you not locking me away in the palace with the others?" She twisted to look into his eyes.

She was not wrong. Kai wanted to hide her away, but that would be selfish. "It is your choice. I would be lying if I denied my fears, and I would ask that you stay away from the frontlines. But then I know you, and I imagine you will go wherever you are needed. Besides, you never miss your target from any distance, and with your Katori speed, you can take down four times what the best Diu archer can. This past week, you fought with the same fierceness as any other, all while pregnant. Ryker was right, I have no right to ask anyone to sit this out because we are fighting for our future—and their future. I hate to admit it, but we need you."

"I am happy to hear you say you need me," she said with a sigh. "This morning I feared you might change your mind."

"If we are being honest, I almost did." Kai released a heavy sigh of his own. "Last night I watched you grow hundreds of arrows for our archers, and I noticed something. Whatever Benmar did, blending your auras is wearing off. I see them—and I do mean *them*—more clearly now. There are two babies." He hugged her again and kissed her forehead.

Her mouth gaped open. "I . . . I did not know." She cupped her hands over her abdomen and then glanced at Kai. "Everything over this last week—" Her voice trailed off as she lowered her head. "Oh, I do see two. They are so tiny, but I see two lights now. How did I not know? I am their mother." She hugged herself and then looked back to Kai. Her face beamed with pride but faded as her eyes pulled her head to the side and her joy shifted to concern.

Kai turned to discover Riome joining them. She was dressed in her usual black Diu attire with her hair pulled into a tight knot atop her head. "Sorry to interrupt, but the Milnosian army is close. Simone spotted them coming around Thade Mountain on the northern road about an hour away. Meanwhile, the Caroco army is marching around the city's western side, hoping to avoid the fires and get closer to our walls for another attack. We will be fighting on two fronts." She handed him a few vials, Kai accepted them.

"Are these for the archers along the wall?" he asked.

"They are for you to coat your darts. Sigry is supplying the archers. You must hit Keegan at least once, no more than twice unless you want to kill him—or unless his Kodama magic allows him to block the toxin. I have never drugged a Katori like him before. The Lioness will take much more; the archers will take aim for her. Say five to seven hits, anything less, and all she will be is angry. Again, I have never tried a sleeping potion on a creature this large. I could have the wrong herbs or the wrong oils, or the amounts could be too weak. This is a foolish risk, but if you mean to take them both alive, I can think of no other way."

As he listened to her concerns, his eyes shifted to the sky above her head. Through the dark wisps of smoke above the Arkin oil blaze, he noticed the golden tips of an eagle flying in their direction. "Sabastian has returned." He jutted his chin at the Beastmaster eagle as his friend swooped and dropped amongst their group atop the Master General's tower.

"Kai, I have news," Sabastian panted with exhaustion while he wiped his brow. "Roark is coming. His troops retook Port Anahita. There will be no Caroco to flank his approach into Diu, but he and his men are hours away. He wanted me to inform you; the Caroco captured your Aunt Helena and severely wounded your Uncle Kaeco. While Roark managed to recover Helena, it is unclear if your uncle will survive the day without a Kodama healer. They are bringing your uncle here, but I came to see if you or Benmar would bring Rayna to him. if he is still alive, he has very little time left." Sebastian stopped, tilted his head, and then motioned to Rayna's abdomen. "Now, I do not think she is the best choice. Should she even be here in her condition?"

Kai smiled proudly. "She gets brighter by the day. Although she is your best option, and we made peace with my uncle after our last encounter in Port Anahita, I am not sure he wishes to see either of us."

"All the more reason I should go," Rayna offered. "I want to stay here, but your uncle needs a healer. I cannot say if it is the babies or me, but my magic grows stronger each day. If he is at death's door, as Sabastian claims, I am his best chance for survival. Let me go with you."

"I agree you should go, but I cannot leave Diu. The Lioness will be here soon, and I need to face her and stop her if I can. Today may be our only chance before they turn on Katori. Keegan will come straight for me in the battle, and I need to be here, and ready. He is counting on me being here, and for our plan to work, he needs to continue to believe he has the upper hand."

The sight of a single dragon in the distance again drew Kai's eyes skyward. Even at this distance, the size and silhouette were familiar—Benmar. He did not let his disappointment show, but his heart sank seeing his grandfather return alone. Not one fellow Katori came to help. The others followed his gaze.

"Gather everyone in the courtyard," Kai instructed, motioning to the exit. "Benmar will be here soon with news from Katori. I will inform the men on the walls he is friendly. I do not want a repeat of last night." He rubbed his shoulder as if the wound still haunted him.

◆ ◆ ◆

Standing next to his father, King Iver, Kai addressed the group. "We have news from Port Anahita." He nodded to Sabastian. "Admiral Roark's men have secured the city and the harbor, but my uncle suffered a nearly fatal wound in the early morning hours. Rayna and Benmar have agreed to fly to the harbor, meet Roark's army, and see if she can save his life. After which, Benmar will return. Tolan, it is up to you, but I think seeing you would do your father good. Keegan and the Lioness are coming, and the rest of us need to prepare."

Tolan nodded. "If it is alright with you, I will join my father. Amelia will stay here; she is hiding with Sigry. She will be safer with him should the baby arrive. He says it could be any day now. My father should know

I am alive and free from Milnos. Leave someone at the southern gatehouse to keep watch for our return. When we arrive, I want to ride straight through the center of Diu; it will be the fastest route to the Milnosian battle in the north."

Kai nodded, understanding his friend's desire to see his father. "I did not want to persuade you either way. Get back to Diu as quickly as possible. I fear we will not last long without reinforcements. I will ask Tenoch or Liam to bring down the stone wall blocking the south end of the city. Not sure what they can do about the fires, but Yulia is letting them burn, keeping the Caroco at bay."

"What of Katori?" Yulia questioned, looking between Benmar and Kai. "Any word? Will they come to help?"

Benmar stepped forward. "Many still fight amongst themselves, and Keegan's followers continue to spread doubt and destruction. I sent word around our great nation that Diu was in peril and that Keegan's machinations left us vulnerable. I reminded them that failing to come to the aid of another—or fighting amongst ourselves—goes against the very spirit of what it means to be Katori. How we respond in this crisis defines how the world will see our nation and our magic, which in turn redefines us as a people." Benmar's eyes grew heavy. "I spoke to the dragons. In the end, they said very little, and they refused to leave the mountain or call on those living in the Mystic Islands. I left knowing none would follow. There was no time to stay and preach."

Kai let the news they were on their own settle in the back of his throat, but then he forced himself to swallow his disappointment. "Benmar, you must reach my Uncle Kaeco with Rayna. Please deliver Tolan to his father, Admiral Roark. If you can come back here, I would welcome you to fight at my side."

Benmar stepped back from the group and transformed. His silver wing lowered for Rayna and Tolan to climb up. Torn between having his wife close by and hoping she would be safer away from the city, Kai watched his grandfather take flight and disappear into the clouds.

The clanging of metal on metal followed by the shouts of men echoed into the palace grounds. The people called for their king and demanded that he let them inside. Iver rushed through the group toward the gatehouse. "Why are they not hiding within the city bunkers as ordered?"

When Kai and Iver arrived at the gatehouse, they climbed the turret to see their numbers. Every able-bodied man stood outside the palace gatehouse, shouting for their King. "Open the gates! Where is our king?" Each man stood armed with swords, shields and a few had both.

Iver shouted to his guards, "Let them inside. Open the gates."

"Sire, we should not." The guard refused and bowed to his king. "I am sorry Your Highness, but their intentions are unclear. We should turn them away. A riot is the last thing we need on the verge of battle."

"Open the gates," Iver ordered in a bolder tone.

Without further rebuttal, the guard did as Iver ordered, and the king stepped out to greet his people. "Citizens, why do you protest and bring weapons to the palace? There are tunnels around the city that lead to underground refuges created by the Katori Stonekings to protect you. Why are you not seeking shelter?"

One man pounded his armor-covered chest. "I am Adam Barton. My great grandfather was a Diu warrior, and while I am a humble fisherman, I have come to fight for my city. As have all of these men." He motioned to the crowd behind him.

A guard came from behind and whispered to Iver. "Your Majesty, there are more men at the other gatehouse all claiming a desire to fight beside their king. Some are retired soldiers, and others are lords of the city. Each is claiming they wish to defend their home. Should we send them away?"

Iver patted the guard on the shoulder then faced his people. "Citizens of Diu, we find ourselves in troubling times. It is with honor I would stand and fight with each of you today. All who need weapons, we will do our best to arm you. If you know how to fight, find a place in the formation. As for the rest, I ask you to stay near the archers. If the time comes and you must fight, you will be our last line of defense."

CHAPTER 25

Trouble in the Skies

The Diu warriors marched across the battlefield, their polished Diu uniforms gleamed in the early morning sunlight. A meager army against the uncountable Milnosian troops Kai knew was coming. He heard them, the sounds of marching, armor clanging, and horse hooves pounding on the ground. His heart raced as he searched the distant hillside; he waited for the enemy to crest the hilltop.

Kai waited for the battle to start as his mind scrambled to consider everything the day might bring. Today he had double the cause for worry. In the distance, the sounds of another confrontation rippled across his city. Diu's military stood divided; one group defended against the Caroco and Katori warriors along the western wall, while Kai and his group watched the northern hillside fill with Milnosian soldiers. Unable to be in both places, he prayed for his fellow warriors and wished them luck.

As the Milnosians marched into view, he was astounded by their numbers—there seemed to be twice what he recalled from the air only the day before. And to his dismay, their numbers increased with each heart-pounding step, sealing Diu's fate with little uncertainty on how the day would end.

Seven Milnosian men stepped from their ranks, one from each section. Their coordinated movements sent chills down Kai's neck. Fifteen feet from their units, they stopped and pounded their chests. In response, the entire Milnosian army repeated the action. Their armor echoed down the field in a wave of confidence. The seven grunted and took an attack posture. Again, the troops repeated, sending a shout of grunts at Diu followed by three heart-pounding steps forward. The ground thundered and shook, and before Kai knew it, the enemy charged in their direction.

As the black flood poured in his direction, his men clamored in anticipation. "Hold," Kai shouted, reminding the Diu soldiers to keep their ground and stay within range of the city walls. "Let them come!" he called again, knowing they needed the protection from the Milnosian longbowmen if they even stood any chance at all. That and he had no intentions of getting surrounded by their superior numbers if they chose to flank them like a fist closing in on its prize.

The enemy's black swords slid from their sheaths as they ran. The sunlight danced along their razor-sharp edges and glinted a gleeful smile. Armed with the dragon-slaying metal, weapons capable of slicing through bone with a single cut, they again shouted—attack! Kai looked down at the matching blade in his hand—weapons acquired in Milnos by Ryker and Dresnor—and then across the Diu frontline to those lucky enough to carry one. They would need to get more of these weapons.

The first clash of swords set everyone in motion. Battle cries bounced around the field. Weapons and bodies slammed together in a free-for-all fight to the death. The eyes of the Milnosian man in front of Kai wavered between anger and excitement. They exchanged blows. The man's jaw clenched as he rose his weapon for another go, but his sneer faded as Kai pulled his blade from the man's ribs.

In battle, Kai moved with great speed. His instinct and years of training reflected in the attacks he wielded and the defensive blocks he used. His weapons: the black sword, a shield, and the new techniques of pressure points taught to him during his Guardian training. He and his Katori brethren thrashed through the Milnosian ranks with a fierce, unyielding fury. With him and his friends stood Katori men and women who called Diu home and fought for the country they chose to love.

Even with the superior black blades, there was no accounting for skill. Disarming three opponents, Kai stepped over the dead, allowing those behind him to collect and distribute additional swords. It wasn't much, but he could see the confidence the stronger blade gave the men on both sides. While the Diu silver swords held, many began to crack or shatter under the strikes from the superior weapons.

Caught in a moment, Kai watched in horror at the devastation war left in its wake. Warriors fought and fell; each man attacked and then moved to their next adversary without looking back. In his twenty years of life, Kai had fought several small battles with his first skirmish at the age of thirteen, but never in his lifetime did he think he would fight in a war, let alone one the world blamed him for starting.

The Milnosian army outnumbered Diu three to one, and Kai knew his meager, divided troops did not stand a chance—but then that was Keegan's plan all along, to divide the Diu resources and allies. With everyone fighting individual battles, no one country could possibly gain an upper hand against him. And it certainly did not help that Nola's duplicitous schemes dismantled King Iver's loyal troops, leaving Diu an unprotected city, ripe for the picking. With Roark and his men miles away and Katori caught in civil war, and Nebea distracted with Keegan's forces, there were but a few soldiers left to defend Diu.

Supercharged from the Katori water, his friends, Dresnor and Drew, fought alongside, both holding their own. Ryker and Haygan worked together further down the line while Sabastian kept them together, unable to take flight for fear of the menacing black weapons that might fly from within the enemy's ranks. The Diu soldiers held their ground, barely inching forward to retrieve weapons before stepping back in place, encouraging the enemy closer. At the same time, the Kodama archers repeatedly launched a volley of arrows. The sight of them made Kai think of Rayna, making him thankful she was far from the battle.

In the distance, the sounds of thunder and war reminded Kai that a second battle took place with the original Caroco warriors on the northern side of Diu. Keegan's men battled against all the Diu warriors they could spare less than a mile away. Even with the distance, he could feel the occasional earthquake and hear lightning crack the sky as the sounds of war mixed with his own. Parts of him wanted to rush to their aid, add his Katori speed and skill to their numbers, but he could not.

Even with the archers' support, the Milnosian soldiers pressed relentlessly against Kai and his fellow warriors. Up until now, his men held their ground, refusing to lose even a step. But when they lost two steps, then two more, Kai saw the fear in his men's eyes. Eager to win their courage back, he pressed forward. Wielding his sword against half a dozen men, he cut a swath in front of him. It was then the front line began to blur. Before he knew it, clumps of men from both sides mingled together. Their once orderly formation was breaking.

Kai noticed a towering figure from the corner of his eye; the man's battle-ax cut through Kai's men with fierce brutality. Nearly a head and shoulder above everyone, the man moved fast. His dark eyes fixed on Kai as he fought through anyone in his path. When they met in battle, the first blow against Kai's shield cracked off a corner, and the second strike cleaved it in half. Useless, Kai thrust the remaining piece at his attacker.

They exchanged blows, and Kai's black steel blade left a few nicks along his opponent's silver blade. Keeping a safe distance, Kai shifted left then right, forcing the man to pivot and block until Kai found his opening to slip around behind to disarm his attacker. He dropped the man in a heap, paralyzed by the Guardian pressure points.

Still, no matter how quick or good Kai was, a new set of Milnosian soldiers replaced those he removed from the fight. Magical or not, they needed reinforcements, or they would die here. Even as the next volley of arrows flew overhead, he knew the mingled mass of Diu and Milnos would make it harder to reach the enemy accurately. They would soon lose this advantage. In the long run, they would not last the hour unless something shifted in their favor.

The sounds of clay pots breaking drew his gaze. First to the right, then back fifteen feet behind him. Protected by four men with large shields, Riome fired her short bow and tossed daggers and silver stars, striking the enemy, pushing them back, or dropping them where they stood. Men with her catapulted ceramic jugs filled with flammable liquids—all Diu could offer—deep into the Milnosian ranks. Captured by the wind, Kai smelled Arkin oil waft back in his direction. The men worked quickly; their slingshots snapped as they fired the remaining vessels.

On the next volley from the walls, flaming arrows struck the doused area. Men screamed in terror as the fire swept through their ranks; man to man, the fire jumped like a jackrabbit. Even from twenty feet away, Kai felt the heat reach his face. The man in front of him pushed into him, more desperate to flee the spreading flames than to fight back. Dozens of men fell to the fire while he and his men cut into the organized chaos. Kai did not know how but the tide seemed to turn in their favor. Small victories mostly, but their strategies seemed to be pushing the enemy back.

Lighting cracked the sky and thunder shook the ground. Kai cut his eye to the sounds of battle cries and trumpeting horns. From the west, a swarm of men flooded the hillside—Caroco men armed to the teeth. They pressed hard on Diu's left flank, blending into the Milnosian ranks. The Arkin oil blaze sank into the ground, smothered in an ocean wave of dirt, and with it went any distance they gained with Riome's explosion. Diu lost ground to the increasing numbers of the enemy as the Caroco rushed to fill the gap.

In the distance, a second wave of Milnosian soldiers crested the hillside and charged. They marched with fresh determination, turning the hillside into a sea of enemy soldiers. The arrival of the new men pushed against Kai's troops. They were losing the hill. As a line of Caroco men pressed into their flank, Kai expected them to cut into their ranks and crush them, but the ground shook and grumbled, raising like a ramp below him and his men. The wall of dirt blocked the Caroco attempt to shatter their formation. Kai gleaned the area; a bright figure slid across the ramped ground—Tenoch.

Thankful for the arrival of his Stoneking friend, he could not help but wonder what happened to drive the Caroco men around the city. He could only imagine the other Diu unit had failed, and now they were in worse shape than before. Still, Kai kept fighting—blocking and attacking.

Cannons fired from both sides, sending debris vaulting into the sky and chunks of the Diu walls crumbling to the ground.

Stonekings battled with rocks and earthquakes. The ground heaved beneath Kai's feet then suddenly fell flat. Silence. Thunder rumbled, and lightning cracked the sky. Strikes hit the Milnosian soldiers on the hillside, followed by a hit on the city. A third bolt cut across the sky but swerved and shrank into nothingness seconds before it could strike the gatehouse. Weathervanes on both sides attacked, evenly matched but wreaking havoc on the battlefield. Storm clouds rolled in, turning the sky dark.

Arrows launched, arched, and fell on Kai's position. Hundreds would die as many, including him, no longer held a shield. Holding his swords at the ready, he waited to slice away the oncoming projectiles. But then a plume of fire exploded across the sky, followed by a silver streak and the screech of a dragon. "Benmar!" Kai shouted as dragon's fire consumed the arrows, and his grandfather twisted midflight to fly back toward Diu—back to safety only seconds before a volley of dark arrows fired into the sky.

The ground heaved once more, left, up, then right, and down again. Kai used the distraction to dispatch two adversaries, but in the chaos, a Diu shield struck him in the side of the head. The blow brought stars into his eyes and put Kai on his knees. As the dead Diu warrior fell to the ground at his side, Kai snatched the man's abandoned shield. His watery vision blurred his surroundings, leaving him vulnerable to attack.

On instinct, he closed his eyes and gleaned the battle in time to see his next adversary preparing to strike. Tears ran down his cheeks as he blocked the blow and hopped back to his feet. As his head and vision cleared, a strange sound came from the sky, drawing his gaze. He imagined the mechanical racket came from the war machines, but he still refused to believe Milnos could create flying vessels capable of carrying weapons and men of any magnitude.

Above the battlefield, a new threat loomed in the clouds, announced by foreign rumbles, clinks, and clangs. The clouds rolled like waves around dark shadows pushing through the storm. Kai watched lightning flicker through the sky, illuminating the ship's silhouettes—the airships were real. Like him, everyone stopped to watch the Weathervanes' magic scatter the stormy mist, revealing their wooden flatbottom hulls, white sails angled around a large silver puffy pillow where the mast should be and followed by a black smoke puffing contraption at the rear. The gears and blades spun at a furious rate, the source of the mechanical racket.

Kai could not believe his eyes, but there they were real as can be—ships capable of riding the clouds without wings. As he watched in horror, seven of the sixteen Milnosian warships lowered to the ground west of the battlefield and began to spew thousands of men before returning to the sky. The new men poured through the Caroco forces, mingling with their ranks, and shouting, "Milnos forever!" Their cries of unity echoed around the battlefield, bolstering the enemy. Everything looked hopeless, and his men stepped back in response. They lost ground closed quickly as the Milnosian soldiers consumed the gap, but Kai and his fellow Katori pushed harder. He could not let them lose heart.

As the battle raged, Kai kept a fierce pace. Rounds of attack—defend—attack. The frenzy left little time to consider anything as he fell into a rhythmic trance against the enemy. When the sounds of something new rang in the distance, Kai cocked his head and then shouted to Ryker, "Do you hear that?" he asked. "I hear bells and trumpets."

Ryker nodded his head in agreement, but his friend did not stop fighting.

Taking the risk, Kai looked back toward the city. A new line of archers filled the empty spaces—the Fort Pohaku banners were a rejoiceful sight. As the new group launched a volley of arrows, he saw Rayna among their ranks. Her appearance was both a relief and a distraction. She was back, which he could only hope meant that Roark's reinforcements had arrived.

When the city gates opened, the Diu troops parted, and a swarm of riders emerged. The men leading the charge were two he knew very well by their fiery red hair—Admiral Roark Raebun and his son, Tolan. They rode fast and fierce through his ranks up the hill to the front lines and slammed into the never-ending wave of Milnos soldiers. With them, hundreds of riders poured into the enemy lines, followed by countless men on foot bolstering their ranks.

The riders carved a swath through the Milnosian invaders in a mad rush, and Roark's Fort Pohaku troops filled in the gaps. The disruptive attack spread into the enemy with like fingers through weeds, yanking and pulling without mercy. Battle-seasoned men poured through his troops, taking his place along the front, crushing the Milnos force across the hillside. Taking a step back, Kai managed to catch his breath. In the wake of Roark's arrival, his troops followed with renewed confidence. The day was not yet theirs, but the armed riders turned the tide with devastating results against the enemy.

Although he wanted to believe the Admiral's naval forces and the Fort Pohaku army would arrive to save them all, his heart clinched ever so slightly, sending a wave of anxiety rippling down his spine. He shared strong connections with a few special people in his life, but none more powerful than the one with his mother. Even without her necklace around his neck, he knew she was close. He felt her rage followed by a warning. Although the hate and anger were not her truth, they resonated the loudest. Behind the raw madness, a soft note—the real her—begged for a chance to live. And still, a part of her pleaded for an end to her suffering and the terrible things she might do.

The golden Lioness crested the hilltop. His mother's roar reverberated through the air, and her magical energy washed over the battlefield pushing against Kai. She was angry—angry with him. Jumping into the sky, she took flight. This was the moment he was dreading; time to face his mother and Keegan. He pressed his hand against his vest and felt Riome's the poison-tipped black darts. As his mother flew over the Milnosian soldiers toward the front line, toward him, Kai felt her rage spike. Her dark rider pointed his finger directing her forward. Her softness was gone, leaving only her fury.

Keegan was coming, as promised. Every part of Kai wanted to panic, but there was no time; everyone counted on him to set this right. He shouted desperately to her with his Beastmaster mind. *You are stronger than Keegan! Fight him! Show him your truth. Let him feel the love and hope within your heart.* He implored his mother's spirit as he watched the distance between him and her close.

The only emotion Kai felt was rage. Not only from his mother, but Keegan's anger pounded into him. His father's influence was more potent than he remembered. The Lioness bounded into the middle of the Milnosian army. Golden waves of red and orange emanated a vengeful glow from her beastly form. Dozens of men screamed as her flames consumed them while others ran to avoid her deadly heat.

The Lioness spoke to Kai's mind, *You had your chance, boy. Now you will submit or burn; either way, I do not much care. Time for you to feel my wrath.*

Her words stung, but they were not hers; they couldn't be her. Needing more time to persuade his mother to fight against Keegan, Kai leaped into the sky, transforming into his silver dragon, drawing her away from the battlefield. Barely a few feet into the air, he heard the twang and swoosh of darts launched toward his underbelly. With a quick pivot and a roll, he avoided their deadly strikes as he flew out of range over the battle toward his parents.

The closer he came, the angrier she felt; there did not seem to be an ounce of the real Mariana left. It was as if Keegan's hatred was now his mother's. *Mother, remember who you are?* He spoke back to her, but he felt the *NO* hit his heart more than he heard it. Any hope Kai once had that her true self could change his father was slowly fading away. She no longer had the will to fight; she was becoming like his father.

The Lioness's fire-consumed eyes followed his flight pattern as Kai pivoted and rolled, avoiding the arrows raining down from the hovering ships fighting from the clouds. As predicted, she launched into the air in quick pursuit. Up and into the clouds, he led her above it all. Although he avoided the dark arrows and the large dragon-killer bolts, he saw three darts stuck in his mother's hind leg. Blood dripped around the wounds.

Bright flames pulsed down her body, engulfing and disintegrating the unwanted projectiles. Keegan's hands slid along the Lioness, and Kai saw a ripple of pale green dance across her fur and heal the open wounds.

On his next pass, Kai glanced between the flying war machines and his mother. Keegan pointed to the ground, but she did not listen; she seethed, roared, and pursued Kai.

Mother, help me stop this war. Fight Keegan. He is poisoning your mind. His madness is infecting your heart, but you are stronger. Love is stronger than hate. Please, mother. He begged, but hatred was all he felt in response.

The roaring ships and the battle below caught his ear. He dove. She followed. The wind rushed past his face and over his wings. *Fight the enemy, mother. Milnos will turn on you next.* On his next pass, he belched thick smoldering flames at one of the silver balloons, which he assumed held up the flying contraptions. Again, archers fired from the ships. The black-powdered metal scraped his scales. Dozens of tiny scrapes, but luckily, nothing pierced his body. Glancing back, he saw a few ropes set alight and men scrambling to extinguish the blaze, but the balloon remained intact, secured by dozens of metal chains.

Below him, on the ground, he saw the Caroco army and the Milnosian forces pushing toward Diu, but Admiral Roark's men held them back. Bursts of Katori animals popped along the front, transforming in and out of beast forms, fighting and ripping through the enemy. To his dismay, some were not quick enough to avoid the dark arrows and blades, and far too many fell in a heap: great eagles, vultures, and even a bear lost their lives to the dark weapons. The airships fired cannons, arrows, and hot Arkin oil on the men below.

Joining in the fight, Kai saw Benmar and Simone dive into the action, skimming the ground and breathing waves of fire and ripping through the enemy ranks. While their attacks reaped a deathly toll on the Milnosian forces, the endless supply of Milnosian men filled in the gaps and continued to attack Diu and fire a steady supply of dark arrows at the sky. Continuing to chase his mother, Kai dodged one airship as it weaved through the sky, firing at both he and his mother when they came too close.

To his left, he saw two airships making aggressive maneuvers in pursuit after Simone's black dragon; his aunt's beautifully erratic flight pattern kept the enemy just out of reach. She avoided the dark arrows and dragon-killer bolts with dives and climbs and led them straight toward Benmar's superior-sized dragon. The Lioness snapped and roared at Benmar as she passed, but his grandfather paid her no mind.

His grandfather's massive, spiked head and shoulders rammed the hull of an airship, sending it into an uncontrolled spin. Tilted to one side, it careened into another vessel at full speed. The shouts and cries of men were cut short as the sky erupted in a ball of fire that consumed the two vessels. The thunderous blast of heat rippled across the sky, disrupting Kai's flight. Regaining his balance, he watched and listened to the sounds of metal crashing into the ground with one final blast.

So, it is possible to destroy these vessels! Kai heard his grandfather exclaim.

CHAPTER 26

Redemption

The Lioness rebounded from her injury and returned in full force to claw and spit fire at Kai. Her sharp claws sparked and scrapped down his tail but did not cut. He twisted and turned midflight and swatted her from the sky with his powerful claws. Her mighty wings slowed her descent, and she attacked with a relentless fury, pouncing on his back. He felt the burning sensation of her claws as they pressed into his backside. Her massive weight set him into a downward spiral, and they crashed into one of the enormous flying ships.

The horns on Kai's dragon head struck the silver balloon, ripping a huge gash in the metallic fabric and releasing a gust of putrid air. Kai jerked his head free. Men scrambled in fear as the airship wavered, while others attacked with blades and darts. Chains used to hold the balloon caught on his wing, holding him in place. Thrashing to get loose, Kai fell overboard. Two men clung to his horny spine as they plummeted toward the ground alongside the vessel. To save himself, Kai dropped his dragon form and punched the one man who managed to grab his arm. Kai's dragon wings sprang from his back at the last second, pulling him skyward as everyone else on the ship collided with the hillside in a gigantic explosion.

The heat from the blast bloomed in Kai's direction. With seconds to spare, he completed his transformation, covering his delicate human skin with silver scales. The smoke and fire consumed the air around him but the eruption did not harm him, and within three beats of his wings, he soared clear of the destruction. Amidst the clouds, he searched for the orange glow of the Lioness. Her fiery silhouette bloomed in the clouds, and Kai flew in her direction. This time he aimed for her dark rider, breathing fire at his father, but the Lioness twisted to use her wiry wings to deflect the flames and protect Keegan.

Fight him, Mother, he encouraged her, taking another shot at Keegan.

His mother weaved and dodged his attacks but did not return fire. She kept her movements erratic, setting an extreme pace, and Kai lost sight of her in the clouds. He called to her again. *Let me help you, mother, and together we can stop Keegan. You are not alone in this fight.*

We are one now, boy. There is no separation—Mariana is Keegan, Keegan is the Lioness.

Her words again broke his heart. He refused to believe she was beyond saving. Still, they could keep this up all day, and neither could burn the other, but he feared Keegan's ability to heal his mother meant she held the advantage given the dozen-plus cuts and gashes scattered across his body. Thoughts of the potion and the dark darts reminded him he had another way to fight. He needed to separate her from Keegan—maybe then she would listen to him.

It was a feeling more than anything that drew his eyes over his outstretched wing. A speck at first, but as they drew near, there was no way to distinguish, let alone identify, one dragon from another. Their numbers were so great they blocked out the sun. They dove at the ships, dodging dragon-killing bolts and dark arrows to ram the floating vessels. Other dragons skimmed the ground in coordinated attacks, dropping dozens of Katori warriors left and right around the field. They ripped through the enemy troops, decimating their numbers in a path of destruction a hundred feet wide.

The ground heaved and cracked, gobbling men. Lightning cracked the sky and struck the ground with deadly results. Beastmasters transformed and thundered into the enemy—bears, shuks, leopards, and gorillas. The elite Milnosians chanted, "Milnos forever," instilling a renewed desire as their forces turned, attacking the new threat with unyielding mercy; they let loose their dark arrows and charged with their dark blades. The swarm of darts struck many, but only a few beasts fell. The Beastmaster attack slashed through the Milnosian ranks. People and beasts clashed, each fighting to their last breath.

From above and below, Milnosian men fired dark darts and dragon-killer bolts. One dragon fell from the sky with deadly results while two others limped off, struggling to stay airborne before they careened into the ground down near Baden Lake. Kai swooped around just out of range of the lethal attack, searching the sky for the Lioness. Her golden form darted around the ships as she chased the attacking dragons. Breathing fire back and forth, neither did any damage, except his mother's volley provided the perfect distraction, drawing the pursing dragons closer to the hovering ships.

Even with the dragon's superior speed and agile maneuvers, Kai watched three dragons struck by deadly bolts plummet to the ground. Two remained as dragons, while one returned to her natural form. An older gray-haired woman, struck in the chest, grasped at the air before she gave up her last breath and died.

Even with the magical support, Kai found it impossible to tell who was winning. Men and women died on both sides. Stonekings and Weathervanes attacked, and it came to a point he could no longer tell friend from foe in the heaving cluster. It was chaos. Then he noticed one ship, the vessel under King Landon's command with Maxwell's magnifying eyeglass lens focused on the battle. The airship hovered in the clouds out of range, watching and waiting.

Landon and Maxwell stood proudly in their silver raven armor as they ordered the Katoris killed and tossed from their ship. They cast out the dead and unnecessary Katori Weathervanes. They had done their work, bringing the war machines swiftly to the Diu kingdom; now they were unwanted baggage. Their trumpets echoed from ship to ship, and the announcement set a chain of events in motion that shocked Keegan's Katori followers and the Caroco.

Desperate to understand what was happening, Kai dove toward the battle below. It was then he noticed new Milnosian troops and their odd behavior. They were swift, light-footed, and direct. Unopposed, they began cutting down every Caroco and Katori on their side, stabbing the unsuspecting men in the back. It was unbelievable, the double-cross that Maxwell had promised. The new Milnosian reinforcements, Maxwell's elite men with silver raven armor, began to chant —*Milnos forever*— killing every Caroco warrior, encouraging the regular Milnosian army to join in the slaughter.

Launched into a three-way war, it became a free for all as the Milnosian forces turned against their Caroco and Katori allies. Kai could only imagine that once they finished with the Caroco, their entire might would again fall upon Diu.

The Lioness swerved away from Kai, and he could only imagine Keegan's eyes were scanning the battlefield, watching his men slaughtered at the hands of his deceitful Milnosian allies.

Keegan yelled in anger, and the Lioness roared. Kai felt their rage.

Along the eastern part of the battle, the last few ships lowered, allowing more soldiers to disembark. Kai watched the ground heave. Keegan's remaining Katori warriors—men and women fighting from the forest—joined forces with the new Katori forces and attacked the grounded vessels. Four dragons swooped down, spewing fire. Clouds rolled in, and lightning cracked the sky, and two bolts struck the metal balloons. Both ships exploded in burnt orange and yellow balls, sending shards of wood and metal debris in all directions.

His heightened dragon nose caught the scent of Arkin oil behind the explosion. Men set ablaze writhed in uncontrolled agony as they spewed from the remains. Again, he heard the Lioness. Her roar grew louder over the cries of battle and the sounds of destruction. She landed with a thud near the center of the Milnosian forces. The force shook the ground, and her flames licked at any foolish enough not to get clear.

Keegan slid from her back, and he stepped into the mass of Milnosian warriors. The men turned, their eyes curious, their blades angled in his father's direction. Kai hovered above them. His wings pumped to keep him airborne, yet he lowered himself to listen. His father spoke, shouting at the onlookers. At first his words did not carry, but Kai felt the raw hatred ripple through the air, which felt oddly amplified.

Now within range, Kai heard his father's words. "Did you think I gave you this world on a platter?" He laughed at them. "Fools! You would turn on me, a god among men? I gave you a gift, and you double-cross me. You have no idea my power; you are but pawns. This world is mine, all of it! My dark powder not only gives the armor and weapons strength, but it also allows my darkness to consume the user." Keegan grinned and touched a man to his left and a man to his right; their eyes turned dark and black lines crept across their face.

Kai watched in horror as each man touched the next, spreading the hate in a wave across the battlefield. The grass beneath Keegan's feet withered and died, spreading under their feet, converting more men to his dark warriors. Every warrior wearing or holding the dark metal turned. Kai shouted with his mind to Ryker and Sabastian. *Drop your dark sword! The metal is connected to Keegan's magic!*

His friends tossed their weapons and began knocking weapons from anyone they could. The dark circle stopped. The uninfected Milnosian men stepped away from their counterparts, ripping off their dark armor and casting down the dark swords.

The Lioness roared, and Kai turned around. Keegan touched her face, and her golden fur turned shades of black and gray. Her flames became blue-violet and yellow-white. Ryker yelled in sorrow and charged through the dumbfounded battlefield. The second his foot touched the spoiled ground, his eyes went black, and he stood motionless among the others.

Keegan cocked his head at Ryker's cry but gave him no response; instead, his eyes rose to the sky and the hovering vessel that carried King Landon. "You think you are safe from my wrath in your airship? Think again!" he yelled, raising one arm while touching the Lioness with the other. White hot flames shot from her mouth and consumed the vessel igniting the silver balloon. The explosion sent a shockwave across the sky and Kai felt the heat of the blast followed by the smell of Arkin oil.

With his traitorous allies destroyed, Keegan turned his eyes back to the battlefield.

Electricity tickled Kai's spine, and he felt a wave of hate and darkness push against his chest. *The tainted darts.* He cringed, anxious to rip the evil weapons from his pocket. He dropped his dragon body, letting only his wings remain holding him aloft. His mind clouded as he reached for the arrows, he clutched them in his hand. Darkness consumed his mind, and he felt a seething anger boil in his heart. His father's voice resonated in his mind darkening his soul—*follow me.*

Kai's arm went slack, and he felt compelled to land. A black haze covered his eyes, and then everything went sideways. When he came to, Benmar stood in front of him, and the darkness was gone. Simone stood to the side. "We removed the dark arrows from your grip," his grandfather announced, "but not without help." He motioned behind Kai.

Rayna stepped around Kai. Her smiling face warmed his heart. "You should not be out here," he cautioned, then he pulled her into a hug. "Thank you," he whispered.

"You are not the only one Rayna saved." Kai turned to see Ryker restored. "Her Kodama magic undoes the effects of your father. The weapons are still tainted, as is the ground, but it does not affect her for some reason. We are not sure if there is a range limit to Keegan's spell, but the one ship draws his focus for now. In due time, he will again turn his sights and magic on us. We need a plan."

No sooner did Ryker speak than Keegan once again turned and walked into his waiting army. They had little time to plan; Riome's potion was no longer a viable option. All the sleeping potion they had was useless on the contaminated dark arrows. Kai looked to his grandfather, but Benmar shook his head. They both knew it was up to them. "We need to pull the tainted magic out of Keegan, out of the metal, and out of the ground," Kai heard himself say as he looked to Rayna. He knew he could not do this without her.

The dark horde attacked with Keegan leading the charge, and the Lioness took to the sky, striking random places with her fiery breath.

The Diu army fought against Keegan's possessed soldiers. They were no match. The Lioness swooped around behind the dark forces and flew toward Kai. He felt her anger and rage directed at him. *Please, Mother, fight back. I know you are still in there.* She did not respond.

"Kai, this is that once in a lifetime shot," Sabastian insisted. "We have no choice but to take the Lioness down. I can do this, but you will need to lift me into the sky in front of her."

Kai's dragon wings sprouted, and he took hold of Sabastian; he could feel magic pouring into his friend as they flew into the sky in front of his mother. When Sabastian clapped his hands together, a blast of light struck the Lioness. She fell and skidded across the ground, crushing and burning everyone in her path. For a moment, she did not move, then her body shook, and she stumbled to her feet, dazed.

While the Lioness shook her head in recovery, four Kodama arrows pierced her in the side. She wavered but did not fall. Kai dropped to the ground, ready to run to his mother. If he could just lay his hands on her, maybe he could reach her soul. Before he took one step, she pounced into the Diu army, biting and clawing the men. Kai saw her dark fur begin to glow blue as her mouth opened, and she spewed fire in every direction.

Dozens of arrows launched at Keegan, but he deflected each one with his curved black swords. Like an angry demon, Keegan sliced through the Diu soldiers who were foolish enough to get in his way. Three Katoris charged, but they too were no match for Keegan's skill. The Lioness returned to the sky, and with a roar of anger, she burst into flames. The fire burned through the arrows embedded into her fur.

Milnosian archers fired deep into the Diu mass, and a second volley launched toward the Kodama warriors on the wall, followed by the Lioness and her flaming breath. Frustrated, Kai gritted his teeth. *We had her,* he thought as he blocked an oncoming attack.

"We are one!" Keegan shouted from across the battlefield. "I am coming for you, my boy." His father's foot stepped into the healthy green grass, and the foliage did not die, not at first—then once again a blackness spread across the ground. Many died as ooze seeped up their bodies and sucked them into the soil, while others raged like black-eyed monsters, attacking anyone in their way.

"Kai!" Benmar shouted. "We must stop Keegan. We are the only ones who can. Steal his magic and repurpose it," he yelled, charging his son, lost in his chaos.

With every ounce of speed, Kai followed his grandfather. The black ground swelled with anger-filled ooze that clung to his feet, slowing him down and creeping up his ankles. The dark magic pulled at the edges of his faith, and he stumbled. The strange goo slid up around his waist; it sucked at his arms, drawing his face to the ground. Rayna helped him to his feet. Her hand felt warm on his arm. As she ran her hand from his waist to his knees, the substance receded. It was then he noticed her glow; even without gleaning, he could see her shine.

The grass beneath her feet was green and free from darkness. "Go, Kai, you must hold your father and pull on the energy within his magic. We must stop the spread of this darkness." Rayna turned and ran after Benmar.

Kai started to go as he looked to the Lioness as she roared, crashing into a cluster of warriors. She trashed and chomped at men from both sides; in her anger, she did not choose sides, only destruction and chaos. Men ran from her, screaming in fear. Kai called to her, *Help us, mother, help us stop Keegan.* Unable to reach her mind, Kai pushed the essence of his soul in a wave of magic. As the wave of emotion struck his mother, for a moment, her fur glistened gold, then faded back to blacks and grays. His mother did not respond to his plea; she continued attacking troops and burning the ground beneath her feet.

Before he could try again, Rayna and Benmar shouted for him to follow. They needed him to help stop Keegan and the spread of his darkness.

Stealing magic was a foreign concept. The Katori borrowed from nature, taking a little here or there but never from each other. Kai sensed the magic within the ooze and pulled it inward, and the thick muck receded. Before he could reach his father, Kai saw an aberration pass him on the battlefield from out of nowhere. It was the moment from his vision, the sight of himself running headlong toward his father. His doppelganger charged Keegan, and his father gleefully grabbed the man by the neck.

Keegan pulled their faces close together. "Who are you?" he asked seconds before a dagger stabbed him. "You are not my son," he seethed and growled, shaking the would-be attacker.

The face contorted and shifted, turning into Riome. "No, I am not Kai," she writhed, trying to free herself, her dark auburn hair turned completely white.

"You think your little dagger can kill me?" he laughed, pulling the blade from the side of his collarbone. "You missed my heart, my dear."

Riome laughed. "I was not aiming for your heart."

She flung Mariana's freed pendant over her shoulder, and Kai caught the crystal. The crystal glowed in his hand, and he felt his mother. Her soul was still there, the real her. Trapped within the crystal, she called to him—*Free me, Kai.*

Keegan's anger manifested in an angry howl as he sucked the remaining years from Riome and tossed her unwanted carcass into the ooze. Her loss was devastating. Kai could not tell if she was alive or dead, but there was no time to check; he pulled his legs free and ran as best he could.

Come back to us, Mother. Burn away the hate. I believe in you. Kai looked to the Lioness; her dark fur fluttered in the wind as she stopped to look at him. He offered his own heart to the essence within his mother's crystal. *Remember who you are. Share your heart with Keegan.* Kai reached for his father, taking hold of his arm while Benmar held the other. "We are still one, my son. Your mother and I can never be separated." His father's face snarled.

Unable to move, Kai thought about movements Riome taught him and the flow of magic. The ooze was an extension and manifestation of his father's emotions, but the energy within was raw and neutral; it was that source Kai focused on within his mind.

The world outside fell away as his mind concentrated on the energy. It felt rough, like breathing sand. His father yanked and pulled to get free, emanating a visceral growl as his eyes and skin turned black. Terrified by the changes in his father, Kai continued to steal the magic from Keegan. The hate was powerful, and it seeped up his arms, but he did not let go. He felt his mind begin to cloud when he saw Rayna place her hands on Keegan. One hand on his head, the other on his heart. Golden white light poured from her hands into his father. Everything about her began to glow.

Rayna's magic stopped the flow of death. The ground rumbled, and the wind whipped around them. As her glow grew, it reclaimed the land. The raging battle stopped, but everyone remained infected. Continuing to steal his father's power, Kai started giving magic to Rayna, helping her restore the land, and with it, everyone else.

The light was small at first, but a tiny illumination sparked inside of Keegan's crystal. It ebbed and went out, then returned, struggling to burn away decades of anger and hate. *Please, Father,* Kai begged with his mind, unsure if Keegan could hear him. *Remember the man you were before the hate. Feel my mother's truth, feel mine.* Kai gave a little of his heart to Keegan.

The Lioness roared, and her thunderous footsteps shook the ground. Kai looked to see the emotional battle within the beast when he noticed her dark eyes turning a golden hue once more. Her body shook, and the ripple transformed her fur into a soft white, and her wings changed from dark wiry leather to soft white feathers. The Lioness approached them in her new beauty.

Standing behind Rayna, the Lioness transformed back into Mariana, just as Kai remembered her. Her white gown flowed around her in a golden shimmer. Smiling at him, she rested her hands on Rayna's shoulders. The two of them shined bright white like the sun. The dark ooze turned to dust and blew away, and the light from Keegan's crystal increased, taking with it all the darkness.

Kai held firm to his father, who no longer fought against him. Light beamed from his eyes until the last of the darkness was gone, and their natural blue returned, yet the soft haze of old age slowly clouded their brilliance. As Keegan's black, hate-covered skin became its natural bronze, it changed. As the hate left, it took Keegan's youth, carving decades of life in age lines over his body and turning his dark hair stark white. Now Keegan sank back on his heels as an old man. Tears streamed down his face, and a joyful sadness swept over this expression.

"I am so sorry," he wept.

Benmar touched Keegan's face. The father had become the younger man. "I am here, my son."

The large dome of light engulfed everything as far as Kai could see, burning away the darkness within all it touched. The men dropped to the ground, restored but asleep. Unsure what to do, Kai refused to let go. *Is it over?* he wondered.

"The hate is gone, my child." Alenga's angelic voice echoed as she stepped through an iridescent watery curtain, standing behind Keegan. "All of it. There are no dark crystals left. Keegan had collected them all, crushing them to create the dark powder, which he planned to use to control those who would not bend to his will."

Keegan tried to stand and Kai helped him. his eyes swelled with the newness of hope. "Alenga, can you forgive me? I do not remember losing my faith, all I remember is hate. From the first dark crystal to the last, they called to me. I do not remember why, but I always felt angry. Mariana, Kai, father, please forgive me." He looked at each one.

Rayna dropped to the ground, screaming in pain. Her hands cupped her abdomen. "The babies," she cried.

"Alenga, please, help her," Kai begged.

She shook her head. "I cannot. My magic cannot enter this plain. I am here in spirit only because of the vast amount of magic created at this moment, but when it fades, I will return to my place. You all must help her." She looked to Keegan and Mariana.

Keegan looked at his hands as if he did not recognize that his gifts could do anything but destroy. Mariana knelt and cradled Rayna's head in her lap. "Keegan, we can do this, this one last thing." Mariana extended her hand. "Save our grandchildren. You are the only one with the power of life. Set this right and give back to the world the life you stole."

Rayna's screams echoed through the trees. Keegan's hands cupped Rayna's belly as tears streamed down his face. His white crystal beamed brightly. Kai held his wife's hand as she lay in the center of the battlefield. His mother's hands soothed Rayna as her light comforted and flowed into her daughter-in-law. "There, there, my dear. You can do this, just a little longer. The babies are coming."

Kai knelt across from Keegan and watched as his father's true power nurtured and gave life. A man once so consumed with hate, now he gave himself so that Kai's unborn children would live. Offering the gift of life, Keegan's body shook. Power from the sun, sky, and plants flowed through him as he gave it purpose and pushed the energy into Rayna. The surge of magic surrounding Keegan touched the edges of Kai's aura, and he felt the magnitude of his father's might and the essence of love wrapped in the life he gave.

As Rayna's stomach bloomed with life, Mariana's hand joined Keegan's, and together they offered their everything to save Rayna and the children before they both collapsed.

It was Yulia's voice that called Kai from his father's dazed expression. "You can do this, Rayna," she instructed.

Rayna's screams reached a crescendo as the first baby girl emerged. She was so small and perfect. Holding his firstborn, Rayna delivered their second child. Yulia offered the second baby girl to Rayna. Staring into his wife's eyes, Kai could not be happier.

Next to him, he noticed Alenga's celestial presence; her iridescent form touched his head, sending a wave of magic washing over him, and then she knelt by his side. "Your mother's stone, if you please," she whispered.

He retrieved the crystal from his pocket and found it cracked—or rather cut with purpose. The stone now consisted of a circle divided into two halves by a curved line. "Keegan and Mariana's power is now a part of your children. With the inherited power, they will need a crystal to harness and soften the raw power. When they reach the age of Conhaspriga, they will come into their magic. Raise them well, my children, for they embody the magic of Lumens, Beastmaster, and

Kodama. It is their destiny to reunite the Katori people with the rest of their magical family and bring them to my dimension."

Keegan sagged like an empty sack. "I have little left, but I owe someone her life back." His father stood and moved to Riome's still form. His hands blossomed with light, and Kai saw the remaining years begin to drain from his father as he gave Riome life. "I cannot undo all the years, but you will have a long life, longer than most." His wrinkled hands dropped to his side, and he fell back in a slump.

Riome sat up. Her hair remained white, but her face regained much of her youthfulness, minus a few years. The magical Katori crystal hanging from her neck returned to dust and blew away in the wind. Drew rushed to her side.

The white dome around them shrank only to include Kai, Rayna, Benmar, and his parents—Mariana and Keegan. It was then Kai noticed his mother was now a spirit; her body lay in the grass to his right. Next to her, Keegan's spirit stood, his face at peace.

"What are their names?" Mariana asked.

Kai looked to Rayna. He had not thought of names, not yet. "Luciana and Marica," Rayna responded. "After your grandfather Lucca and your mother, Mariana." She smiled, and he agreed.

Alenga's shimmering figure wavered. "It is time for us to go, my children." She extended a hand to Mariana and glanced at Keegan before taking his hand in hers. "You have much to atone for, my child." Then she turned her eyes on Kai and his family. "Kai, I cannot tell you for certain what awaits once time resumes, but much has changed in the hearts of those who survived. Let Amelia speak to her people, and I believe she can convince them to go home and wait for her return." Alenga turned, and Mariana and Keegan followed; together, they vanished into the brightness. As if waking from a dream, Kai and his family returned to the grassy field as time resumed.

❖ ❖ ❖

Dawn eased into the sky as Amelia stood at the Diu gates. Milnosian soldiers wandered the battlefield, no longer interested in fighting. Given the reports of King Landon and Maxwell's death, her people had no remaining leadership; they were a people with no ruler. King Iver and Admiral Roark pulled back their men to the city as she stepped forward to speak with her people. At her side, Tolan carried their child, which gave her strength. Joined by her husband's men, she stopped and stood in front of her people.

She was cautious but remembered not all her people believed war was the answer, but a good soldier follows orders. "My people, citizens of Milnos. Much has changed in our world these many months. I offer you my service, but I ask first, do you want war or peace? I have no interest in war, not with Diu or Katori. I offer you peace and relations with our neighboring nations. In the coming weeks, I wish to return to Milnos if you would have me as your queen." The men cheered her name. "But I have conditions. Tolan Raebun will rule by my side as your king. Do you accept these terms?"

The growing crowd again cheered her name. "I would meet with any remaining captains willing to stay behind here in Diu to negotiate a peace treaty before returning to be crowned queen. We will return united and cleanse our city, retore it to glory, and set a new path for our people." The soldiers cheered.

Tolan looked down at her. She could see the pride in his eyes, and he handed her their child. "One last order of business, this is my son, your royal prince, Emery!" Her people cheered.

EPILOGUE

The wind blew through the Kodama glade, tucked into the Katori hillside. Kai watched his two young daughters, now nearly five years of age, chase their mother. Marica's long brown hair like her mother's, and Luciana's sandy blonde hair like his, fluttered in the wind. Their carefree lives were filled with lighthearted moments and magical lessons far beyond their years.

The sun warmed his face, and the scent of sweet apple blossoms filled his lungs. A sense of remembrance washed over the moment; this was the vision Alenga had blessed him with all those years ago of Rayna's future. His family's giggles tickled his heart, and Rayna's smile lifted the corner of his mouth. He felt at peace and lucky to be with them.

They were happy.

Luciana and Marica danced and twirled each other around the garden; the two halves of his mother's crystal bounced as they moved, dangling on silver chains about their necks. Each crystal, he knew, helped to contain the magic they were born with and keep it from consuming their young bodies. In their wake, wildflowers bloomed, and butterflies danced on the breeze.

Tired, Rayna dropped into his lap, her breathing heavy and her cheeks pink from play. She fanned her face, and Kai kissed her cheek. "I love you," he whispered.

She blushed and wrapped her arms around his neck. "I love you too."

Luciana plucked magic like grapes from the air, and Marcia touched her sister's outstretched hand. Together they traced the air creating a golden outline in their wake. The form looked like a horse, and Kai smiled until Marcia finished the head with a long spiral horn, the addition unique and elegant. Then the girls snickered and clapped their hands together, the beautiful creature pranced around the meadow before scattering its golden magic-filled particles back into nature.

"Beautiful creation, my little ones," Kai called to them, and his daughters ran and jumped into their parent's open arms with joy-filled smiles. "I am so blessed for having three beautiful girls in my life." He hugged them all tight.

Luciana laughed, winking at her sister. "Daddy, what if Mommy has a boy? Will you love him just as much?"

"Girls," Rayna smirked more than chastised, "that was our little secret."

Kai swiveled his head between them. "Secret? You are pregnant?" He beamed with pride.

"Barely a few weeks. It is really so early, but the girls see things, even the tiniest light." Rayna gleamed, and Kai kissed her.

Kai tickled his daughters. "Yes, I will love each of you with all my heart."

The End

www.ingramcontent.com/pod-product-compliance
Lightning Source LLC
Chambersburg PA
CBHW071417200726
48294CB00002B/430